More praise for
A Kiss of Shadows

"Packed with brownies, ogres, action, and adult-style
sexuality, this magical adventure is for grown-ups."
—*The Dallas Morning News*

"A sizzling new series that blends supernatural fantasy
with detective adventure . . . Memorable characters
and wicked wit make it all delicious, ribald fun."
—*Publishers Weekly*

"Entertaining . . . Highly recommended."
— *Library Journal*

"Spellbinding."
—*Southern Pines Pilot (NC)*

By Laurell K. Hamilton
Published by Random House

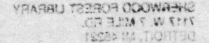

A KISS OF SHADOWS
A CARESS OF TWILIGHT
SEDUCED BY MOONLIGHT
A STROKE OF MIDNIGHT
MISTRAL'S KISS
A LICK OF FROST
SWALLOWING DARKNESS
DIVINE MISDEMEANORS

A KISS OF SHADOWS

Laurell K. Hamilton

BALLANTINE BOOKS · NEW YORK

For everyone who kept the old stories alive in small rooms and great houses, by firelight and electricity, for all who kept the faith and for those who just liked a good story.

2014 Ballantine Book Mass Market Edition

Published in the United States by Ballantine Books, an imprint of Random House, a division of Random House LLC, a Penguin Random House Company, New York, and simultaneously in Canada by Random House of Canada Limited, Toronto.

The phrase elf-struck is used by the kind permission of Larry Hammer from an as of yet unpublished novel. Finish the book Larry, I'd love to read the rest of it.

BALLANTINE and the HOUSE colophon are registered trademarks of Random House LLC.

Originally published in hardcover in the United States by Del Rey, an imprint of Random House, a division of Random House LLC in 2000.

ISBN 978-0-345-42340-5
eBook ISBN 978-0-345-44688-6

Printed in the United States of America

www.ballantinebooks.com

First Hardcover Edition: October 2000
First Mass Market Edition: March 2002

19   18   17   16   15   14

Acknowledgments

Robin Bell for so many things, the Celtic research being but a small part. Darla Cook, without whom so much would go undone. Deborah Millitello, who read this book and pronounced it good. All my writing group, who due to time constraints did not get to read this final version: Tom Drennan, Rett MacPherson, Marella Sands, Sharon Shinn, and Mark Sumner. And everyone at Ballantine and Del Rey, especially my editor, Shelly Shapiro.

· Chapter 1

TWENTY-THREE STORIES UP AND ALL I COULD SEE OUT THE windows was grey smog. They could call it the City of Angels if they wanted to, but if there were angels out there, they had to be flying blind.

Los Angeles is a place where people, those with wings and without, come to hide. Hide from others, hide from themselves. I'd come to hide and I'd succeeded, but staring out at the thick, dirty air, I wanted to go home. Home where the air was blue most of the time and you didn't have to water the ground to get grass to grow. Home was Cahokia, Illinois, but I couldn't go back because they'd kill me if I did, my relatives and their allies. Everyone wants to grow up to be a faerie princess. Trust me. It's overrated.

There was a knock on the office door. It opened before I could say anything. My boss, Jeremy Grey, stood framed in the doorway. He was a short, grey man, four feet eleven inches, an inch shorter than me. He was grey from his dark Armani suit to his button-up shirt and silk tie. Only his shoes were black and shiny. Even his skin was a pale uniform grey. Not from illness or age. No, he was a trow in the prime of life, just a little over four hundred. There were some lines around his eyes, along the thin mouth, that made him appear mature, but he'd never be old. Without the aid of mortal blood and a pretty serious spell, Jeremy might live forever. Theoretically. Scientists say that in about five billion years the sun will expand and engulf the Earth. The fey won't survive that. They will die. Does five billion years count as forever? I don't think so. Though it's close enough to make the rest of us envious.

1

I leaned my back against the windows and the thick, hanging smog. The day was as grey as my boss, but his color was a cool, crisp grey, like clouds before a spring rain. What lay outside the window felt heavy and thick like something you would try to swallow, but you'd never get it down. It was a day to choke on, or maybe it was just my mood.

"You look gloomy, Merry," Jeremy said. "What's wrong?" He closed the door behind him, making sure it shut. Privacy, he was giving us privacy. Maybe it was for my benefit, but somehow I didn't think so. There was a tightness around his eyes, a set to his thin, well-tailored shoulders that said I wasn't the only one in a bad mood today. Maybe it was the weather or the lack of it. A good rain shower or even a good wind would have cleared out the smog and let the city breathe again.

"Homesick," I said. "What's wrong, Jeremy?"

He gave a small smile. "Can't fool you, can I, Merry?"

"No," I said.

"Nice outfit," he said.

I knew I looked hot when Jeremy complimented my clothes. He always looked impeccable even in jeans and T-shirt, which he only wore if he absolutely had to be undercover. I'd seen Jeremy do a three-minute mile in Gucci loafers once, chasing a suspect. Of course, it helped that his dexterity and speed were more than human. When I thought I might have to actually chase someone, a rare occasion, I got out the jogging shoes and left the high heels at home.

Jeremy put into his eyes that look a man gives you when he's appreciating the view. It wasn't personal, but among the fey it's an insult to ignore someone who's obviously trying to be attractive, a slap in the face telling them that they'd failed. Apparently, I hadn't failed. I'd woken up to the smog and dressed brighter than normal to try and cheer myself up. Royal blue suit jacket, double-breasted, silver buttons, a matching blue pleated skirt that was so short, it was only a fringe across my thighs underneath the jacket. The outfit was short enough that if I crossed my legs wrong, I'd flash the tops of my black thigh-highs. Two-inch patent leather high heels helped show off the legs. When you're as short as I am, you've got to do something to make your legs look long. Most days the heels were three inches.

My hair was a deep rich red in the reflections of the mirrors. A color more red than auburn, a color that had black highlights instead of the usual brown that most redheads had. It was as if someone had taken dark red rubies and spun them out into hair. It was a very popular color this year. Blood auburn it was called in the high court of the fey royalty. Faerie Red, Sidhe Scarlet, if you went to a good salon. It was actually my natural color. Until it became popular this year and they finally got the shade right, I'd had to hide my true color. I'd gone for black, because it looked more natural than human red with my skin tone. A lot of people getting the dye job made the mistake of thinking that Sidhe Scarlet complements a natural redhead's coloring. It doesn't. It's the only true red color I know of that matches a pale, pure white skin tone. It's the red hair for someone who looks great in black, true reds, royal blues.

The only things I still had to hide were the vibrant green and gold of my eyes and the luminosity of my skin. I used dark brown contacts for the eyes. My skin—that I had to tone down using glamour, magic. Just a steady concentration like music in the back of my head, to never let down my guard and start to glow. Humans don't actually glow, no matter how luminous they may be. No glowing, which was why the contacts covered my eyes. I also wove a spell around myself like a long familiar coat, an illusion that I was just a human with lesser fey blood in my background who had some psychic and mystical abilities that made me a really excellent detective, but nothing too special.

Jeremy didn't know what I was. No one at the agency knew. I was one of the weakest members of the royal court, but being sidhe means something even on the weak end of the scale. It meant that I had successfully hidden my true self, my true abilities, from a handful of the best magicians and psychics in the city. Maybe in the country. No small feat, but the kind of glamour I was best at wouldn't keep a knife from finding my back or a spell from crushing my heart. For that I needed skills that I didn't have, and that was one of the reasons I was in hiding. I couldn't fight the sidhe, not and live. The best I could do was hide. I trusted Jeremy and the others. They were my friends. What I didn't trust was what the sidhe might do to them if I were discovered, and my relatives found out my friends had known my secret. If they were truly ignorant, then the sidhe would leave them alone and only hurt me. Ignorance was bliss on this one. Though I thought that some of my very good friends would see it as a type of betrayal. But if the choices were them alive, with all their body parts intact, but angry at me, or dead by torture but not angry at me, I'd take angry. I could live with their anger. I wasn't sure I could live with their deaths.

I know, I know. Why not go to the Bureau of Human and Fey Affairs and get asylum? My relatives would probably kill me when they found me, but if I went public and aired our dirty laundry for the world media, they would most definitely kill me. And they'd kill me slower. So no police, no ambassadors, just the ultimate game of hide-and-seek.

I smiled at Jeremy and gave him what I knew he wanted: the look that said that I appreciated the slender potential of his body under his perfect suit. To humans it would have looked like flirting, but for the fey, any fey, it wasn't even close to flirting. "Thanks, Jeremy, but you didn't come in here to compliment my clothes."

He walked farther into the room, running manicured fingers along my desk edge. "I've got two women in my office. They want to be clients," he said.

"Want to be?" I said.

He turned, leaning against the desk, arms crossed over his chest. Mirroring my stance at the windows, either unconsciously, or purposefully, though I didn't know why. "We don't usually do divorce work," Jeremy said.

I gave him wide eyes, pushing away from the windows. "Day one lecture, Jeremy: The Grey Detective Agency never, ever, does divorce work."

"I know, I know," he said. He pushed away from the desk and came to stand beside me, staring out into the fog. He didn't look any happier than I felt.

I leaned back against the glass so I could see his face better. "Why are you breaking your cardinal rule, Jeremy?"

He shook his head without looking at me. "Come meet them, Merry. I trust your judgment. If you say we stay out of it, we'll stay out of it. But I think you'll feel the same way I do."

I touched his shoulder. "And how are you feeling, boss, other than worried?" I ran my hand down his arm, and it made him look at me.

His eyes had gone dark charcoal grey with anger. "Come meet them, Merry. If you're as angry afterward as I am, then we'll nail this bastard."

I gripped his arm. "Jeremy, relax. It's just a divorce case."

"What if I told you it was attempted murder?" His voice was calm. Matter of fact, it didn't match the intensity in his eyes, the vibrating tension in his arm.

I moved back from him. "Attempted murder? What are you talking about?"

"The nastiest death spell that's ever walked into my office."

"The husband is trying to kill her?" I made it a question.

"Someone is, and the wife says it's the husband. The mistress agrees with the wife."

I blinked at him. "Are you saying that the wife and the mistress are in your office?"

He nodded, and even through all the outrage, he smiled.

I smiled back. "Well, that's got to be a first."

He took my hand. "It might be a first even if we did do divorce work," he said. His thumb rubbed back and forth over my knuckles. He was nervous, or he wouldn't be touching me this much. A way to reassure himself, like a touchstone. He raised my hand to his lips and planted a quick kiss on my knuckles. I think he'd noticed what he was doing, that his nerves were showing. He flashed me a white smile, the best caps money could buy, and turned toward the door.

"Answer one question first, Jeremy."

He adjusted his suit, minute movements to tug it back into place as if it needed it. "Ask away."

"Why are you scared of this?"

The smile faded until his face was solemn. "I've got a bad feeling about this one, Merry. Prophecy isn't one of my gifts, but this one has a bad smell to it."

"Then pass it by. We aren't the cops. We do this for a very nice paycheck, not because we've sworn to serve and protect, Jeremy."

"If after you meet them, you can honestly walk away from it, then we will."

"Why is my vote suddenly a presidential veto? The name on the door is Grey, not Gentry."

"Because Teresa's so empathic she couldn't turn anyone away. Roane is too much the bleeding heart to turn tearful women away." He adjusted his dove grey tie, fingers smoothing over the diamond stickpin. "The others are good for grunt work, but they aren't decision makers. That leaves you."

I met his eyes, trying to read past the anger, the worry, to what was really going on inside his head. "You're not an empath, and you're not a bleeding heart, and you make dandy decisions, so why can't you make this one?"

"Because if we turn them away, they won't have anywhere else to go. If they leave this office without our help, they're both dead."

I stared at him, and finally understood. "You know we should walk away from this one, but you can't bring yourself to pass judgment on them. You can't bring yourself to condemn them to death."

He nodded. "Yes."

"What makes you think that I can do it, if you can't?"

"I'm hoping one of us is sane enough not to be this stupid."

"I won't get you all killed for the sake of strangers, Jeremy, so be prepared to walk away from this one." Even to me, my voice sounded hard, cold.

He smiled again. "That's my little cold-hearted bitch."

I shook my head and walked toward the door. "It's one of

the reasons you love me, Jeremy. You count on me not to flinch."

I walked out into the hallway that led between offices, sure that I would turn these women away. Certain that I would be the wall that kept us all safe from Jeremy's good intentions. Goddess knows, I'd been wrong before, but seldom as wrong as I was about to be.

Chapter 2

I THOUGHT FOR SOME REASON I'D BE ABLE TO TELL WHICH OF the two women was wife and which was mistress just by looking at them. But at first glance they were just two attractive women, casually dressed, like girlfriends out for a day of shopping and lunch. One woman was small, though a few inches taller than either Jeremy or myself. Blond hair cut just above the shoulders, with a careless curl to it that said it was natural and she hadn't done anything special to it this morning. She was pretty in a girl-next-door sort of way, with extraordinary blue eyes that took up most of her face. Her eyebrows arched thick and black, balancing out a lace of dark lashes that framed those eyes in a very dramatic fashion—though the dark brows made me speculate about how natural the blond hair might be. She wore no makeup and still managed to be very pretty in an ethereal, very natural way. With makeup and a little effort she'd have been a knockout. But it would have taken more than makeup and a better fit of clothes.

She sat huddled in the client chair, shoulders hunched as if waiting for a blow to fall. Her lovely eyes blinked at me like the eyes of a deer caught in headlights, as if she were powerless to stop what was happening, and what was happening was bad.

The other woman was tall, five feet eight inches or better, slender, with long pale brown hair that swung straight and shining to her waist. At first glance she seemed early twenty-something. Then I met her eyes and there was an intensity in their brown depths that made me add on ten years. You just didn't get that look much before thirty. Her look was more confident than the blonde's, but there was a flinching around her eyes, a tightness in her shoulders, as if something deep inside was hurting. There was also a delicacy of bone as if what lay under the skin had been formed of daintier things than mere bone. There is only one thing that can give a tall, commanding person that look of daintiness: she was part sidhe. Oh, it was a few generations back, nothing as intimate as my ties to the court, but somewhere a several-times-great-grandmother had lain down with something not human and walked away with a child. Fey blood of any kind marks a family, but sidhe blood seems to stay in the genes forever, as if once in the mix, it never gets cleaned out.

I was betting the blonde was the wife, and the other one the mistress. The blonde seemed the more beaten down of the two, which is usually the case with an abusive man. They may abuse all the women in their lives, but they'll usually save the best or worst for immediate family. My grandfather had always done it that way.

I came into the room smiling, hand out to shake hands, like they were any other clients. Jeremy made the introductions. The small blonde was the wife, Frances Norton; the tall brown-haired one was the mistress, Naomi Phelps.

Naomi's handshake was firm, hand cool to the touch, those extraordinary bones moving under her skin. I held her hand just a little too long, luxuriating in the feel of her touch. It was the closest thing I'd had to another sidhe in three years. Even a touch of some other fey isn't the same. There is something in the royal bloodline that is like some drug. Once tasted, you miss it.

She looked puzzled at me, and it was a very human puzzlement. I let her hand go and tried to pretend to be human. Some days I was better at it than this. Some days I was worse. I could have tried to get the measure of her psychically, to see if she had more than bone structure going for her, but it was impolite to try and read another person's magical ability at first introduction. Among the sidhe it's considered an open challenge, an insult that you don't believe that the other person can shield himself from your most casual magic. Naomi probably wouldn't have taken it as an insult, but her ignorance was no excuse for me to be rude.

Frances Norton held out her hand like she was afraid to be touched, the arm half bent so she could tuck it back into her body as soon as I was finished with it. I'd have given her the same polite treatment that I'd given the other woman, but with my fingers just above her skin I could feel the spell. That small line of energy that surrounds all of us, her aura, pushed against my skin like it was trying to keep me from touching her. Someone else's magic was so thick in her body that it had filled her aura up like dirty water in a clean glass. In a way, the woman wasn't herself anymore. It wasn't possession, but it was a close cousin. It was certainly a violation of several human laws, all of them felonies.

I forced my hand through that roil of energy, gripping her hand. The spell tried to surge through my skin up my arm. There was nothing to see with the eyes, but just as you can see things in your dreams, so I could sense a faint darkness trying to creep up my arm. I stopped it just below my elbow and had to concentrate on peeling it down my arm like stripping off a glove. It had breached my shields like they hadn't been there. Not many things can do that. None of them human.

She was staring at me with wide, wide eyes. "Wh . . . what are you doing?"

"I'm not doing anything to you, Mrs. Norton." My voice sounded a little detached, distant, because I was concentrating on peeling the spell off of me so that when I let go of her hand none of it would cling to me.

She tried to take her hand back, and I wouldn't let her. She started to tug on it, weak but frantic. The other woman said, "Let Frances go, now."

I was almost free, almost ready to let her go, when the other woman gripped my shoulder. The hair on the back of my neck stood up, and I lost concentration on my hand, because I could sense Naomi Phelps now. The spell poured back over my hand and was halfway to my shoulder before I could concentrate enough to stop it. But all I could do was stop it. I couldn't push it back because too much of my attention was on the other woman.

You never touch someone while they're working magic, or doing psychic stuff, unless you want something to happen. This more than anything told me that neither woman was a practitioner or an active psychic. No one with even minimal training would have done it. I could feel the remnants of some ritual clinging to Naomi's body. Something complex. Something selfish. The thought that came unbidden to my mind was gluttony. Something had been feeding off of her energy, and it had left psychic scars behind.

She jerked back from me, cradling her hand against her chest. She'd sensed my energy, so she had talent. Not a big surprise. What was surprising was that she was untrained, maybe totally untrained. Nowadays they go into preschools and test people for psychic gifts, mystical talent, but it was a new program in the sixties. Naomi had managed not to be spotted, and now she was over thirty and still hadn't dealt with her abilities. Most untrained psychics are either crazy, criminals, or suicides by the time they're thirty. She had to be a very strong person to be as together as she looked. But this very strong woman looked at me with tears trembling in her eyes. "We didn't come here to be abused."

Jeremy had stepped closer to us, but was being careful not to touch any of us. He knew better. "No one is abusing you, Ms. Phelps. The spell on Mrs. Norton tried to . . . leach onto my colleague. Ms. Gentry was merely trying to push the spell off of her when you touched her. You should never touch anyone when they're working magic, Ms. Phelps. The results can be unpredictable."

The woman looked from one to the other of us, and her face said clearly she didn't believe us. "Come on, Frances. We're getting the fuck out of here."

"I can't," Frances said in a voice grown small and submissive. She was staring up at me, fear plain in her eyes, but it was fear of me.

She felt the energy wrapped around our hands, pressing us together, but she thought I was doing it. "I swear to you, Mrs.

Norton, I am not doing this. Whatever magic has been used against you, it thinks I'm tasty. I need to peel it off of me and let it flow back into you."

"I want to get rid of it," she said, voice high with a faint edge of hysteria trailing around the edges.

"If I don't pull it off of me, then whoever did this to you will be able to trace me. They'll be able to find me. They'll know that I work at a detective agency that specializes in supernatural problems, magical solutions." It was our slogan. "They'll know that you came here for help. I don't think you want that, Mrs. Norton."

A fine trembling started in her hands and spread up her arms, until she stood there shivering as if she were cold. Maybe she was, but it wasn't the kind of cold that an extra sweater would fix. No amount of outer warmth would cure the coldness inside. She'd have to be warmed from the damaged core of her soul out to her fingertips. Someone would have to pour power into her, magic into her, a little bit at a time, like thawing some ancient body found frozen in ice. If you thawed it too fast, you'd cause more damage than if you just left it alone. Such delicate use of power was beyond my abilities. All I could have done was give her a measure of calmness, taken some of her fear—but whoever laid the spell on her would sense that, too. They wouldn't be able to trace me by it, but they'd know she'd been to see a practitioner, someone who'd tried to help her on a psychic level. Call it a hunch, but whoever laid the spell wouldn't like that. They might do something rash, like speed up the process.

I could feel the sucking energy of the spell, trying to breech my defenses, to feed on me, too. It was like magical cancer, but as easy to catch as the flu. How many people had she infected? How many people were walking around with this spell draining little bits of their energy? Someone who was only a little bit psychic might know something had happened, but not what. They'd avoid Frances Norton because she'd hurt them, but they might not realize for weeks, months, that the tiredness, the vague feelings of hopelessness, the depression, were being caused by a spell.

I started to tell her what I was about to do, but staring into her wide eyes, I didn't bother. She'd just tense up, be more afraid. The best I could do was make it as invisible to her as possible. I would try to make sure she didn't feel it slide back inside her, but that was the best I could do.

The spell had grown thicker, blacker, more real, just from those few extra moments of sitting against my skin. I began to peel it down my arm. It clung like tar, and it took a lot more concentration to push it back, rolling it back on itself like thick cloth. Every inch of my skin that I freed up felt lighter, cleaner. I could not imagine living totally encased in this thing. It would be like going through your entire life faintly oxygen-deprived, shoved in a dark room, where the light never came.

I had freed my arm, my hand, and began to slowly pull my fingers away from her hand. She stayed utterly still against my skin like a rabbit hiding in the grass, hoping desperately that the fox will pass her by if only she can lie quiet enough. What I don't think Frances Norton realized yet was that she was halfway down the fox's throat, with her little legs kicking in the air.

When I pulled my fingers away, the spell clung to them, and then fell back into place around her with an almost audible sound. I wiped my hand on my jacket. I was clear of the spell, but I had a terrible urge to wash my hand with very hot water and lots of soap. Ordinary water and soap wouldn't help, but some salt or holy water might.

She collapsed into the chair, hiding her face in her hands, shoulders shaking. I thought at first she was crying without making any noise. But when Naomi hugged her, she raised a face devoid of tears. Frances was shaking, just shaking, as if she couldn't cry anymore, not because she didn't want to, but because all the tears had been drained out of her. She sat there while her husband's mistress hugged her, rocked her. She was shaking so badly her teeth began to chatter, but she never cried. It seemed worse somehow because she didn't cry.

"Excuse us for a moment, ladies. We'll be right outside," I

said. I looked at Jeremy and headed for the door, knowing he'd follow. In the hallway he closed the door behind us.

"I'm sorry, Merry. I shook her hand, and nothing happened. The spell didn't react to me."

I nodded. I believed him. "Maybe I just taste better."

He grinned at me. "Well, I don't know from experience, but I'd almost bet on it."

I smiled. "Physically, maybe, but mystically, you're as powerful in your own way as I am. Lord and Lady, you're a better magician than I'll ever be, yet it didn't react to you."

He shook his head. "No, it didn't. Maybe you're right, Merry. Maybe it's too dangerous for you."

I frowned at him. "Now he gets cautious."

He looked at me, fighting to make his face neutral. "Why do I get the feeling that you're not going to be the cold-hearted bitch I was hoping for?"

I leaned against the far wall and glared at him. "This thing is so malignant that we'll be able to get some police help."

"Bringing in the police won't save them. We don't have enough to prove it's the husband. If we can't prove it in court, he doesn't do jail time, and that means he'd be free to work more magic on them. We need him locked away in a warded cell where he can't harm them."

"They'd need magical protection until he was in custody. This isn't just a detective job. It's a baby-sitting job."

"Uther and Ringo are great babysitters," he said.

"I guess."

"Still not happy. Why?"

"We should walk away from this one," I said.

"But you can't do it," he said. He was smiling now.

"No, I can't do it." There were lots of detective agencies in the United States that said they specialized in supernatural cases. It was big business, the preternatural, but most agencies couldn't back up their advertising. We could. We were one of only a handful of agencies that could boast a staff made up entirely of magic practitioners and psychics. We were also the only one that could boast that all but two employees were fey. There aren't that many full-blooded fey who can stand to live in a big, crowded city. L.A. was better than New York or Chicago, but it was still exhausting to be surrounded by so much metal, so much technology, so many humans. It didn't bother me. My human blood allowed me human tolerances for steel and glass prisons. Culturally and personally, I preferred the country, but I didn't have to have it. It was nice, but I didn't sicken and fade without it. Some fey would.

"I wish I could turn them away, Jeremy."

"You've got a bad feeling about this one, too, don't you?"

I nodded. "Yeah." But if I cast them out, I'd see her trembling, tearless face in my dreams. For all I knew, they might come back to haunt me after whoever was killing them finished the job. They could come back as righteous ghosts and bemoan me for having knowingly taken their last chance at survival away. People always think ghosts haunt the people who actually killed them, but that's just not true. Ghosts seem to have an interesting sense of justice, and it would be just my luck to have them following me around until I could find someone to lay them. If they could be laid. Sometimes spirits were tougher than that. Then you could end up with a family ghost like a banshee howling at every death. I doubted either woman had that kind of strength of character, but it would have served me right if they had. It was my own sense of guilt that made me walk back into that office, not fear of ghostly reprisals. Some people say that the fey have no souls, no sense of personal responsibility. For some that's true, but it wasn't true for Jeremy, and it wasn't true for me. More's the pity sometimes. More's the pity.

Chapter 3

NAOMI PHELPS DID MOST OF THE TALKING WHILE FRANCES SAT there and shivered. Our secretary got her hot coffee and an afghan. Her hands shook so badly that she spilled coffee on the afghan, but she got some of it down. Whether it was the warmth or the caffeine, she looked a little better.

Jeremy had called Teresa in to listen to the women. Teresa was our resident psychic. She was two inches shy of six feet, slender, with high sculpted cheekbones, long silky black hair, skin the color of pale coffee. The first time I'd seen her, I'd known she had sidhe blood in her, along with African American, and something fey that hadn't been high court. The last was what gave her the slight points to the tops of her ears. A lot of faerie wanna-bes get cartilage implants to make their ears pointy. They grow their hair down to their ankles and try to pretend to be sidhe. But no pure-blooded sidhe has ever had pointed ears. It's a mark of mixed blood, less than pure. But some bits of folklore die harder than others. To a vast majority of people if you were truly sidhe, you had to have pointed ears.

Teresa had that same delicacy of bone that Naomi did, but I'd never been tempted to hold Teresa's hand. She was one of the most powerful touch clairvoyants that I'd ever met. I spent a goodly amount of energy making sure she didn't touch me for fear that she'd learn my secrets and endanger us all. She sat in a chair to one side, dark eyes watching the two women. She hadn't offered to shake their hands. In fact she'd walked wide around them so that she didn't accidentally touch either of them. Her face betrayed nothing, but she'd felt the spell, the danger, when she walked into the room.

"I don't know how many mistresses he's had," Naomi was saying, "a dozen, two dozen, hundreds." She shrugged. "All I know for sure is that I'm the latest in a long line of them."

"Mrs. Norton," Jeremy said.

Frances turned her eyes up to him, startled, as if she hadn't expected to be asked to contribute to the story.

"Do you have any proof of all these women?"

She swallowed, and said in a voice that was almost a whisper, "Polaroids, he keeps Polaroids." She stared down into her lap, murmuring, "He calls them his trophies."

I had to ask. "Did he show these pictures to you, or did you find them?"

She looked up, and her eyes were empty—no anger, no shame, empty. "He showed them to me. He likes . . . he likes to tell me about what he's done with them. What each one is good at, better at than me."

I opened my mouth, closed it, because I couldn't think of a single helpful thing to say. I was outraged for her sake, but it was Frances Norton that needed to be angry on behalf of Frances Norton. My anger might help us solve the immediate problem, but it wouldn't make her strong again. If we could take the husband out of the picture, that wouldn't heal all the damage he'd done. There was a lot more wrong with Frances than just a spell.

Naomi touched her arm, comforting her. "That's how she met me. She saw my picture, and then we just ran into each other one day. I caught her staring at me in a restaurant. He had woken her when he got home and told her what he'd done to me." It was Naomi's turn to look down into her lap, her hands lying upright and empty against her legs. "I had bruises showing." She looked up, met my eyes. "Frances came over to my table. She rolled back her sleeve and showed me her bruises. Then she just said, 'I'm his wife.' And that was how we met." She gave a shy smile at the last, the sort of smile you give when you've explained how you met your lover. A tender story to be related to others.

I gave her blank eyes, but I wondered if the bond between them was more than just the abuse and the husband. If they were lovers, it could change how the healing was done. So often in mystical things the emotions have to be taken into account. Because love and hate have different energies, you work with them differently. We'd need to know exactly what the bond between the two women was before serious healing work was begun, but not today. Today we'd listen to what they wanted to tell us.

"That was very brave of you," Teresa said. Her voice, like everything about her, was somehow soft and feminine with an underlying strength, like steel covered by silk. I'd always thought Teresa, though she'd never traveled farther south than Mexico, would have made an excellent Southern belle.

Frances's eyes flicked to her, then back to her lap, then up, and her mouth moved. It was almost a smile. That one small movement made me feel better about the woman. If she could begin to smile, begin to take pride in what strength she'd shown, then maybe she would be all right with time.

Naomi squeezed her arm and gave her a smile of pride and affection. Again, I got the impression that they were very close. "It was my salvation. From the moment that I met Frances, I started trying to break away from him. I don't know how I allowed him to hurt me. I'm not like that. I mean, I've never, ever let a man abuse me." Her face showed the shame she felt, as if she should have saved herself.

Frances put her hand over the other woman's hand, giving comfort as well as getting it.

Naomi smiled at her, then turned puzzled eyes to us. "He's like a drug. Once he's touched you, you crave his touch. Not just him either. It's like he wakens you sexually, until your body aches to be touched." She looked down again. "I've never been so sexually aware of other people. It was embarrassing, and exciting, at first. Then he started to hurt me. At first it was just little things, tying me up, then . . . spanking." She made herself look up, forced herself to meet our eyes. Such anger, as if defying us to think the worst of her. There was a great deal of strength here. How had this man tamed her? "He made the pain part of the pleasure, but then he started doing worse things. Things that just hurt. I tried to get him to stop the kinky stuff, and that's when he started beating me for real, no pretending that it was part of sex." Her mouth trembled, eyes still defiant. "But beating me did excite him. The fact that it didn't excite me, that it scared me, he liked that, too."

"Rape fantasies," I said.

She nodded, her eyes wide as she tried to keep the tears glistening in her eyes from falling. She held herself very still, trying to hold it all inside. "Not just fantasies at the end."

"He likes to take you by force." This from the wife.

I looked at both of them and fought the urge to shake my head. I'd spent the years from sixteen to thirty in the Unseelie Court, the years of my sexual awakening, so I knew about combining pleasure with pain. But the pain was shared, and it was never done against anyone's will. If the other person didn't think pain was pleasurable, it wasn't sex. It was torture. There is a vast difference between torture and a little hard sex. But for sexual sadists, there is no difference. In the extreme forms they are incapable of sex without the violence, or at least the terror of their victim. But most sadists are capable of more normal sex. They can use that to fool you, but in the end they can't keep up a normal relationship. In the end what they truly desire must come out, and they must have it.

How was I such an expert? Like I said, I spent my sexual awakening years at the Unseelie Court. Don't get me wrong. The Seelie Court has its own brand of unusual activities, but they do share the more mainstream human view of dominance and submission. The Unseelie Court is much more welcoming of such things or maybe just more open about it. It could also be that the Queen of Air and Darkness, my aunt, the overall ruler of the court for the last thousand years, give or a take a century, is very into dominance and borders on being a sexual sadist. She has shaped the court in her image, as my uncle, the King of Light and Illusion of the Seelie

Court, has shaped his court in his image. Strangely, you can scheme and lie more easily in the Seelie Court. They're into illusion. If everything looks good on the outside, then it must be good. The Unseelie Court is more honest, most of the time.

Teresa said, "Naomi, was this your first abusive relationship?"

The woman nodded. "I still don't understand how I let it get so bad."

I looked at Teresa, and she gave a very small nod. It meant that she'd listened to the answer and that the woman was telling the truth. Like I said, Teresa is one of the most powerful psychics in the country. It's not just her hands you have to watch out for. Most of the time she can tell if you're lying or not. I've had to be very careful around her these three years we've worked together.

"How did you meet him?" I asked. I didn't use his name or say Mr. Norton because both women had been very careful to say only him or he, as if there was no other man, and you would know whom they were talking about. We did.

"I answered a personal ad."

"What did the ad say?" I asked.

She shrugged. "The usual stuff, except for the end. At the end of the ad it said he was looking for a magical relationship. I don't know what it was about the ad, but after I read it, I had to meet him."

"A compulsion spell," Jeremy said.

She looked at him. "What?"

"If you're powerful enough, you can put a spell on an ad so that the ad brings to you what you truly desire, not necessarily what the ad says you want. It's the way I ran the ad that Ms. Gentry answered. Only people with magical ability would have noticed the spell on the ad, and only people with exceptional gifts would have been able to see through to the true writing underneath. The true writing listed a different phone number than the ad. I knew that anyone who called that number was capable of the job."

"I didn't know you could do that with a newspaper," Naomi

said. "I mean, it's printed, and he couldn't have touched every paper." Just by knowing that not touching the paper physically made the spell harder to cast meant Naomi knew more about magic theory than I thought she did. But she was right.

"You have to be powerful enough that the ad, the words that you read into it, carry the spell. It is very difficult, and that he was capable of it lets us know the kind of skill we'll be up against."

"So the ad called me to him?" she asked.

"Maybe not you specifically," Jeremy said, "but something about you was exactly what he wanted or needed."

"Most of the women look fey," Frances said.

We all looked at her. She blinked at us. "Pointed ears. One woman had these cat-green eyes that seemed to glow out of the picture. Skin colors that no human has, like green, blue. Three of them had more . . . parts than a human would have, but not like it was a deformity, like it was just part of the way they looked."

I was impressed. Impressed that she'd noticed and put it together in her head. If we could save her, get her away from him, she'd make it. "What did he say about Naomi?"

"That she was part sidhe. He really got off on that, if the women were part sidhe. He called them his royal whores."

"Why fey women?" Jeremy asked.

"He never said," Frances answered.

"I think it had something to do with the ritual," Naomi said.

We all turned to her. Jeremy and I asked in unison, "What ritual?"

"The first night he took me to the apartment he's rented. The bedroom has mirrored walls and this huge circular bed. The floor was this beautiful gleaming wood with a Persian carpet under the bed. Everything seemed to glow. When I climbed up on the bed, I felt something, like I'd walked through a ghost. I didn't know what it was that first night, but one night I slipped on the rug, and underneath was a double circle set into the wood of the floor with symbols in a band around the circle. I realized the bed was the center of the circle. I didn't recognize the symbols, but I knew enough to know it was a circle of power, a place to work magic."

"Did he ever do anything in the bed that seemed like ritual magic?" I asked.

"Nothing that I recognized. We just had sex, lots of it."

"Was there anything that was the same every time?" Jeremy asked.

She shook her head. "No."

"Was the sex always in this apartment?" Jeremy asked.

"No, sometimes we met at a hotel."

That surprised me. "Is there anything he does in the apartment inside the circle that he doesn't do anywhere else?"

She blushed bright red. "It's the only place he brings other men."

"Other men to have sex with him?" I asked.

She shook her head. "No, with me." She looked up at us, as if waiting for the cry of horror, or maybe whore. Whatever she saw reassured her. We all knew how to give good blank face when we needed it. Besides, a little group sex seemed tame after knowing that he showed pictures of his lovers to his wife, with details. That was a new one. Group sex had been around a lot longer than Polaroids.

"Was it always the same men?" Jeremy asked.

She shook her head. "No, but they knew each other. I mean, it wasn't like he brought in strangers off the street." She sounded defensive, as if that would have been so much worse, and it wasn't as bad as all that.

"Were there any repeats?" Jeremy asked.

"There were three men that I saw more than once."

"Do you know their names?"

"Just their first names. Liam, Donald, and Brendan."

She seemed very sure of the names. "How many times did you see these three men?"

She wouldn't meet our eyes. "I don't know. Many times."

"Five times," Jeremy asked, "six, twenty-six?"

She looked up, startled. "Not twenty times, not that many."

"Then how many?" he asked.

"Maybe eight, maybe ten, but no more than that." It seemed important to her that it hadn't been more than ten. Was that the magical cut-off? More than ten times and you were worse than just eight?

"And the group sex, how many times for that?"

She blushed again. "Why do you need to know?"

"You called it a ritual, not us," Jeremy said. "So far there doesn't seem much ritual to it, but numbers can have mystical significance. The number of men inside the circle. The number of times you were inside the circle with more than one man. Believe me, Ms. Phelps, this is not how I get my jollies."

She looked down again. "I didn't mean to imply . . ."

"Yes, you did," Jeremy said, "but I understand why you'd be suspicious of any male, human or not." I saw the idea float over his face. "Were all the men human?"

"Donald and Liam both had pointed ears, but other than that they all seemed human."

"Were Donald and Liam circumcised?" I asked.

Her voice came out in a hurried rush, color high in her cheeks again. "Why do you need to know that?"

"Because a real male fey would be hundreds of years old, and I've never heard of a Jewish fey, so if they were fey, they wouldn't be circumcised."

She met my eyes. "Oh," she said, then she thought about the original question. "Liam was, but Donald wasn't."

"What did Donald look like?"

"Tall, muscular, like a weight lifter, blond hair to his waist."

"Was he pretty?" I asked.

She had to think about that one, too. "Handsome, not pretty, handsome."

"What color were his eyes?"

"I don't remember."

If they'd been one of the more colorful shades of eyes that the fey are capable of, she'd have remembered. Except for the pointed ears he could have been any of a dozen men at the Seelie Court. There were only three blond men at the Unseelie Court, and none of my three uncles lifted weights. They had to be more careful of their hands than that for fear they'd rip the surgical gloves they always wore. The gloves kept the poison that their hands naturally produced from rubbing off on anyone else. They'd been born cursed.

"Would you recognize this Donald if you saw him again?"

"Yes."

"Was there anything the same about all the men?" Jeremy asked.

"They all had long hair like he has, shoulder-length or longer."

Long hair, possible cartilage implants in the ears, Celtic names—sounded like faerie wanna-bes to me. I'd never heard of a sex cult of faerie wanna-bes, but you should never underestimate people's ability to corrupt an ideal.

"Good, Ms. Phelps," Jeremy said. "How about tattoos, symbols written on their bodies, a piece of jewelry that they all wore?"

"No to all of it."

"Did you meet only at night?"

"No, sometimes in the afternoon, sometimes at night."

"No special time of the month, not close to a holiday?" Jeremy asked.

She frowned at him. "I've been seeing him only a little over two months. There haven't been any holidays, but no special time."

"Did you have sex with him or others a certain number of times a week?"

She had to think about that one, but finally shook her head. "It varied."

"Did they chant or sing?" Jeremy asked.

"No," she said.

It didn't sound like much of a ritual to me. "Why did you use the term ritual, Ms. Phelps? Why didn't you say spell?"

"I don't know."

"You do know," I said. "You're not a practitioner. I don't think you'd use the term ritual without a reason. Just think for a minute. Why that word?"

She thought about it, eyes staring into space, seeing nothing, tiny frown lines between her eyebrows. She blinked and looked at me. "I heard him talking on the phone one night." She looked down, then up, defiant again, and I knew she didn't like what she was about to say. "He'd tied me to the bed, but he'd left the door open a little. I could hear him talking. He said, 'The ritual will be good tonight,' then his voice dropped too low for me to hear, then he said, 'The untrained ones give it up so easily.' " She looked at me. "I wasn't a virgin when we met. I was . . . experienced. Before him, I thought I was good in bed."

"What makes you think you're not?" I asked.

"He told me that I wasn't good enough at straight sex to satisfy him, that he needed the abuse to spice it up, so he wouldn't be bored." She tried to stay defiant and failed. The hurt showed in her eyes.

"Were you in love with him?" I tried to make the question gentle.

"What difference does that make?"

Frances took her hand, held it in her lap. "It's all right, Naomi. They're going to help us."

"I don't see what love has to do with any of this," she said.

"If you love him, then it will be harder to free you of his influence, that's all," I said.

She didn't seem to notice that I'd changed loved to love. She answered the question. "I thought I loved him."

"Do you still love him?" I hated having to ask, but we needed to know.

She gripped the other woman's small hand in both of hers, knuckles whitening with the strength of her grip. The tears finally slid down her face. "I don't love him, but . . ." she had to take a few deep breaths before she could finish, "but if I see him, and he asks for sex, I can't seem to say no. Even when it's awful and he's hurt me, the actual sex is still better than anything I've ever felt before. I can say no over the phone, but if he shows up, I let him . . . I mean, I fight if he's beating me, but if it's during sex . . . it gets all confused."

Frances stood, moving behind the other woman's chair, spreading the afghan over both of them while she hugged her from behind. She made soothing noises, kissing the top of her head like you'd do with a child.

"Have you been hiding from him?" I asked.

She nodded. "I have, but Frances . . . He can find her no matter where she is."

"He follows the spell," I said.

Both women nodded as if they'd figured that much out for themselves. "But I've hidden from him. I moved out of my apartment."

"I'm surprised he didn't hunt for you," I said.

"The building is warded," she said.

I widened eyes at that. For a building to be warded, not just an apartment but the entire building, meant that the protective spells had to be put into the foundation of the building. The wards had to be poured with the concrete, riveted into place with the steel beams. It took a coven of witches, or several covens. No single practitioner could do it. It was not a cheap process. Only the most expensive high-rises or homes could boast of it.

"What do you do for a living, Ms. Phelps?" Jeremy asked, because I think that he, like me, had actually not expected the two women to be able to meet our fee. We had enough money in the bank under the agency's account and in our own accounts so we could do charity work from time to time. We didn't make a habit of it, but some cases you don't do for money but because you simply can't say no. We both thought this was going to be one of those.

"I've got a trust fund that matured last year. I have access to all of it now. Trust me, Mr. Grey, I can pay your fee."

"That's very good to know, Ms. Phelps, but truthfully I wasn't worried about it. Don't spread it around, but if someone's in deep enough trouble, we don't turn them away because they can't meet our fees."

She blushed. "I didn't mean to imply that you were . . . I'm sorry." She bit her lip.

"Naomi didn't mean to insult you," Frances said. "She's been rich all her life, and a lot of people have tried to take advantage of that."

"No offense taken," Jeremy said. Though I knew that there probably was some offense taken. But he was a very business-like businessman. You didn't get mad at a client, not if you were taking the case. Or at least not until they'd done something really awful.

Teresa asked, "Has he ever tried to get your money?"

Naomi looked at her, and you could see the surprise on her face. "No, no."

"Does he know you have it?" I asked.

"Yes, he knew, but he never let me pay for anything. He said he was old-fashioned that way. He didn't care about money at all. It was one of the things I liked about him at first."

"So he's not after money," I said.

"He's not interested in money," Frances said.

I met those big blue eyes, and they didn't look scared now. She was still standing behind Naomi, still comforting her, and she seemed to gain strength from that. "What is he interested in?" I asked.

"Power," she said.

I nodded. She was right. Abuse is always about power in one way or another. "When he said the untrained ones give it up so easily, I don't think he was talking about your sexual prowess."

Naomi was holding on to Frances's hands, pressing them to her shoulders. "Then what did he mean?"

"You're untrained in the mystic arts."

She frowned at me. "Then what was it that I gave up so easily, if it wasn't sex?"

Frances answered, "Power."

"Yes, Mrs. Norton, power."

Naomi frowned at all of us. "What do you mean, power? I don't have any power."

"Your magic, Ms. Phelps. He's been taking your magic."

She looked even more astonished, mouth open in a little "o" of surprise. "I don't know any magic. I get feelings sometimes about things, but that's not magic."

And that, of course, was why he'd been able to do it. I wondered if all the women were untrained mystics? If they were untrained, then we were going to have trouble infiltrating his little world. But if all they had to be was part fey and magically talented . . . well, I'd done decoy work before.

Chapter 4

THREE DAYS LATER I WAS STANDING IN THE MIDDLE OF JER-emy's office wearing nothing but a black lace push-up bra, matching panties, and black thigh-highs. A man I'd never met was fishing down the front of the bra. Normally, I have to be planning to sleep with a man before I let him fondle my breast, but it was nothing personal, just business. Maury Klein was a sound expert, and he was trying to fit a tiny wire with a tiny microphone under my right breast where the un-derwire of the bra would keep Alistair Norton from feeling it if he brushed his hand across my ribs, or breast. He'd been fiddling with the wire for about thirty minutes, fifteen of that trying to find the best place to hide the wire in my cleavage.

He was kneeling in front of me, the tip of his tongue bitten between his teeth, eyes behind the wire-frame glasses staring fixedly at his hands, one plunged almost out of sight inside the cup of the bra, the other holding the material of the bra away from my breast so he could work better. By pulling the bra out, he'd exposed my nipple and most of the rest of my right breast to the room.

If Maury hadn't been so obviously oblivious to both my charms and our audience, I'd have accused him of taking so long because he was enjoying himself, but he had that inner stare that said he wasn't really aware of what he was doing, except for the job part. I understood why he'd had complaints from female undercover people before. The complaints had been why he insisted on not doing all this in private. He wanted witnesses that he hadn't overstepped the bounds. Though frankly, if all the witnesses had been human, they might have been on my side anyway. He'd poked, lifted, and otherwise manhandled my chest as if it weren't attached to anyone. What he was doing was very intimate, but he didn't mean it to be. He was the proverbial nerd or maybe the absent-minded professor. He had only one love, and that was his hidden mikes, hidden cameras. In Los Angeles if you wanted the best, you went to Maury Klein. He put in security systems for Hollywood stars, but his true passion was undercover work. How to get the equipment even smaller, better concealed.

He'd actually at one point suggested that the wire might be best hidden inside my body. I'm not shy, but I vetoed that idea. Maury had shaken his head and muttered, "Don't know how the sound quality would hold up, but I wish someone would let me try it." He did have an assistant, read "keeper," and probably emergency diplomat.

Chris—if he had a last name, I'd never heard it—had cautioned Maury not to be so rough or so indelicate. He'd hovered until I assured him I was fine. Now he stayed near Maury like a surgical nurse ready to hand him whatever esoteric piece of equipment he needed.

Jeremy sat behind his desk watching the show, fingers steepled, an amused smile on his face. He'd shown polite heat in his eyes when I first took my dress off and stripped to the lingerie, but after that he'd just tried to keep from laughing at Maury Klein's total lack of heat. Jeremy had complimented me on the amazing contrast between the perfect white of my skin and the blackness of the lingerie. You're always supposed to say something nice the first time you see someone in a state of undress.

Roane Finn was sitting on the corner of Jeremy's desk, feet kicking in the air in a soft unconscious movement, as he, too, enjoyed the show. He didn't have to compliment me. He'd seen me naked last night and many nights before that. His eyes are the first things you notice about him, huge, liquid brown orbs that dominate his face like the moon dominates the night sky. Then it's a toss-up whether you notice his dark auburn hair, and the way it clings to his face, rolls down the back of his collar, or his lips, which are a perfect red-tinged pouting bow. You'd think he used lipstick to get the color, but he doesn't. It's all natural. His skin looks white, but it isn't really, or not pure white. It's as if someone took my own pale complexion and added a drop of the red-brown of his hair. When he wears brown or other autumn colors, his skin seems to darken.

He was my height exactly, and it made him appear delicate at first glance, but the body that showed under the black clothing he'd donned for tonight looked firm and muscular. I knew for a fact that he wasn't just strong. He was limber. I also knew that there were burn scars along his back and shoulders, like white calluses on the smooth silk of his body. The scars had been caused when a fisherman burned his sealskin. Roane was a roane, one of the seal people. Once he'd been able to don his sealskin and become a seal, then slip the skin and be human, or rather human form. Then a fisherman had found his skin and burned it. The skin was not just a magical device for shape-shifting. It wasn't even just part of Roane. The skin was as much him as his eyes or his hair. Roane is the only seal person I've ever heard of that survived the destruction of his other self. He survived but he could never again change form. He was doomed to be forever landbound, forever denied the other half of his world.

Sometimes at night I'd find the bed empty. If we were at my apartment, he'd be gazing out the window at nothing. If we were at his place, he'd be looking out at the ocean or vanishing into the waves as I watched from the balcony. He never woke me and asked me to join him. It was his private pain, not to be shared. I guess it was fair because in the two years we'd been lovers, I'd never dropped my glamour completely. He'd never seen the dueling scars. The injuries would have marked me as someone intimate with the sidhe. I might have been hopeless at offensive spells, but there were few better at personal glamour in all the courts than me. It helped me hide, but not much else. Roane couldn't breech my shields, but he knew they were there. He knew that even in that moment of release, I held back. If he'd been human, he would have asked why, but he wasn't human, and he didn't ask, just like I never questioned him about the call of the waves.

A human wouldn't have been able not to pry, but a human lover also wouldn't have been able to sit calmly while another man fiddled with my breasts. There was no jealousy in Roane. He knew this meant nothing to me, so it meant nothing to him.

The only other woman in the room was Detective Lucinda—call me Lucy—Tate. We'd worked with her on several cases where the perpetrator wasn't human, and their decoys were getting bewitched, bewildered, or killed. In fact, having Jeremy and the rest of us as temporary police had been the first time the Magical Dispensation Act had been stretched to include police work. But we'd all met the criteria of having magical abilities that made us ideal for the job, which meant they could waive all training that a nonmagic cop would have needed and just put us straight on the job. Sort of like emergency deputies. The Magical Dispensation Act is how I got to be a detective fresh off the bus, so to speak, with none of the hours and hours of training that you normally need to get your license in California.

Detective Tate leaned against the wall, shaking her head. "Jesus, Klein, no wonder you've got sexual harassment complaints against you."

Maury blinked as if having to draw his attention back from a long way off. It was the way people looked at the end of a powerful spell, like they were just waking and the dream hadn't finished yet. You couldn't fault Maury's powers of concentration. He finally turned to the detective, hands still in my bra.

"I don't know what you mean, Detective Tate."

I looked at her over Maury's kneeling head. "He really doesn't," I said.

She smiled at me. "Sorry about the manhandling, Merry. If he wasn't the best at what he did, nobody would tolerate him."

"We don't use sound equipment and hidden cameras much," Jeremy said, "but when we do I like to pay for the best."

Tate looked at him. "The department certainly couldn't afford him."

Maury spoke without turning his attention from my chest. "I've done free work for the police in the past, Detective Tate."

"And we really appreciate that, Mr. Klein." The look on her face didn't quite match the words—a more mischievous twinkle in the eye and cynicism in the face. Cynicism seemed to be an occupational hazard. The mischievous twinkle was pure Lucy Tate. She always seemed to be laughing softly at everything. I was pretty sure it was a defense mechanism to keep the real her hidden, but I still hadn't figured out what she was hiding from. None of my business, but I will admit to a certain amount of very unfeylike curiosity about Detective Lucy Tate. It was the very perfection of her camouflage, the fact that you never saw beyond that faintly amused shield, that made me want to breech it. I could see Roane's pain, so I could leave it alone. But I could see nothing in Lucy, and neither could Teresa, which meant, of course, that Detective Tate was a psychic of considerable power. But something had happened at an early age that made her hide her powers so far under that even she didn't know she had them. None of us had explained this to her. Detective Tate's life seemed to work well. She seemed happy. If she tore the scar open that had forced her powers underground, that could all change. It might be something traumatic enough that she'd never rebuild from it. So we left her alone, but we wondered about her, and sometimes it was harder than it should have been not to poke at her with magic or psychic feints, just to see what would happen.

Maury leaned back, hands to himself at last. "There, I think that'll do. I'll put just a touch of tape to make sure it doesn't shift, and you're set." Chris handed him some small bits of tape on his hand all ready to go, anticipating the need. Maury took the tape without comment. "You've seen what I had to do to put the mike in. Well, this guy will have to do the same thing to find it." He actually had me hold the bra out so he could tape with both hands. It was the kindest thing he'd done in the last forty-five minutes.

He stood and moved back. "Fix the bra the way you'd normally wear it."

I frowned at him. "This is the way I normally wear it."

He made a small motion with his hands at about chest level. "You know, fluff that one, so it matches the other one."

"Fluff," I said, but I smiled because I finally understood what he meant.

He sighed and moved forward. "I'll show you."

I held a hand out. "I don't need help." I bent over and shook my right breast into the cup of the bra, having to use my hand to get everything into place. The bra was push-up enough that my already nice chest looked positively obscene, but when I ran my hand over the area where I should have felt the mike, all I could feel was the underwire and material.

"It's perfect," Maury said. "You can strip down to this, just keep your bra on, he'll never know." He cocked his head to one side, as if he'd just thought of something. "I've taped the mike to the bra so if you have to you can take it off, just leave it within a five-foot radius. Closer is better. If I make the mike more sensitive, we'd start picking up your heartbeat and the cloth moving. I can filter it out, but it's easier to do after the tape's made than before. I'm assuming you want to be able to hear tonight, in case your bad guy gets out of hand."

"Yes," Jeremy said, "it'd be nice to know if Merry needs help." The sarcasm was too mild for Maury.

"We might have been able to tape the mike to the elastic top of the hose, but I couldn't swear that the hose wouldn't roll down and flash the mike. If you take the bra off, make sure and roll the cloth so the mike doesn't show."

"I don't plan on taking it off."

Maury shrugged. "Just wanting to give you all the options I can."

"I appreciate that, Maury," I said.

Maury nodded. Chris was already picking up the bits and pieces that had gotten scattered on the floor.

Roane jumped down from the desk, lifting my folded dress from the top of it. He held the square of black cloth out to me. I'd had to buy a black dress on the advice that it was easier to hide things in black than in lighter colors. I never wore unrelieved black if I could help it, even though it was a color that looked good on me. It was the color favored by the Unseelie Court because it was their queen's favorite color to wear.

Roane let the silk dress unfold from his hands, holding it by the shoulders, then he began very slowly, very deliberately to roll the dress up in his hands, watching my face the entire time he did it. When the dress was just a thin black fringe hanging from his small strong hands, he knelt in front of me, holding the dress open so I could step into it.

I placed my hand on his shoulder for balance and stepped into the circle of cloth. Roane began to let the dress slide from his hands, raising his hands at the same time so the dress fell around me like a theater curtain coming down. When his arms were raised as far as they'd go kneeling, the dress was to my waist. He stood, hands resting lightly on my hips. The movement put him kissably close. His eyes were exactly at the same level as mine. There was an intimacy to the eye contact that I'd never had with anyone else. I'd never been with anyone as short as I was before. It made missionary position unbelievably intimate.

Roane raised the dress until I could slip my arms through the sleeves, then he raised it over my shoulders, moving around me until he was at my back and could pull the last of the silk into place. He began to zip the dress up in back. The dress tightened as it zipped, like it was slowly constricting across my waist, my ribs, over the breasts. The neckline was a very daring V, which was another reason for the uplift bra. It was the only one I'd found that you could wear under the dress and not flash the bra. The dress was sleeveless and fit like a shiny second skin, leaving my flesh very white against the dark fabric. I'd chosen the tightness very deliberately. The bodice looked like it was barely there and all it left was a view of my breasts, but if you tried to slide your hand into the top, you couldn't do it without risking ripping the dress. If Alistair

Norton wanted to play with my breasts, he'd have to keep his play to the exposed tops, unless we were planning a rape scenario, and according to Naomi the rape fantasies had only come out at two months or more. The first month had been a perfect affair. Since this was the first date, Alistair would probably be on his best behavior. I'd have to take the dress off for him to have a chance at finding the mike, and I wasn't planning on taking the dress off.

Roane finished zipping me, fastening the small hook at the top. He traced his thumbs over the bare skin of my upper back, the barest of movements, then stepped away from me. He actually ran his thumbs over the scars on my back that he could neither see nor feel. I was confident enough in my abilities that the dress would have shown the scars, except for my glamour. They were like ripples in the skin, frozen forever. Another sidhe had tried to change my shape during a duel. Many of the fey can shape-shift, but only the sidhe can change the form of others against their will. I can't change my shape or anyone else's, another mark against me in the courts.

"How do you do that?" Detective Tate asked.

The question startled me, made me turn to her. "Do what?" I asked.

Chris was glancing up as he repacked equipment. Maury was already fiddling with a medium-sized transmitter, working at it with a tiny screwdriver. The rest of us might as well not have been in the room.

"You stand there for nearly an hour in nothing but your underwear with a man fondling your breasts, but it's not sexual. It's like an R-rated comedy routine. Then Roane helps you on with your dress, never touches your bare skin, just zips you up, and suddenly the sexual tension in the room is thick enough to walk on. How the hell do you do that?"

"Us, as in Roane and me, or us, as in . . ." I let the thought trail off.

"Us as in the fey," she said. "I've seen Jeremy do it with a human woman. You guys can walk around buck naked and make me comfortable being in the same room with you, then fully clothed you do something small and suddenly I feel like I should leave the room." She shook her head. "How do you do that?"

Roane and I looked at each other, and I saw the same question in his eyes that I knew was in mine. How do you explain what it is to be fey to someone who is not? The answer, of course, is you don't. You can try, but you rarely succeed.

Jeremy tried. He was, after all, the boss. "It is part of what it means to be fey, to be a creature of the senses." He rose from his chair and walked to her, face, body neutral. He took her hand and raised it to his lips, laying a chaste touch of lips to her knuckles. "Being fey is the difference between that and this." He took the same hand again and raised it much slower, eyes on her face filled with that polite heat that any fey male might have given to the tall, attractive woman. The look alone made her shiver. He kissed her hand this time, a slow caress of lips, the upper lip catching just a little on her skin, as he drew back from her. It had been polite, no open mouth, no tongue, nothing rude, but color had spread up her cheeks, and from across the room I could tell her breathing had deepened, pulse quickening.

"Does that answer your question, Detective?" he asked.

She gave a shaky laugh, holding her hand with the other hand, cradling it against her body. "No, but I'm afraid to ask again. I don't think I could handle the answer and still work tonight."

Jeremy gave a little bow. Whether Tate knew it or not, she'd just given a very fey compliment. Everyone likes to be appreciated. "You warm the cockles of this old man's heart."

She laughed then, high and delighted. "You may be a lot of things, Jeremy, but you'll never be old."

He gave another bow, and I realized something I hadn't before. Jeremy liked Detective Tate, liked her the way a man likes a woman. We all touch humans more than they touch each other, or at least more than most American humans touch each other. But he could have chosen other ways to "explain" to Tate. He'd chosen to touch her in a way he'd never touched her before, taken a liberty with her, because she'd given him the excuse to do it without seeming forward. That was how the fey flirted when invited. Sometimes it was just a glance, but the fey do not go where they are not asked. Though our men will make the same mistake that human males make sometimes, mistaking a little flirting for sexual advance, outright rape is almost unknown among us. Our version of date rape on the other hand has been popular for centuries.

Funny how the thought of date rape brought me back to the job at hand. I went to the desk where I'd left my shoes and slipped into them, gaining three inches of height. "You can tell your new partner that he can come back in now," I told Lucy.

It was an insult to insist on modesty in a nonsexual situation among most of the fey, certainly among the sidhe. That's why the audience. To send them away would imply lack of trust, or outward dislike. There were only two exceptions. The first was if the person couldn't behave in a civilized manner. Detective John Wilkes had never worked with non-humans before. He didn't blink when Maury asked me to disrobe, but when I took the dress off without warning or clearing the room, the detective had spilled hot coffee down his shirt. When Maury plunged his hand down my bra, Wilkes had said, "What the hell is he doing?" I asked him to wait outside.

Lucy gave a low laugh. "Poor boy, I think he got second-degree coffee burns when you took off your dress."

I shrugged. "He must not see a lot of naked women."

She smiled, shaking her head. "I've dealt with fey, even a few visiting sidhe, and you're the only one I've met that was humble."

I frowned at her. "I'm not humble. I just think that if seeing me strip to my underwear is enough to make your partner nearly swallow his tongue, he must not be very experienced."

Lucy looked at Roane and Jeremy. "Does she not know what she looks like?"

"No," Roane said.

"I think, though I don't know, that our Merry was raised

somewhere where she was considered the ugly duckling," Jeremy said.

I met his eyes, my pulse thudding in my neck. That one comment was a little too close for comfort. "I don't know what you guys are talking about."

"I know you don't," Jeremy said. There was a knowledge in his dark grey eyes, a guess that was close to a certainty. In that moment, I knew he suspected who I was, what I was. But he would never ask. He would wait until I was ready to talk, or the question would remain forever silent between us.

I looked at Roane. He was the only fey lover I'd known had not come to my bed to further his political ambitions. To him I was just Merry Gentry, a human with fey ancestry, not Princess Meredith NicEssus. Now I stared into that familiar face and tried to read his expression. He was smilingly blank. Either it had never occurred to him that I might be the missing sidhe princess, or he'd guessed long ago, but would never be rude enough to bring it up. Or had Roane known from the first? Had that been why he'd come to me? Suddenly, all the security that I'd built up with these people, my friends, began to crumble around me.

Some of it must have shown on my face because Roane touched me. I drew back from him. His face showed the hurt, confusion. He didn't know. I hugged him suddenly, hiding my face from him, but I could still see Jeremy.

As the look on Roane's face had reassured me, so the look on Jeremy's frightened me. All it would take was my true name being mentioned after dark, and it would float back to my aunt. She was the Queen of Air and Darkness, and that meant that anything said in the dark was hers to hear, eventually. The fact that spotting the missing Elven American Princess had become more popular than spotting Elvis helped. Her magic was always chasing blind leads. Princess Meredith skiing in Utah. Princess Meredith dancing in Paris. Princess Meredith gambling in Vegas. After three years I was still a front-page story for the tabloids, though the latest headlines had been speculating that I was as dead as the King of Rock and Roll.

If Jeremy spoke my name aloud to my face, the words would resonate, and when they finally floated back to her, she'd know I was alive, and she'd know that Jeremy had spoken my name. Even if I ran, she'd question him, and if polite methods didn't work, she'd use torture. I am told she is a creative lover. I know she is an inventive torturer.

I drew back from Roane and gave them part of the truth. "My mother was the beautiful one."

"How do you know that?" Jeremy asked.

I looked at him. "She told me so."

"You mean your mother told you you weren't beautiful?" Lucy asked. It took a human to be that direct.

I nodded.

"Don't take this wrong, but what a bitch."

To that there was only one thing to say—"I agree, now let's get out of here."

"We wouldn't want to keep Mr. Norton waiting," Jeremy said.

"I still wish we were going after him for proof on the attempted murder," Lucy said.

"We can't guarantee proof that will stand up in court about the death spell," I said.

"But," Jeremy said, "we might be able to prove tonight that he is using magic to seduce women. Magically aided seduction is rape under California law. We need him in jail away from his wife, and this is the surest way to do it. He won't get bail on a felony charge that includes magic."

Lucy nodded. "I agree that the plan is great for Mrs. Norton, but what about Merry? What if this guy pulls out the magical aphrodisiac that he's used on the other mistresses, the ones who just couldn't get enough of him like Naomi Phelps?"

"We're counting on it," I said.

She looked at me. "What if it works? What if you start panting over the microphone?"

"Then Roane breaks down the door playing the jealous lover and drags me out."

"If I have trouble getting her to leave, then Uther will come in as my friend and help me take my woman back home."

Lucy rolled her eyes. "Well, what Uther wants, Uther gets." Uther was thirteen feet tall, with a head that was more pig than human, and two curling tusks on either side of his snout. He was a jack-in-irons, but he was named Uther Squarefoot. He wasn't much good for undercover work, but he was hell on wheels when we needed muscle.

Uther had excused himself from the room when he realized the dress was coming off. He'd said only, "It's nothing personal, Merry, don't make more of it than there is, but seeing any attractive female nearly naked is not good for a man when there's no hope of relieving the thoughts that spring unbidden." It wasn't until he made for the door, stooping his great shoulders low enough to squeeze out the doorway, that I realized something I should have known before. Uther is thirteen feet tall, the size of a large ogre or a very small giant, and there aren't many females his size in the Los Angeles area. He'd been here nearly ten years. That was a long time to be without the touch of another naked body. How terribly lonely.

If no one guessed who I really was, and if I didn't get bespelled out of my mind by Alistair Norton, I'd see about fixing Uther up with someone. Uther wasn't the only giant-sized fey wandering outside the courts, just the only one in the immediate area. If we couldn't find someone his size, we might be able to come up with other solutions. Sex doesn't have to mean intercourse. There are women on the streets that will do just about anything for a couple of hundred dollars, especially if twenty is their going rate. If I were truly fey down to my toes, I'd do Uther myself. That's what a real friend would do. But I was raised outside the court, out among the humans, from age six to sixteen. It meant that no matter how fey I was, some of my attitudes were human.

I can't be human because I'm not. But I can't be completely fey because I'm not that either. I am half Unseelie Court, but I am not one of them. I am part Seelie Court, but I do not belong among the shining throng. I am part dark sidhe, part light sidhe, and yet neither side wishes to claim me. I have always been on the outside looking in, my nose pressed to the window, but never welcomed inside. I understood isolation and loneliness. It made me hurt for Uther. Made me regret that I wasn't comfortable helping him with a little friendly, casual sex. But I wasn't, and I wouldn't. As usual, I was fey enough to see the problem, but too human to fix it. Of course, if I'd been pure Seelie sidhe, I wouldn't have touched Uther at any price. He would have been beneath my notice. The Seelie do not fuck monsters. Unseelie sidhe . . . well, define monster.

Uther wasn't a monster by Unseelie standards, but Alistair Norton might be. Either a monster, or a kindred spirit of the dark.

Chapter 5

ALISTAIR NORTON DIDN'T LOOK LIKE A MONSTER. I'D EX-
pected him to be handsome, but it was still disappointing.
There is something in all of us that believes deep down that
evil shows on the outside, that we should be able to pick out
the bad people just by looking at them, but it just doesn't
work that way. I'd spent enough time at both courts to know
that beautiful and good were not the same. I, if anyone, knew
that beauty was perfect camouflage for the darkest of hearts,
and still I wanted Alistair Norton's face to show what he was
inside. I wanted some visible mark of Cain on him. But he
came smiling into the restaurant, tall, broad-shouldered, face
full of clean angles, so masculine it was almost painful. His
lips were a little thin for my taste, face a little too masculine,
eyes a very ordinary brown. The hair that was tied back in a
neat ponytail was an odd shade of brown, neither light nor
dark. But I had to look for imperfections because there just
weren't any.

His smile was quick and softened his face to something
more approachable, less model-perfect. The laugh was deep
and charming. His large hands wore a silver ring with a diamond as big as my thumb, but no wedding ring. There wasn't
even a telltale pale line where the ring had been removed. His
skin was dark enough that there should have been a tan line.
He'd never worn a ring. I always felt that any man who didn't
want to wear a wedding band was probably planning to cheat.
There are always exceptions, but not many.

For his part, he seemed pleased. "Your eyes glow like green
jewels."

I'd left the brown contact lenses at the office. My natural eye color really did glow. I thanked him for the compliment, playing shy, looking into my drink. It wasn't shyness. I was trying to keep him from seeing the contempt in my eyes. Both human and sidhe culture abhor an adulterer. The sidhe don't worry about fornication, but once you get married, give your word that you will be faithful, then you must be faithful. No fey will tolerate an oath breaker. If your word is worthless, then so are you.

He touched my shoulder. "Such perfect white skin." When I didn't chase him away, he leaned in and placed a soft kiss on my shoulder. I stroked his face as he drew back, and that seemed to be a signal of some kind. He kissed the side of my neck, hand touching my hair. "Your hair's like red silk," he breathed against my skin. "Is it your natural color?"

I turned into him, answering him with my mouth just above his, "Yes."

He kissed, and it was gentle, a good first kiss. I hated the fact that he seemed so sincere. What was truly horrible was that he might be sincere, that at the beginning of the seduction he might mean every word. I'd met men like that before. It's as if they believe their own lies, that this time it will be true love. But it never lasts because no woman is perfect enough for them. Of course, it isn't the women who aren't perfect enough. It's the man. He tries to fill some void in himself with women or sex. If the love is true enough, the sex good enough, then this time he'll feel complete. This time he'll finally be whole. Serial womanizers are like serial killers in one respect. They both believe that next time will be perfect, that the next experience will complete them and stop this unending need. But it never does.

He whispered, "Let's get out of here."

I nodded, not trusting my voice. I'd be doing a lot of eyes-closed kissing because sometimes I could lie with my eyes, and sometimes I couldn't. It was going to be hard enough to keep the reluctance out of my body as he touched me. Expecting my eyes to show lust and love was asking too much.

His car matched the rest of him: expensive, sleek, fast. A black Jaguar with black leather seats so that it was like sliding into a pool of darkness. I put my seat belt on. He didn't. He drove fast, weaving in and out of traffic. It would have been more impressive if I hadn't been driving in L.A. for three years. Everyone drove like this out of sheer self-defense.

The house was neat and small, the smallest in the neighborhood, but it had the largest yard. There was actually enough land on either side that even a Midwesterner would say it had a good-sized yard. The house looked like a place for kids to wait for daddy to come home, while mom rushed around in her power suit trying to fix dinner after a hard day's work.

For a moment I wondered if he'd actually taken me to his home, the one he shared with Frances. If so, it was a break in his pattern, and I didn't like that. Why would he break his pattern? I knew he hadn't found the bug, and he hadn't touched my purse, which meant he didn't know about the hidden camera in it. I was saving turning it on until we got to his love nest. He couldn't know.

Ringo was posted outside the Norton house watching over Mrs. Norton. If Alistair got too violent before we could get him in jail, Ringo was on his own best judgment over whether to intercede. I didn't look around for Ringo. If he was here, I didn't want to draw attention to him.

Alistair opened the door for me, helping me out of the car. I let him because I was trying to think. I finally tried for honesty, sort of. "You sure you're not married?"

"Why do you ask?"

"This looks like a house for a family."

He laughed and drew me into the circle of his arm. "No family, just me. I just moved in."

I looked up at him. "Are you buying with an eye for the future? Munchkins and the family thing?"

He raised my hand to his lips. "With the right woman anything's possible."

Lord and Lady, but he knew just how much carrot to dangle in front of most women. Imply that you could be the woman to tame him, make him settle down. Most women love that. I knew better. Men don't settle down because of the right woman. They settle down because they are finally ready for it. Whatever woman they're dating when they get ready is the one they settle down with, not necessarily the best one or the prettiest, just the one who happened to be on hand when the time got to be right. Unromantic, but still true.

He'd moved out of his apartment. Why? Did it have something to do with Naomi Phelps leaving him abruptly? Did it make him nervous enough to move? Or had he been planning the move all along? No way to know without asking, and I couldn't ask. As Alistair Norton ushered me through the door, I fought an urge to look back, to search for Jeremy and the rest. I knew my backup was out there. I knew because I trusted them. Alistair hadn't driven fast enough to lose both vehicles. The van for the sound system and to hide Uther, and the car with Jeremy at the wheel in case they needed more maneuverability to follow Norton, or just to switch off so that he wouldn't notice the same car behind him for too long. They were out there, listening to us. I knew that, but still I would have liked to have glanced back and seen them. Just sheer insecurity on my part.

I felt the warding before the door opened. When I stepped over the threshold, power shivered over my skin. He noticed. "Do you know what you're feeling?"

I could have lied, but I didn't. I'd like to say it was a hunch that Alistair would be pleased that I was a trained mystic, but that wasn't it. I wanted him to know that I wasn't helpless. "You've got the door warded," I said. The air in the room pressed against my skin, and it was as if I couldn't breathe deep enough, like there wasn't enough air. I stepped off the tiled entryway, hoping the atmosphere would get better. It didn't. If anything the atmosphere grew heavier, like wading into deeper water. Hot, close, skin-crawling water.

I'd known he was powerful by the spells he'd laid on his wife and his mistress. But the amount of power that filled that empty living room was more than human. The only way for a human witch to get that much power was to bargain with things not human. I hadn't counted on that. None of us had.

He was talking to me, but I hadn't heard. My mind was screaming, "Leave! Leave now!" But if I did that, Alistair was still free to kill his wife and torture other women. Me leaving would keep me safe, but it wouldn't help our clients. It was one of those moments when I had to decide, was I going to earn my paycheck or not.

One thing I did know. The guys in the van needed to know what I'd found out. "The ward isn't to keep things out, is it, Alistair? Though it will keep out other powers. The ward is to keep anyone else from sensing how much power you've got in here." My voice sounded breathy as if I was having trouble breathing.

He looked at me then, and for the first time I saw something in his eyes that wasn't pleasant or smiling. For an instant the monster was there in those brown eyes. "I should have known you'd sense it," he said. "My little Merry, with her sidhe eyes, hair, and skin. If you were tall and willowy, you'd pass for sidhe."

"So I've been told," I said.

He held his hand out to me. I reached for his hand, but I had to reach through the power in the room, like pushing my hand through an invisible, skin-tingling thickness. His fingers touched mine, and a jolt of energy like static jumped between us. He laughed and wrapped his hand around mine. I forced myself not to pull back, but I couldn't make myself smile. I was having too much trouble breathing through the power. I'd lived in places so full of power, the walls groaned with it, but this power had been allowed to fill the space available like water until there was no air space left. Alistair probably thought he was a big, powerful witch to be able to call this much power, but he was a baby witch if he couldn't control it better than this. A lot of people can call power. Calling is not the measure of your strength as a practitioner. It's what you can do with the power that counts. Though as he pulled me, gently, through the brush of the hovering energy, I did wonder what he was doing with all this magic. He might be wasting a lot of it just letting it swirl around, but you don't get this much energy without having some idea of what you're doing and some plan of what to do with it.

My voice sounded strange even to me, strained, and breathy. "The living room is full of magic, Alistair. What are you going to do with all of it?" I hoped everyone in the van was getting this.

"Let me show you," he said. We were at the closed door in the left-hand wall.

"What's behind the door?" I asked. It was the only door visible from the entrance. There was an open hallway that led from the rear of the living room farther into the house, and an open entranceway into the kitchen. It was the only closed door, and if the guys had to come save me, I didn't want them wandering around. I wanted them to come straight in and get me out.

"Let's not pretend, Merry. We know why you're here, why we're both here. It's the bedroom." He opened the door, and it was the bedroom. It was red from the four-poster bed to the drapery that covered every wall to the carpet. It was like standing inside a crimson velvet box. Mirrors were set between the heavy drapes like jewels set to charm the eye. There were no windows. It was a closed box and the center of the magic that had been called to this place.

The power rolled over me like suffocating fur, warm, close, choking. I couldn't breathe, couldn't speak. My feet stopped working, but Alistair didn't seem to notice. He kept leading me, pulling me into the room, so that I stumbled, and the only thing that kept me from falling to the polished wood of the floor was his arms. He tried to lift me in his arms, but I collapsed the rest of the way to the floor so that he couldn't lift me up. I wasn't fainting. I just didn't want to be picked up because I knew where he'd take me: to the bed. And if that was the center of all this power, I didn't want to go there, not yet.

"Wait," I said, "wait. Give a girl a second to catch her breath." There was a small chest of drawers about waist high just inside the door. I used the edge of the chest of drawers to get to my feet, though Alistair was there to help, very solicitous. I set my purse on the edge of the chest, squeezing the handle twice to turn on the hidden camera. If the camera was on, it had a near perfect view of the bed.

He came up behind me, arms wrapping around me from behind, managing to pin my arms to my sides, but not hard. He meant it to be a hug. The fact that it panicked me wasn't his fault, not really. I tried to relax against his body, in the circle of his arms, but couldn't. The power was too thick, and I couldn't relax. The best I could do was not to pull away.

He nuzzled the side of my face, lips moving down my skin. "You're not wearing any base."

"I don't need any." I turned my head just enough to encourage him to continue kissing down my face to my neck. It was all the invitation he needed to work his way lower. His lips stopped at my shoulder, but his hands slid from my arms to encircle my waist. "God, you're a tiny thing. I can reach around you with my hands."

I moved gently away from him toward the bed. My senses were dulling to the magic. I'd had years of practice at ignoring amazing amounts of power. If you're sensitive to such things and you don't want to go mad, you adapt. Magic can become like white noise, like the sounds of the city itself, only coming to your attention when you concentrate.

I stood on the bright Persian rug that surrounded the bed, just like Naomi had described it. But I couldn't force myself to walk those last few feet to the bed because I could feel the circle that lay under the rug like a great hand pushing me away. It was a circle of power, something to stand inside while you conjured, so that whatever you called wouldn't come inside and eat you, or so you could call something inside the circle and remain safely outside. I wouldn't know until I saw the runes which kind of circle it was, whether it was a shield or a prison. Even seeing the runes and the construction of the circle might not tell me. I knew sidhe witchery, but there are other kinds of power, other mystical languages to work magic with. I might not recognize any of it, and then there would be only one way to know what the circle was . . . by walking into it.

The real trouble was that some circles are constructed to hold fey captive, and once I was inside, I might have trouble getting back out. If they were really a bunch of fey wanna-bes, they probably wouldn't be trying to capture us, but you never know. If you love something hard enough but can never touch it or keep it, the love can curdle into a jealousy more destructive than any hate.

Alistair loosened his tie as he walked toward me, an antici-patory smile curling his lips. He was utterly arrogant, sure of himself and of me. It was so tempting to just walk out, just so I could watch that arrogance slide away. He hadn't done any-thing mystical yet, let alone illegal. Was I being too easy? Did he save the mystical stuff for the reluctant ones? Did I need to be more reluctant? Or more aggressive? Which would get Alistair Norton on tape doing something illegal? I was still trying to make up my mind whether to be the unwilling virgin or the eager whore when he was there in front of me, and I was out of time.

He bent down to kiss me, and I raised my head up to meet him, rising on tiptoe, hands balancing on his arms. His biceps flexed under my hands, swelling against the cloth of his jacket. I don't think he was even aware of it, just habit. He kissed like he seemed to do everything, with a practiced ease, smooth skill. His arms wrapped around my waist, pressed me to his body, lifted me off the floor. He started moving me backward toward the circle. I drew back from the kiss enough to say, "Wait, wait." But we were in it, and it stole my breath for a second until we were on the other side, inside the circle. It was like being in the eye of a storm. Inside the circle was quiet, the most restful place I'd felt in the entire house. A tightness I hadn't known was there eased from my shoulders and back.

Alistair scooped my legs up and walked us both onto the bed with his knees. When we were near the center of the bed, he laid me down and stayed on his knees, looking at me, tow-ering over me. But I'd worked alongside Uther for three years. Six feet was nothing when you'd been having lunch with thirteen.

I don't think I looked impressed enough because he took off the tie and tossed it to the bed, fingers going to his shirt buttons. He was going to undress first. I was surprised. A control freak usually wants their victim naked first. He was out of his jacket and shirt, hands going to his belt before I could figure out what to do. Slowing him down seemed to be good.

I sat up, touching his hands. "Slow down. Let me enjoy the unveiling. You're rushing through it like you've got another date tonight." I held on to his hands, rubbing across his skin, stroking his bare arms. I concentrated on the feel of the tiny hairs on his forearms and how they slid under my touch. If I concentrated just on the physical sensations one at a time, I could make my eyes lie or at least show a genuine interest. The trick was not to think too hard about who I was touching.

"There's no one but you tonight, Merry." He drew me to my knees, then ran his hands through my hair, letting it slide through his fingers so that he held my face in his big hands. "There will be no one else for either of us after tonight, Merry."

I didn't like the sound of that, but it was the first thing he'd said that was sort of psychotic so I was doing something right. "What do you mean, Alistair? We eloping to Vegas?"

He smiled, still holding my face, staring into my eyes like he'd memorize them. "Marriage is just a ceremony, but tonight I'll show you what it means to be truly one with a man."

I raised an eyebrow before I could help myself. Knowing my face already showed it, I said, "My, you do have a high opinion of yourself."

"It's not idle boasting, Merry." He kissed me, softly, then crawled past me to the headboard of the bed. He pressed on the wood, and a little door sprang open. A secret compartment, how nifty. He turned with a small glass bottle in his hands. It was one of those glass bottles with curves and frills to it that you're supposed to keep expensive perfume in, but no one ever does.

"Take off the dress," he said.

"Why?"

"It's massage oil." He held the bottle up so I could see the thick oil in the light through the ruby glass.

I smiled at him, and I tried to make it everything he wanted: sexual, flirtatious, a little cynical. "The pants first."

He grinned at me, evidently pleased. "I thought you said you wanted to go slow."

"If we're getting naked, you first."

He started to turn and set the bottle inside the compartment again. "I'll hold it for you," I said.

He stopped in midmotion, turning back to me with a heat in his eyes that was almost touchable. "Only if you put some on your breasts while I undress."

"Will it stain my dress?"

He actually seemed to think about that, face becoming thoughtful, intelligence showing through. "I'm not sure, but I'll buy you a new one if it's ruined."

"Men will promise anything in the heat of the moment," I said.

"Let me see the oil run down that pure white skin. Make them glisten for me." He handed the bottle to me, wrapping my hands around it. He kissed me again, mouth lingering on me, his tongue probing, opening my mouth so the kiss could be more. He drew back, slowly. "Please, Merry, please."

He moved back, but not far, hands at his belt again. He drew the leather tongue slowly through the gold buckle, drawing out each movement while he watched me. It made me smile because he was doing what I'd asked. He was slowly unveiling himself.

The least I could do was do what he'd asked. The push-up bra left enough of my breasts bare so that I didn't have to lift anything out of the dress. I drew the stopper out of the bottle. It had one of those long glass rods on the end of it, to glide along your skin. I sniffed the oil. It smelled of cinnamon and vanilla. There was something familiar about the odor, but I couldn't place it. The oil was nearly clear. "Aren't you supposed to warm it first?" I said.

"It reacts to your body's heat." He pulled the belt out of the last loop and tossed it between us on the bed. "Your turn."

I lifted the stopper out of the bottle. The oil clung to it in a heavy strand. I touched the end of the glass rod to the top of my breast. The oil was already warm, body temperature. I trailed the rod across the mounds of my breasts and tiny trails of oil followed it, tracing like thick tears across my skin. The smell of cinnamon and vanilla seemed to soak into my skin like a warm rush.

Alistair undid the snap on his pants and slowly drew down the zipper. He wore red bikini underwear, like he'd dressed to match the bedroom. The scarlet was very bright against his skin, clinging over the front of his body like a second skin. He lay down on the bed to get the pants off, gazing up at me so that I towered over him on my knees as he had towered over me earlier.

He reached up, still flat on his back, running his fingertips across the oil, spreading it over my skin. He came to his knees, hands smoothing over the tops of my breasts, fingers trying to get inside the dress and touch more, but it was too tight. Prior planning prevents embarrassing groping. He rubbed his oiled hands down his own chest, then took the bottle from me and trailed the glass stopper across my mouth like he was putting on lip gloss. It was sweet upon my lips, thick and sweet. He kissed me, both his hands still holding the bottle, so that it was just his mouth on mine. He kissed me like he was going to eat the oil off my lips. I melted into the kiss, hands stroking over his oiled chest, feeling the muscles of his stomach moving under my hands. My hand slid lower, over the front of him, finding him hard and ready. The feel of him thrilled through my body like a jolt of energy. That was when I realized that I was enjoying myself and had forgotten why I was there.

I drew back from the kiss and tried to focus, to think. I didn't want to think. I wanted to touch him and have him touch me. My breasts ached to be touched. My mouth almost burned with the need to close the distance between us. He leaned in for another kiss, and I crawled backward, falling onto my back in my rush to put distance between us.

Alistair crawled to me on knees and one hand. The other hand held the bottle. He straddled me the way a horse stands over her colt. My gaze kept sliding down his body to the hard front of him. I couldn't keep my eyes on his face. It was embarrassing, and frightening.

"Stupid," I said, "so stupid. It's in the oil. There's a spell in the oil."

His voice came in an almost harsh whisper. "The oil is the spell."

I didn't understand what he meant at first, but I knew I didn't want any more of it on me. He started to open the bottle, and I sat up, taking his hands in mine, keeping the lid on the damn thing. The moment I touched his hands, I lost. We were kissing again, and I hadn't meant to. It was as if the more we kissed, the more I wanted to be kissed, like it fed on itself.

I threw myself back on the bed, hands covering my face. "No!" I knew what it was now: Branwyn's Tears, Aeval's Joy, Fergus's Sweat. It could make a human into a sidhe lover for one night. It could turn even a sidhe into a sexual slave, if that sidhe had no access to other sidhe. No fey, no matter how talented, how powerful, can rival the sidhe, so it's said. You can forget what the touch is like. You can fight not to dream of glowing flesh and eyes like molten jewels, a sweep of ankle-length hair across your body. But the desire is always there just under the surface, like an alcoholic who can never take another drink for fear that one drink will never be enough to satisfy that thirst.

I screamed, loud and long and wordless. There was another side effect of Branwyn's Tears. No glamour can stand against it. Because your concentration can't stand against it. I felt my glamour leaking away, felt my skin as if my entire body took a deep breath.

I lowered my hands slowly until I was staring up into the mirror on the ceiling. My eyes glowed like tricolor jewels. The outer edge of my irises was molten gold, within that was a circle of jade green, and last came emerald fire to chase around the pupil. Only the sidhe, or a cat, could have such eyes. My mouth was a mixture of crimsons: the remains of my lipstick, and the scarlet gleam of the lips themselves. My skin was a white so pure, it shimmered, like the most perfect of pearls. Again there was light coming out of my skin, like a candle behind a veil. The red-black of my hair fell around the shining colors like a spill of dark blood. If my hair had been pure black, I'd have looked like Snow White carved from jewels.

This wasn't just me without the glamour. It was me when my power was upon me, when magic was in the air.

"My God, you're sidhe," he whispered.

I turned those glowing eyes to Alistair. I expected fear in his eyes, but there was a kind of soft wonderment. "He said you would come if we were faithful, if we truly believed, and here you are."

"Who said I'd come?"

"A sidhe princess to feast upon." He spoke in a voice that held awe, but his hands slid under my dress, fingers curling over the band of my panties. I grabbed his wrist and slapped him with the other hand. Slapped him hard enough to leave a red imprint of my hand on his face. We had all the proof we needed to put him in jail. I didn't have to play along anymore. You can take the energy of Branwyn's Tears and turn it from sex to violence, or so they say in the Unseelie Court. I was going to try. I was really going to try.

If he'd hit me back, it might have worked, but he didn't. He collapsed his body on top of mine, pinning me to the bed. He was so low on my body that his face was level with mine. There was a moment where I looked into his eyes, and I saw the same stricken need in his eyes that I felt in mine. The Tears cut both ways. You could not use it to seduce without being seduced.

He made a small sound low in his throat and kissed me. I ate at his mouth, one hand going to the ponytail holder that held his hair back. I jerked it out, spilling his shoulder-length hair around me like a silken curtain. I plunged my hands into his hair, two fistfuls of it, held tight, while I explored his mouth.

His free hand tried to reach down the dress for my breast, but it was still too tight. He pulled at the cloth, and my body jerked with the force of it as the cloth ripped, and his hand spilled inside my bra.

The touch of his hand on my breast jerked my head back, freed my mouth from him. I was suddenly looking behind us at the mirrors on the far wall. It took me a few seconds to realize something was wrong. Part of it was distraction. Alistair was kissing my neck, working his mouth over my skin, ever lower. Part of it was someone else's magic. Someone powerful didn't want me to know they were watching. But the mirrors were blank like the eyes of the blind. I looked up at the mirror above the bed, and it was empty, too, as if Alistair and I weren't there.

Then I felt the spell like a great sucking wound, drawing my power to the surface until it spilled from the pores of my skin, and up, up into that mirrored surface. Whatever it was, it was feeding off my power like a psychic leech. It pulled the power slowly like sucking up a straw. I did the only thing I could think of. I shoved the power into the throat of the spell, force-fed my power into the magic. They hadn't expected that, and the magic shuddered. There was a figure in the mirror, but it wasn't Alistair or me. The figure was tall, slender, covered in a hooded grey cloak that hid every inch of the body. The cloak was illusion, an illusion to hide the witch at the other end of the spell. Every illusion can be stripped away.

Alistair's mouth bit gently on my breast, and my concentration shattered. I looked down at him as he drew my nipple into his mouth. It felt as if his mouth drew on a hot line that went directly from my breast to my groin. It tore a gasp from my throat, made me writhe under his touch. A small part of me hated that this man could make my body react, but the larger part of me had turned to nothing but nerve endings and engorged flesh. I was sinking deeper into Branwyn's Tears, drowning in them. Soon there'd be no thinking, just sensations. I couldn't think to draw power. All I could smell, feel, taste was cinnamon, vanilla, and sex. I took that sex, that need, and wrapped it in my mind, and shoved it into the spell. The cloak wavered, and for a second I almost saw what lay behind it, but Alistair went to his knees, blocking my view.

He pulled his underwear down his hips, his thighs, and I was suddenly staring at the hard, gleaming length of him. It took my breath away for a second, not because he was so wonderful, but just out of pure need. It was as if my body saw the cure for all this need, and the cure was lying flat against Alistair's belly. I don't know if it was the sight of him nude or the power I'd shoved into the spell, but I was feeling more myself. A throbbing, nymphomaniac self, but still it was an improvement.

I sat up. The front of the dress was torn away, my bra pulled down so that my breasts were bare. I said, "No, Alistair, no. We are not doing this."

A prickle of energy spilled over the bed, running in goose bumps on my body. Alistair looked up as if he saw something I didn't, and said, "But you said to only use small amounts. Too much could drive her mad." He listened, face intent. I heard nothing.

Whatever was in the mirror wasn't hiding from Alistair, just from me.

Alistair opened the bottle. I had time to say "No." My hand went out as if to ward off a blow. He threw the oil on me. It was like being touched by some great liquid hand. I couldn't move, couldn't do anything but scream. He poured the oil down the front of my body. It soaked through my dress, to the skin underneath. He raised the skirt, and this time I couldn't stop him. I was frozen, overwhelmed. He poured the oil over the satin of my panties, and I fell back onto the bed, my spine bowing, hands scrambling at the sheets. My skin felt like it was swelling, stretching with a desire that narrowed the world down to the need to be touched, to be held, to be had. It wouldn't have mattered who it was. The spell did not care, and neither did I. I opened my arms to the naked man kneeling over me. He collapsed on top of me. I could feel him tight and heavy against the satin of the panties. Even that thin piece of cloth was too much. I wanted him inside me, wanted it more than I'd ever wanted anything or anyone.

Then something floated down from the mirror. It was a tiny black speck, but it held my attention, compelled it. It got closer, and I could see that it was a small spider, hanging from a silken thread. I watched the spider float slowly to Alistair's shoulder. The spider was small and black and shiny like patent leather. My body was cooler, my head clearer. Jeremy had managed to get something through to me. I knew now that the magician on the other end of the spell had kept them all trapped outside the house.

I felt the smooth head of Alistair's penis slip around the edge of the panties, touching my swollen wetness. It made me cry out, but I could still talk, still think. Now if I couldn't get away, it really was going to be rape. "Stop it, Alistair, stop it!" I struggled to get out from under him, but he was too big, too heavy. I was trapped. He started to push inside me. I got a hand between his groin and mine. He could have penetrated me, but it seemed to distract him. He fumbled at my hand, trying to move it, so he could finish.

I screamed, "Jeremy!"

Alistair and I fought over where my hands were, and I glimpsed the mirror. It was full of grey, swirling fog. It shivered, rippling like water. It bowed out like a bubble. It was only then that I knew that the magician was sidhe. He or she was hiding themselves from me, but the mirrors, that was sidhe magic. Then Alistair won the fight and slid the tip of himself inside me. I cried out, and it was half protest and half pleasure. My mind didn't want this, but the oil still rode my body. I screamed, "No!" but my hips twitched under him, trying to help him slide inside me. I wanted, needed him to be inside me, to feel his naked body inside of mine. Still, I screamed, "No!"

Alistair flinched and pulled out of me the small distance he'd won, rising to his knees, brushing at his back. He came away with a small smear of crimson. He'd crushed the spider.

Another small black spider crawled down his arm. He batted it away. Two more spiders crawled over his shoulders. He tried to touch the middle of his own back and turned like a dog chasing its tail, and I saw his back. The skin had split open, and a wave of tiny black spiders poured out. They swarmed over him like black water, a moving, biting second skin. He screamed, clawing at his back, crushing some of them, but there were always more, until he was a moving mass of them. They poured into his open mouth as he shrieked, and he choked, and still he screamed.

All the mirrors were pulsing, breathing, the glass stretching out and in like something elastic and alive. I heard a man's voice in my head: "Get under the bed, now." I didn't argue. I rolled off the bed and crawled under it. The red sheets spilled down over the edge, hiding everything but a thin sliver of light.

There was a sound of breaking glass, like a thousand windows breaking all at once. Alistair's screams vanished under the sound of falling glass. The glass burst on the carpet like brittle hail, a tinkling, sharp sound.

Silence filled the room by degrees, as the glass settled over the room. There was a sound of splintering wood. I couldn't see it, but I thought it was the door. "Merry, Merry!" It was Jeremy.

Roane yelled, "Merry, dear God."

I crawled to the edge of the bed and lifted the rim of the sheet to see the floor glittering silver. I called, "I'm here. I'm here." I reached my hand out from under the bed, waving it, but unable to move farther without getting cut on the glass.

A hand gripped mine, and someone laid a suit jacket over the glass so that Roane could pull me out from under the bed. It wasn't until he was cradling me in his arms that I realized I was still covered in Branwyn's Tears, and what that might mean for us. But I'd gotten a glimpse of what lay on the bed, and it stole the words from my mouth. I think I forgot to breathe for a second or two.

Roane carried me toward the door. I stared back over his shoulder at what lay on the bed. I knew it was a man. I even knew it was Alistair Norton, but if I hadn't known what I was looking at, I'm not sure I'd have known it was human. The shape was as crimson as the sheets it lay on. The glass had turned him into so much raw meat. I couldn't see the spiders under all that blood. I knew two things, maybe three. First, the magician on the other end of the spell was sidhe; second, he or she had tried to kill me; third, if it wasn't for Jeremy getting a spell through the ward, I'd be just a smaller red lump on the blood-soaked bed. I owed Jeremy a very big favor.

Chapter 6

THE POLICE WOULDN'T LET ME SHOWER. THEY WOULDN'T
even let me wash my hands. Four hours after Roane carried
me out of the bedroom, I was still trying to explain to the police exactly what had happened to Alistair Norton. I wasn't
having much luck. No one believed my version of events.
They'd all watched the tape, and they still didn't believe me.
I think the only reason I hadn't been charged with Alistair's
murder was that I'd been outed as Princess Meredith NicEssus.
They knew and I knew that all I had to do was claim diplomatic immunity and I could walk out the door. So they were
taking their time about charges.

What they didn't know was that I was almost as eager to
avoid bringing in the diplomats as they were. Once I claimed
diplomatic immunity, they'd contact the Board of Human-
Fey Relations. They would contact the ambassador to the
sidhe courts. The ambassador would contact the Queen of Air
and Darkness. He'd tell her exactly where I was. Knowing my
aunt, she'd tell them to keep me "safe" until her guard could
arrive to bring me back home. I'd be trapped like a rabbit in a
snare until someone came along to snap my neck and take me
home like a prize.

I sat at the small table with a glass of water in front of me. I
had a blanket that the paramedics had given me draped over
the back of the chair. The blanket had been to keep me warm
in case of shock and to cover the ruined front of my dress. I'd
spent part of the last few hours being cold and needing the
blanket, but the rest of the time it was as if my blood ran hot. I
was either shivering or almost sweating, a combination of

shock and Branwyn's Tears. Going from one extreme to the other had given me an amazing headache. No one would get me anything for the headache because they were all planning on getting me to the hospital soon—always soon, never now.

I'd still been glowing softly when the first police backups had arrived. I wouldn't be able to do glamour as long as the oil was in my system. So I couldn't hide. Some of the first uniforms recognized me; one of them had said, "You're Princess Meredith." The soft California night had taken a breath around us, and I knew it was only a matter of time until the Queen of Air and Darkness sent someone to investigate this latest whisper. I had to be out of town before that happened. I had at least one more night, maybe two, before my aunt's guard would arrive. I had time to sit here and answer questions. But I was getting tired of answering the same questions.

So why was I still sitting in the hard-backed chair, looking across a small table at a detective I'd never met before? First, even if I walked out of here without being charged or claiming diplomatic immunity, they would contact the politicians. They'd do it to cover their asses. Second, I wanted Detective Alvera to believe me about Branwyn's Tears and just how serious it would be if there was more of the oil out there. Probably it was a gift from whatever sidhe had set up the leech spell. The one bottle may have been all anyone outside the courts had. That was the best-case scenario. But if there was even the slightest chance that humans, with or without sidhe help, had figured out how to manufacture Branwyn's Tears and it was out on the market, then it had to be stopped.

Of course, there was another possibility. The sidhe that set Norton up in his little magic-rape scam might have been giving Branwyn's Tears to lots of others. This was probably the more likely of the two worst-case scenarios, but I couldn't tell the police that another sidhe had been involved with Alistair Norton. You do not take sidhe business to the human police, not if you want to keep all your body parts attached.

Police are good at smelling lies, or maybe, to save time,

they just assume everyone is lying. Whatever the reason, Detective Alvera didn't like my story. He sat across from me, tall, dark, slender, with hands that looked too big for his narrow shoulders. His eyes were a solid brown with a fringe of dark lashes that made you notice them, or maybe that was just me tonight. Jeremy had laid a warding over me to help me control the Tears. He'd traced runes across my forehead with his finger and his power. Nothing visible to the police, but I could feel them like a cold fire if I concentrated. Without Jeremy's spell, Goddess knew what I'd have done by now. Something embarrassing and slutty. Even protected by the runes I was very aware of all the men in the room.

Alvera stared at me with lovely, distrustful eyes. I watched how the shape of his lips formed words, such a generous mouth, a kissable mouth. "Did you hear what I just said, Ms. NicEssus?"

I blinked at him and realized I hadn't. "I'm sorry, Detective. Could you repeat it?"

"I think this interrogation is coming to an end, Detective Alvera," my lawyer said. "It's obvious that my client is very tired and in shock."

My lawyer was a partner at James, Browning, and Galan. She was Galan. Usually Browning handled the Grey Detective Agency's legal affairs. I think Eileen Galan was here because Jeremy had mentioned the rape part. A woman would be more sympathetic, or at least that was the theory.

She sat beside me in her dark pinstriped skirt suit, so neat and pressed she looked like she'd just been unwrapped. Her greying blond hair was styled perfectly; her makeup was flawless. There was even a shine on her black high-heeled pumps. It was two o'clock in the morning, and Eileen looked like she'd just finished a power breakfast and was eager to greet the day.

Alvera's gaze went over me from the push-up bra shoving my breasts in plain view to my eyes, last. "She doesn't look like she's in shock to me, Counselor."

"My client was raped, Detective Alvera. Yet, she has not been taken to a hospital, or examined by a doctor. The only reason I have not demanded these things is my client's determination to answer your questions and aid you in this investigation. Frankly, I'm beginning to think my client is not capable of protecting her own interests tonight. I saw how she was brutalized on the tape. I must step in for Meredith's rights even if she doesn't want me to."

Alvera and I looked at each other across the table. He spoke the next words staring directly at me, major eye contact. "I saw the tape, too, Counselor. It looked like your client was enjoying herself most of the time. She said no, but her body kept doing yes."

If Alvera thought that I was going to crack under the pressure of his steely gaze and his insults, he just didn't know me. Even normally it wouldn't have worked, but tonight I was too numb to rise to such poor bait.

"That is insulting, not just to my client, but to women everywhere, Detective Alvera. This interview is over. I'll expect a police escort to the hospital for the rape kit."

He just looked at her with those pretty, jaded eyes. "A woman can keep saying no, stop, but if she's playing with a man's dick, you can't blame him for getting mixed messages."

I smiled, shaking my head.

"You think this is funny, Ms. NicEssus? The tape may make a case for rape, but it also shows you turning Alistair Norton into so much raw meat."

"One more time, I did not kill Alistair Norton. About the rape, you're either trying to be deliberately insulting to get me angry enough to say something indiscreet, or you're a male chauvinist asshole. If the first is true, you're wasting your time. If the second is true, you're wasting mine."

"I'm sorry that answering questions about a man you left to bleed to death in his own bed at his own house is a waste of your time."

"What kind of man has a house that his wife doesn't know about?" I asked.

"He was cheating on his wife, so he deserved to die, is that it? I know you fey have a thing about marriage and monogamy, but execution seems a bit harsh."

"My client has said repeatedly that she did not do the spell that caused the mirrors to crack."

"But she's alive, Counselor. If she didn't do the spell, then how did she know to take cover?"

"I said already that I recognized the spell, Detective Alvera."

"Why didn't Norton recognize the spell? He's got a rep as a big-time magician. He should have seen it coming, too."

"I told you that Branwyn's Tears affects humans more strongly than it effects the sidhe. He wasn't paying as much attention to his surroundings as I was."

"Where did the spiders come from?"

"I don't know." I wasn't telling him that Jeremy had done the spiders because then they'd start blaming him for the mirrors, or maybe charge us both as conspirators.

He shook his head. "Just say you did it. It was self-defense."

"The only reason I am still sitting here is because I want you, the police, to understand how dangerous this spelled oil can be. If there is more Branwyn's Tears out there, you need to find it and destroy it."

"Lust spells don't work, Ms. NicEssus. Aphrodisiacs don't work. Some magic potion that'll make a woman drop her pants for a man she doesn't want is bullshit. It doesn't exist."

"You'll wish it didn't if it gets out into the general population. Maybe Norton had the only bottle, but just in case there is more of it out there, please look for his friends."

He riffled back through the notebook that had been lying untouched on the table for a very long time. "Yeah, Liam, Donald, and Brendan, no last names. Two of them have faerie ears, all of them with long hair. Yeah, we'll be able to find them, no problem. Of course, they might be a lower priority since they aren't wanted on murder charges."

Eileen stood again. "Come on, Meredith, this interview is over, and I mean it." She looked at both of us as if we were naughty first graders, and we would not dare argue with her. I was tired, and they weren't going to believe me about Branwyn's Tears. I stood up.

Alvera stood, too. "Sit down, Meredith."

"Are we on a first name basis, Alvera? I don't know yours."

"It's Raimundo. Now sit down."

"If," I said, "if I claim diplomatic immunity, I walk out of here and it doesn't matter who's right or who's wrong." I looked at him, and thanks to Jeremy's ward, I was able to just meet his eyes. If I concentrated, I hardly noticed the line of his upper lip.

He looked at me a long time before saying, "What would keep you from claiming diplomatic immunity and walking out that door, Princess?"

"You believing me about the lust oil, Raimundo."

He smiled. "Sure, I believe you."

I shook my head. "No joy, Detective. A lie won't keep me in this room." I was bluffing, sort of. I hoped he didn't call it.

"What will?" he said.

I had an idea. I needed to prove to the police just how serious Branwyn's Tears could be. Sex with a sidhe would haunt a human forever, but a taste of it wouldn't do permanent harm. Some dreams, perhaps, or extra eagerness in the bedroom for a while, but nothing bad. You needed the joining of flesh and magic in a major intimate way to be beyond the point of safety. If we all shared the merest taste, everyone would survive.

"What if I could prove to you that the lust oil worked?"

He crossed his arms over his chest and managed to look even more cynical, which I hadn't thought possible. "I'm listening."

"You believe that no spell can make you instantly lust after some stranger, right?"

He nodded. "That's right."

"Do I have your permission to touch you, Detective?"

He smiled, his gaze roaming over the front of my dress. I hoped he was being deliberately insulting because otherwise he wasn't very bright, and I needed him to be good at his job. With a politically sensitive case like this one, Alvera was either the best they had or the worst. They either hoped for super detective to clear it all up or were offering him up as a sort of preemptive scapegoat for when the shit hit the fan. I'd hoped for super detective, but I was beginning to lean toward scapegoat. Of course, since I was lying about several things, maybe I didn't want him to be good at his job. But I wasn't lying about what he thought I was lying about. Honest.

"A minute ago I was Raimundo. Now you want permission to touch me and I'm back to detective."

"It's called a distancing technique, Detective Alvera," I said.

"And here I thought you wanted to get up close and personal, not distant."

I heard Eileen Galan draw a breath to speak and I stopped her, holding up my hand. "It's okay, Eileen, he can't be this stupid and still have made detective, so he's baiting me. I don't know what he hopes to gain from it."

The humor drained from his eyes, leaving them cold and dark, unreadable as stone. "The truth would be nice."

"You behaved yourself for hours in here. Suddenly in the last thirty minutes you've managed to insult me sexually several times, and you've been staring at my breasts. Why the change?"

Those cold eyes stared at my face for a heartbeat or two. "Being businesslike and professional wasn't getting me shit."

"I'm listed as a rape victim in the initial reports whether you believe that or not. Your conduct in the last half hour could get you on the wrong end of a sexual harassment suit."

His eyes flicked to my still silent lawyer, then back to me. "I've seen rape victims, Princess. I've taken them to the hospital, held their hands while they cried. One girl was only twelve. She was so traumatized, she couldn't speak. It took me nine days, working with a therapist, to get her to name her attackers. You don't act like a rape victim."

I shook my head. "You arrogant . . . man." I made the last word sound like the worst of insults. "Have you ever been raped, Raimundo?"

He blinked, but his eyes stayed neutral. "No."

"Then don't you dare presume to tell me how I'm supposed to be acting or feeling or any fucking thing. I'm not so broken up tonight. Part of it's the damn spell, but part of it,

Detective, is that as rapes go this one wasn't that bad. Eileen said I'd been brutalized. Well, she's a lawyer. I can forgive her the choice of words, but she can't know what the word means. She's never seen what a man can do to a woman if he really wants to hurt her. I've seen brutal, Detective, and what happened tonight wasn't brutal, but just because I'm not bleeding my life away through tubes or my face is still recognizable under the bruises, doesn't mean it wasn't rape."

Something passed through his eyes, something I couldn't read, then his eyes were back to giving nothing away. "This wasn't your first time, was it?" His voice was soft, gentle.

I looked at the floor, afraid to meet his eyes. "Not me, Detective, not me."

"A friend," he said in that same gentle voice.

I looked up then, and the sudden show of compassion almost did me in, almost made me want to confide in him. Almost. I remembered Keelin's face a mask of blood, one eye socket crushed so that her eye had lolled out onto her cheek. If she'd had a nose, it would have been broken, but her mother was a brownie, and they don't have human noses. Three of her arms had been held at awkward angles like the broken legs of a spider. No sidhe healer would lay hands on her because she was so near death and they would not risk their own lives for a goblin-brownie half-breed. My father had carried her to a human hospital and reported the attack to the authorities. My father had been Prince of Flame and Flesh, and even his sister the Queen feared him, so he was not punished for inviting the humans in. It was on record. I could talk about it without being punished. So good to know there was something I could tell the whole truth on tonight.

"Tell me," he said, voice grown even softer.

"When we were both seventeen, my best friend Keelin Nic Brown was raped." My voice was bland and empty, as Alvera's eyes had been moments before. "They broke the bones around one of her eyes so that the eye was just lying there on her face, hanging by threads." I took a deep breath and pushed the memory away, not aware that I'd pushed it away with my hands, as if that would help, until I'd finished the movement. "I've seen people beaten, but not like that, never like that. They tried to beat her to death and very near succeeded." I had myself under control again. I wasn't going to cry. I was glad. I hated to cry. It always made me feel so weak.

"I'm sorry," he said.

"Don't be sorry for me, Detective Alvera. Watching Keelin heal gave me a measuring rod for violence. If it wasn't as bad as what happened to Keelin, then it can't be that bad. It's gotten me through some very harsh things without having hysterics."

"Like tonight," he said in that same talk-the-jumper-down-from-the-ledge voice.

I nodded. "Yeah, like tonight, though I will admit that what happened to Alistair Norton was one of the worst things I've ever seen, and I've seen some bad things. I did not kill him. I'm not saying I might not have killed him if he'd completed the rape. When I recovered from the lust spell, I might have hunted him down. I don't know. But someone else took care of it for me."

"Who?" he asked.

My voice dropped to a whisper. "I wish I knew, Detective. I really wish I knew."

"Do you need to touch me to prove this lust oil of yours is real?"

I nodded.

"You have my permission," Alvera said.

"If I prove that the lust spell is real, you'll bring in narcotics?"

"Yeah."

"You swear it," I said, "your word of honor."

His eyes got all serious. He seemed to understand that his word meant something to me that it might not to a human. Finally, he nodded. "Yeah, I give you my word."

I glanced at Eileen Galan and back to the one-way glass on the far wall. "Spoken before witnesses. The Gods themselves beware of it if you break your promise."

He nodded. "Should I be expecting a lightning bolt?"

I shook my head. "No, not a lightning bolt."

He'd started to smile, but when I didn't seem to think it was funny, his smile faded. "I keep my word, Princess."

"I hope so, Detective, for all our sakes."

Eileen took me to one side, a few steps away from the detective. "What are you planning to do, Meredith?"

"Are you a practitioner of any mystic art?" I asked.

"I'm a lawyer, not a witch."

"Then just watch. It's sort of self-explanatory." I drew away from her gently and walked back to Alvera. I stayed farther away than I would have normally, just close enough that I could touch him. I'd had oil on my fingers, but some of it had rubbed off. I wanted this to work so I drew my fingers across my breasts where the oil was still slick and shining. Branwyn's Tears had a long shelf life. I reached out toward Alvera's face.

He leaned back out of reach.

I raised an eyebrow at him, hand extended in midair. "You said I could touch you."

He nodded. "Sorry, habit." He moved a step closer to me but maneuvered us so that we were in full view of our audience behind the one-way glass. He visibly steeled himself not to flinch away from me. I wasn't sure if he didn't want me touching him because I was fey or because he thought I'd murdered someone by magic or because of some esoteric cop thing.

I traced my fingertips along his full mouth until they glistened like lip gloss. His eyes widened, and he looked softly stunned. I stepped away from him, and he reached toward me, then stopped himself. He folded his arms across his chest and tried to talk, then shook his head.

I went back to my chair and sat down. I crossed my legs, and the skirt was short enough that I flashed the lacy edge of the thigh-highs. Alvera noticed. He watched every move of my hands as I smoothed the skirt into place. I could see his pulse in his neck jumping under his skin. The wide eyes, the

half-parted lips as he fought to control himself were very in-
triguing. It took more self-control than was pretty to not close
the distance between us and make the first move. I was still
safe behind Jeremy's runes, but it was an act of will not to go
to him.

Eileen Galan was looking from one to the other of us, a
puzzled expression on her face. "Did I miss something?"

Alvera just kept staring at me, arms hugging himself, as if
afraid to move or even speak, for fear that any forward motion would spill him over the edge and into my arms.

I answered her. "Yes, you missed something."

"What?"

"Branwyn's Tears," I said softly.

Alvera closed his eyes, his body beginning to sway slightly.

"Are you all right, Detective?" Eileen said.

He opened his eyes, and said, "Yeah, I'm . . ." He looked
back at me. ". . . fine." But that last was barely audible. There
was a kind of a panic on his face as if he couldn't believe what
he was thinking.

I don't know how long he might have been able to stand
there, but I had run out of patience tonight. I ran my fingertip
over the white, glistening mounds of my breasts, and that was
all it took.

He crossed the room in three strides, grabbing my forearms, lifting me to my feet. He was nearly a foot taller than I
was, and he had to bend at an awkward angle, but he managed. He put those kissable lips against mine, and the first
taste tore Jeremy's careful spell away. I was suddenly a throbbing, needful thing. My body still wanted to finish what had
been denied it earlier. I kissed him like I was feeding off of
his soft lips, my tongue seeking for something deep inside
him. My oiled hands caressed his face. The more oil that
touched him, the stronger the spell. He lifted me around the
waist, raising me to eye level so he didn't have to bend.

I wrapped my legs around his waist, and I could feel him
through the layers of cloth that separated us. My body pulsed
with the contact, and I broke from the kiss, not to breathe but
to cry out.

He pressed me to the tabletop, his groin grinding into me. Lying on the table he was too tall to maintain the kiss and keep our lower bodies pressed together, so he raised himself up on his arms like a push-up, keeping his body pressed into mine.

I stared up the length of his body and finally met his eyes. They held the darkness that usually doesn't come to a man's eyes until later when the clothes are gone and there's no turning back. I grabbed two handfuls of his shirt and pulled them, sending his buttons flying, baring his chest and stomach. I raised up, doing a sort of sit-up so I could lick down his chest, run my hands across the flatness of his stomach. I tried to put my hand down his pants, but his belt defeated me.

Suddenly, the room was full of uniforms and plainclothes detectives. They pulled Alvera off me, and he fought them. They had to pile on top of him, ride him to the floor in a mountain of uniforms. He was screaming, wordlessly.

I lay on the table, the skirt hiked to my waist, my body so full of blood and need that I couldn't move. I was angry, angry that they'd stopped us. I knew that was stupid. I knew I didn't want to have sex in an interrogation room in front of an entire precinct, and yet . . . I was still angry, still wanting.

A young uniformed cop was standing beside the table. He was trying not to stare and failing. It was easy to grab his hand, to press the Tears over the pulse point in his wrist. His blood beat against my hand, and he bent over me, kissed me before anyone noticed what was happening.

Someone said, "Jesus, Riley, don't touch her!"

Hands grabbed Riley, tore him from my lips, my hands. I reached for him, sitting up, screaming, "No!" I started off the table to go to one of them, when another detective grabbed my arms, held me sitting on the table's edge. He stared down at his hands as if he'd burned them against my bare arms. He said, softly, "Oh, my God."

Just before he bent and kissed me, he yelled, "Get some women officers in here." I learned later that this medium-build, slightly balding man with the strong hands and the muscled body was Lieutenant Peterson. They had to handcuff him before they could carry him out of the room.

I was buried under a mound of female officers until I couldn't move. A couple of the female officers had the same trouble that the men had, just as at least one of the men had had no problem not manhandling me. Nothing like being outed at work!

They got Jeremy back in to redo the warding. I calmed, eventually, but I was in no shape to talk to anyone. Jeremy assured me that he'd talk to narcotics for me, though he was pretty sure that the officers who had been in the room with me would be persuasive on the dangers of Branwyn's Tears.

Roane was waiting for me, a pair of surgical gloves on his hands so he could touch me, a jacket to throw over my head to keep people from recognizing me. The police took us out the back way. So far the media didn't seem to know that I'd finally surfaced and under what circumstances. But someone at the police station or on the ambulance would talk. They might do it for money, they might do it by accident, but the media would find out. It was only a matter of time. A race to see which hounds would find me first: the tabloids or the Queen's Guard. If I'd been well, I'd have gotten in my car and driven out of state that night or caught the first plane to anywhere. But Roane took me to his apartment because it was closer than mine. I didn't care where we went as long as there was a shower. If I didn't get my body free of the Tears or have sex soon, I was going to lose my mind. I was voting for a shower. What I didn't realize until too late was that Roane was voting for sex.

Chapter 7

THE FRONT PART OF MY BRAIN KNEW I SHOULD HAVE HAD Roane take me to my car. There was a packet taped under the driver's seat with money, a new identity complete with a driver's license and credit cards. I'd always planned on simply driving out of the city or to the airport and taking the first plane that caught my fancy. It was a good plan. The police would be contacting the embassy by now, and before dawn my aunt would know where I was, who I was, and what I'd been doing for three years.

The primitive rear of my brain wanted to jump Roane while he was driving eighty on the freeway. My skin felt large and swollen with need. I actually sat on my hands in the car so I wouldn't touch him. The last thing we needed was for me to contaminate him with the Tears. At least one of us needed to be sane tonight, and until I had a shower, it wasn't going to be me.

I mounted the stairs to Roane's apartment, hugging myself, fingers digging into my arms hard enough to leave nail marks. It was all that kept me from touching Roane as he moved up the stairs just ahead of me.

He left the door open behind him, and I followed him into the room. He stood in the center of the large open space. Even in the dark the room was strangely bright, the white walls gleaming in the moonlight. Roane stood a dark figure in the midst of all that silver gloaming. He stared out at the sea as he did every time we entered his apartment, stopped and stared out the bank of windows that made up the west and south walls. The sea rolled out and out from the windows in a gleaming, rushing spill of silver and dark, with a rim of white foam riding like an edge of lace as the waves spilled toward the shore.

I would always be second in Roane's heart because his love belonged to his first mistress—the sea. He would mourn her loss when I was just dust in a grave. There was a loneliness to that knowledge. The same loneliness I'd felt at court, watching the sidhe squabble about insults that occurred a hundred years before I was born, and that the sidhe would still be quarreling about a hundred years after I died. Bitter, a little, but mostly just very aware that I was an outsider. I was sidhe so I couldn't be human, and I was mortal so I couldn't be sidhe. Neither fish nor fowl.

Even feeling isolated, left out, my gaze slid to the bed. It was a mound of white sheets and scattered pillows—Roane had stripped it but had only done a haphazard job of remaking it. If the sheets were clean, he never understood the reason for getting the wrinkles out. I had a sudden image of him naked against those white sheets. The vision was so sharp that it hurt, tightening my stomach, twisting lower things, until it was hard to breathe. I leaned against the closed door until I could move, then straightened. I would not be controlled by chemicals and magic. I was sidhe, a weak, lesser sidhe, but that didn't change that I was the height of all we and men called magical. I wasn't some human peasant with my first taste of faerie. I was a princess of the sidhe, and I would, by Goddess, act like it.

I locked the door behind me, and even the sound of the lock going home didn't make Roane turn. He would commune with his view until he was ready for me. I didn't have the patience for it tonight. I walked past him through the darkened room to the bathroom. I turned the bathroom light on and was left blinking in the brightness. The bathroom was tiny, barely room for the stool, small sink, and the bathtub. The tub might have been original to the house because it was deep and claw-footed and very antique-looking. The shower curtain had been strung on a rail above the tub. The curtain had seals from all over the world on it, with their common names in print by each image. I'd ordered it from one of those catalogs that you always seem to get when you have a background in biology, found it in among the animal-motif T-shirts, candles shaped like animals, books about trips to the Arctic Circle and summers spent watching wolves in remote places. Roane had loved the curtain, and I'd loved giving it to him. I loved having sex in the shower surrounded by my gift for him.

I had a sudden image of his body wet and naked, the feel of his skin slick with soap. I cursed softly and flung the curtain aside. I turned the water on so it would get warm. I needed the Tears off of me before I did something regrettable. I would be safe tonight. No one would be able to show up on my doorstep until tomorrow at the earliest. I could take Roane, fill my hands with the silk of his skin, coat my body in the sweet scented closeness of his body. Who would it hurt?

It was the Tears talking, not me. I needed tonight for my head start if I was to get out of town. The police wouldn't like me leaving town, but the cops wouldn't kill me, and my family would. Hell, California wasn't even a death penalty state.

The dress was ripped enough that I tried to pull the sleeves down over my shoulders like a jacket, but the zipper still held it in place. The front of the dress was soaked thick and heavy with the oil. I'd never known anyone to waste so much of something that even the sidhe considered so valuable. But if I'd died with Alistair Norton, then maybe the sidhe wizard was hoping that no one would know what Branwyn's Tears were. The sidhe were very snobbish about what the lesser fey did and did not know. He, she, or they might have thought with me dead, they'd be safe.

The sidhe, whoever they were, had given Branwyn's Tears to a mortal to be used against other fey. It was punishable by eternal torture. There are a few downsides to being immortal. One of the biggest is that punishment can last a very, very long time.

Of course, so can pleasure. I closed my eyes as if that would chase away the images that came flooding back. It wasn't Roane I was thinking of. It was Griffin. He'd been my fiancé for seven years. If we'd managed to get with child, we'd have been wife and husband. But there had been no child, and in the end there had been only pain. He'd betrayed me with other sidhe women, and when I had the bad taste to protest, he'd told me he was tired of being with a half-mortal. He wanted the real thing, not a pale imitation. I could still hear the words stinging in my ears, but it was his golden flesh I saw behind my eyes, his copper hair spilled across my body, the way candlelight glistened along the shining length of him. I hadn't thought about him in years, and now I could taste him on my lips.

For this one night while the oil lasted, it could make a lesser fey, or a human, sidhe. They would shine with our power and give and take pleasure as one of us. It was a great gift, but like most gifts of faerie it was a double-edged one. Because the human or fey would spend the rest of their life longing for that power, that touch. A human could waste and die from lack of it. Roane was a fey without his magic, without his sealskin. He had no magic of his own to protect him from what the Tears could do to him.

I'd known how much I missed the touch of another sidhe, but until this moment I hadn't realized how much. If Griffin had been in the other room, I'd have gone to him. I might have driven a knife through his heart in the morning, but tonight, I'd have gone to him.

I heard Roane in the doorway behind me but didn't turn. I didn't want to see him standing there. I wasn't sure my abused strength of will could take it. The front of the dress was ripped, ruined, but I still couldn't get the zipper myself. "Could you, please, unzip me?" My voice sounded strangled as if the words had to be pulled from my lips. I think because what I wanted to say was, "Take me, you rowdy beast," but that lacked a certain dignity and Roane deserved better than to be left craving something he could never touch again. I could drop my glamour and sleep with him after this night, but every night he touched me in true form would only draw the addiction tighter.

He unzipped me, hands moving up to help slide the dress from my shoulders. I jerked away from him. "My skin is soaked with the Tears. Don't touch me."

"Even with the gloves on?" he asked.

I'd forgotten about the surgical gloves. "No, I guess with the gloves you'll be safe enough."

He lifted the cloth off my shoulders, slowly, carefully, as if he were afraid to touch me. I slipped my arms out, but the cloth was so thick with oil that the dress wouldn't slide. It clung to me like a thick, heavy hand, sucking against my skin as I peeled it down my body. Roane helped me pull the wet cloth over my hips, kneeling so I could step out of it. I was unsteady on the high heels and cursed softly that I hadn't taken them off sooner. I'd closed my eyes so I wouldn't see him as he helped me undress. I touched his shoulder to steady myself on the high heels and nearly fell anyway because my hand touched bare skin.

I opened my eyes and found him kneeling in front of me, nude except for the gloves. I stumbled back from him so violently that I ended up in the tub, on my ass, one hand held out in front of me to ward him off. I was sitting in about an inch of water and fumbled for the faucets to turn the water off. Though I might have been better off leaving it on and crawling under it.

Roane was laughing. "I thought I'd get you unzipped before you noticed, but I didn't know you'd close your eyes." He stripped the gloves off using his teeth, my dress still in his arms. He plunged his naked hands into the oil-soaked cloth, hugged it against his bare chest.

I was shaking my head over and over. "You don't know what you're doing, Roane."

He looked at me over the tub edge, and there was nothing innocent in his big brown eyes. "For tonight I can be sidhe for you."

I sat in the tub like I was about to take a shower in my underwear, and tried to sound reasonable. All the blood seemed to have left my brain and gathered in other places. It made it hard to think. "I can't do glamour tonight, Roane."

"I don't want you to do glamour. I want to be with you, Merry. No masks. No illusions."

"Without your own magic, you'll be like a human. You won't be able to protect yourself from the charm. You'll be elf-struck."

"I won't wither and die for want of sidhe flesh, Merry. I may have lost my magic, but I am immortal."

"You may not die, Roane, but forever is a long time to want what you cannot have."

"I know what I want," he said.

I started to open my mouth, to tell him at least part of the truth, part of the reason that I had to clean myself off and get out of town. But he stood up, and my voice died in my throat. I couldn't breathe, let alone talk. All I could do was stare.

He wadded the dress in his hands so tight that the muscles in his arms strained with the movement. Oil squeezed out of the cloth, gliding in slow lines from his chest, across the flat smoothness of his stomach, trailing ever lower. He was already smooth and hard, but when the oil slid over him, his breath caught in a sharp hiss. He ran one hand down his stomach, spreading the oil in a gleaming sheet across the pale perfection of his skin. I should have told him to stop, should have screamed for help, but I watched his hand move lower, until he cupped himself, slid the oil over the hardness of himself. His head threw back, eyes closed, and words tore in a loud gasp from his strained throat. "Oh, Gods."

I remembered that there was something important I should have been saying or doing, but for my life I couldn't remember what it was. I was thinking things, but not words. Words had deserted me, leaving only images: sight, touch, smell, and finally taste.

Roane's skin tasted overwhelmingly of cinnamon and vanilla, but under that was something green, herbal, a light clean taste like drinking spring water straight from the heart of the Earth. Under all that was the taste of his skin, sweet, smooth, and lightly salted with sweat.

We ended on the bed. My clothes were gone, though I didn't remember them going. We were naked and slick with oil on the clean white sheets. The feel of his body sliding over mine brought my breath shuddering from between half-parted lips. He kissed me, tongue probing, and I opened to him, rising from the bed to force his tongue deeper inside my mouth. My hips moved with the kiss, and he took it as invitation, sliding inside me, slowly, until he found me wet and ready, then he slammed the length of him inside me, as fast, as far as it would go. I cried out under him, body rising off the bed, then falling back against the sheets, staring up at him.

His face was inches from mine, his eyes so close they filled my view. He watched my face as he moved inside me, half-raised on his arms so he could watch my body writhe underneath him. I couldn't stay still. I had to move, had to rise up to meet him, until a rhythm built between us, a rhythm forged of pounding flesh, the thundering of our hearts, the slick juices of our bodies, and the throbbing of every nerve. It was as if one touch was many caresses; one kiss, a thousand kisses. Each movement of his body seemed to fill me like warm water spreading out and out, filling up my skin, my muscles, my blood, my bones, until it was all one rush of warmth that built and built like the press of light as night fades. My body sang with it. My fingertips tingled, and just when I thought I couldn't hold any more, the warmth turned to heat and roared over me, through me. Distantly, I heard noises, screaming, and it was Roane, and it was me.

He collapsed on top of me, suddenly heavier, his neck lying against my face so that I felt his pulse like a racing thing jumping against my skin. We lay there entwined as intimately as man can be with woman, holding each other until our hearts slowed.

Roane raised his head first, propping himself on his arms to look down at me. The look was one of wonderment, like a child who had learned a new joy that until that moment he hadn't known existed. He said nothing, just stared down at me, smiling.

I was smiling, too, but there was a vein of wistfulness to mine. I remembered now what I'd forgotten. I should have showered and fled the city. I should never have touched Roane with Branwyn's Tears on our bodies. But the damage was done.

My voice came soft, strange to my own ears, as if we hadn't spoken for a very long time. "Look at your skin."

Roane glanced at his own body and hissed like a startled cat. He rolled off my body to sit staring at his hands, arms, everything. He was glowing, a soft, nearly amber light as if fire were being reflected through a golden jewel, and that jewel was his body.

"What is it?" he asked, voice low and almost frightened.

"You are sidhe, for tonight."

He looked at me. "I don't understand," he said.

I sighed. "I know."

He put his hand just above my skin. I glowed with a white, cold light, like moonlight caught behind glass. The amber glow of his hand reflected off the white glow, turning it pale yellow as his hand moved just above my skin. "What can I do with it?"

I watched him move that glowing hand down my body, still careful not to touch my skin. "I don't know. Every sidhe is different. We all have different abilities. Different variations on a theme."

He laid his hand against the scar on my ribs, just under my left breast. It hurt like the twinge of arthritis when it's cold, but it wasn't cold. I moved his hand away from the mark. It was the perfect imprint of a hand, bigger than Roane's, longer, more slender fingers. It was brown and raised slightly above my skin. The scar turned black when my skin glowed, as if the light could not touch it, a bad spot.

"What happened?" he asked.

"I was in a duel."

He started to touch the scar again, and I grabbed his hand, pressing our flesh together, forcing that amber glow into my white. It felt as if our hands melded together, the flesh parting, swallowing. He jerked away, rubbing his hand against his chest, but that slid the oil over his hand, and that didn't help.

Roane still didn't understand that he'd had only the first taste of what it could mean to be sidhe.

"Every sidhe has a hand of power. Some can heal by touch. Some can kill. The sidhe I fought placed her hand against my ribs. She broke my ribs, tore through muscle, and tried to crush my heart, all without ever breaking the skin."

"You lost the duel," he said.

"I lost the duel, but I survived, and that was always win enough for me."

Roane frowned. "You seem saddened. I know you enjoyed it. Why such gloom?" He trailed a finger along my face, and the glow intensified where we touched. I turned my face from him.

"It's too late to save you, Roane, but it's not too late to save myself."

I felt him lie down beside me, and I moved my body just enough to keep him from lying the length of himself along the length of me. I looked at him from inches away.

"Save you from what, Merry?"

"I can't tell you why, but I need to leave tonight, not just this apartment, but the city."

He looked startled. "Why?"

I shook my head. "If I told you that, you'd be in more danger than you already are."

He accepted that and didn't ask again. "Is there anything I can do to help?"

I smiled, then laughed. "I can't go to my car, let alone the airport glowing like a rising moon, and I can't do glamour until the oil wears away."

"How long?" he asked.

"I don't know." I stared down the length of his body and found him limp, though he recovered quickly, as a rule. But I knew something he didn't. Tonight, like it or not, I was sidhe.

"What is your hand of power?" he asked, though it had taken him a long time to ask the question. He must have truly wanted to know, to ask that which was not offered.

I sat up. "I don't have one."

He frowned. "You said all sidhe have one."

I nodded. "It's one of many excuses the others have used over the years to deny me."

"Deny you what?"

"Everything." I ran my hand just above the line of his body, and the amber light intensified, following my touch like a fire when you breathe on it to make it glow. "When our hands melded, it was one of the side effects of the power. Our entire bodies can do the same."

He raised eyebrows at that.

I cupped him in my hand, and he responded, but I spilled power into him, and he was instantly hard, instantly ready. It made his stomach contract, made him sit up, moving my hand away from him. "It felt almost too good. It almost hurt."

I nodded. "Yes."

He gave a nervous laugh. "I thought you didn't have a hand of power."

"I don't, but I am descended from five different fertility deities. I can bring you back to strength all night, as quickly and as often as we want." I leaned my face toward his. "You are like a child tonight, Roane. You can't control the power, but I can. I could bring you again and again until you rubbed yourself raw and begged me to stop."

He'd lain down on the bed as I moved over him, until he was staring up at me, eyes wide, his auburn hair spilled around his face. Tonight, it was almost the same shade as mine . . . almost. He spoke in a breathy rush. "If you do that, it will be your flesh that gets rubbed raw, too."

"Think if I was not the only sidhe in this room, Roane. Think what we could make you do, and you could not stop us." I spoke the last into his half-parted lips. When I kissed him, he jumped as if it had hurt, and I knew it hadn't.

I pulled back enough to see his face. "You're afraid of me."

He swallowed. "Yes."

"Good. Now you begin to understand what you have called to life in this room. Power comes with a price, Roane, and so does pleasure. You have called both, and if I were a different sidhe, you would pay dearly for them." I watched the fear slide across his face, fill his eyes. It pleased me. I liked the edge that fear could give sex. Not the big fear, where you truly weren't sure you'd both come out alive, but the lesser fear, where you risked blood, pain, but nothing that wouldn't heal, nothing you didn't want. There is a vast difference between a little game playing and cruelty. I wasn't into cruelty.

I stared down at Roane, that sweet flesh, those lovely eyes, and I wanted to scratch nails over that perfect body, sink teeth into his flesh, and draw just a little bit of blood in a lot of different places. The thought tightened my body in places where most people didn't respond to violence, no matter how mild. Bad wiring, maybe, but there comes a point when you either embrace who and what you are, or condemn yourself to be miserable all your days. Other people will try to make you miserable; don't help them by doing the job yourself. I wanted to share a little pain, a little blood, a little fear, but Roane wasn't into any of that. Hurting him wouldn't bring him pleasure, and I wasn't into torture. I was not a sexual sadist, and Roane would never know how lucky he was that that particular miswiring was not part of my urges. Of course, there are always other urges.

I wanted him, wanted him so badly that I didn't trust myself to be careful. Roane would carry the desire for this experience to his grave, whenever that would be, but he could carry more than psychological scars away from this night. If I wasn't careful. Even now, even here with him sidhe for this one night, I couldn't drop all my control. I was still going to have to be the one in charge, the one that said what we would do and what we wouldn't. The one that said how far things would go. I was achingly tired of being the one who drew the line. It wasn't just the magic I missed. It was having someone else in charge or, at least, someone equal. I didn't want to have to worry about hurting my lover. I wanted my lover to be able to protect himself so that I could truly do what I wanted to do without fearing for his safety. Was that really too much to ask?

I glanced back at Roane. He lay on his back, one arm flung over his head, the other arm lying across his stomach, one leg drawn up so that he was displayed, in all his glory. The fear had faded from his face, leaving only desire behind. He had no idea how bad things could get in the next few hours if I wasn't ever so careful.

I hid my face in my hands. I didn't want to be careful. I wanted everything that the magic could give me tonight and to hell with the consequences. Maybe if I hurt him enough, Roane wouldn't look back on it as something wonderful. Maybe he wouldn't crave it like some golden dream. Maybe he'd fear it like a nightmare. A small voice in my head said it would be kinder in the long run. Make him fear us, our touch, our magic, so that he would never want the touch of sidhe hands on his body again. A little pain now to save him from an eternity of suffering later on.

I knew it was lies, and still I couldn't look at him.

His fingertips brushed my back, and I jumped like he'd hit me. I kept my hands over my face. I wasn't ready to look again.

"Those aren't burn scars on your shoulders, are they?"

I lowered my hands, but kept my eyes closed. "No."

"What then?"

"It was another duel. He used magic to try and force me to shape-shift in the middle of the fight." I heard, felt, Roane moving along the bed, closer to me, but he didn't try and touch me again. I was grateful.

"But changing shape doesn't hurt. It feels wonderful."

"Maybe to a roane, but not to one of us. Changing shapes is painful, like all your bones breaking at once and re-forming. I can't change shape on my own at all, but I've seen it in others. You're helpless for the minutes it takes to change form."

"The other sidhe was trying to distract you."

"Yes." I opened my eyes and stared into the blackness of the windows. They acted like a dark mirror, showing Roane sitting just behind me, body half-lost to sight, glowing like the sun behind the moon of my body. The three rings of color in my eyes glowed bright enough that even from that distance you could see the individual colors: emerald, jade, liquid gold. Even Roane's eyes had lightened to a dark honey brown like glowing bronze. Sidhe magic suited him.

He reached for me, and I tensed. He traced his hand over the rippled skin of the scars. "How did you stop him from changing you into something else?"

"I killed him." I saw Roane's eyes widen in the windows, felt his body tense.

"You killed a sidhe royal?"

"Yes."

"But they are immortal."

"I am truly mortal, Roane. What is the one way for all the eternal fey to die?"

I watched the thoughts flicker across his face and finally saw the realization in his eyes. "To invoke mortal blood. The mortal shares our immortality, and we share the mortal's mortality."

"Exactly."

He sat close to me, going up on his knees, but he spoke to my reflection not directly to me. "But that is a very specific ritual. You can't invoke mortality by accident."

"The ritual for a duel binds the two participants together in mortal combat. Among the Unseelie sidhe they share blood before they fight."

His eyes went wider still, until they were like two huge pools of darkness. "When they drank your blood, they shared your mortality."

"Yes."

"Did they know that?"

I smiled then. I couldn't help it. "Not until Arzhul died with my dagger sticking out of him."

"You must have put up a hard battle for him to try and change your form. It's a major spell for the sidhe. If he didn't fear death, then you must have hurt him badly."

I shook my head. "He was showing off. It wasn't enough that he meant to kill me. He wanted to humiliate me first. For one sidhe to force a shape-shift on another is proof that they are the more powerful magician."

"So he was showing off," Roane said. It was the closest he would probably get to asking what happened next.

"I stabbed him, just hoping to distract him, but my father always taught me never to waste a strike. Even if you know you face an immortal, strike as if they could die because deathblows hurt more, even if they won't kill."

"Did you kill the one who scarred you here?" His hand came from behind to trace my ribs.

I shuddered at his touch, and not because it hurt. "No, Rozenwyn is still alive."

"Then why didn't she crush your heart?" His hands slid around my waist, holding me against his body, cradling me. I let myself rest in the curve of his arms, the solid warmth of his body.

"Because her duel was after Arzhul, and when I stabbed her, she panicked, I think. She called the duel won without making the kill."

He rubbed his cheek along mine, and we both watched the colors mingle as our skins touched. "It was the last duel then," he said.

"No," I said.

He kissed my cheek, very softly. "No."

"No, there was one more." I turned my face to him. His lips brushed mine, not quite a kiss.

"What happened?" He spoke the words in a warm breath against my mouth.

"Bleddyn had been one of the Seelie Court once, before he did something so awful that no one will speak of it, and he was cast out. But he was so powerful that the Unseelie Court took him in. His true name was lost, and he became Bleddyn. It means wolf or outlaw, or did once very long ago. It meant he was an outlaw even among the dark court."

Roane kissed the side of my neck where my pulse beat just under the skin. My pulse sped at that light touch. He raised his face enough to ask, "How was he an outlaw?" Then he began to kiss his way down my neck.

"He was subject to horrible rages for no reason. If he hadn't been surrounded by immortals, he'd have killed people, friends as well as enemies."

Roane's kisses had worked down to my shoulder, then my arm. He stopped just long enough to say, "Just rages?" Then lowered his head and kissed until he found the bend in my arm. He lifted my arm so that he could lock his mouth around the fragile skin at the bend. He sucked sudden and sharp on the skin, teeth sinking into my arm enough to hurt, enough to make me gasp. Roane didn't care for pain, but he was an attentive lover, and he knew what I liked, as I knew what he liked. But I suddenly couldn't concentrate on what I was saying.

He raised his face from my arm, leaving a round, nearly perfect imprint of his small sharp teeth. He hadn't broken the skin. I'd never been able to persuade him to go that far, but the mark against my flesh pleased me, made me bend toward him.

He stopped me, asking, "Was it just rages, or were there other things that marked Bleddyn as dangerous?"

It took me a second to remember. I had to sit back from him. "If you want to hear the story, behave yourself."

He lay on his side, one arm flung underneath his head for a pillow. He stretched his body so that I had to notice the way the muscles moved under that gleaming skin. "I thought I was behaving myself."

I shook my head. "You'll make me forget myself, Roane. You don't want that."

"I want you tonight, Merry. I want all of you, no glamour, no hiding, no holding back." He sat up suddenly, peering so close to my face that I started to move back, but he grabbed my arm. "I want to be what you need tonight, Merry."

I shook my head. "You don't understand what you're asking."

"No, I don't, but if you're ever going to have everything, tonight is the night." He grabbed my other arm, pulling us both to our knees, his fingers digging in enough that I knew I'd be bruised tomorrow. That one forceful movement made my heart beat faster. "I've lived for centuries, Merry. If either of us is a child, it's you, not me." His words were fierce, and I'd never seen him like this, so forceful, so demanding.

I could have said, "You're hurting me, Roane," but I was enjoying that part, so instead I said, "You don't sound like yourself."

"I knew you held your glamour in place even when we lay together, but I never dreamed how much you were hiding." He shook me twice, hard enough that I almost told him it did hurt. "Don't hide, Merry." He kissed me then, bruising his lips against mine, forcing his mouth against mine, until if I hadn't opened my mouth he might have cut either his lips or mine on our teeth. He forced me back on the bed, and I wasn't having a good time. I liked pain, not rape.

I stopped him with a hand on his chest, pushing him away from me. He was still above me, eyes strangely fierce, but he was listening. "What are you trying to do, Roane?"

"What happened in your last duel?"

The change of subject was too fast for me. "What?"

"Your last duel, what happened?" His voice, his face was all seriousness while his naked body pressed against mine.

"I killed him."

"How?"

Somehow I knew he wasn't asking about the mechanics of the kill. "He underestimated me."

"I have never underestimated you, Merry. Don't do less for me. Don't treat me as less just because I'm not sidhe. I am a thing of faerie with not a drop of mortal blood in my veins. Do not fear for me." His voice was normal again, but there was still an undercurrent of fierceness.

I stared up into his face and saw the pride there, not a masculine pride, but the pride of the fey. I was treating him as less than fey, and he deserved better, but . . . "What if I hurt you without meaning to?"

"I'll heal," he said.

It made me smile because in that moment I loved him, not the kind of love that the bards sing of, but it was love all the same. "All right, but let's pick a position that puts you dominant, not me."

A thought filled his eyes. "You don't trust yourself."

"No," I said.

"Then trust me. I won't break."

"Promise?" I said.

He smiled, and kissed my forehead, gently like you'd kiss a child. "Promise."

I took him at his word.

I ended with my hands gripping the cool metal rods of the headboard. Roane's body pinned mine to the bed, his groin cupped against my buttocks. It was a position that gave him a great deal of control and kept most of my body turned away from him. I couldn't touch him with my hands. There were so many things I couldn't do from this position, and it was why I'd chosen it. Short of being tied up, it was the safest thing I could think of, and Roane didn't like bondage. Besides, the real dangers had nothing to do with hands or teeth or anything purely physical. Bonds wouldn't really have helped, except to serve as a reminder for me to be careful. I was very afraid that somewhere in the welter of power and flesh I would forget everything but pleasure, and Roane would suffer for it, and I didn't mean suffer in a good way.

The moment he slid inside me, I knew I was in trouble. He was a fearsome thing, holding himself up on his hands so that he could force himself into me with all the strength of his back and hips. I'd once seen Roane punch his fist through a car door to impress a would-be mugger that we weren't worth the trouble. It was like he was trying to push his way into my body and out the other side. I realized something I hadn't before. Roane had thought I was human with fey blood, but still human. He'd been as careful of me, as I had of him. The difference was that I feared my magic would harm him, and he'd feared his physical strength. Tonight there would be no holding back, no true safety net for either of us. For the first time I realized that I might be the one injured, not Roane. Sex with an edge of true danger, there's nothing like it. Add magic that could melt your skin, and it was going to be a very good night.

His body caught a harsh rhythm coming in and out of mine; there was the sound of flesh hitting flesh every time he thrust into me. This, this was what I'd wanted for so very long. He took my body, and I felt the first wave of pleasure. I suddenly worried that he'd bring me before the magic had time to build.

I opened my metaphysical skin as I'd opened my legs, but instead of letting him enter me, I reached up to him. I opened his aura, his magic, like he'd unzipped my dress earlier. His body began to sink into mine, not physically, but the effect is surprisingly similar. He hesitated with his body sheathed inside mine, stopping. I could feel his pulse speeding, speeding, not from physical exertion but from fear. He drew himself out of me completely, and for one heartrending moment I thought he was going to stop, that it would all stop. Then he entered me again, and it was as if he gave himself completely to me, to us, to the night.

The amber and moonlight glow of our skins expanded until we moved in a cocoon of light, of warmth, of power. Every thrust of his body raised the power. Every writhe of my body underneath him drew the magic like a choking shield around us, close and suffocating. I knew that I was trying to draw him inside me, not his organ, but him, like my magic was trying to drink him up. I dug my fingers into the metal rods of the bed until the metal bit into my skin and made me think again. Roane collapsed his body on top of mine, so that the line of his chest and stomach molded against my back, while his groin thrust between my legs. He couldn't get as much power from this angle, but the magic flared between us at the touch of so much skin. Our bodies melded as our hands had earlier, and I could feel him sinking into my back until our hearts touched, fluttering together in a dance more intimate than anything we'd known before.

Our hearts began to beat together, closer and closer until the rhythm was identical and it was one heart, one body, one being, and I no longer knew where I stopped and Roane began. It was in that moment of near perfect unison that I first heard the sea. A soft, murmuring rush of waves on the shore. I floated bodiless, formless in a shining place of light with nothing but the beating of our joined hearts to let me know I was still flesh and not pure magic. And in that shining, formless place, with no bodies to hold us, there was a hurrying, flowing, spilling sound of water. The sound of the ocean chased our heartbeats, filled that bright place. Our heartbeats sank into the waves. We sank deeper and deeper in a blinding circle of light, under the water, and there was no fear. We had come home. We were surrounded by water on every side, and I could feel the pressure of the depth pushing against our hearts as if it would crush us, but I knew it wouldn't. Roane knew it wouldn't. The thought, a separate thought, sent us rising up, and up toward the surface of the invisible ocean that held us. I was aware of how frighteningly cold it was, and I was afraid, and Roane wasn't. He was joyous. We surfaced, and though I knew we were still pressed to the bed in his apartment, I felt the air hit my face. I drew a great breath of air, and I was suddenly aware that the sea was warm. The water was so warm, warmer than blood, warm enough to be almost hot.

I was suddenly aware of my body again. I could feel Roane's body inside mine. But the swirl and rush of warm ocean flowed over us. My eyes told me I was still on the bed, hands holding to the headboard, but I could feel the warm, warm water swirling over us. The invisible ocean filled the glowing light of our two mingled bodies like water inside a goldfish bowl, the ocean held by our power like metaphysical glass. Our bodies were like the wicks of some floating candle, caught in the water and the glass, fire, water, and flesh. Our bodies began to be more real, more solid. The feel of invisible ocean began to fade. The light of our skins began to shrink back inside the shields of our skins. Then the pleasure took us, and the warmth that had been in the water, in the light, crashed over us. We cried out. The warmth became heat, and it filled me up, spilled out my skin, my hands. Sounds tore from my mouth, too primitive to be screams. Roane's body bucked against mine, and the magic held us both, drawing out the orgasm until I felt the metal of the bed begin to melt under my hands. Roane screamed, and it wasn't a scream of pleasure. Finally, finally, we were free. He rolled off of me, and I heard him fall onto the floor. I turned, still lying on my stomach.

He was lying on his side, one hand flung up, reaching for me. I had one quick glimpse of his face, eyes wide and terrified, before fur spilled over that face, and he collapsed in a roil of sleek fur.

I sat up on the bed, reaching for him, knowing there was nothing I could do. Then there was a seal lying on the apartment floor. A large, reddish-furred seal, staring at me with Roane's brown eyes. All I could do was stare. There were no words.

The seal moved clumsily toward the bed, then a seam that hadn't been there opened up the front of the animal, and Roane crawled out. He stood up, holding the new skin in his arms. He stared at me, a look of soft wonder on his face. He was crying, but I don't think he knew it.

I went to him, touching the skin, touching him, as if neither one was real. I hugged him, and my hands found his back was whole, untouched, the skin as smooth and perfect as the rest of him. The burn scars were gone.

He slipped the skin back on before I could find words. The seal stared up at me, moving around the room in awkward almost snakelike movements, then Roane stepped out of the skin again. He turned to me and began to laugh.

He picked me up around the thighs, lifting me up above his head, wrapping us both in the sealskin. He danced us around the room laughing while the tears hadn't even dried on his face. I was crying, too, and laughing.

Roane collapsed on the bed, spilling me across it, lying on top of his sealskin. I was suddenly so tired, horribly tired. I needed to shower and leave. I wasn't glowing anymore. I was almost sure I could do glamour again. But I couldn't keep my eyes open. I'd been drunk only once in my life, and I'd passed out. That was what was happening. I was about to pass out from Branwyn's Tears or just too much magic.

We fell asleep curled in each other's arms, with the skin wrapped around us. The last thing I thought before we fell into a sleep deeper than anything natural wasn't a thought for my safety. The skin was warm, as warm as Roane's arms around me, and I knew that the skin was just as alive, just as much a part of him. I fell into darkness curled between pieces of Roane's warmth, Roane's magic, Roane's love.

Chapter 8

A VOICE WAS SAYING, SOFTLY, "MERRY, MERRY." A HAND stroked the side of my face, smoothing back my hair. I turned, cuddling against the hand, opening my eyes. But the overhead light was on, and I was blinded for a second. I flung a hand up to guard my eyes and turned on my side, burying my face in the pillow.

I managed to say, "Turn off the light."

I felt the bed move, and a second later the rim of brightness under the pillow was gone. I raised my head from the pillow and found the room in near perfect darkness. It had been nearly dawn when Roane and I fell asleep. It should have been light outside. I sat up and looked around the darkened room. Somehow I wasn't surprised that Jeremy was standing by the light switch. I didn't bother looking for Roane. I knew where he was. He was in the ocean with his new skin. He hadn't left me unprotected, but he had left me. Maybe it should have hurt my feelings, but it didn't. I'd given Roane back his first love, the sea.

There is an old saying: never come between a faerie and his magic. Roane was in the arms of his beloved, and it wasn't me. We might never see each other again, and he hadn't said good-bye. But I knew that if ever I needed something he could give me, I could go down to the sea and call him, and he would come. But he couldn't give me love. I loved Roane, but I wasn't in love with him. Lucky me.

I knelt naked in the wrinkled sheets, staring out at the black windows. "How long did we sleep?"

"It's eight o'clock Friday night."

I slid off the bed and stood. "Oh, my God."

"I take it that means that you still being in town after dark is a bad thing."

I looked at him.

He stood near the door, and the light switch. It was hard to tell in the dark but he seemed dressed in one of his usual suits, impeccably tailored, compact and elegant. But there was an underlying tension to him, as if he wanted to say other things, more direct things, or maybe, he knew something already. Something bad.

"What's happened?"

"Nothing yet," he said.

I stared at him. "What do you think is going to happen?" I couldn't quite keep the suspicion out of my voice.

Jeremy laughed. "Don't worry, I haven't made any calls, but I'm sure the police have by now. I don't know why you've been hiding all this time, but if you're hiding from the sluagh, the Host, then you're in deep trouble."

"Sluagh" was a rude name for the lesser Unseelie fey. The Host was the polite phrase. Rude first, polite was an afterthought. Oh, well. Only another Unseelie could say "sluagh" and not have it be a mortal insult.

"I'm an Unseelie princess. Why should I be hiding from them?"

He leaned back against the wall. "That is the question, isn't it."

Even across the room in the dark I could feel the weight of his gaze, the intensity of it. It was impolite for a fey to ask another direct questions, but, oh, he wanted to ask. You could feel the unasked questions like something touchable in the air between us.

"Jump in the shower like a good girl." He lifted a bag from the floor near his feet. "I brought you clothes. The van is downstairs with Ringo and Uther in it. We'll get you to the airport."

"Helping me could be very dangerous, Jeremy."

"Then hurry."

"I don't have my passport."

He tossed a small paper-wrapped packet onto the bed. It was the packet of papers that stayed taped under the seat of my car. He'd brought my new identity. "How did you know?"

"You've hidden from the human authorities, your . . . relatives, and their henchmen for three years. You're not stupid. You knew you'd be found, thus you had a plan to cover yourself. I will say that the next time I'd hide the secret papers in a different spot. It was one of the first places I looked."

I stared at the packet, then at him. "That wasn't all that was under the seat."

He opened his jacket like a model on the runway showing off the smooth line of his shirt and tie. But he was flashing the gun tucked into the waistband of his pants. It was just a darker shape against the paleness of his shirt, but I knew it was a 9-mm LadySmith because it was my gun. He took an extra clip out of one pocket. "The box of extra ammo is in the sack with your clothes." He laid the gun on top of the taped packet and stepped back around the bed, so that it stood between us.

"You seem nervous, Jeremy."

"Shouldn't I be?"

"Nervous of me. I didn't think you'd be impressed with royalty." I watched his face, tried to read what lay underneath, and couldn't. He was hiding something.

He raised his left hand in the air. "Let's just say that Branwyn's Tears has a long shelf life. Take the shower."

"I don't feel the power of the spell anymore."

"Good for you, but trust me about the shower."

I looked at him. "It's bothering you to see me nude."

He nodded. "My apologies for that, but it's why Ringo and Uther are down in the van. Just as a precaution."

I smiled at him, and I found myself wanting to step closer to him, to close a little of that careful distance. I didn't want Jeremy in that way, but the urge to see just how much of a hold I could have on him was there like a dark thought. It wasn't like me to want to push the envelope with a friend. An enemy maybe, but not a friend. Was it a leftover urge from last night, or were the Tears still affecting me more than I realized? I didn't think about it again. I just turned and walked to the bathroom. A quick shower and we'd be on our way to the airport.

Twenty minutes later I was ready, my hair still soaking wet. I was dressed in a pair of navy blue dress slacks, an emerald green silk blouse, and a navy suit jacket that matched the pants. Jeremy had also chosen a pair of black low-heeled pumps and included a pair of black thigh-highs. Since I didn't own any other kind of hose, that I didn't mind. But the rest of it . . . "Next time you pick out clothes for me to run for my life in, include some jogging shoes. Pumps, no matter how low-heeled, just aren't made for it."

"I never have any problem in dress shoes," he said. He was reclining in one of the stiff-backed kitchen chairs. He made the chair look comfortable, and he looked graceful as he reclined in it. Jeremy was too in control, in a tight modern sort of way, to ever be called catlike. But cat was what came to mind as I watched him curled around the chair. Except that cats didn't pose. They just were. Jeremy was definitely posed and trying to appear at ease and failing.

"I am sorry that I forgot your brown contact lenses. Not that it seems to be a problem. I like the eyes as jade green, striking. Matches the blouse, but very human. Though I'd have kept more red in the hair and made it less auburn."

"Red hair stands out at a glance even in a crowd. Glamour is supposed to help you hide, not single you out."

"I know a lot of fey that use glamour for nothing but attracting attention, being more beautiful, more exotic."

I shrugged. "That's their problem. I don't need to advertise."

He stood. "All this time and I never guessed you were sidhe. I thought you were fey, true fey, and hiding that for some reason, but I never guessed the truth." He stood away from the table, hands at his sides. The tension that had been in him since he woke me vibrated from him.

"That bothers you, doesn't it?" I said.

He nodded. "I'm this great magician. I should have seen through the illusion. Or is that an illusion, too? Are you a better magician than I am, Merry? Have you hidden your magic, too?" For the first time I felt the power growing around him. It could be just a shield. Then again, it could be the beginnings of something more.

I faced him, feet apart, hands at my side, mirroring him. I called my own power, slowly, carefully. If we'd been gunslingers, he'd have had his gun out, but not pointed. I was still trying to keep my gun in its holster. You'd think after all this time I wouldn't trust anyone, but I just couldn't believe that Jeremy was my enemy.

"We don't have time for this, Jeremy."

"I thought I could treat you like nothing had changed, but I can't. I have to know."

"Know what, Jeremy?"

"I want to know how much of the last three years has been a lie." I felt his power breathe out around him, fill up that small tight space that was his personal aura. He was pumping a lot of power into his shields. A lot of power.

My shields were always in place, tight, and loaded for bear. It was automatic for me. So automatic that most people, even very sensitive ones, mistook the shielding for my normal power level. It meant that I faced Jeremy with shields at full strength. I didn't have to do anything to add to it. My shielding was better than his, just a fact. My offensive spells on the other hand, well, I'd seen Jeremy work magic. He'd never get through my shields, but I'd never be able to hurt him magically. It would come down to blows or weapons. I was hoping it wouldn't have to come to anything.

"Is the ride to the airport still open, or did you change your mind while I was in the shower?"

"The ride to the airport is still on," he said. Most of the sidhe can see magic in colors or shapes, but I've never been able to do that. I can feel it though, and Jeremy was crowding the room with all the energy he was pouring into his shields.

"Then what's with the power trip?"

"You're sidhe. You're Unseelie sidhe. That's just a step above being a member of the sluagh." Jeremy's Highland accent leaked through onto the phrases. I'd never heard him lose his all-American-from-the-middle-of-nowhere accent. Made me nervous because many of the sidhe pride themselves on retaining their original accents, whatever they may be.

"And your point is what?" But I had a sinking feeling that I knew where he was going with it. I'd almost have rather had a fight.

"The Unseelie thrive on deception. They are not to be trusted."

"Am I not to be trusted, Jeremy? Does three years of friendship mean less to you than old stories?"

Some bitter thought crossed his face. "It is not stories," and again his accent thickened. "I was cast out as a boy from the trow lands. The Seelie Court would not deign to notice a trow boy, but the Unseelie Court, they take in everyone."

I smiled before I could stop myself. "Not everyone." I don't think Jeremy got the sarcasm.

"No, not everyone." He was so angry that a fine trembling had started in his hands. I was about to pay the bill for a centuries-old grievance. It wouldn't be the first time. It probably wouldn't be the last, but it still pissed me off. We didn't have time for his temper tantrum, let alone one of mine.

"I'm sorry that my ancestors abused you, Jeremy, but it was before my time. The Unseelie Court has had a publicist for most of my lifetime."

"To spread the lies," he said in a brogue so thick, it was guttural.

"You want to compare scars?" I lifted my shirt out of my pants and let him see the handprint scar on my ribs.

"Illusion," he said, but he sounded doubtful.

"You can touch it if you want. Glamour fools vision, but not touch, not for another fey." This was a partial truth at best, because I could use glamour to fool every sense, even of another fey, but it wasn't a common ability even among the sidhe, and I was betting that Jeremy would believe me. Sometimes a plausible lie is quicker than an unwanted truth.

He walked toward me slowly, distrust clear on his face. It made my chest tight to see that look on Jeremy's face. He peered at the scar, but stayed out of touching range. He knew that the sidhe's most powerful personal magic was touch-activated, which meant he knew the sidhe more intimately than I'd thought.

I sighed and laced my fingers on top of my head. The shirt slid down over the scar, but I figured Jeremy could move the cloth. He kept peering up at me as he moved forward into arm's reach. He touched the green silk, but stared into my eyes for a long time before he raised it, as if he were trying to read my thoughts. But my face had gone back to that familiar polite, slightly bored, empty look that I'd perfected at court. I could watch a friend be tortured or put a knife into someone's gut with the same look on my face. You don't survive at the court if your face betrays your feelings.

Jeremy lifted the cloth slowly, never taking his eyes from my face. He finally had to look down, and I was very careful to make no move, however small, to spook him. I hated that Jeremy Grey, my friend and boss, was treating me like a very dangerous person. If he only knew how very undangerous I was.

He ran fingertips over the raised, slightly roughened flesh.

"There's more scars on my back, but I just got dressed, so if you don't mind, this is as far as I'm going."

"Why didn't I see them when you were naked or in my office being fitted for the wire?"

"I didn't want you to see them, but I don't bother hiding them when they're under my clothes."

"Never waste magicial energy," he said, as if to himself. He shook his head, as if he were hearing something I couldn't hear. He looked at me, and his eyes were puzzled. "We don't have time to stand here and argue, do we?"

"I've been saying that?"

"Shit," he said. "It's a spell of discontent, distrust, discord. It's means they're coming now." Fear flowed over his face.

"They could still be miles away, Jeremy."

"Or they could be just outside," he said.

He had a point. If they were just outside the door, then a safer bet might be calling the police and waiting for help to arrive. I wouldn't say that Unseelie bad guys were hiding in the bushes, but I was pretty sure that if I called up Detective Alvera and said that Princess Meredith was about to be killed on his turf, they'd send help.

But if I could, my preference was sneaking away. I needed to know what was out there.

Jeremy was looking at me strangely. "You've thought of something. What is it?"

"The Host isn't made up of sidhe, except for one or two sent along as keepers, masters of the hunt. It's part of the horror of being chased by them. I may not be able to find the sidhe if they don't want to be found, but the rest of the Host, them I can find."

He made a sweeping motion with his hands. "Then by all means."

He didn't argue. Didn't ask if I could do it, or if it was safe. He just accepted it. He wasn't acting like my boss anymore. I was Princess Meredith NicEssus, and if I said I could search the night for the Host, he believed me. He would never have believed Merry Gentry, not without proof.

I cast outward, keeping my shields in place, but flinging my power wide. It was dangerous, because if they were on top of us then that opening might be all they needed to overwhelm me, but it was the only way to know how close they were. I felt Uther and Ringo outside, felt their beings, their magic. There was the force of the sea and a thrumming to the land, the magic of all living things, but nothing else. I cast farther and farther outward. Mile after mile and there was nothing, then, there, almost at the edge of my limit something pressed on the air like a storm moving this way, but it wasn't a storm, or at least not a storm of wind and rain. It was too far away for me to get a clear sense of what creatures of faerie rode with the sidhe, but it was enough. We had some time.

I pulled back inside my shields, squeezing them tight. "They're miles from here."

"Then how did they do the spell of discord?"

"My aunt could whisper it on the night wind and it would find its target."

"From Illinois?"

"It might take a day or three, but yes, from Illinois. But don't look so worried. She would never dirty her hands personally with fetch-and-carry duties. She may want me dead, but not from a distance. She'll want to make an example of me, and for that they'll need to get me home."

"How much time do we have?"

I shook my head. "An hour, maybe two."

"We can get you to the airport in time then. Getting you out of town is the only thing I can offer. One sidhe magician, one not even on the spot, kept me out of Alistair Norton's house. I can't break sidhe magic, and that means I'm not going to be any help to you."

"You sent the spiders through the warding at Norton's house. You warned me to hide under the bed. You did great."

He gave me a strange look. "I thought you did the spiders."

There was a moment when we stared at each other. "It wasn't me," I said.

"It wasn't me, either," he said, softly.

"I know this is a cliché, but if it wasn't you, and it wasn't me . . ." I left the rest unsaid.

"Uther isn't capable of something like that."

"Roane doesn't do active magic," I said. I was suddenly cold, and it had nothing to do with the temperature. One of us had to say it out loud. "Then who was it? Who saved me?"

Jeremy shook his head. "I don't know. Sometimes the Unseelie can befriend you before they break you."

"Don't believe all the stories you hear, Jeremy."

"It's not a story." Anger made those simple words hot and unpleasant. I realized suddenly just how afraid he was. The anger was a shield for the fear. His reactions all had a personal taste to them. He wasn't just afraid in a general way. It was specific, based on something besides stories or legends.

"Have you been up close and personal with the Host?"

He nodded and unlocked the door. "We may only have an hour. Let's get out of here."

I pressed my hands to the door, stopped him from opening it. "This is important, Jeremy. If you've been in thrall to one of them, then that sidhe will have . . . power over you. I need to know what was done."

Then he did something I hadn't expected. He started unbuttoning his shirt.

I raised eyebrows. "You're not still being affected by Branwyn's Tears, are you?"

He smiled, then, not his usual smile, but still an improvement. "I was befriended once before by a member of the Host." He left the tie and collar tight, but unbuttoned the rest, slipped his jacket off, folded it over one arm, and gave me his back. "Lift the shirt."

I didn't want to lift the shirt. I'd seen what my relatives could do when they got creative. There were so many awful possibilities, none of which I wanted to see carved into Jeremy's flesh. But I lifted the crisp, grey cloth because I had to know. I didn't gasp because I was prepared. Screaming was overkill.

His back was covered in burn scars, as if someone had pressed a red-hot brand into his flesh again and again. Except this brand was in the shape of a hand. I touched his scars, as he had mine, lightly, fingers tracing them. I started to put my hand over one of the hand marks, then hesitated, and warned him. "I want to place my hand over one of the scars to see the size."

He nodded.

The hand was much bigger than mine, bigger than the mark on my own body. A man's hand, the fingers thicker than most of the sidhe. "Do you know the name of the one who did this?"

"Tamlyn," he said. He sounded embarrassed, and he should have.

Tamlyn was the John Smith of faerie aliases. Tamlyn along with Robin Goodfellow and a handful of others were favorite false identities when true names were to be hidden.

"You must have been very young not to suspect something when he gave that name," I said.

He nodded. "I was that."

"May I check your aura?"

He smiled back at me over his shoulder. The movement wrinkled the skin on his back, making the scars form shapes. "Aura is a New Age word. The fey don't use it."

"Personal power then," I said, but I was staring at his back. I pushed the cloth of his shirt over his shoulders. "Were you tied while this was done?"

"Yes, why?"

"Can you put your hands in the position they were tied in?"

He took a breath as if he'd ask why, but he finally just raised his hands above his head, and moved into the door so that his body was flush against it. He raised his arms until they were held extended as far as they would go, slightly out from his body until he formed a Y shape.

The shirt had slipped back into place and I had to raise it again. But when I did, I saw what I thought I'd find. The hand-shaped burns had formed a picture. It was the image of a dragon, or maybe more accurately a wyrm, long and serpentine. It was vaguely oriental-looking because of the hand shape, but it was most definitely a dragon. But the burns only formed the picture if Jeremy was in exactly the same position as when he was tortured. When he lowered his arms the skin separated and it was just scars.

"You can lower your arms," I said.

He did, turning so that he could look at me. He started tucking in his shirt. I don't think he even realized he was doing it. "You look grim. What did you see in the burns that no one else has seen?"

"Don't tuck your shirt in, yet, Jeremy. I need to lay a warding on your back."

"What did you see, Merry?" He stopped fussing with his shirt, but didn't untuck it for me.

I shook my head. Jeremy had carried the scars for centuries and had never known that the sidhe had played a little game upon his flesh. It showed such disdain for the victim, a callousness that was hard to wrap your mind around. Of course, it might be very practical; cruelty with a purpose, as it were. The sidhe, whoever it was, could have laid a spell on the burns. They might be able to call a dragon out of his flesh or shape-shift him into one. Probably not, but better safe than sorry.

"Let me ward your back, then I'll tell you on the way down to the van."

"Do we have time?" he asked.

"Sure. Hold the shirt out of the way so the burns are bare."

He looked like he didn't believe me, but when I turned him to face the door, he didn't argue. He held the silk shirt out of the way so I could work.

I spilled power into my hands like holding warmth cupped between my palms. I slowly opened my hands, palms facing Jeremy's bare back. I placed my hands just above his skin. That trembling warmth caressed his back, and Jeremy shivered under its touch.

"What runes are you using?" he asked, voice just a touch breathless.

"I'm not," I said. I spread that warm power across the scars, down his back.

He started to turn.

"Don't move."

"What do you mean, you're not using runes? What else can you use?"

I had to kneel to make sure the power covered every scar. When I was sure that everything had been covered, I sealed it, visualizing the power like a coating of glowing yellow light just above his skin. I sealed the edges of that glow so that it clung tight to his skin like a shield.

Jeremy's breath came out in a shivering gasp. "What are you using, Merry?"

"Magic," I said, and stood.

"Can I let the shirt down?"

"Yes."

The grey silk slid into place, and the warding was so solid in my mind's eye that I felt like the cloth should bunch over the magic, but it didn't. The silk slid over his back as if I'd done nothing to it. But I never doubted that I'd done my job.

He began to tuck the shirt in, before he even turned to face me. "You used just your own personal magic for that?"

"Yes."

"Why not use runes? They help empower our magic."

"Many runes are actually ancient symbols for long-forgotten deities or creatures. Who knows? I might be invoking the very sidhe that injured you. I couldn't risk it."

He slipped his jacket on, straightened his tie. "Now tell me what scared you about the scars on my back?"

I opened the apartment door. "While we go to the van." I went out into the hallway before he had time to argue. We'd used up too much time, but not to ward his back would have been too careless for words.

We clattered down the stairs in our dress shoes. "What was it, Merry?"

"A dragon. A wyrm actually, since it didn't have legs."

"You saw a vision in the scars?" He got to the outside door before me, and held it open out of long habit. I drew the gun from behind my back, clicking the safety off.

"I thought the Host was miles away," Jeremy said.

"One lone sidhe could hide from me." I held the gun down at my side so it wouldn't be immediately noticeable. "I won't be taken back, Jeremy. Whatever it takes."

I stepped into the soft California night, before he could say anything. A lot of the fey, especially the sidhe, considered modern weapons cheating. There was no written rule against using guns, but it was still considered bad form, unless you were a member of the Queen's, or the Prince's, elite guard. They got to carry guns if they were protecting the royal body from harm. Well, I was a royal body, a wee, disowned royal body, but still royal whether the rest of them liked it or not. I had no guard to protect me, so I'd do it myself. Whatever that took.

The night was never truly dark here—there were too many electric lights, too many people. I searched that gentle darkness for a lone figure. I searched with eyes, and energy, casting outward in a straining circle as we hurried to the waiting van. There were people in the other houses. I could feel them moving, vibrating. A line of seagulls moved along one of the roofs, half-asleep, moving in protest, aware of my magic sweeping over them. There was a party on the beach. I could feel the energy rising higher, excitement, fear, but the normal fear; should I do it, should I not; is it safe? There was nothing else, unless you count the shivering energy of the sea that was constantly with you near the shore. It got to be like white noise, something ignored, like the crush of so many people, but it was always there. Roane was somewhere in that huge rolling power. I hoped he was having a good time. I knew I wasn't.

The sliding door of the van opened, and I got a glimpse of Uther crouched in the dimness. He held his hand out to me, and I gave him my left hand. His hand engulfed mine, pulling me into the van's interior. He slid the door closed behind me.

Ringo looked back over the driver's seat at me. He barely fit in the driver's seat, all that muscle, those inhumanly long arms, that huge chest squeezed down into a seat made for humans. He smiled, revealing a mouth of some of the sharpest teeth I'd ever seen outside of a wolf. The face was slightly elongated to accommodate the teeth, which made the rest of his more human face seem out of proportion. The teeth flashed out of a solid brown of skin. Once upon a time, Ringo had been a fully human gang member. Then a group of visiting sidhe from the Seelie Court had gotten lost in the wilds of deepest, darkest Los Angeles. A group of gang members had found them. Cultural interaction at its best. The sidhe got the worst end of the fight. Who knows how it happened? Maybe they were too arrogant to fight a bunch of inner-city teenagers. Maybe the inner-city teenagers were just a hell of a lot more vicious than the visiting royals had expected. However it happened, they were losing. But one of the gang members got a bright idea. He switched sides on condition that he get his wish.

The sidhe agreed, and Ringo shot his fellow gang members to death. His wish was to be one of the fey. The sidhe had given their word to grant his wish. They couldn't go back on their word. To make a full human into a part fey, you have to pour wild magic, pure power, into them, and it is the human's will or desire that chooses the shape of that magic. Ringo had been in his early teens when it happened. He'd probably wanted to appear fierce, frightening, to be the toughest son of a bitch around, so the magic had given him his wish. By human standards he was a monster. By sidhe standards, ditto. By fey standards, he was just one of the gang.

I don't know why Ringo left the gangs. Maybe they turned on him. Maybe he got wise. By the time I met him, he'd been an upstanding citizen for years. He was married to his child-hood sweetheart and had three kids. He specialized in body-guard work and did a lot of celebrities that just wanted some exotic muscle to follow them around for a while. Easy work, no real danger, and he got to rub elbows with the stars. Not bad for a kid whose mother had been a fifteen-year-old junkie, father unknown. Ringo keeps a picture of his mom on his desk. She's thirteen, bright-eyed, well groomed, pretty, with the world in front of her. By the next year she was on drugs. She died at seventeen, overdose. There are no pictures of his mother after age thirteen in his office or in his home. It's as if, for Ringo, everything after that wasn't real, wasn't his mother.

His oldest daughter, Amira, looks eerily like that smiling picture. I don't think she'd survive if he found her doing drugs. Ringo says that being on drugs is worse than dead; I think he believes it.

Neither of them remarked on the gun as I slipped it back into the waistband of my pants. They'd probably been with Jeremy when he found the gun and the papers.

Jeremy got in the passenger-side seat. "Let's get to the airport" was all he said. Ringo put the car in gear and away we went.

Chapter 9

THE BACK OF THE VAN WAS EMPTY EXCEPT FOR CARPET AND A modified seat-belt harness that Jeremy had had installed on one side. Uther's seat. I started to crawl into the middle row of seats but Uther touched my arm. "Jeremy has suggested that if you sit with me my aura may serve to overlap yours, thus confusing our pursuers." Each word was carefully enunciated, because the tusks may have looked like they came out of the skin over the mouth, out of the face, but in reality the tusks were modified teeth, attached inside the mouth. It meant if he were careless, he had a tendency to slur his speech. He'd worked with one of Hollywood's leading speech coaches to learn his Midwestern college professor voice. It did not match a face that was more pig than human, with a double set of tusks curling out of it. We'd had one client faint after he spoke to her for the first time. Always fun to shock the humans.

I glanced up at Jeremy. He nodded. "I may be the better magician, but Uther's got that older-than-God energy whirling around him. I think it'll help them overlook you."

It was a great idea, and a simple one. "Gee, Jeremy, I knew there was a reason you were the boss."

He grinned at me, then turned to Ringo. "It's a straight shot up Sepulveda to the airport."

"At least we won't hit rush hour," Ringo said.

I settled into the back of the van, next to Uther. The van came out on Sepulveda a little too fast, and Uther caught me before I had time to fall. His big arms pulled me against him, cradling me against a chest nearly as big as my entire body. Even with my shields firmly in place he was like a large, warm, vibrating thing. I'd met other fey who had no real magic to speak of, just the very barest of glamour, but they were so old and had been around so much magic all their lives that it was as if they'd absorbed the power into the very pores of their skin. Even the sidhe wouldn't find me caught within Uther's arms. They'd sense him, not me. Probably. Initially.

I relaxed against Uther's broad chest, the warm safety of his arms. I don't know what it was about him, but he always made me feel safe. It wasn't just the sheer physical size. It was Uther. He had a center of calm like a fire that you could huddle around in the dark.

Jeremy turned in his seat, as far as the seat belt would allow, wrinkling his suit, which meant what he had to say was serious. "Why did you ward my back, Merry?"

"What?" Uther said.

Jeremy waved the question away. "I had an old sidhe injury on my back. Merry put a ward on it. I want to know why."

"You are persistent," I said.

"Tell me."

I sighed, cuddling Uther's arms around me like a blanket. "It's possible that the sidhe that injured you could call the dragon out of your back or force you to shape-shift into one."

Jeremy's eyes widened. "You can do that?"

"I can't, but I'm not a full-blooded sidhe. I've seen similar things done."

"Will the warding hold?"

I'd have liked to have simply said yes, but it was too close to a lie. "It will hold for a while, but if the sidhe that did the spell is here, he may be powerful enough to breech my magic, or he could simply keep hitting the ward with his own power until he wears the magic away. The chances of the same sidhe being on this hunt are very slim, Jeremy, but I couldn't let you help me, and not ward it."

"Just in case," he said.

I nodded. "Just in case."

"I was very young when this was done, Merry. I can protect myself now."

"You're a powerful magician, but you're not sidhe."

"It makes that big a difference?" he asked.

"It can."

Jeremy fell silent and turned in his seat to help Ringo find the quickest way to the airport. Uther said, "You are tense."

I smiled up at him. "And you're surprised?"

He smiled, that very human mouth under the curved bone of the tusks, the piggish snout. It was like part of his face was a mask, and underneath was just a man, a big one, but just a man.

He ran thick fingers through my still-wet hair. "I take it Branwyn's Tears were still active when Jeremy went up?"

I'd have never taken time for a shower otherwise, and Uther knew that. "So Jeremy told me." I sat up so that I wasn't soaking his shirt with my hair. "Didn't mean to get you wet. Just forgot. Sorry."

He pressed my head, gently, back to his chest with a hand as big as my head. "I was not complaining, just remarking."

I settled back against him, my cheek resting on his upper arm.

"Roane left just after we arrived. Did he go for help?"

I explained about Roane and his newfound skin.

"You didn't know you could heal him?" Uther asked.

"No."

"Interesting," he said. "Very interesting."

I looked up at him. "Do you know something I don't about what happened?"

He gazed down at me, small eyes almost lost in his face. "I know that Roane is a fool."

That made me stare at him, searching his face, trying to read what lay behind those eyes. "He's a roane, and I've given him back the ocean. It's his calling, his heart of hearts."

"You're not angry with him?"

I frowned, shrugging awkwardly in his arms. "Roane is what he is. I can't blame him for that. It would be like yelling at the rain for being wet. It just is."

"So it does not bother you, at all?"

I shrugged again, and his arms settled around me, cradling me almost like a baby, so I could gaze up at him more comfortably. "I'll admit to being disappointed, but not surprised."

"Very understanding."

"I might as well be understanding, Uther—I can't change things." I rubbed my cheek against the warmth of his arm and realized what part of Uther's charm was. He was so large and I was so small, it was like being a child again. That feeling that if someone could hold you in their arms completely, nothing could hurt you. It hadn't been true when I believed it as a very little girl, and it certainly wasn't true now, but it was still nice. Sometimes false comfort is better than no comfort at all.

"Damn," Jeremy said, raising his voice for our benefit. "There's a wreck up ahead—looks like Sepulveda is completely blocked off. We'll try to take side streets around it."

I rolled my head back against Uther's arm to see Jeremy. "Let me guess, everyone else is trying to exit here, too."

"Of course," he said. "Settle in. It's going to take a while."

I moved my head so I was looking up at Uther again. "Heard any good jokes lately?"

He gave a small smile. "No, but my legs are going to fall asleep if I must keep them tucked under like this for long."

"Sorry." I started to move away so he could adjust.

"No need to move." He put one arm under my thighs, kept the other arm behind my back, and picked me up. He held me like a baby, effortlessly, while he straightened his legs out in front of him. He settled me onto his lap, one arm behind my back, the other lying loosely across my legs and his.

I laughed. "Sometimes I wonder what it would be like to be . . . big."

"And I wonder what it would be like to be small."

"But you were a child once. You remember what that was like."

He gazed into the distance. "Childhood was a very long time ago for me, but yes, I do remember. But that is not the kind of small that I mean." He looked down at me, and there was something in his eyes, something lonely, needy. Something that pierced that calmness in him that I valued so much.

"What's wrong, Uther?" My voice was soft. There was something very private about us being back there alone with no one in the middle seats.

His hand rested lightly on my thigh, and I was finally able to read the look in his eyes. It wasn't a look I'd ever seen in Uther's face. I remembered his comment when I was getting fitted for the wire, how he'd wait in the other room because it had been so long since he'd seen a naked woman.

The surprise must have shone on my face, because he turned his face away from me. "I'm sorry, Merry. If this is completely unwelcome, tell me so, and I will never mention it again."

I didn't know what to say, but I tried. "It's not that, Uther. I'm about to get on a plane and go Goddess knows where. We may never see each other again." Which was partially true. I mean, I was leaving town. I couldn't think of any way to finish this in this short drive without hurting his feelings or lying to him. I wanted to avoid both.

He spoke without looking at me. "I thought you were human with some fey blood in you. I would never have suggested this to someone who was raised human. But your reaction to Roane's desertion is proof that you don't think like a human." He turned almost shyly back to me. The look in his eyes was so open, so trusting. It wasn't that he thought I'd say yes. He didn't know, but he was trusting me not to react badly.

It had just been yesterday that I'd first thought of how very alone Uther must be out here on the coast. How many times had I cuddled against him like this, thinking of him as some kind of big brother, a father substitute? Too many. It had been unfair, and he'd always been the perfect gentleman because he thought I was human. Now he knew the truth, and it had changed things. Even if I said no, and he took it well, I'd never be able to treat him this casually again. I'd never be able to cuddle in his big arms in innocence. That was gone. I mourned that, but there was no recovering it. All I could do now was try and keep Uther from getting hurt. The trouble was I didn't know how to do that because I didn't have a clue what to say.

My thinking had taken too long. He closed his eyes and moved his hand off my thigh. "I'm sorry, Merry."

I reached up and touched his chin. "No, Uther, I'm flattered."

He opened his eyes, looked at me, but the hurt was there, plain to see. He'd put his heart on his sleeve, and I'd put a knife through it. Dammit, I was about to get on a plane and never see these people again. I didn't want to leave him like this. He was too good a friend for that.

"I am part human, Uther. I can't . . ." There was no delicate way to put it. "I can't take the damage that a full-blooded fey could take."

"Damage?"

So much for being coy. "You're too large for my body, Uther. If you were . . . smaller, I could have sex with you for an afternoon, but I don't see us dating. You're my friend."

He looked at me, gaze searching my face. "You could truly sleep with me and not be repulsed?"

"Repulsed? Uther, you have been too long among the humans. You are a jack-in-irons and you look exactly as you are supposed to look. There are others of your kind. You are not a freak."

He shook his head. "I am exiled, Merry. I can never go back to faerie, and here among the humans I am a freak."

It made my chest tight to hear him say that. "Uther, don't let other people's eyes make you hate yourself."

"How can it not?" he asked.

I laid a hand over his chest, feeling the sure thick beat of his heart. "Inside is Uther, my friend, and I love you as a friend."

"I've been among humans long enough to know what the friend speech means," he said. Again he turned away from me, his body growing stiff and uncomfortable, as if he couldn't bear for me to touch him.

I got to my knees. I would have said I straddled his legs, but the best I could do was to put a knee on each thigh. I touched his face with my hands, exploring the slope of his forehead, the thick eyebrows. I had to lower my arms and come from underneath to trace his cheeks. I ran my thumb along his mouth, rubbing my hands along the smooth bone of the tusks. "You are a handsome jack-in-irons. The double tusk is highly prized. And that curve in the end—the jacks consider it a sign of virility."

"How do you know that?" His voice was soft, a whisper.

"When I was a teenager, the queen took a jack named Yannick as her lover. She said, after she'd been with him, that no sidhe could fill her as her Jack of Hearts could." In the end she'd called him her Jack of Fools, and he'd fallen out of favor. He'd gotten away with his life, which was more than most of the queen's nonsidhe lovers managed. The humans usually ended up committing suicide.

Uther stared at me. With me kneeling on his legs we were almost eye to eye. "What did you think of Yannick?" he asked, voice low and lower, so that I had to lean in to hear him.

"I thought he was a fool." I leaned in to kiss him and he turned away. I put a hand on either side of his face and brought him back to face me. "But I thought that all the queen's lovers were fools." I had to sit on Uther's lap, a leg to either side of his waist to get an angle to kiss him. The tusks got in the way for kissing. But if it would take that hurt from his eyes, it would be worth the effort.

I kissed him as my friend. I kissed him because I didn't find him ugly. I'd grown up around fey that made Uther look like a GQ cover boy by human standards. One thing the Unseelie teaches is the love of every form of fey. There is beauty in all of us. Ugly is simply not a word you use at the Unseelie Court. At the Seelie court I was considered ugly, not tall enough, not slender enough, and my hair was the blood auburn of the Unseelie Court, not the more human red of the Seelie Court. Among the Unseelie I hadn't had many "boyfriends" either. Not because they didn't find me attractive, but because I was mortal. A sidhe that was mortal frightened them, I think. They treated it like a contagious disease. Only

Griffin had been willing to try, and in the end I hadn't been sidhe enough for him either.

I knew what it was to be forever the outsider, the freak. I put all that into the kiss, closing my eyes, cupping his chin in my hands. I kissed him hard enough to feel how the bones of his upper jaw widened before they curled upward.

Uther kissed like he spoke, carefully, each movement, like each syllable, well thought out. His hands kneaded my lower back, and I could feel the amazing strength in them, the potential in his body to break me like some fragile doll. Only trust would take you to his bed and let you expect to come out the other side unharmed. But I did trust Uther, and I wanted him to believe in himself again.

"I hate to interrupt," Jeremy said, "but there's another wreck up ahead. There's a wreck at every side street we've tried."

I drew back from the kiss. "What did you say?"

"We're two wrecks for two side roads," Jeremy said.

"Coincidence does not stretch so large," Uther said. He kissed me gently on the cheek and let me slide out of the embrace to sit beside him, still staying in the shadow of his energy. The hurt look in his eyes had vanished, leaving something more solid, more sure of itself behind. It had been worth a kiss.

"They know I was at Roane's apartment, but they don't know where I am now. They're trying to cut off all the escape routes."

Jeremy nodded. "Why haven't you sensed them?"

"She's been too busy," Ringo said.

"No," I said. "But as Uther's aura keeps them from spotting me, so his aura interferes with me sensing them."

"If you move away from him, you'll be able to sense them," Jeremy said.

"And they me," I said.

"What do you want me to do?" Ringo asked.

"We seem to be stuck in traffic. I don't think there's anything you can do," I said.

"They've blocked all the roads," Jeremy said. "They'll

start searching among the cars now. Eventually, they will find us. We need a plan."

"If Uther will move up with me, I'll look and see if my eyes can sense something that the rest of me can't."

"My pleasure," Uther said, and smiled.

We were both smiling as I crawled into the second row of seats. Uther hovered over the back of the seats, one big hand on my shoulder. There were cars parked on one side of the street, and two lanes of traffic trailing from the streetlight. The reason we weren't moving was a three-car pileup at the light. One car was upside down on the pavement. The second car had smashed into it, and a third into both, so the three cars formed a pile of twisted metal and broken glass. I could visualize how the second and third car smashed into the first. What I couldn't figure out was how that first car had gotten on its side, upside down in the middle of the road. No scenario that I could come up with would have flipped the car dead center into the middle of the road. Flipped it so that it formed as large a barrier across the street as possible. I was betting that someone or some things had turned the car over and let the other cars hit it. They'd formed a dam of machines and bleeding people. As long as they could use glamour to hide themselves and not be blamed, they wouldn't give a damn about injured bystanders. My family—how I hate them sometimes.

There were people gathering on the sidewalks, people getting out of their cars, standing in the open doors. There were two police cars parked in the middle of the intersection, stopping the traffic that was still trying to drive on the cross street. The lights on the police cars cut the night in splashes of colored light, competing with the signs and lighted windows of the businesses and clubs that were on either side of the street. I could hear the wail of an ambulance coming closer, probably what the police were clearing the traffic for.

I searched the crowd with my eyes, and there was nothing unusual to see. I cast out with that other sense. I'd be limited with Uther's energy leaking all over me, but not completely helpless. I might be able to spot how close they were before I revealed myself.

The air wavered two cars ahead of us, like a ripple of heat, except it wasn't heat, and you never got that effect after dark. Something large was moving between the cars, something that didn't want to be seen. I cast out farther and found three more ripples. "Four shapes moving out there, all bigger than a human. Closest one is only two cars up from us."

"Can you see shapes?" Jeremy asked.

"No, just ripples."

"To be able to hold glamour in place when you're tipping over cars is more than most fey can manage," Jeremy said.

Apparently, none of us believed the first car had gotten on its roof by itself. "Even most of the sidhe couldn't do it, but some of them can."

"So four larger than human, and at least one sidhe close by," Uther said.

"Yes."

"What's the plan?" Ringo asked.

A good question that. Unfortunately, I didn't have a good answer. "We've got four policemen at the intersection. Are they going to be a help or a hindrance?"

"If we could break their glamour, make them visible to the police, and they didn't know it right away . . ." Jeremy said.

"If they did something harmful in full sight of the police . . ." I said.

"Merry, my girl, I think you've grasped my plan."

Ringo looked back at me. "I don't know much about sidhe magic, but if Merry isn't a full-blooded one, is she powerful enough to break their glamour?"

They all looked at me. "Well?" Jeremy said.

"We don't have to break the spell. All we have to do is overload it," I said.

"We're listening," Jeremy said.

"The first car was turned over, but the rest just crashed. They're peering in the cars, looking for me but not touching anyone. If we get out and fight them, the sidhe won't be able to keep them unseen."

"I thought we wanted to avoid a direct fight if possible," Ringo said.

The ripple was almost here. "If anyone's got a better idea, you've got about sixty seconds to share it. We're about to be searched."

"Hide," Uther said.

"What?"

"Merry hides," he said.

It was a good idea. I slipped behind the secondary seats, and Uther moved away from the wall just enough for me to worm behind him. I didn't think it would work, but it was better than nothing. We could fight later if they found me, but if I could hide . . . I pressed myself against the cool metal wall and Uther's warm back and tried not to think too hard. Some sidhe can hear you thinking if you're agitated enough. I was completely hidden from sight. Even if they opened the big sliding door, which I didn't think they would risk, they wouldn't see me. But it wasn't really their eyes I was worried about. There are all types of fey, and not all of them have a human's reliance on their vision. That wasn't even counting the sidhe who was doing the glamour. If we were the only car with fey occupants, the sidhe would come to investigate before they left this area. He, or she, would have to see for themselves.

I wanted badly to watch that wavering in the air peer in all the windows. But that would have defeated the purpose of hiding, so I crouched behind Uther and tried to be very still. I heard, felt, something brush against the metal wall at my back. Something large was pressed against the metal. Then I heard it, a loud sniffing like of some gigantic hound.

I had a heartbeat to think, "It smells me," then something smashed through the metal inches from me. I screamed, scrambling out from behind Uther, before my mind had fully registered the fist, large as my head, stuck through the side of the van.

A sound of shattering glass whirled me around. An arm big as a tree trunk and a chest wider than the car window was pressed through the driver's-side window. Ringo beat at the arm, but it grabbed the front of his shirt and started pulling him through the broken window.

The gun was in my hand but there wasn't a clear shot. Jeremy moved across the seats, and I saw the flash of a blade in his hand.

Metal screamed as giant fists pulled the side of the van apart until a huge leering face peered into the hole. He looked past Uther like he wasn't there, yellow eyes on me. "Princess," the ogre hissed, "we've been looking for you."

Uther smashed his fist into the huge face. Blood sprayed from the ogre's nose, and the face fell back from the hole. There were screams from outside, human screams. The glamour had collapsed under the violence. The ogres had simply appeared to the humans like magic. I heard a man's voice yelling, "Police, stop where you are!"

The police were coming. Yeah. I put the gun back in my waistband. I didn't want to explain it.

I turned back to the front seat. Ringo was still in the driver's seat. Jeremy was leaning over him, and there was blood on his hands. I moved through the middle seats to them. I started to ask if Ringo was hurt, but the moment I saw his chest, I didn't have to ask. The front of his shirt was soaked with blood, a piece of glass as wide as my hand stuck out of his chest.

"Ringo," I said his name softly.

"Sorry," he said, "I'm not going to be much help to you." He coughed, and I could see it hurt.

I touched his face. "Don't talk."

I could hear the police talking to the ogres, telling them things like, "Hands on top of your heads! On your knees! Don't fucking move!" Then I heard another man's voice, a smooth masculine voice, with just a touch of accent. I knew the voice.

I scrambled to the big sliding door, while Jeremy was still saying, "What? What is it?"

"Sholto," I said.

His face remained puzzled. The name meant nothing to him.

I tried again. "Sholto, Lord of That Which Passes Between, Lord of Shadows, King of the Sluagh."

It was the last title that widened his eyes, and drove fear sharp in his face. "Oh my God," he said.

Uther said, "Shadowspawn is here?"

I glanced at him. "Never say that to his face." I could hear the voices through the broken window, so very clearly. I felt like I was moving in slow motion. The door didn't want to open, or I'd grown clumsy with fear.

That voice was saying, "Thank you so much, Officers."

"We'll wait for transport for the ogres," the policeman said.

The door slid open and I had a frozen moment to see everything. Three of the ogres were on their knees on the sidewalk, hands clasped on their heads. Two policemen had their guns out. One officer was on the sidewalk in front of the ogres; the other one, separated from them by the line of parked cars. A tall figure, though only human tall, stood by the cars and that policeman. The figure was dressed in a grey leather trench coat with his white hair trailing down the back of it. The last time I'd seen Sholto, he'd been wearing a grey cloak, but the effect was surprisingly similar as he turned, as if he felt me standing there. Even from yards away in the electric-kissed darkness I could see that his eyes were three different shades of gold: metallic gold around the pupil, then amber, and last a circle the color of yellow autumn leaves. I was afraid of Sholto, always had been, but when I saw those eyes, I realized how homesick I was for the sidhe, because for a second, I was glad to see another person with a triple iris. Then the look in those familiar eyes sent a chill across my neck and the moment of connectedness was gone.

He turned, smiling, back to the police. "I will attend the princess." He started walking toward the van, and they didn't stop him. I realized why as he moved closer. He had the queen's emblem, a badge that her Guard carried, hanging from his neck. It looks surprisingly like a police badge, and it had been well publicized that to use one of the emblems if you didn't deserve it came with a curse. A curse that not even a sidhe would risk.

I didn't know what he'd told them, but I could guess. He'd

been sent to stop the attack on me. He'd see me safely home.
All so very reasonable.

Sholto moved toward me in a long-legged, graceful stride.
He was handsome, not the heartbreaking beauty of some of
the sidhe, but striking. I knew that the humans watched him
as he walked, because they could not help themselves. The
grey coat blew back and there was the faintest bulk around
his middle. Sholto had the hair, the eyes, the skin, the face,
the shoulders, everything—except that from just below his
nipples to vanish into his pants was a nest of tentacles, things
with mouths. His mother had been sidhe, his father had not.

Something touched my shoulder and I jerked, screaming.
It was Jeremy. "Close the door, Uther."

Uther slid the door shut, almost in Sholto's face. He leaned
against it, so that it couldn't be opened from the outside
without some effort. "Run," Uther said.

"Run," Jeremy said.

I understood. Outside of a war, the sluagh hunted one prey
at a time, and I was it. Sholto wouldn't hurt them if I weren't
here. I slipped out the jagged metal hole that the ogres had
made on the other side, managing to worm through without
cutting myself. I could hear Sholto knocking, oh so politely,
on the van's big door. "Princess Meredith, I've come to take
you home."

I dropped low to the ground and used the parked cars to
hide me as I made it to the sidewalk and the crowd that had
gathered to watch the show. I threw another coating of glamour over me. Hair a nondescript brown, skin darker, tanned. I
moved through the crowd, changing my appearance a little at
a time so that no one would point and draw attention to me.
By the time I made it out the other side and started down the
side street, the only thing that still looked the same was the
clothes. I slipped the suit jacket off, took the gun in my hand,
and rolled the jacket around my hand and arm. Sholto had
seen an auburn-haired woman with pale skin in a navy jacket.
Now I was a brown-haired woman with a tan, and a green
shirt. I walked calmly down the street, though there was a

place between my shoulder blades that itched as if he were staring a hole through me.

I wanted to turn around and glance back, but I forced myself to keep walking. I made it to the corner without anyone yelling, "There she is!" When I got to the corner, I stopped for a second. Dear Goddess, I wanted to look back over my shoulder. I fought the urge and stepped around the corner of the building. When I was safely out of sight, I let out a breath I hadn't known I was holding. I wasn't out of danger, not with Sholto on this coast, but it was a start.

A noise came from overhead. A high, thin sound, almost too high to hear, but it pierced through the normal sounds of the city like an arrow through the heart. I scanned the night sky, but it was empty, except for the distant trail of an airplane glowing against the darkness. The sound came again almost painfully high, like the sounds of bats. There was nothing there.

I started walking backward, slowly, still scanning the sky, when a movement caught my eye. I followed that flicker to the top of the nearest building. A line of black shapes huddled on the building's edge. They were like a line of ink-black hoods the size of small men. One of the "hoods" shook itself like a bird settling its feathers. The blackness raised its head to flash a pale, flat face. A slit of a mouth opened and that high-pitched cry sounded.

They could fly faster than I could run. I knew that, but I turned and ran anyway. I heard their wings unfurl with a sharp sound like thick, clean sheets snapping in the wind. I ran. Their high-pitched calls chased me into the night. I ran faster.

Chapter 10

THEY CAME LIKE A WIND AT MY BACK, THEIR SOUND MELDING into a rush of wind like a chasing storm. That's what humans would hear: wind, storm, or a flight of birds. If there'd been humans to hear anything. The street stretched deserted to the end of the block. Eight o'clock on a Saturday night in prime shop district, and there was no one. It almost seemed arranged, and maybe it was. If I could run out of the spell area, there would be people. The wind buffeted against my back, and I threw myself onto the sidewalk, rolling with the impact. I kept rolling, over and over, getting dizzying glimpses of the nightflyers spilling over me, less than a yard off the sidewalk like a run of airborne fish, moving too fast after their leader to change direction.

I rolled into the nearest doorway, surrounded by a roof and glass on three sides. The flyers only took from above. They wouldn't come down on the ground for me. I lay there for a few heartbeats listening to the thud of my own blood in my ears, when I realized I wasn't alone.

I sat up, my back against the window display of books, trying to think of any excuse good enough to explain to a human what I'd just done. The man had his back to me. He was short, about my height, wearing a loud Hawaiian shirt and one of those soft-rimmed caps that come down over the eyes. Not something you see at night much.

I pushed to my feet, using the glass of the window. Why was he wearing a hat to keep the sun out of his eyes at night?

"Some wind," he said.

I eased around the window, keeping the shop awning over me. I still had the gun in my hand. The jacket was loose, flapping like a matador's cape, but it still shielded the gun.

The man turned, and the light from the shop fell upon his face. The skin was black, eyes like dark, shiny jewels. He grinned, flashing a mouthful of razor-sharp teeth. "Our master wants to speak with you, Princess."

I felt movement behind me and turned my head to see, but I was afraid to turn completely around and give my back to the grinning figure. Three figures emerged from the next shop. It was dark, no lights to hide from. The figures were taller than me, cloaked and hooded.

"We've been waiting for you, corr," one of the cloaked figures said. It was a female voice.

"Corr?" I made it a question.

"Slut." A second female voice.

"Jealous?" I said.

They rushed me, and I spilled the jacket to the ground, pointing the gun two-handed at them. Either they didn't know what a gun was, or they didn't care. I shot one of them. The figure collapsed in a pile of cloth. The two others huddled back, clawed hands extended as if to ward off a blow.

I pressed my back to the window, spared a glance for the grinning man behind me, but he was standing in the doorway with his small hands clasped on top of his hat, as if he'd done it before. I kept the gun and most of my attention on the women, though that was a loose term for them. They were hags. I wasn't being mean. It was what they were . . . night hags.

The one I'd shot struggled to sit, cradled in the second one's arms. "You shot her!"

"So happy you noticed," I said.

The wounded one's hood had fallen back to reveal a huge beaked nose, small glittering eyes, skin the color of yellowed snow. Her hair was a dry ragged mass, like black straw coming barely to her shoulders. She hissed as the second hag spread the cloak enough to see the wound. There was a bloody hole between her sagging breasts. She was nude except for a heavy golden torc around her neck, and a jeweled belt that rode low on her thin hips. I caught a glimpse of the dagger that hung from the belt and was tied to her thigh with a golden chain.

She writhed, unable to get enough air to curse me. I'd hit her heart, and maybe a lung. It wouldn't kill her, but it hurt.

The second hag raised her face into the light. Her skin was a dirty grey with huge pockmarks covering her face, tracing along the sharp nose like craters. Her lips were almost too thin to cover the mouth full of sharp carnivorous teeth. "I wonder if he'd still want you if you didn't have all that smooth white flesh."

The last hag was still standing, hooded, hidden. Her voice was better than theirs, more cultured somehow. "We could make you one of us, our sister."

I sighted at the grey one's face. "The second someone starts a curse, I'll shoot her through the face."

"It won't kill me," Grey said.

"No, but it won't help your looks either."

She hissed at me like some great crooked cat. "Bitch."

"Ditto," I said.

It was the one still standing that I was worried about. She hadn't panicked or let anger get the better of her. She'd suggested using magic against me when she was still partially hidden by shadows and night. Smarter, more cautious, more dangerous.

I had purposefully not used glamour to hide. I was standing in front of a lighted bookstore window with a gun in plain sight, obviously pointed at someone. The gunshot alone should have sent someone to the door or to call the police. I gave a quick flare of power, searching, and found the thick folds of the glamour. Heavy and well made. I was good at glamour, but not this kind. Sholto had covered the entire street with it, like an invisible wall. The humans in the shops would just want to stay inside. No one would see or hear anything to alarm them. Their minds would explain the gunshot as some ordinary noise. If I screamed for help, it would be the wind. Short of throwing someone through the window in back of me, into the shop itself, no one would see anything.

I'd have been willing to throw any and all of them through the glass, but I didn't trust them up close. The hands that clasped at the wound had black claws like the talons of some great bird. The teeth that bared when she hissed were made for tearing flesh. I would never win a one-on-one battle. I needed them at bay, and the gun kept them there, but Sholto would come, and I needed to be gone before that happened. Once he arrived I'd lose. Come to think of it, I wasn't doing too well now. They couldn't hurt me, but I was trapped. If I moved out from under the awning, the nightflyers would get me or at least mob me, then the hags and the grinning man could take me. I'd be disarmed or worse before Sholto showed up.

I had no offensive magic. The gun wouldn't kill any of them, only hurt and slow them. I needed a better idea, and I couldn't think of anything. I tried talking. When in doubt, talk. You never know what the enemy might let slip.

"Nerys the Grey, Segna the Gold, and Black Agnes, I presume."

"Who are you? Stanley?" Nerys said.

I had to smile. "And they say you have no sense of humor."

"Who're they?" she asked.

"The sidhe," I said.

"You are sidhe," Black Agnes said.

"If I were truly sidhe, would I be here on the shores of the Western Sea hiding from my queen?"

"The fact that you and your aunt are enemies makes you suicidally foolish, but it doesn't make you one ounce less sidhe." Agnes stood so straight and tall, like a black pillar of cloth.

"No, but the brownie blood on my mother's side does. I think the queen would forgive the human taint, but she can't forget the other."

"You're mortal," Nerys said. "That's the unforgivable sin for a sidhe."

My hands were starting to cramp. My arms would start to tremble soon. I had to either shoot something, or lower the gun. Even a two-handed stance isn't meant to be held indefinitely.

"There are other sins my aunt finds just as unforgivable," I said.

A man's voice said, "Like having a nest of tentacles in the middle of all that perfect sidhe flesh."

I turned the gun toward the voice, keeping my vision on the three hags. I was soon going to have so many targets in so many different directions that I'd never be able to shoot them all in time. At least the movement and the fresh rush of adrenaline had helped chase away the muscle fatigue. I was suddenly sure I could hold the shooting stance forever.

Sholto was standing on the sidewalk, hands at his side. I think he was trying to appear harmless. He failed. "The queen said that to me once, that it was a shame that I had a nest of tentacles in the middle of one of the most perfect sidhe bodies she'd ever seen."

"Great. My aunt's a bitch. We all knew that. What do you want, Sholto?"

"Give him his title," Agnes said, that cultured voice holding an edge of anger.

It never hurts to be polite, so I did what she asked. "What do you want, Sholto, Lord of That Which Passes Between?"

"He is King Sholto." Segna spat the words at me, almost literally.

"He's not my king," I said.

"That could change," Agnes said, the implied threat nicely subtle.

"Enough," Sholto said. "The queen wants you dead, Meredith."

"We've never been friends, Lord Sholto. Use my title." It was an insult for him to have omitted my title after I'd used his. It was also an insult to insist on it from someone who was king of another people. But Sholto had always complicated his life by trying to play lord of the sidhe and king of the sluagh.

A look passed over the strong bones of his face—anger, I

think, though I didn't know him well enough to be sure. "The queen wants you dead, Princess Meredith, daughter of Essus."

"And she sent you to fetch me home for the execution. I figured that much out."

"You couldn't be more wrong," Agnes said.

"Silence!" Sholto put the bite of command in that one word. The hags seemed to shrink in upon themselves, not bowing, but like they thought about it.

The grinning man to my right stepped closer. I didn't take the gun off Sholto, but I said, "Take two big steps back or I shoot your king."

I don't know what the man would have done because Sholto said, "Gethin, do what she asks."

Gethin didn't argue, just stepped back, though I noticed out of the corner of my eyes that his hands were folded across his chest. He wasn't doing the hands on top of your head routine anymore. Fine as long as he stayed out of immediate reach. They were all too close. If everyone rushed me at once, it was over. But Sholto didn't want me crowded. He wanted to talk. Fine with me.

"I don't want you dead, Princess Meredith," Sholto said.

I couldn't keep the suspicion off my face. "You'd go up against the queen and all her sidhe to save me?"

"Much has happened in the last three years, Princess. The queen relies more and more on the sluagh for her threat. I do not think she would start a war over you being alive if you were safely out of her sight."

"I'm as out of her sight as I can get and still be on dry land," I said.

"Ah, but perhaps there are others at court that whisper in her ear and remind her of you."

"Who?" I asked.

He smiled, and it made that handsome face almost pleasant. "We have many things to discuss, Princess. I have a room in one of the better hotels. Shall we retire to it and discuss the future?"

Something about the way he worded that bothered me, but

it was the best offer I was going to get tonight. I lowered the gun. "Swear by your honor and the darkness that eats all things, that you mean all of what you just said."

"I swear on my honor, and by the darkness that eats all things, that every word I have spoken on this street to you is the truth."

I clicked the safety on the gun and tucked it at the small of my back. I picked my jacket up off the ground, shook it out, and slipped it on. It was a little wrinkled, but it would do. "How far is your hotel?"

The smile this time was wider, it made him less perfect, but more . . . human. More real. "You should smile more often, Lord Sholto. It becomes you."

"I hope to have reason to smile more often in the near future." He offered me his arm, even though he was yards away. I went to him because he'd sworn the Unseelie's most solemn oath. He could not break it without risking a curse.

I slipped my hand in the crook of his arm. He flexed under my hand. Sometimes a male is a male is a male, no matter what flavor they are. "Which hotel are you staying at?" I smiled at him. It never hurts to be pleasant. I could always be unpleasant later if I needed to be.

He told me. It was a very nice hotel.

"That's a little far to walk," I said.

"If you like, we can get a taxi."

I raised eyebrows at that, because once inside the metal of a car he wouldn't be able to do major magic. Too much refined metal interfered with it. I could do major spells inside solid lead if I had to. My human blood was good for a few things. "Won't you be uncomfortable?" I asked.

"It's not that far, and it's our mutual comfort I've come to see to."

Again, I felt there were shades of meaning in his words that I was missing. "A taxi would be lovely."

Agnes called after us. "What are we to do with Segna?"

Sholto looked back at them and his face was cold again, that carved handsomeness that made him seem distant. "Make your way back to your rooms any way you can. If Segna had not tried to attack the princess, she wouldn't have been wounded."

"We have served you for more centuries than that piece of white flesh will ever see, and this is the treatment you give us," Agnes said.

"You get the treatment that you earn, Agnes. Remember that." He turned, patting my hand on his arm, smiling at me, but his triple-golden eyes still held the edge of that coldness.

Gethin appeared at Sholto's side, floppy hat in his hands, a bow curving him toward the sidewalk. He had impossibly long ears, like those of a donkey. "What would you have of me, Master?"

"Help them get Segna to the rooms."

"Happily." Gethin flashed another toothy grin as he stood, ears flapping down to frame his face almost like a dog's or maybe a lop-eared rabbit's. He turned and almost skipped back toward the hags.

"I feel like I'm missing something," I said.

His hand wrapped over my hand, warm, strong fingers sliding over mine. "I will explain all when we get to the hotel." There was a look in his eyes that I'd seen in other men's, but it couldn't mean the same thing. Sholto was one of the Queen's Guard, which meant he couldn't sleep with any sidhe except her. She didn't share her men, not with anyone. The punishment for breaking the taboo was death by torture. Even if Sholto was willing to risk that, I was not. My aunt might execute me, but she'd make it quick. If I broke her most strict taboo, she'd still kill me, but it would not be quick. I'd been tortured before. It was hard to avoid it if you lived at the Unseelie Court. But I'd never been tortured at the queen's own hand. I had seen her handiwork, though. She was creative, very, very creative.

I'd promised myself years ago that I would never give her an excuse to be creative on me. "I'm already under a death sentence, Sholto. I won't risk torture on top of it."

"If I could keep you alive and safe, what would you risk?"

"Alive and safe? How?"

He just smiled, held his hand up, and yelled, "Taxi!" Three of them appeared within minutes on the empty street. Sholto just meant to call a taxi. He had no idea how impressive it was in Los Angeles to be able to call three taxis within minutes to an empty street. He could also re-animate corpses that hadn't grown cold yet, and that was impressive. But I'd lived for three years in the city, and a taxi when you wanted it was more impressive than a walking corpse. After all, I'd seen walking corpses before. A convenient taxi was a completely new animal.

Chapter 11

AN HOUR LATER SHOLTO AND I WERE SITTING IN TWO LOVELY but uncomfortable chairs around a small white table. The room was elegant, if a little too pink and gold for my tastes. There'd been wine and a tray of hors d'oeuvres waiting on the table. The wine was a very sweet dessert wine. It complemented the cheese on the tray but clashed with the caviar. Of course, I'd never tasted anything that could make caviar palatable. No matter how expensive it was, it still tasted like fish eggs.

Sholto seemed to like the caviar and the wine. "Champagne would have been more appropriate, but I've never liked it," he said.

"Are we celebrating something?" I asked.

"An alliance, I hope."

I took a minute sip of the too-sweet wine and looked at him. "What sort of alliance?"

"Between the two of us."

"That much I'd assumed. The big question, Sholto, is why would you want an alliance with me?"

"You're third in line to the throne." His face had become very closed, very careful, as if he didn't want me to know what he was thinking.

"And?" I said.

He blinked those triple-golden eyes at me. "Why wouldn't a sidhe want to join himself to the woman who is only two steps away from the throne?"

"Normally, that would be fine reasoning, but you and I both know that the only reason I'm still third in line for the throne is that my father got the queen's oath before he died. She'd have had me disqualified on the grounds of my mortality alone, except for that. I have no standing at the court, Sholto. I am the first princess of the line who has no magic."

He sat his wineglass carefully on the table. "You are one of the best of all of us at personal glamour," he said.

"True, but it's the greatest of my powers. For Goddess sake, I am still called NicEssus, daughter of Essus. A title that I should have lost after childhood when I came into my power. Except I didn't come into my power. I may never come into my power, Sholto. That alone could have gotten me removed from the line of succession."

"Except for the oath the queen made to your father," Sholto said.

"Yes."

"I am aware how much your aunt loathes you, Meredith. Much the same way she loathes me."

I sat the wineglass down, tired of pretending to enjoy it. "You have magic enough for a court title. You're not mortal."

He looked at me, and it was a long, hard, almost harsh look. "Don't be coy, Meredith, you know exactly why the queen can't stand the sight of me."

I met that hard glance, but it was . . . uncomfortable. I did know, all the court knew.

"Say it, Meredith, say it out loud."

"The queen disapproves of your mixed blood."

He nodded. "Yes." He seemed almost relieved. The harshness in his eyes had been uneasy to see, but at least it had been genuine. For all I knew everything else was false. I wanted to see what truly lay behind that handsome face.

"But that's not why, Sholto. There's more mixed blood among the sidhe royals now than pure."

"Fine," he said, "she disapproves of my father's bloodline."

"It's not the fact that your father is a nightflyer, Sholto."

He frowned. "If you have a point, make it."

"Except for the odd pointy ear, until you came along sidhe genetics won out no matter what we mated with."

"Genetics," he said. "I forget that you are our first modern college graduate."

I smiled. "Father was hoping I'd be a doctor."

"You can't heal with your touch, what kind of doctor is that?" He took a big drink of wine, as if he were still agitated.

"Someday I must take you on a tour of a modern hospital," I said.

"Whatever you wish to show me would be a pleasure." Whatever real emotion had almost peeked through, vanished in a wave of double entendre.

I ignored the double meaning and went back to digging. I'd seen real emotion, I wanted to see more of it. If I was going to risk my life I needed to see Sholto without the masks that the court taught us to wear. "Until you, all the sidhe looked like sidhe no matter what we mated with. I think the queen sees you as proof that the sidhe blood is growing weak, just as my mortality shows the blood is thinning."

That handsome face grew tight with anger. "The Unseelie preach that all fey are beautiful, but some of us are only beautiful for a night. We are diversions, but nothing more."

I watched the anger eat across his shoulders, down his arms. His muscles tightened as the anger flowed over him. "My mother," and he spat that last word out, "thought she would have a night of pleasure and pay no price. I was that price." He bit off the words, rage intensifying the light in his eyes so that the rings of color in them blazed like yellow flame and molten running gold.

I'd broken through that so careful exterior and found a nerve. "I would say that you're the one that paid the price, not your mother," I said. "Once she gave birth to you, she went back to the court, to her life."

He looked at me, the rage still naked on his face.

I talked carefully to that anger, because I didn't want it to spill over on me, but I liked the anger. It was real, not some mood calculated to get him something. He hadn't planned this mood, it had just come over him. I liked that, I liked that a lot. One of the things I'd loved about Roane had been that his emotions were so close to the surface. He never pretended anything he did not feel. Of course, that was the same trait that had allowed him to go off to the sea with his new seal-skin, and never bother to say good-bye. No one was perfect.

"And she left me with my father," Sholto said. He looked down at the table, then slowly raised those extraordinary eyes to me. "Do you know how old I was before I saw another sidhe?"

I shook my head.

"I was five. Five years old before I saw anyone with skin and eyes like mine." He stopped talking, eyes distant with remembering.

"Tell me," I said, softly.

His voice came soft, as if he were talking to himself. "Agnes had taken me into the woods to play on a dark, moon-less night."

I wanted to ask if Agnes was the hag Black Agnes that I'd met tonight, but I let him talk. There'd be time for questions when his mood had changed, and he stopped telling his se-crets. It had been surprisingly easy to get him to open up to me. Usually when it's this easy to peel away someone's pro-tections they want to talk, need to talk.

"I saw something shining through the trees as if the moon had come down to Earth. I asked Agnes, what is that? She wouldn't tell me, just took my hand and led me closer to the light. At first, I thought they were human, except humans didn't glow like they had fire beneath their skins. Then the woman turned her face toward us, and her eyes . . ." His voice trailed off, and there was such a mixture of wonder and pain in him that I almost let it go, but I didn't. I wanted to know, if he wanted to tell me.

"Her eyes . . ." I prompted.

"Her eyes glowed, burned, blue, darker blue, then green. I was five, so it wasn't her nakedness, or his body on top of hers, but the wonderment of that white skin and those swirling eyes. Like my eyes, like my skin." He stared past me as if I weren't there. "Agnes dragged me away before they saw us. I was full of questions. She told me to ask my father."

He blinked and took a deep breath as if he were literally coming back from someplace else. "My father explained about the sidhe, and that I was one of them. My father raised me to believe I was sidhe. I could not be what he was." Sholto gave a harsh laugh. "I cried the first time I realized I would never have wings."

He looked at me, frowning. "I've never told anyone at court that story. Is this some kind of magic that you have over me?" He didn't actually believe it was a spell, or he'd be more upset, maybe even frightened.

"Who else at the court but me would understand what the story meant?" I asked.

He looked at me for a long moment, then slowly nodded. "Yes, though your body is not marred as mine, you, too, do not belong. They won't let you belong." That last was said for both of us, I think.

His hands lay on the table so tightly clasped that they were mottled. I touched his hands, and he jerked away as if I'd hurt him. He'd slid his hands out of reach, but stopped in midmotion. I watched the effort it took for him to put his hands back within my reach. He acted like someone who expected to be hurt.

I covered his large hands with one of mine, or covered as much as I could. He smiled, and it was the first real smile I'd seen, because this one was uncertain, not sure of its welcome. I don't know what he saw on my face, but whatever it was it reassured him, because he opened his hands, and took my hand in his, raising it slowly to his lips. He didn't so much kiss my hand, as press his mouth to it. It was a surprisingly tender gesture. Loneliness can be a bond stronger than most. Who else at either court understood our hearts better than each other? Not love, or friendship, but a bond nonetheless.

His gaze rose to meet mine, as he raised his face from my hand. The look in his eyes was one I rarely saw among the sidhe, open, raw. There was a need in his eyes so large it was like staring into an endless void, a deep yawning pit of some missing thing. It made his eyes wild like some creature's, or a feral child's. Something untamed, but badly wounded. Did my eyes ever look like that? I hoped not.

He let go of my hand slowly, reluctantly. "I have never been with another sidhe, Meredith. Do you understand what that means?"

I understood, probably better than he did, because the only thing worse than never was to have had it, and be denied it. But I kept my voice neutral because I was beginning to fear where we were heading, and no matter how much sympathy I had with him, it wasn't worth being tortured to death. "You wonder what it would be like."

He shook his head. "No, I crave the sight of pale flesh stretched underneath me. I want my shine matched by another. I want that, Meredith, and you can give it to me."

He was heading where I'd feared. "I told you, Sholto, I won't risk death by torture for any pleasure. No one, nothing, is worth that." I meant it.

"The queen joys in making her guards watch her with her lovers. Some refuse to watch, but most of us stay on the off chance that she may beckon us to join. 'You are my bodyguards—don't you want to guard my body?' " He did a fair imitation of her voice. "Even when it is meant for cruelty, the love of two sidhe is still a wondrous thing. I would give my soul for it."

I gave him my best blank face. "I don't have any use for your soul, Sholto. What else can you offer me that would be worth risking death by torture?"

"If you are my sidhe lover, Meredith, then the queen will know what you mean to me. I will make sure she understands that if anything happens to you that she will lose the sluagh's loyalty. She can't afford that right now."

"Why not make this deal with other more powerful sidhe women?"

"The women of Prince Cel's Guard have him to have sex with, and unlike the queen, Cel keeps them busy."

"When I left, some of the women were beginning to refuse Cel's bed."

Sholto smiled happily. "The movement has become quite popular."

I raised eyebrows. "Are you saying that Cel's little harem is turning him down?"

"More and more of them." Sholto still looked pleased.

"Then why not make this invitation to one of them? They're all more powerful than I am."

"Perhaps it's what you said earlier, Meredith. None of them would understand me as you do."

"I think you underestimate them. But what could Cel possibly be doing to them that's making them leave him in droves? The queen herself is a sexual sadist, but her guardsmen would crawl over broken glass to bed her. What is Cel offering that is worse than that?" I didn't expect an answer, but I couldn't even begin to think of anything that bad.

The smile faded from Sholto's face. "The queen did that once," he said.

"What?" I asked, frowning.

"Made one of us strip and crawl over broken glass. If he made it without showing pain, then she'd fuck him."

I blinked. I'd heard worse, hell, I'd seen worse. But part of me wanted to know who it was, so I asked, "Who was it?"

He shook his head. "We of the Guard have sworn to keep the humiliations among ourselves. Our pride, if not our bodies, survives the better for it." His eyes looked lost again.

Again, I wondered what Cel could be doing that was worse than the queen's games. "Why not make this offer to a more powerful sidhe woman who isn't a member of the Prince's Guard?" I asked.

He gave a faint smile. "There are women at court who are not members of the Prince's Guard, Meredith. They would not touch me before I joined the Guard. They fear bringing more perverse creatures into the world." He laughed, and it had a wild sound to it, almost like crying. It hurt to hear it. "That's what the queen calls me, her 'perverse creature'— sometimes, simply 'creature.' In a few centuries I will be like Frost and her Darkness. I will be her Creature." He gave that painful laugh again. "I will risk much to keep that from happening."

"Does she really need the sluagh's backing that much, so much that she'd give up my death, give up punishing us for going against her strictest taboo?" I shook my head. "No, Sholto, she can't let this stand. If we find a way around her celibacy taboo, then others will try. It will be like the first crack in a dam. Eventually it breaks."

"She is losing control, Meredith, losing her hold on the court. These three years have not been good ones for her. The court is splitting under the weight of her erratic behavior, and Prince Cel's growing . . ." He seemed at a loss for words, then finally said, "When he comes into power, Cel is going to make Andais look sane. It will be like Caligula after Tiberius."

"Are you saying, if we think it's bad now, we ain't seen nothing yet?" I tried to make him smile, and failed.

He turned haunted eyes to me. "The queen cannot afford to lose the support of the sluagh. Trust me on this, Meredith, I have no desire to end up at the queen's mercy, any more than you do."

"The queen's mercy" had become a saying among us; if you feared something, you said, "I'd rather be at the queen's mercy than do that." It meant that nothing scared you more.

"What do you want of me, Sholto?"

"I want you," he said, his gaze very direct.

I had to smile. "You don't want me, you want a sidhe in your bed. Remember that Griffin rejected me because I was not sidhe enough for him."

"Griffin was a fool."

I smiled, and it made me think of Uther's words earlier that night, that Roane was a fool. If everyone was a fool for leaving me, why did they keep doing it? I looked at him and tried to be just as direct. "I've never been with a nightflyer."

"It is considered perverted by those that consider nothing perverse," Sholto said, and his voice was bitter. "I would not expect you to have experience with us."

Us. An interesting pronoun. If you asked me what I was, I

was sidhe, not human, not brownie. I was sidhe, and if you pushed me, I was Unseelie, for better or worse, even though I could claim the blood of both courts. But I would never have said "us" when speaking of anything but Unseelie sidhe.

"After my aunt, our beloved queen, tried to drown me when I was six, Father made sure I had my own sidhe body-guards. One of them was a crippled nightflyer, Bhatar."

Sholto nodded. "He lost a wing in the last real battle we fought on American soil. We can grow back most of our body parts, so it was a grave wound."

"Bhatar stayed in my room at night. He never left my side when I was a child. Father taught me chess, but Bhatar taught me how to beat Father." It made me smile.

"He still speaks well of you," Sholto said.

I started to ask, then shook my head. "No, he would never have suggested that you do this. He would never have risked my safety, or yours. You see, he spoke well of you, too, King Sholto. The best king the sluagh had had in two hundred years, that's what he used to say."

"I'm flattered."

"You know what your people think of you." I tried to read that face. The need was there, but need could mask so many things. "What of the hags, your little harem?"

"What of them?" he asked, but there was a look in his eyes, that gave lie to his casual words.

"They wanted to hurt me to keep me from you. What do you think they'll do if you actually bed me?"

"I am their king. They will do as they are told."

I laughed then, but it wasn't bitter, just ironic. "You are a king of a fey people, Sholto, they never do quite what you tell them, or quite what you think they will. From sidhe to pixie, they are free things. Take for granted their obedience and you do so at your peril."

"Like the queen has done for a millennium?" He made it half question, half statement.

I smiled, nodding. "As the king of the Seelie Court has done for even longer."

"I am a new king compared to them and not quite so arrogant."

"Then tell me truly what will your hag lovers do if you desert them for me?"

He seemed to think about it for a minute, long and slow, then he looked at me. His face was serious. "I don't know."

I almost laughed. "You are new at being king. I've never heard one of them admit ignorance before."

"Not knowing a thing is not ignorance. Feigning knowledge you don't have, can be," he said.

"Wise, as well as modest; how terribly unique for fey royalty." I remembered a question I'd wanted to ask. "The Agnes that took you into the woods as a boy, your nanny, is she Black Agnes?"

"Yes," he said.

I fought not to frown. "Your ex-nanny is now your lover?"

"She has not aged," he said, "and I am all grown up now."

"Growing up around immortal beings is confusing, I admit, but there are still fey that helped raise me that I don't think of in that way."

"As there are among the sluagh for me, but Agnes is not one of them."

I wanted to ask why, but didn't. First, it was none of my business; second, I might not understand the answer even if he gave it to me. "How do you know the queen intends to execute me for certain?" Back to the important topic.

"Because I was sent to Los Angeles to kill you." He said it like it meant nothing—no emotion, no regret, just fact.

My heart beat a little faster, my breath catching in my throat. I had to concentrate to ease the air out without making it noticeable. "If I don't agree to sleep with you, then you carry out the sentence?"

"I gave my oath that I meant you no harm. I meant it."

"You would go against the queen for my sake?"

"The same reasoning that keeps us safe if we bed each other, keeps me safe if I leave you alive. She needs my sluagh more than she needs to be vindictive."

He seemed so certain of that last part. Certain of what he was certain of, uncertain of everything else; like most of us if we're honest. I looked at that strong face, the jaw a little wide for my taste, the bones of the cheek at little too sculpted. I liked a softer look to my men, but he was undeniably handsome. His hair was a perfect white, thick and straight, held back in a loose ponytail. The hair fell to his knees like one of the older sidhe, even though Sholto was only about two hundred years, give or take. The shoulders were broad, the chest looked good under the white, button-down shirt. The shirt fell absolutely smooth, and I wondered if he were using some sort of glamour to make it so, because I knew that what lay under the shirt was not smooth. "The offer is very unexpected, Sholto. I'd like some time to think about it, if I may?"

"Until tomorrow night," he said.

I nodded, and stood. He stood as well. I found myself staring at his chest and stomach trying to see that movement I'd noticed on the street. Nothing showed, he was wasting glamour on keeping it hidden. "I don't know if I can do this," I said.

"What?" he asked.

I motioned at him. "I saw you once without a shirt when I was much younger. The sight . . . stayed with me."

His face paled, eyes hardening. He was throwing his walls back in place. "I understand. The thought of touching me frightens you. I do understand, Meredith." He let out a long breath. "It was a pretty thought while it lasted." He turned away from me, gathering his long coat from the back of the chair where he'd laid it. The heavy tail of hair lay like a white furred stripe down his body.

"Sholto," I said.

He didn't turn around, just held the length of hair over one shoulder while he put on his coat.

"I didn't say no, Sholto."

He turned then. His face was still closed, careful, all the emotions I'd worked so hard to find buried again. "Then what are you saying?"

"I'm saying, no sex tonight, but I can't say yes, I'll have sex with you, until I see everything."

"Everything?" He made it a question again.

"Now who's being coy," I said.

I watched the idea take shape on his face, in his eyes. A strange little smile played on his lips. "Are you asking to see me naked?"

"Not all of you." I had to smile at the look on his face. "But down to your thighs, yes, please. I have to see how I truly feel about your . . . extras."

He smiled and it was warm with an edge of uncertainty. It was his real smile, that edge of charm and fear. "That is the kindest way anyone has ever described them."

"If I can't be with you in joy and shared pleasure, then your dream of matching your glow with another falls apart. A sidhe does not glow for things that are duty and not pleasure."

He nodded. "I understand."

"I hope so, because it's more than seeing you nude. I need to touch and be touched to see if . . ." I spread my hands wide. "If I can do this."

"But no sex tonight?" His voice was as close to playful as I'd ever heard it.

"You dream of sidhe flesh and have never had it. I have had it, and for three, nearly four years, I've gone without. I miss home, Sholto. Strange and perverse as it is, I miss it. If I agree to this, then I get a sidhe lover and home. Not to mention I'm escaping a death sentence. You are not a fate worse than death, Sholto."

"Some have thought so over the years." He tried to make it a joke, but his eyes gave him away.

"That's why I need to see what I'm getting myself into."

"Do I raise the question of love, or is that too naive for a king and a princess?" he asked.

I smiled, but this time it was sad. "I tried love once; it betrayed me."

"Griffin is a worthless thing, Meredith, unworthy of such depth of emotion, and certainly incapable of returning it."

"I found that out, eventually," I said. "Love is grand while it lasts, Sholto, but it doesn't last."

We looked at each other. I wondered if my eyes were as tired and full of regret as his.

"Am I supposed to argue with you, and tell you some love does last?" Sholto asked.

"Are you going to?"

He smiled, and shook his head. "No."

I held my hand out to him. "No lies, Sholto, not even the pretty ones." His hand was very warm wrapped around mine. "Let me take you to bed, and see what I'm bargaining for."

He let me lead him toward the bed. "Do I get to see what I'm bargaining for?"

I pulled him backward toward the bed so I could watch his face. "If you like."

A look passed through his eyes that was neither sidhe, nor human, nor sluagh, but simply male. "I like," he said.

Chapter 12

I LET GO OF HIS HAND SO I COULD CRAWL ONTO THE BED, STILL working backward so I could watch him. I took the gun out of my waistband and slid it under one of the pillows, then lay back in the middle of the bed, propping myself up on my elbows. Sholto stood beside the bed looking at me. He had a strange half-smile on his face. His eyes looked uncertain, not unhappy, just uncertain.

"You look terribly pleased with yourself," he said.

"It's never a bad thing to see a handsome man naked for the first time."

His smile vanished. "Handsome? I've never had anyone who knew what lay under the shirt call me that before."

I let my gaze speak for me. I lingered over his face, the eyes, the strong, nearly perfect nose, the thin wide mouth. The rest of the body looked wonderful, but I knew at least part of what I was looking at was magically enhanced. I just didn't know how much. But I kept my gaze on the parts that I was pretty sure were real, like the slender width of his hips, the strong length of legs. Until I saw him without the pants I wasn't sure what the bulge in the pants was, so I passed that by in mind as well as by eye. The queen was right, it was a shame; he truly was magnificent.

"I've fantasized about a sidhe woman looking at me like that." He still looked too solemn.

"Like what?" I asked. I made the question low, sexual, teasing.

That made him smile. "Like I'm something to eat."

I smiled, and made it everything he wanted it to be, everything he needed it to be. "Eat, eh. Lose the coat, and the shirt, and maybe we'll get to that."

"No sex tonight remember," he said.

"How about just no orgasm?"

He threw back his head and laughed, a loud, joyous sound. He looked at me with shining eyes, and it wasn't magic that made them glitter, just laughter. He looked younger, more relaxed. I realized that with his white hair and skin, those gold eyes, that he'd be welcomed at the Seelie Court. If he could keep his shirt on they'd never suspect.

The laughter faded round the edges. "Now you look solemn," he said.

"I was just thinking that you look more Seelie Court than I do."

He frowned. "You mean the blood auburn hair?"

"And my lack of height, and the breasts are a little too plentiful for sidhe style."

He grinned then, wide and sudden. "It has to be the women who are complaining about the breasts. No man would dream of it."

That made me smile. "You're right. My mother, my aunt, my cousins."

"They're just jealous," he said.

"Pretty to think so," I said.

He let the grey overcoat fall to the floor, then undid a button of his cuff. He watched my face while he did it. He undid the other sleeve, and moved to the first shirt button, the second, fanning the cloth to expose a triangle of white, gleaming skin. A third button, and the first swell of chest muscle came into view. His fingers went to the fourth button, but he didn't undo it. "I would ask for a kiss now, before you see."

I would have asked why, but I thought I knew. He was afraid that once I saw all of him, he wouldn't get his kiss.

I crawled across the bed toward him. Sholto put his hands on the bed and lowered himself to his knees. He moved down until his chin was nearly touching the bed, his hands flat on the bedspread.

I stayed on all fours above him. He gazed up at me, and I lowered my face toward his in a sort of push-up position. I gave him his kiss. A soft brush of lips and Sholto started to pull away. I touched his face gently. "Not yet," I said.

Sholto was right, once I saw all his "extras" he might not get another kiss. If it was the only touch of sidhe hands that he would ever know, I wanted it to be memorable. A kiss couldn't make up for not having ever felt the touch of sidhe flesh, but it was all I could offer. In his own way he was as alone as Uther.

Sholto laid his chin back on the bed, rolling his eyes up at me. He waited for me patiently, totally passive, waiting for me to do whatever I was going to do. In that instant I had another question answered. If I was going to tie myself to any one person for a lifetime, we'd have to have more in common than just sidhe blood. He'd have to share my love of pain.

I lay flat on the bed so that our faces were even. "Open your mouth, just a little," I said.

He did it without question. I liked that. I kissed his upper lip, softly, gently. I used my tongue to open his mouth wider, then used lips and tongue to explore his mouth. He was completely passive at first, letting me feed softly at his mouth, then he began to kiss me back. He kissed slowly, almost hesitantly, as if it were his first time, and I knew it wasn't. Then his mouth pressed against mine harder, more demanding.

I bit his lower lip, gently, but firmly. He made a small noise in his throat, and rose to his knees, pulling me with him, hands on my arms. His kiss mashed against my lips. The kiss was hard enough it hurt, and I had to open my mouth wider, letting his lips, his tongue, his mouth inside mine completely, as deeply as he wanted to probe and lick and feed, just to keep from being bruised.

He pushed me back against the bed, and I let him, but I noticed that he kept his body above mine, using his hands to prop himself up so only our mouths touched. I drew back from the kiss enough to look down the line of his body. I could feel his body above mine like a trembling line of energy. It was as if the weight of his body was already pressed against mine, as if I could already feel the heaviness of him against me. His aura, his magic, had substance like a second body pressing outward from him. The press of power trapped my breath in my throat, brought my pulse racing. His magic drew the blood in my body like a magnet draws metal.

Even with Roane covered in Branwyn's Tears it hadn't been like this. It had been wondrous, but it hadn't been this. And this was what I wanted, needed, craved. Sholto stared down at me with a kind of soft wonder on his face. "What is that?"

I realized he could feel my power as I felt his. I could have simply said, "Magic," but the last time I'd been with another sidhe had been Griffin, and he had explained to me how my power was a lesser glow, a paltry thing. Once I'd believed him; now I didn't. I had to ask, because I might never be with another sidhe. I might never be able to answer the doubts that Griffin had put in my mind. "What does it feel like?" I asked.

"Warm, like heat rising off your body, pressing against my skin." He balanced on one arm, using his free hand to caress the air between us like he was stroking something that had shape, weight. The feel of him stroking his hand along my aura made me close my eyes, my body writhing under that not-touch.

He pushed his hand through the energy, and even with closed eyes I knew where his hand was. "It clings to my hand like it's a bowl of something that sucks against my skin as I reach into it," Sholto said, voice breathy, filled with the wonder his face had shown.

I felt his hand thrust through the power, as if my body were underwater and his hand brought cool air with it. His hand didn't just touch my side, it breeched my shields, forced his magic inside me. It brought my eyes wide open, froze my breath in my throat. It forced me to lash out with my own power, to cover it like holding a hand over a wound.

His body jerked at the touch of my magic. He looked at me with half-parted lips, his pulse thudding like a trapped thing against the fragile skin of his throat. "I had no idea what I was missing."

I nodded, staring up at him, flat on the bed, his hand like a throbbing weight over my ribs. "This is only the beginning," I said, and my voice had fallen to a hoarse whisper. I wasn't trying to sound sexy, it was all the voice left me with the press of him above me. In that moment I couldn't think of any deformity that would keep me from saying yes.

I reached for his shirt. He moved his hand off of me, so he could support his weight on both hands and I could reach the buttons of his shirt. I undid the next button; nothing popped out. I undid another button. The power wavered like heat rising from pavement. "Let go of the illusion, Sholto, let me see."

His voice was a whisper. "I'm afraid."

I stared up at him. "Do you really think I want to lose a chance at this? I want to end this exile, Sholto. I'm tired of pretending, of settling. I want it all back." I caressed a hand over the front of his throat, and the mix of our power flowed behind my hand like an invisible veil. "Sidhe flesh, pleasure to equal mine, to walk into the hollow hills and be welcome; I want to go home, Sholto. Drop your glamour and let me see what you look like."

He did what I asked. The tentacles spilled out of the shirt, and analogies like nest of snakes, or the spill of intestines when you open someone's gut, came to mind. I froze, and this time when my breath caught in my throat it wasn't from passion.

Sholto started to back away immediately, standing, turning so I couldn't see. I had to grab his arm to stop him. My reaction had shut down the magic between us, or rather his reaction to my reaction had. His arm was just an arm under my hand, warm and alive, but nothing more.

I gripped his arm tight with both my hands. I tried to turn him back toward me, but he resisted. I rose on my knees, keeping one hand on his arm, but reached across his body to grab the far side of his shirt. Nothing touched me as I reached across his body, and there should have been a lot of things touching me. He'd called the glamour back in place. I wasn't feeling what was really there.

I dragged him back around to face me. The shirt was open to midstomach. The chest and stomach were pale, muscular, smooth, perfect. I undid another button and the stomach that showed was cobblestone, like an ad for the after shot in a gym commercial. Sholto let me unbutton the shirt and pull it out enough that he was exposed down to the leather of his belt, but he wouldn't look at me.

"I guess if you're going to hide behind glamour, it might as well be handsome."

He did look at me then, and he looked angry. "If this was my true appearance you wouldn't turn from me."

"If this was your real appearance you'd have never become king of the Host."

Something passed through his eyes, something I couldn't read, but anything was better than the anger tinged with bitterness. "I would have been a noble of the sidhe court," he said.

"A lord, nothing better—your mother's bloodline isn't good enough for a greater title."

"I am a lord," he said.

I nodded. "Yes, on your own power, your own merit. The queen could not let such a power walk away from our court without a title."

He smiled, but it was bitter, and that anger crept back into his eyes. "Are you saying it's better to rule in hell than serve in heaven?"

I shook my head. "Never, but I am saying that you have everything your mother's blood could have given you, and you are a king."

He stared down at me, his face that arrogant mask again. The one I saw so often at court. "My mother's blood could have given me you."

"I haven't turned you down," I said.

"I saw the look on your face, felt the reluctance in your body. You don't have to say it out loud for it to be true."

I started to pull his shirt out of his pants. He grabbed my hands. "Don't."

"If you walk away now then it's finished. Drop your illusions, Sholto, let me see."

"I did that." He jerked the shirt out of my hands so hard that he almost dragged me off the bed as he moved away.

"It'd be nice if I could have embraced you without flinching. I am sorry that I couldn't, but give a girl a chance. The first look is a little overwhelming."

He shook his head. "You're right, I am king of the sluagh. I will not be humiliated."

I sat on the edge of the bed and looked at him. He looked perfect if a little sulky. But it wasn't real, and I'd spent the last few years hiding, pretending. Pretense, no matter how pretty, can grow very old. Though they rejected him, there was no one that epitomized the Unseelie Court better than Sholto did. A combination of unbelievable beauty and horror, not just side by side but entwined. One could not exist without the other. In his way Sholto was the perfect marriage of all the court stood for, and they rejected him because they feared that he was indeed the ultimate Unseelie sidhe. I doubted they thought of it that clearly, not in so many words, but that was what frightened them about Sholto—not that he was alien, but that he wasn't alien.

"I can't give my word that I won't turn away a second time, but I can give my word that I will try."

He looked at me, arrogance like a shield in his eyes. "That's not good enough."

"It's the best I have to offer. Is fear of rejection really worth losing your first touch of sidhe flesh so quickly?"

Doubt flickered in his eyes. "If you can't . . . stomach it," something about the phrase amused him, but not in a happy way, "then can I call glamour and . . ."

I finished when his voice trailed off. "Yes, we can."

He nodded. "That is the closest I have ever come to begging."

I laughed. "Lucky you."

He looked puzzled then, and it was almost a relief to see the real Sholto peeking through that careful mask. "I don't understand."

"Your magic is powerful enough that you probably don't." It was my voice that held bitterness now. I shook it off, literally shaking my head, sending my hair sliding around my face. I held my hands out to him. "Come here."

Distrust showed on his face. I guess I couldn't blame him, but I was getting tired of holding his emotional hand. I didn't want to hurt him, but I wasn't sure I wanted to tie myself to him forever. It wasn't the tentacles—it was the heavy emotions that seemed to swing back and forth so quickly. He was going to be a high-maintenance partner when it came to his feelings. Men like that are so damned exhausting that I usually avoid them, but Sholto could offer me things that the others couldn't. He could give me back my home—for that I could shovel emotional shit for a while. But truthfully, it was almost a bigger mark against him than his extras.

"Drop the shirt and come here, or don't. It's your choice."

"You sound impatient," he said.

I shrugged. "A little." I motioned him closer with my hands.

He slid the shirt off his shoulders to spill to the floor. A flurry of emotions crossed his face; he finally settled on defiance. Fine with me, because I knew that whatever was on his face wasn't how he really felt. He'd use a mask until he was sure of his welcome.

He dropped the glamour.

Chapter 13

I TRIED TO WATCH ALL OF HIM AS HE WALKED TOWARD ME, BUT finally gave up and stared. The tentacles were the same gleaming white as the rest of him. There was the faintest marbling effect in the thickest tentacles, and I knew from Bhatar that those were the muscular arms, the tentacles that did the heavy work. There were longer, thinner tentacles in groupings around the ribs and upper stomach. They were the fingers, but a hundred times more sensitive than a sidhe's. Then just above the belly button was a fringe of shorter tentacles with slightly darker tips. That he had those made me wonder even more if what lay in his pants was sidhe, or not.

I sat on the bed and stared until he was standing in front of me. He kept his face turned away, hands clasped behind his back, as if he didn't want to see or touch me. I reached out and touched one of those smooth muscular tentacles. It jerked away at my touch. I stroked it, and I felt Sholto's gaze before I looked up to meet it.

I stroked the outer skin of the tentacle again. "These are for hard work, lifting, capturing prey, or prisoners." I traced my finger on the underside of the tentacle, feeling the slightly different texture. It wasn't unpleasant, but it was thicker than human skin, almost rubbery, like the skin on a dolphin.

"I suppose Bhatar told you that." His voice was angry.

"Yes." I grabbed the base of the tentacle where it melded into his body. I pulled gently but firmly down the length of it. It wrapped around my hand, holding it, moving it away from him.

155

"Don't," he said.

"It felt good didn't it?" I asked.

He looked at me, so angry, so scared. "How do you know what feels good to a nightflyer?"

"I asked."

He looked startled then, and I was able to pull my hand free of him.

I touched one of the groupings of thinner tentacles. They retracted like sea fans when a diver brushes them below a coral sea. "Bhatar could do the most intricate needlework with his fingers."

I moved my hand lower, not quite touching the last visible line of tentacles. "These are very sensitive—they can be used for the finest tactile work, but they're actually a secondary sexual organ."

He looked startled. "We do not usually share that bit of information with outsiders."

"I know." I smiled. "Bhatar used to caress visiting ladies with them. They were often afraid to tell him to go away for fear of offending him, and offending my father. I noticed when I finally went back to court that the Host often caressed nonsluagh with the lower tentacles. It's a sort of in-joke that you all have on us. You touch us with what amounts to a breast, and we're none the wiser."

"But you know," he said.

"I like a good in-joke when I'm not the butt of it." I ran my hand in a long movement over that last line of organs.

His breath went out in a sigh. His eyes stayed defiant, protective. I didn't even blame him for it. I had enough mixed genetics in my own ancestors that there but for the grace of Deity go I.

I touched them gently, and they began to weave around my fingers. The ends were slightly prehensile, not nearly as much so as the upper ones, but there was a slight depression on one side of each of the tentacles. I stroked a finger into one of the depressions; it made him shudder.

"I take it that has a specific job if you're with a female nightflyer?"

He nodded, wordlessly.

"What can they do for me?" I asked the question for several reasons. First, I was curious. Second, I had to know if I could stand for him to touch me intimately with them. I was touching him in almost a detached scientific way. You do x, and y happens. Detachment might allow me to touch him, but it wouldn't get me through sex.

He reached down with his hands, but that put the thicker tentacles in a mass against my face. It made me jerk back. Sholto instantly straightened. Maybe he would have stepped away again, but I grabbed a handful of the lower tentacles. It froze him in place, and his breath caught in his throat. The reaction reminded me of what happens when you touch a man's penis when he's not expecting it.

He reached down with his hands and jerked my shirt out of my pants. The movement put the thick muscular limbs against my face. This time I didn't pull away, but it was an effort.

He pulled the shirt over my head, and let it drop to the floor. The defiance was tinged with something else, something darker and more real. He used two of the muscular tentacles to gently move my hands away from the lower organs. Then the long thin tentacles grew, stretching longer and thinner, like muscular clay. The tips caressed the mounds of my breasts in quick teasing movements. It made me both startle and gasp.

The tips plunged inside my bra, and it was like a snake crawling against my skin. I was about to tell him, no, I couldn't do it, when those reddened tips found my nipples and I discovered what the depressions on the underside were for. They had suction, and the touch was expert. My nipples hardened under the sucking, squeezing sensation.

A second organ played low on my belly, tickling along the top of my pants. He asked without asking. I pushed him gently away. "Enough, please."

He pulled away from me, but this time he wasn't hurt. The look on his face was almost, not quite, but almost triumphant. "The look on your face just now, that alone is worth much to me."

I took a shaking breath and tried to think. "Glad to hear it, but there's one more thing I have to check before I know for sure."

He looked at me.

"Lose the belt, please," I said.

I didn't have to ask twice. He took the belt out, but left the pants buttoned. I liked that he had done exactly what I asked, no more, no less.

I undid the pants, exposing the line of his briefs. The bulge in them was straight and firm, and looked very . . . human. But after what I'd just seen, I had to be sure. I pulled the underwear carefully over that bulge, and saw him nude for the first time.

He was as straight and perfect as his face had promised, like a carved alabastar sculpture. I wrapped my hand around him, and he cried out.

I wasn't teasing, I was looking for something. Bhatar had had a spine inside his penis nearly as long as my hand. Something no human woman would survive. Only the royals of their kind had it, and it meant they were fertile males— without the spine the females didn't ovulate during sex.

Sholto watched me, eyes eager. "A man's control is only so good."

"That's why my pants are staying on." He was like thick muscled velvet in my hands, but there was nothing there but flesh, no nasty surprises. "Your father wasn't royal?"

"You're looking for the spine." His voice was low, hoarse.

"Yes."

"My father was not one of the royal drones." He whispered those reasonable words in a voice that was growing less reasonable after every touch.

"Then how did you get to be king?" My voice was calm. I hadn't stayed excited once the tentacles stopped touching me. It hadn't lasted, because I wasn't aroused by the sight of him. Lord and Lady forgive me, but I saw the extras as a deformity.

"King of the sluagh is not an inherited title. It is earned."

"Earned," I said. "How earned?"

He shook his head. "I am having trouble thinking."

"I wonder why that is." I made it teasing, but I didn't mean it. I wished I did. I could have taken him a piece at a time. Maybe if he'd had just one or two tentacles, but he had over a dozen. The thought of pressing my naked body against him, of being embraced by the nest of tentacles . . . The thought made me shudder.

Sholto mistook my reaction, and one of the muscular tentacles brushed my hair like another man would use his hand. I closed my eyes, raised my face to the touch, tried to enjoy the caress, but I couldn't. For a night, maybe, but not night after night. I just couldn't.

I lowered my face, and the tentacle moved away. I held him in my hand as solid and lovely as any man I'd been with, and because of what lay writhing just above, I couldn't take the pleasure in it that I should have.

Sholto was watching me expectantly, as if I'd already said yes. The logical thing would have been to stand up, kiss him, and bow out, but if I kissed him the mass of tentacles would wrap around me and Sholto would know how I truly felt. I didn't want him to see me pull away in horror. I wanted perhaps his last touch of sidhe flesh to be something pleasant, not humiliating. If I couldn't stand to go higher up his body, well, there was only one way to go: lower.

I slid off the bed, to my knees in front of him. The movement forced him to take a step back from the bed, and put my face even with that length of solid silken flesh. He drew breath to say something, but I stopped his words by taking him into my mouth. I ran my hands up the backs of his thighs to cup his buttocks, digging my fingernails into his flesh.

He cried out, his body thrusting a little to meet my mouth. Normally I liked to watch up the line of a man's body to see his reaction, but not this time. I didn't want to see. I fed at him, sucking him, using tongue, mouth, lips, and gently, teeth.

His breathing took on that quick, panting rhythm that said I would have to stop soon or break the queen's taboo. The

power, too, was back, like a solid hum of energy against my
body, and where I touched him, the energy thrummed; inside
my mouth it was as if he vibrated, and I had a sudden vision of
what it might feel like to have this warm, power-filled thing
between my legs. The image was so strong, I had to pull away.
I opened my eyes and found his skin white, nearly translus-
cent with power.

I looked up slowly, and every inch of him was a shimmering, glowing thing. The ends of the smaller tentacles
glowed like red embers, and the higher tentacles showed a
play of marbled color like colored lightning under the skin.
The play of soft red, softer violet, bands of gold like the color
of his eyes pulsing against the white-white light of his skin
was beautiful.

I stared up at him, and in that moment all I could see was
beauty. He was as he was meant to be, a thing carved from
light, filled with color and magic. That power rose off of him
in a skin-caressing, body-vibrating roll, embracing me like
some invisible, living silken blanket. I wanted to step into it,
to feel it enfold me.

"Undo your hair." My voice sounded strange, like someone else was speaking.

Sholto undid the clasp of his hair, and shook it out around
his body. The hair fell past his knees in a glittering fall like
new snow. I grabbed two handfuls of it and pulled gently. It
had been so long since I'd had hair that could cascade over my
body like this. It was like holding heavy living satin. I pushed
the cups of my bra down so that my breasts spilled out and I
could brush his hair across them. That one touch made me
shudder, and this time it was passion.

I looked up at him, still on my knees. "Do you think we
could behave ourselves if you ran all this lovely hair over my
nude body?"

Each color in his irises was glowing; the rings seemed almost to be whirling like the eye of a storm. The heat in his
face changed to laughter. "Shall I lie and say yes?"

I raised a hand gone shining, nearly translucent, to stroke
along his body. "Yes, lie to me, if it will keep us from stopping."

"Dangerous talk," he said, softly.

"Dangerous times," I said, and licked him, making his body react from legs to shoulders, head going back, breath coming in a shuddering sigh.

"Meredith," he said in that tone that a man saves for only the most intimate of occasions. The sound of it made my body tighten in places he hadn't seen, let alone touched.

The door burst open with a crack of tearing wood and a roil of power that slammed into us like a giant hand. Sholto staggered but stayed on his feet; I ended on my butt on the floor, peering around his legs. I had an image of a dark figure moving in a blur, then Sholto was gone, over the bed and onto the floor beyond.

Nerys the Grey stood framed in the doorway for a heartbeat, then she was moving like a blur of mist toward me. I went for the bed and the gun under the pillow, and knew I'd never make it in time.

Chapter 14

I HAD TO TURN MY BACK ON THE HAG, TO HAVE ANY CHANCE OF reaching the gun. I gave her my back; my hand was under the pillow, and claws slashed my bare back. I screamed, still reaching for the gun. Clawed hands wrapped around my arms and flung me to the floor. I hit the floor hard, unarmed, and Nerys was on me before I could catch my breath.

I kicked at her, and she slashed my legs through the slacks. I kept trying to kick at her and get to my feet, but she never gave me the chance. She attacked, slashing the air, my slacks, the flesh underneath, until I crawled to the wall, and there was nowhere else to run.

She was shrieking at me. "He's ours! Ours! Ours!" Each word was punctuated with a slash. I had my arms in front of my body, but she was going to strip the flesh from my arms, and it wouldn't stop her.

I'd expected the glow to be gone in a wash of terror and pain, but I was still a shining thing. Blood spilled out of my arms in a wash of glittering crimson as if my very blood glowed. I felt power like a warm fist rising up inside my body, spreading out, but not like any magic I'd ever felt before. The power flared through me, and my body shone so brightly that the hag hesitated.

Then she yelled, "I'll eat your skin off, girl, and you won't glow anymore." She slashed my arms until I cried out, and I saw that black-taloned hand coming at my face, my eyes.

I pushed my hand into her bony chest between her breasts, and power spilled up my arm, out my hand. I felt it smash into the hag. She stopped trying to slash me, and just knelt frozen above me. The power flowing through me hurt, it felt like every fiber of my body was being burned all at once. I screamed and tried to stop it, but the pain grew, grew until I looked at Nerys through vision gone grey and spotted. I was close to passing out from the pain, and if I did that, Nerys would kill me.

My body felt like it was being pulled apart with red-hot knives. I finally found voice to scream again, and Nerys joined me. She pulled away from me, crawling to lean against the side of the bed. She watched me with wide eyes, a look of disbelief on her twisted face. Her skin began to . . . flow—it was the only word I had for it. Her skin began to flow like thick water, spilling over her hand like a glove.

Nerys was screaming, "No, no!"

Her body began to fold upon itself, the bones sliding out of place, the muscles sliding to the surface like logs rising in water. Blood spilled onto the carpet, then thicker, darker fluids burst in an acrid wash from her. I watched her heart move to the surface of her body and draw the rest of her internal organs with it like a string of fish. She screamed for a very long time, and even when she was reduced to a large round ball of flesh, you could still hear her screams, muffled, distant, but alive. Nerys was immortal—being turned inside out didn't stop that.

My pain was fading now like an amputated limb that still hurt. I'd seen my father do similar things. It had been one of his hands of power, the one that earned him the title Prince of Flesh.

I started crawling for the door, watching that pulsing, moving thing that I had made. When I cleared the end of the bed I could see Black Agnes straddling Sholto. She'd taken that shining piece of him inside the dull black of her body. He was struggling, but she held his arms down, pinning his body as she rode him. There are things among the fey physically stronger than the sidhe. The hags are one of them.

I went for the splintered door and heard Agnes's voice chase me down the hall. "Nerys, kill that white bitch." The last thing I heard was a plaintive, "Nerys?"

I was in the elevators before the next round of screaming started. If Black Agnes had wanted me dead before, what I'd done to her sister wouldn't make her change her mind. It seemed to take a long time to ride down to the lobby. I was shaking, cold. I raised my arms in front of my face. Both arms were bloodied, hurting with that sharp pain that only slash cuts give, but my left arm was the worst. I could see bone in the cut on the side of my left forearm. Blood flowed from it to run in a steady, red stream from my elbow to the elevator floor. My slacks were soaked nearly purple with blood.

I was hurt enough for shock, but I didn't think that was it. It was the magic. I'd done what could only be a hand of power. I'd done something my father could have done. It was his most terrible power. One that even he used with regret, because they don't die. Nerys wouldn't die. She would be trapped in a prison of her own flesh and fluids forever. Blind, unable to feed or breathe, but never dying. Never dying.

A scream built at the back of my throat, and I knew that if it came out that I would just keep screaming until Agnes found me and pulled out my eyes. I'd left my shirt, my jacket, and the gun in the room. I didn't even have anything to bind my wounds with. I did rearrange my bra so that my breasts were covered.

The elevator doors opened, and a couple almost got in, then saw me. Shock, fear showed on their faces, and they let the doors slide shut. I'd forgotten my glamour. I couldn't go through the lobby looking like this.

Personal glamour is my very best spell, yet I struggled, struggled as never before, to throw a veil of it over me. The best I could do was make people not see me as hurt, and not notice I was wearing nothing above the waist but a bra. I couldn't seem to concentrate on changing my appearance. I needed to use glamour to hide myself from the sluagh, and I couldn't see myself in my head. I couldn't visualize it, and without that, I couldn't do glamour.

The doors opened to the lobby, and I walked out. No one screamed or pointed, so the glamour was working. I was all right. I was going to be all right. Then I saw Segna the Gold sitting on the plush oval couch in the center of the lobby. She watched me with narrowed yellow eyes.

I turned on my heel and went for the back entrance, and found Gethin of the Hawaiian shirt and the baseball cap a few yards away, in front of the other doors. I searched that bright, busy lobby, all the smiling people, the line for checking in and checking out, and knew that they could kill me here on this flowered carpet and no one would know until my body hit the ground and my murderers had fled.

The ladies' room was visible from where I stood. I didn't question it, just walked calmly to it. When the door shushed behind me, I turned and wrote the symbols for protection and strength on the door. I had enough blood coming out of my body that I could have written a letter. I pressed my hands to the door and I called power. I might have feared doing it so soon after what I'd accidently done in the room, but I had no choice. I poured my power into that door, those runes, and I knew that no one of the blood would be able to pass. I knew it, because I willed it so, and I was sidhe, and I had warded the door with my own blood. No one uses blood—it's too power-ful to waste on small things, not to mention unsanitary—but a little overkill wasn't a bad thing tonight. I needed time to think.

I walked through the small lounge area with its sofa and line of mirrors, to the real bathroom beyond. What I saw in the far wall made me realize I didn't need time to think: I was leaving. There was a window set high in the wall. All I had to do was get to it.

I grabbed a handful of paper towels to shove against the worst of the arm wounds while I looked for something to stand on. Once outside I was going to have to find medical help. But I had to survive first, or the only medical help I'd be getting was from the medical examiner.

Gethin's voice—or I assumed it was him, as it wasn't the hag—said, "Little sidhe, little sidhe, let me come in."

I didn't give the next line. If he wanted to quote children's stories he was welcome to it. I was getting out of here. I finally dragged one of the curve-backed chairs from the lounge to the stall closest to the window. I had to jump to grab the metal top bar above the stall, which knocked the chair over. I hung there by my arms for a second, then started using my feet to climb up the wall and get the rest of my body close to my hands. The wounds that had been slowing down, bled faster. I slipped twice in my own blood before I could perch on top of the stall and look at the small window. It was a very small window, and it was one of those moments when I was glad I was small.

I was balanced between the bathroom stall and the window-sill when something slammed into the window. I had a glimpse of tentacles and a razored mouth snapping at the glass, as I fell to the floor. I had to climb back to the window—not to escape through it, but to ward it. They couldn't get in, but now I couldn't get out.

I was trapped, losing more blood than my body could handle, and out of ideas. If I couldn't do anything else, I could at least try to slow the bleeding on my arms. I got a pile of paper towels and went to the sink. What I really needed was a cloth or strong thread to hold the towels in place. I was using the mirror to see how deep the wound on my left arm was when I noticed something in the mirror. Down, down in the depths of the reflection, something small and dark was moving.

I turned, paper towels pressed to the wound, to search the room. The stalls were pale pink and plain, the walls pale pink. Even the few pipes that peeked out of the walls and ceiling had been painted pale pink to match. There was nothing dark in the room except my slacks and bra, and that wasn't what I was seeing.

I turned back to the mirror and it was still there. It was like a dark shadowy figure walking down some crystal hall, coming closer, growing minutely larger. I didn't instantly think it was the sidhe that had tried to kill me at Alistair Norton's, because a lot of sidhe can do mirror magic. For all I knew it was the sluagh coming through the mirror to spill over me. I couldn't ward the mirror—it wasn't a door or a window, not as I understood it. To come through the mirror meant they had better magic than I did, and I couldn't stop them.

The door opened, and my heart almost stopped beating, but it was just two women. Two ordinary, human women, who couldn't have been the least bit sensitive or they would never have been willing to come through the door. They came in laughing, gave me some strange looks, but went into adjoining stalls still laughing and talking. They saw me dressed and not bleeding, because it was the image I'd projected. Good to know something was working.

I didn't know what to do. Then I noticed something new in the mirror. There was a tiny spider crawling over it. No, not over it—inside it. The spider was inside the mirror, crawling on the other side of the glass. It was just like the spiders that had helped save me at Norton's house. It was the fey who had saved me. He, or she, had saved me once. If I ever needed saving again, this was it.

I tore off a piece of paper towel and wrote in blood: HELP ME. I waited until the blood had dried a little then I crumbled the paper into a hard, tight ball. The toilet flushed behind me. I was running out of time.

I passed my fingertips just above the surface of the mirror, careful not to touch it. I didn't want to touch the mirror directly until I had a sense of exactly what spell it was. I could feel the trembling line of power where the magic pulled like a string against the solidness of it. The magic was like a weak spot, a metaphysical crack. Whether the practitioner had found a weakness in the mirror and exploited it, or made the weakness, I didn't know. I pressed my fingers against the cool glass and thought of the heat that had forged the mirror. I spread my fingers apart and the glass fell to pieces like cotton candy on a summer day. A hole opened in the mirror, and a line of white, dazzling light spilled out of it like a distant flash of diamonds.

I threw the ball of paper into that melted hole. I smoothed

the mirror back into place like molding clay. I spread it even with my bare hand. The door opened behind me. I was out of time. There was a lump in the glass, not perfect. I leaned into the mirror, pretending to check my nonexsistent lipstick, blocking the view.

The first woman had opened a tiny purse and was really fixing her lipstick.

But I wasn't looking at my lips. I was watching that shadowy figure low in the mirror. I could see tiny shadow arms moving, unwrapping my message. I heard a male voice ring like a bell in the room. "Done."

The woman froze in front of the mirror. "Did you hear that?" she asked.

"What?" I asked.

"Julie, did you hear that?"

The other woman still in the stall said, "Hear what?" The toilet flushed, and Julie joined her friend at the sink.

To my horror the shadowy figure started growing larger. He was going to come out of the mirror. He was going to walk out of the freaking mirror. I didn't have enough glamour left in me to cover this. Dammit.

I tried to think of some way to distract the women, when I realized exactly what to do. I crossed the room to the light switch and flipped it off. As the darkness slammed around us like a black wall, I felt the pressure in the room change. I knew someone was crawling through the mirror as if pulling aside a thick crystalline curtain. I swallowed to clear my ears and wondered what to do with the two yelling women.

Chapter 15

I STOOD IN THE DARK, FEELING SOMEONE, SOMETHING MOVING in the dark, and knew it wasn't the women, and it wasn't me.

One woman said, "What the hell is going on?"

"Lights are out in the ladies' room," I said.

"Brilliant," the other woman said. "Let's get out of here, Julie." I heard the two of them stumbling toward the door in the dark.

They slid out into the hallway, a flash of brightness against the pitch black, before the door closed behind them.

A wavering yellow-green flame sprang to life in the dark. The flames cast flickering shadows on a dark, dark face.

Doyle's skin wasn't brown—it was black. He looked as if he'd been carved from ebony. His cheekbones were high and sculpted, the chin a little too sharp for my taste. He was all angles and darkness. Those angles looked deceptively delicate, like the bones of a bird, but I'd seen him be hit full in the face with a war hammer once. He'd bled, but he hadn't broken.

The moment I saw him, fear rushed through me in a wave of coldness that left my fingertips tingling. If he hadn't saved my life once already, I'd have been sure he meant my death now. He was the queen's right hand. She would say, "Where is my Darkness? Bring me my Darkness." And someone would die or bleed or both. It was Doyle that should have been given the task of my death, not Sholto. Had he saved me earlier, to kill me now?

"I mean you no harm, Princess Meredith."

The moment he said it out loud, I could breathe again.

Doyle didn't play word games. He said what he meant, meant what he said. The problem was that most of the time he said things like, "I've come to kill you." But this time, he meant me no harm. Why, or rather, why not?

I was standing trapped in a ladies' room with wards that would not hold on the door and window. Eventually the sluagh would break through, and I didn't trust Sholto to save me from them. If it had been almost anyone but Doyle I'd have fallen into his arms with relief, or just let myself faint from blood loss and shock. But it was Doyle, and he simply wasn't a person that you fell into the arms of, not without checking for knives first.

"What do you want, Doyle?" The words came out harsher than I meant them to, angry, but I didn't take them back or apologize for the tone. I was fighting not to shiver visibly, and failing. I was still bleeding from a half dozen wounds on my arms, blood sliding inside my slacks like a warm worm working against my skin. I needed help, and I couldn't hide that fact from him. It put me in a very weak bargaining position. When dealing with the queen, that was a bad place to be. And make no mistake about it, when dealing with Doyle you were dealing with the queen, unless things had changed drastically in the court in three short years.

"To obey my queen in all things." His voice was like his skin, dark. It made me think of molasses and other thick, sweet things. A voice so deep it could hit notes low enough to make my spine shiver.

"That's not an answer," I said.

His hair looked very short and clipped close to his head, black but not as black as his skin. But I knew the hair wasn't short—it was long. His hair was always in a tight thick braid down his back. I couldn't see it, but I knew the braid reached to his ankles. The braid left the tips of his pointed ears bare and visible.

The green flame glittered off the earrings in those fantastic ears. Two fine diamond studs graced each dark earlobe, and two dark jewels almost the color of his skin sat beside the diamonds like dark stars. Small silver hoops climbed up the cartilage of both ears to the very top where the ear curled into a soft, fleshy point.

The ears showed that he was not full high court, but a bastard mix like myself. Only the ears betrayed him, and he could have hidden them behind his hair but he almost never did.

I glanced down at the small silver necklace that was the only other jewelry he wore. A small silver spider with its fat body in the shape of some dark jewel sat on the black cloth of his chest.

"I should have remembered that your livery is a spider."

He gave a very small smile, which for Doyle was an outrageous amount of expression. "Normally, I would give you time to adjust to my presence, our predicament, but your wards will not hold forever. We must act if you are to be saved."

"Lord Sholto was sent here by the queen to kill me. Why send you to save me? Even for her that makes no sense."

"The queen did not send Sholto."

I stared up at him. Did I dare believe him? We rarely lied outright to each other. But someone was lying to me, because they couldn't both be telling the truth. "Sholto said I was under the queen's order of execution."

"Think, Princess. If Queen Andais truly desired your execution she'd drag you home so that the court could see what happens to sidhe who flee the court against royal orders. She would make an example of you." He motioned at the room, his hands spreading flame as he moved, like afterimages. "She would not have you killed in hiding, where no one would see." The flame collected back upon itself like water droplets sliding over a plate, but stayed dancing above his fingertips.

I put a hand on the edge of the sink. If this conversation didn't end soon I was going to be on my knees, because standing wasn't going to be an option. How much blood had I lost? How much blood was I still losing?

"You mean that the queen would want to see me die," I said.

"Yes," he said.

Something thudded into the window with enough force that the room seemed to shake. Doyle whirled toward the sound, drawing a long knife, or a small sword, from behind his back. The greenish flames hung floating in the air above one of his shoulders like an obedient pet.

The light played on the blade and the carved-bone hilt. The hilt was a trio of crows, their breasts meeting, their wings entwined, their beaks open bearing jewels for the pommel.

I sank to the floor, one hand on the sink. "That's Mortal Dread." It was one of the queen's private weapons. I'd never heard of her loaning it to anyone for any reason.

Doyle turned slowly from the empty window. The short sword caught the wavering light. "Now do you believe that the queen sent me to save you?"

"Either that, or you killed her for the sword," I said.

He looked down at me, and the look on his face said he didn't see the humor in that last remark. Good, because I wasn't being funny. Mortal Dread was one of the treasures of the Unseelie Court. The sword had mortal blood tied to its forging, which meant that a death wound from Mortal Dread was truly a death wound for any fey, even a sidhe. I would have said that the only way to get the sword was to pry it from my aunt's cold, dead hands.

Something large was hitting the window over and over again. I'd hoped they'd try to break the wardings by magic, which would take some time, but they were going to simply destroy what I'd warded. If the window was no longer there then the ward would no longer work. Brute force over magic— sometimes it worked, sometimes it didn't. Tonight it was going to work. There was a sharp crumbling sound as the glass cracked around the wire that ran through it. Without the wire in the glass, it would have already broken.

Doyle knelt by me, sword pointed tip down like you'd hold a loaded gun for safety. "We are out of time, Princess."

I nodded. "I'm listening."

He reached his empty right hand toward me, and I flinched,

falling back on my butt on the floor. "I must touch you, Princess."

"Why?"

The glass cracked enough that wind oozed through the room. I could hear something large rubbing against the wall, and the high twittering calls of the nightflyers urging their beefy brethren on.

"I can kill some of them, my princess, but not all of them. I will lay my life down for you, but it will not be enough, not against the might of nearly the entire sluagh." He leaned in close enough that I had to either let him touch me, or lie on the floor and start crawling crabwise backward away from him.

I laid my hand against him, touching the leather of his jacket. He continued pushing forward, and my hand slid off to the black T-shirt underneath. I felt something wet. I jerked back, and my hand was covered black in the eerie half-light.

"You're bleeding," I said.

"The sluagh were most persistent that I did not find you tonight."

I had to put one hand behind me to keep from falling to the ground, because he was that close. Close enough to kiss, or to kill.

"What do you want, Doyle?"

The glass behind us shattered, spraying the floor in a tinkling shower of shards like a sharp hard rain. "My apologies, but there is no time for niceties."

He let the sword fall to the floor and grabbed my upper arms. He pulled me against him, and I had a second to realize that he meant to kiss me.

If he'd tried to knife me, I'd have been prepared, or at least not surprised, but a kiss . . . I was lost. His skin smelled like some exotic spice. His lips were soft, and the kiss gentle. I was frozen in his arms, too shocked to know what to do, as if he'd bespelled me. He whispered against my lips, "She said, it must be given to you, as it was given to me." There was a thread of anger in his whispered words.

I heard something fall through the window, a heavy plop.

Doyle released me so suddenly that I fell back to the floor. In one fluid movement he picked up the sword, turned, and moved across the floor in a dancelike movement that never left his knees. He drove the sword into a black tentacle as big as he was, that had spilled through the crack in the window. Something screamed on the other side of the broken glass. He pulled the sword from the tentacle, and it began to retract through the window. Doyle stood, moving just ahead of its motion. He raised the sword above his head and brought it down with a force that made the blade a shining blur. The tentacle fell in pieces in a wash of blood that spilled like black water in the greenish-yellow light.

The rest of the tentacle retracted through the window to a sound like the wind howling. Doyle turned back to me. "That will make them hesitate, but not for long." He strode toward me, bloody sword naked in his hand. It had all happened in seconds. He'd even managed to stand to one side so the blood had missed him, as if he'd known where to stand, or what the blood would do.

Watching him move toward me, I couldn't stay on the ground. He was here to keep me alive, but as he moved closer every instinct I had screamed out. He was an elemental thing carved of darkness and half-light, armed with a killing sword and moving toward me like death incarnate. In that one moment I knew why humans had fallen down and worshiped us.

I used the sinks to pull myself to my feet, because I could not meet him crouched like a hunted thing. I had to stand before that dark grace, or bow down before it like a human worshiper. Standing made the room waver in lines of color and darkness; I was so light-headed I was afraid I'd fall, but I kept my feet with a death grip on the sinks. When my vision cleared, I was still upright, and Doyle was close enough that I could see green flames reflected in the dark mirrors of his eyes.

He was suddenly holding me so close that the blood on his shirt slapped cool against my skin. His hands were so strong as they moved up my back, pressing me against his body.

"The queen put her mark within me, to give to you. Once you have it, all will know that to harm you is to risk the queen's mercy."

"The kiss," I said.

He nodded. "She said, I must give it to you, as she gave it to me. Forgive me." He kissed me before I could ask what he was seeking forgiveness for.

He kissed me like he was trying to climb inside me through my mouth. I wasn't ready for it and hadn't given permission for it. I tried to pull away, and his arm locked against my back, pressing the leather into my skin. His other hand held my face, fingers digging into my chin. I couldn't pull away from the kiss, I couldn't pull away from him.

Struggling was getting me nowhere, so I stopped and opened my mouth to him, kissing him back. A tension went out of his body, as if he thought I'd given permission. I hadn't. I grabbed his black T-shirt and began to pull it out of his pants. It was so wet with blood that it clung to his skin, but I pulled it free. I ran my hands over the flatness of his stomach, upward to the smooth swell of his chest.

He melted against me, the hand on my back kneading against my bare skin.

My hands found the wound high up on his chest. It was wide, a deep slash. Three things happened at once: I plunged my fingers into his wound; his body stiffened and I felt him react to the pain. I think he would have released me then, but the third thing happened on the heels of his pain, with my fingers plunged inside the meat of his body. The queen's mark filled his mouth and slid inside mine.

A sweet rush of power filled my mouth, pouring from Doyle's body into mine and melting warm between our lips, as if we were both sucking on the same piece of candy. The power swelled inside us, melting between us in long sweet strands. It filled us to the brim with warmth, like mulled wine poured into twin cups, until power ran down our bodies, through our bodies, to finally pour in liquid warmth across our skin.

Doyle broke the kiss, pulling away from me. I slid to the floor, not from blood loss this time, but because my knees wouldn't hold me.

I couldn't seem to focus on anything, as if I were looking at the world through a haze. Doyle was leaning both hands on the sinks, head down, as if he was light-headed, too. I heard him say, "Consort, save me."

I don't know what my snappy comeback would have been, because the door burst open, slamming into the far stalls. Sholto was silhouetted in the doorway. He'd thrown the grey overcoat across his bare chest, but the nest of tentacles showed like some monster trying to pull itself from his skin.

I had a sense of movement behind me, and turned to see Doyle go for the sword that he'd laid in the sink. I felt Sholto's power rise like a wind in the lighted doorway. I realized suddenly that they both thought the other had come to kill me.

I had time to yell, "No!"

Doyle's flame vanished, swallowed into a darkness that was velvet and perfect and filled with the sounds of moving bodies.

Chapter 16

I SCREAMED, "DON'T! SHOLTO, DOYLE, DON'T HURT EACH other!" I heard flesh hitting flesh, the sliding footsteps as someone glided through the dark, someone drew a hard breath, then small noises.

"Dammit, listen to me, neither of you is here to harm me. You both want me alive." I don't know if they didn't hear me, or didn't care. There was at least one sword being used in the dark, so I didn't get up and walk toward the light switch— I crawled. I kept the weight of the sinks to my right and searched the darkness just ahead with my left hand.

The fight continued in almost utter silence. I could hear them straining against each other. Someone cried out, and I said a silent prayer that no one was dead. I almost crawled into the wall, touching it at the last second. I worked my way up until I found the light switch. I hit the lights, and the room was suddenly blindingly bright. I was left blinking in the brilliance.

The two sidhe were locked together, bodies straining against one another. Doyle was on his knees, a tentacle wrapped around his neck. Sholto was covered in blood, and it took my eyes a second to realize that one of his stomach tentacles had been severed and lay twitching next to Doyle's knee. Doyle still held the sword, but Sholto's hand and two tentacles held it away from the other sidhe. Their other hands were locked against each other as if they were engaged in a game of finger wrestling. Except this was no game. I was actually surprised that Sholto seemed to be holding his own. Doyle was the acknowledged champion of the Unseelie Court. There were very few who could stand against him and almost none who would win. Sholto wasn't on that short list, or so I'd thought. Then I caught something out of the corner of my eye: a small glow. When I looked straight at it, nothing was there. Magic is like that sometimes—only visible through peripheral vision. There was something glowing on Sholto's hand: a ring.

As I watched, the sword slipped from Doyle's grip and he started to go limp in Sholto's grasp. Sholto grabbed the sword in his hand before it could hit the ground. The tentacles stayed around Doyle's arm. I was moving forward before I had time to think of what I'd do when I got there.

Sholto held Doyle's limp body in his tentacles and raised the sword in a two-handed overhead plunge, like you'd use to drive a knife into someone's chest. I was behind Doyle as the sword started down. I curled my body over his, one hand up-raised, my gaze never leaving that glittering blade. I had a heartbeat to wonder if Sholto would stop in time, then he reversed the sword and held it pointed at the ceiling.

"What are you doing, Meredith?"

"He's here to save me, not kill me."

"He is the queen's Darkness. If she desires your death, he will be her instrument."

"But he has Mortal Dread, one of her personal weapons. He carried her mark in his body to give to me. If you'll calm down long enough to look with more than just your eyes, you'll see it."

Sholto blinked at me, then frowned. "Then why would she send me to kill you? Even for Andais that makes no sense."

"If you'll stop strangling him, maybe we can figure it out."

He looked down at Doyle's limp body, still hanging from the tentacles, and said, "Oh," as if he'd forgotten he was still squeezing the life from the other man. Technically, you couldn't strangle a sidhe to death, but I'd never been comfortable test-ing the limits of immortality. You never knew when you'd find a chink in the armor big enough to die through.

Sholto uncurled his limbs from Doyle, and the other man fell into my arms, his weight driving me to my knees. I wasn't losing enough blood for this much weakness. It was either shock or something to do with using a hand of power for the first time. Whatever was causing it, I wanted to close my eyes and rest, and that just wasn't going to be happening.

I sat on the floor, cradling Doyle's head in my lap. The pulse in his neck was strong, steady, but he did not wake. He took two quick breaths, then his head threw back, eyes wide, and he took a great gasp of air. He sat up coughing. I saw him tense, and Sholto must have, too, because the sword was suddenly pointed at Doyle's face.

Doyle froze, staring up at the other man. "Finish it."

"No one is finishing anything," I said.

Neither man looked at me. I couldn't see Doyle's expression, but I could see Sholto's, and I did not like what I saw. Anger, satisfaction—he wanted to kill Doyle, it was there on his face plain to see.

"Doyle saved me, Sholto. He saved me from your sluagh."

"If you had not warded the door, I would have been here in time," Sholto said.

"If I had not warded the door, you would have been in time to mourn over my dead body, but not in time to save me."

Sholto still wouldn't take his gaze from Doyle. "How did he get inside when I could not?"

"I am sidhe," Doyle said.

"So am I," Sholto said. The anger in his face hardened just a bit.

I slapped Doyle's shoulder, hard enough to sting. He didn't turn, but he winced. "Don't bait him, Doyle."

"I was not baiting, merely stating a fact."

This entire fight was beginning to feel very personal, as if there was business between the two of them that had nothing to do with me. "Look, I don't know what you have against each other, but call me selfish, I don't care. I want out of this damn bathroom alive, and that takes priority over whatever personal vendetta the two of you have. So stop acting like little boys and start behaving like members of the royal body-guards. Get me out of here in one piece."

"She's right," Doyle said, softly.

"The great Darkness, bowing out of a fight? Inconceivable. Or is it that I'm the one with the sword now?" Sholto moved the sword a fraction forward, touching the tip to the indentation in Doyle's upper lip. "A sword that can kill any fey, even a sidhe nobleman. Oh, I forget, you're not afraid of anything." There was a bitterness, a mockery, to Sholto's voice that said without doubt that I'd stepped into an old grudge.

"I fear many things," Doyle said, his voice calm, neutral. "Death is not one of them. But the ring on your finger is something that I am wary of. How did you get Beathalachd? I have not seen it used in centuries."

Sholto raised his hand so the dark bronze of the ring glimmered dully in the lights. It was a heavy piece of jewelry, and I would have noticed it on his hand if it had been there earlier. "It was the queen's gift to show her blessing on this hunt."

"The queen did not give you Beathalachd, not personally." Doyle sounded very sure of that.

"What is Beathalachd?" I asked.

"Vitality," Doyle said. "It steals the very life and skill of your opponent, which is the only way that he bested me in a fight."

Sholto flushed. It was considered a sign of weakness to need more magic than you had in your own body to defeat another sidhe. Basically, Doyle had said that Sholto couldn't win a fair fight, and had had to cheat. But it wasn't cheating— just less than chivalrous. Fuck chivalry, come back alive. It was what I'd told any man I'd ever loved, including my father, before every duel.

"The ring proves that I have the queen's favor," Sholto said, his face still colored by his anger.

"The ring did not come from the queen's own hand to yours," Doyle said, "any more than your order to kill the princess came from her mouth."

"I know who speaks for the queen and who does not," Sholto said, and it was his turn to sound certain.

"Really," Doyle said. "And if I had come to you and given you the queen's orders, would you have believed me?"

Sholto frowned, but nodded. "You are the queen's Darkness. When your mouth moves, her words come out of it."

"Then hear these words: The queen wants Princess Meredith alive, and back home."

I couldn't read all the thoughts moving across Sholto's face, but there were a lot of them. I tried to ask the question he would not answer for Doyle. "Did the queen herself tell you to come to Los Angeles and kill me?"

Sholto looked at me. It was a long, considering look, but finally he shook his head. "No," he said.

"Who told you to come to Los Angeles and slay the princess?" Doyle asked.

Sholto opened his mouth to answer, then closed it. The tension flowed out of him, and he stepped back from Doyle, lowering the sword to his side. "No, I will keep the name of the traitor to myself for now."

"Why?" I asked.

"Because Doyle's presence here can mean only one thing. The queen wants you to return to court." He looked at Doyle. "I'm right, aren't I?"

"Yes," Doyle said.

"She wants me to return to court?"

Doyle moved so he could see both Sholto and me, his back to the empty bathroom stalls. "Yes, Princess."

I shook my head. "I left because people were trying to kill me, Doyle. The queen wasn't stopping them."

"They were legal duels," he said.

"They were court-sanctioned assassination attempts," I said.

"I did mention this to her," Doyle said.

"And she said what?"

"She gave me her mark to give to you. If anyone kills you now, even in a duel, they will have to face our queen's vengeance. Trust in this, Princess: even those who desire your death greatly will not want to pay that high a price for it."

I looked up at Sholto; the movement made me slightly dizzy. Shock, definitely shock. "Fine, I'm going back to court, if the queen can guarantee my safety. What does that have to do with you not giving us the name of the traitor? Who used the queen's name to send you to execute me, when she didn't want me dead?"

"I will keep that information to myself for now," Sholto said again. His face was that arrogant mask that he wore so often at court.

"Why?" I asked.

"Because if the queen allows you back to court, you don't need to bargain with me. You will be able to return to faerie, to the Unseelie Court, and I would bet my kingdom that she'll find you another sidhe lover. So, you see, Meredith, you don't need me. You'll have everything I could have offered you, and you won't be tied for a lifetime to a deformed monster."

"You're not deformed, Sholto. If your hags hadn't interrupted, I'd have proved that to you."

Something flickered over his face, rippling on the surface of his arrogance. "Yes, my hags." He turned those tri-yellow eyes on me. "I thought you had no hand of power, Meredith."

"I don't," I said.

"I think Nerys would argue with you on that."

"I didn't know, Sholto, I didn't mean to . . ." I had no words for what I'd done to Nerys.

"What has happened?" Doyle asked.

"Black Agnes lied to the sluagh. She told them that if I mated with Meredith that I would become pure sidhe, and no longer be their king. She convinced them that they were protecting me from myself, protecting me from the wiles of the sidhe witch."

I raised eyebrows at that.

He looked at me. "But I have persuaded Agnes and the rest that you are not a danger to them."

I met his eyes. "I saw the method of persuasion before I ran."

He nodded. "Agnes said to thank you—she's never had better from me. She thinks it has something to do with your magic."

"She's not angry about Nerys?" I asked.

"She wants you dead, yes, but she's afraid of you now, Meredith. The hand of flesh like your father—who would have dreamed it?" There was something in his eyes besides careful arrogance. I realized with a start that it was fear. Fear peeking through his mask. It wasn't just Black Agnes who was afraid of what I'd done up in that room.

"Hand of flesh," Doyle repeated. "What are you saying, Sholto?"

Sholto held the sword out to Doyle, hilt first. "Take this, and come up to my room and see what our little princess has done. Nerys cannot be healed, so I request that you grant her true death before you escort Meredith home. I will see you both safely to a taxi on the off chance that my sluagh are not . . . perfectly obedient." His words, his body language all said that he was not happy with Doyle.

With a small bow of his head, Doyle took the sword. "If it is a favor you need, then I am happy to oblige for the name of the traitor that sent you to Los Angeles falsely in the queen's name."

Sholto shook his head. "I will not give up the name, not now. I will hold it until it is of use to me, or until I decide to deal with the traitor personally."

"If you told us the traitor's name, it would help us keep the princess safe at court."

Sholto laughed then, that strange bitter sound that passed for normal laughter for him. "I will not say who sent me here, but I can guess who wanted the message given, and so can you. Meredith fled the court because Prince Cel's supporters kept challenging her to duels. If it had been anyone else behind the attempts on Meredith's life, the queen would have stepped in and stopped it. Such an insult to the royal family would not have been allowed, not even to a mixed-breed magicless mortal. But it was her precious baby boy who was behind it, and we all knew it. So Meredith fled, and hid herself away, because she didn't trust the queen to keep her alive when Cel wanted her dead."

Doyle met those accusing eyes with a tranquil face. "I

think you will find that our queen is no longer so tolerant of the prince's . . . eccentricities."

Sholto laughed again, and it was a painful sound. "When I left the court only days ago, I'd say she was still very tolerant of Cel's . . . eccentricities."

Doyle's face was still peaceful, as if nothing the other man could do would upset him. I think that bothered Sholto more than any other reaction that Doyle could have given him. I think Doyle knew that. "One problem at a time, Sholto. For now I have the queen's promise, and her magic, to ensure that the princess will not be harmed at court."

"As you wish to believe, Doyle, but for now I would ask you to aid me in bringing death to one that I valued."

Doyle stood easily, as if he hadn't been nearly strangled to death moments ago. I wasn't even sure I could stand. There is more than just immortality that I miss by taking after my human blood.

They both reached out to me at the same time, and I took both hands. They nearly pulled me off my feet. "Easy does it, boys. I just need help standing, not flying."

Doyle looked at me. "You are pale. How badly are you hurt?"

I shook my head and pulled away from them both. "Not that badly. It's mostly shock, and . . . it hurt when I . . . did what I did to Nerys."

"What did you do?" he asked.

"Come see," Sholto said. "It is worth a look, or three." He looked at me then. "The news of what you have done will ride before you to the court, Meredith. Meredith, Princess of Flesh, no longer merely Essus's daughter."

"It is very rare for a child to receive the same gifts as the parent," Doyle said.

Sholto walked toward the door, tying the grey trench coat in place as he moved. Blood soaked into the cloth where the cut tentacle pressed against it. "Come, Doyle, Bearer of the Painful Flame, Baron Sweet-tongue, come and see what you think of Meredith's gifts."

I was familiar with the first title, but not the second. I asked, "Baron Sweet-tongue—I've never heard you called that."

"It is a very old nickname," he said.

"Come, Doyle, you are too modest. It was the queen's pet name for him, once."

The two men looked at each other, and again there was a weight of old grudge in the air. "The name is not for what you assume, Sholto," Doyle said.

"I assume nothing, but I think the sobriquet speaks for itself. Don't you, Meredith?"

"Baron Sweet-tongue does have a certain ambiance," I said.

"It is not for what you think," Doyle repeated.

"Well," Sholto said, "it is certainly not because of your honeyed words."

That was true. Doyle didn't go in for long speeches, and he was not an accomplished flatterer. "If you say it's not sexual, then I believe you," I said.

Doyle made a small bow to me. "Thank you."

"The queen doesn't give out pet names except for sex," Sholto said.

"Yes, she does," I said.

"When, and for what?"

"When she thinks the nickname will bother the person bearing it, and because she enjoys being irritating."

"Well, the last is certainly true," Sholto said. He had his hand on the door handle.

"I'm surprised no one barged in on us," I said.

"I put a small spell of aversion on the door. No mortal would want to pass it, and few fey." He started to open the door.

"Don't you want your . . . limb? They might be able to re-attach it."

"It will grow back," he said.

I must have looked as disbelieving as I felt, because he smiled in a half-superior, half-apologetic way. "There are some benefits to being half nightflyer—not many, but a few. I can regenerate any lost body part." He seemed to think about that for a second, then added, "So far, anyway."

I didn't know what to say to that, so I didn't try.

"I think the princess needs to get some rest, so if we could see your friend . . ." Doyle said.

"Of course." Sholto held the door for us.

"What about the mess?" I asked. "We're just going to leave bits of tentacle and blood all over the floor?"

"The baron made the mess, let him clean it up," Sholto said.

"Neither the body parts nor the blood belong to me," Doyle said. "If you want it cleaned up, I suggest you do it yourself. Who knows what damage a talented witch could do with a body part left lying around?"

Sholto protested, but in the end he slipped the severed tentacle in his coat pocket. They left the body-sized one where it lay. If I were Sholto I would definitely be overtipping the cleaning staff, just to make up for whoever had to do the bathroom.

We rode back up in the elevator, and Doyle knelt on the floor studying what was left of Nerys the Grey. She was a ball of flesh about the size of a bushel basket. Nerves, tendons, muscles, internal organs all glistened wetly on the outside of that ball. They all seemed to be functioning normally. That lump of flesh even rose and fell with breath. The sound was the worst: a high, thin screaming, muffled because her mouth was now on the inside of her body, but still she screamed. She shrieked. The shivering that had been growing less, grew more. I was suddenly cold standing there in my bra and pants.

I got my shirt from the floor where I'd left it, and slipped it on, but knew that mere cloth wasn't going to take care of this particular kind of cold. It was more a shivering of the soul than the body. I could pile myself with blankets and it wouldn't help.

Doyle looked up at me, kneeling beside that pulsing, screaming ball. "Most impressive. Prince Essus himself could not have done better." The words were a compliment, but his face was so empty I couldn't tell if he was pleased or not.

I actually thought it was one of the most horrible things I'd ever seen, but I knew better than to share the observation. It was a powerful weapon, the hand of flesh. If people believed

I'd use it easily, often, it was more of a deterrent. If they thought I feared it, then the threat would be less. "I don't know, Doyle, I saw my father turn a giant inside out once. Do you think I could do something that large?" My voice was dry, interested, but in an academic sort of way. It was the voice I'd cultivated at court. The voice I used when I was trying not to have hysterics or run screaming from a room. I had learned to watch the most awful things and make dry, urbane comments.

Doyle took the question at face value. "I don't know, Princess, but it will be interesting to discover the limits of your power."

I disagreed, but I let the comment stand, because I couldn't think of anything dry and urbane enough to cover the situation. The muffled shrieks continued as fast as the ball of flesh could draw breath. Nerys was immortal. My father had once done this to an enemy of the queen's. Andais kept that ball of flesh in a trunk in her room. Periodically, you'd find it sitting around her bedchamber. To my knowledge no one ever questioned what it was doing out of its trunk. You just picked it up, put it back, locked it away, and fought down any visuals that came to mind when you found it sitting in the queen's bed.

"Sholto asked that you grant Nerys death. Do it, so we can get out of here." I sounded disinterested, even bored. I thought if I had to stand there and hear that thing screaming for much longer, I'd join it.

Still on his knees, Doyle held the sword up to me, hilt first, the blade lying on his hands. "It is your magic—let it be your kill."

I stared at the bone hilt, the three ravens and their jeweled eyes. I didn't want to do it. I stared at the blade for a minute more, trying to think how to get out of this without appearing weak. Nothing came to mind. If I got squeamish now, then Nerys's torment was for nothing. I would have gained a new title but not the reputation that went with it.

I took the sword, and hated Doyle for offering it to me. It should have been easily done. Her heart was trapped and pulsing on the side of the ball. I thrust the blade into it. Blood poured black, and the heart stopped beating, but that thin screaming didn't stop.

I glanced at the two men. "Why isn't she dead?"

"The sluagh are harder to kill than the sidhe," Sholto said.

"How much harder?"

He shrugged. "It's your kill."

In that instant I hated them both, because I realized finally that it was a test. It might be that if I refused the kill they'd leave her alive. That was not acceptable. I couldn't leave her like this, knowing that she'd never age, or heal, or die. She'd just continue. Death was mercy; anything else was madness, hers and mine.

I stabbed the sword into every vital organ I could find. They bled, shriveled, ceased to function, and still the screaming went on. I finally raised the sword in a two-handed motion above my head and just started stabbing. At first I paused between stabs, or slices, but every time the screams just went on and on, trapped inside that ball of meat. Somewhere around the tenth blow, or the fifteenth blow, I stopped pausing, stopped listening, and just kept stabbing.

I had to make the screaming stop. I had to make her die. The world narrowed down to the pounding of the blade into the thick meat. My arms raised and lowered, raised and lowered. The blade bit into the flesh. Blood sprayed across my face, my shirt. I ended on my knees beside something that was no longer round, no longer whole. I'd hacked the thing into pieces, unrecognizable pieces. The screaming had stopped.

My hands were soaked with blood, crimson to the elbows. The sword blade was scarlet, the bone hilt was solid blood, and still the hilt fit my hand well, not slippery at all. The green silk shirt I'd put back on was black with soaked blood. My slacks had gone from purple to a violet black. Someone was breathing too fast, too ragged, and I realized it was me. Sometime during the butchering there had been a fierce satisfaction, almost a joyfulness in the sheer destruction. Now I stared down at what I had done and felt nothing. There wasn't enough of me left to feel anything about this, so I felt nothing. I was numb, and it wasn't a bad way to be.

I got to my feet using the edge of the bed. The bed was already spattered with blood—what was one more handprint? My arms were sore, the muscles shaking from too much exercise. I offered the sword to Doyle as he'd offered it to me. "Good sword, the hilt never got slippery." My voice sounded as empty of emotion as I felt. I wondered if this was what it was like to be crazy. If it was, it wasn't so very bad.

Doyle took the sword and dropped to his knees, head bowed. Sholto echoed him, kneeling, bowing his head. Doyle saluted me with the bloody sword and said, "Meredith, Princess of Flesh, true royal of the blood, welcome to the inner circle of the sidhe."

I stared down at both of them, still echoingly numb. If there were ritual words to answer with, I couldn't think of them. Either I'd never known them, or I just couldn't make my mind work right now. The only thing I could think to say was, "May I use your shower?"

"Be my guest," Sholto said.

The carpet squished under my feet, and when I walked off that section of carpet I left bloody footprints behind me. I stripped and showered in the hottest water I could stand against my skin. The blood wasn't red by the time it ran down the drain; it was pink. It was while I watched that pinkish water swirl down the drain that I realized two things. First, I was glad I'd had the courage to finish Nerys rather than leave her in that horror. Second, part of me had enjoyed killing her. I'd have liked to think that the part that enjoyed the kill was motivated by the mercy of the first thought, but I couldn't afford to be that generous to myself. I had to wonder if the part of me that enjoyed sinking blade into flesh was the same part that made Andais keep her own bit of flesh in a locked trunk in her room. The second you stop questioning yourself is the second that you become the monster.

Chapter 17

I ARRIVED BACK AT MY APARTMENT WITH MY HAIR STILL DAMP from the hotel shower. Doyle insisted on unlocking the door for me, in case it had been magically booby-trapped. He was taking his job of bodyguard seriously, but from Doyle I wouldn't have expected less. When he pronounced it safe I walked onto the grey carpet barefoot. I was wearing a Hawaiian shirt and a pair of loose men's shorts, clothes Sholto had borrowed from Gethin. The only thing I couldn't borrow from the man was shoes. My clothes were still in the hotel room, so blood-soaked that even the underwear had been unusable. Some of the blood had been Nerys's, some of it mine.

I turned on the light switch by the door. The overhead light blazed to life. I'd paid extra to be able to paint the apartment a color other than white. The walls of the front room were pale pink. The couch was mauve, purple, and pink. The overstuffed chair in the corner was pink. The drapes were pink with ties of purple. Jeremy had said it was like being inside an expensively decorated Easter egg. The bookcase was white. The entertainment center was white. I turned on the standing lamp by the overstuffed chair. The light over the small white kitchen table and chairs was next. Lacy white curtains framed the big window in front of the table. The window glass was very black and somehow threatening. I closed the drapes, shutting the night out behind the white blind. I stood for a moment in front of the only painting in the front room. It was a print of The Butterflies' Haunt by W. Scott Miles. The picture was mostly green, and the butterflies were painted to nature, so there was precious little pink or purple in the picture. But you never choose a painting just because it matches a room—you choose a painting because it speaks to you. Because it says something that you want to be reminded of daily. The picture had always seemed peaceful, idyllic, but tonight it was just paint on a canvas. Tonight nothing was going to please me. I turned on the kitchen lights and went for the bedroom.

Doyle had stood quietly to one side as I moved around the room turning on all the lights like a child waking from a nightmare. Light to chase away the bad things. The trouble was that the bad things were in my head now. There was no light bright enough for that.

He followed me as I went into the bedroom. I hit the overhead light as I moved through the door.

"I like what you've done with the bedroom," he said.

The comment made me turn and look at him. "What do you mean?"

His face stayed impassive, unreadable. "The living room was so very . . . pink. I feared the bedroom would be, as well."

I looked around the room at the soft grey walls, the burgundy wallpaper border with its mauve, pink, and white flowers. The bed was a king-sized four-poster, leaving almost no room between the foot of the bed and the closet doors. The bedspread was a deep, rich burgundy with a mound of pillows: burgundy, purple, mauve, pink, and a few black, just a few. The mirrored dresser was cherry wood, varnished so dark it was almost black. The dresser near the window matched it. Jeremy said that my bedroom looked like a man's room with a few touches added by his girlfriend. There was a black lacquer cabinet in the corner farthest away from the bathroom door. The cabinet was Oriental, with cranes and stylized mountains. The crane had been part of my father's livery. When I bought it, I remembered thinking he would have liked it. There was a philodendron plant on top of it, grown so long that the vines fell like green hair around the beautiful wood.

I looked around the room, and suddenly it felt like it wasn't mine and I didn't belong here. I turned back to Doyle. "As if it makes a difference to you what color my bedroom is."

He didn't flinch, but his face became even more unreadable, more passive, a trace of arrogance creeping in, and it reminded me of Sholto's courtly mask.

The comment had been mean, and meant to be. I was angry with him. Angry with him for not killing Nerys for me. Angry with him for forcing me to do what had to be done. Angry with him for everything, even the things that weren't his fault.

He watched me with cool eyes. "You're quite right, Princess Meredith, your bedroom is no concern of mine. I am a court gelding."

I shook my head. "No, that's the problem. You're not a gelding; none of you are. She just won't share."

He shrugged, making it look graceful. The movement caused him to wince.

"How is your wound?" I asked.

"You were angry with me seconds ago, now you are not. Why?"

I tried to put it into words. "It's not your fault."

"What is not my fault?"

"You did not endanger me. You saved my life. You didn't send the sluagh after me. You didn't cause the hand of flesh to manifest tonight. It's not your fault. I'm angry, and I want someone to blame, but you shouldn't pay the price for other people's shit."

He raised black-on-black eyebrows at that. "A most enlightened attitude for a princess."

I shook my head. "Drop the title, Doyle. I'm Meredith, just Meredith."

The eyebrows went up even farther, until his eyes looked impossibly wide, and his expression actually made me laugh. The laughter sounded normal, felt good. I sat down on the edge of the bed and shook my head. "I didn't think I'd be laughing tonight."

He knelt in front of me. "You have killed before—why is this different?"

I looked at him, surprised that he'd understood exactly what was bothering me. "Why was it so important that I kill Nerys?"

"A sidhe comes into their power through ritual, but that doesn't mean that the power will manifest itself. After the first time the power is used, then the sidhe must bloody themselves in combat." He put a hand on the bed on either side of me, but not touching. "It is a kind of blood sacrifice; it will ensure that the powers do not go back to sleep, but continue to grow."

"Blood makes the crops grow," I said.

He nodded. "Death magic is the oldest of all magics, Princess." He gave that small smile. "Meredith." He said my name softly.

"So you had me chop Nerys up so that my powers wouldn't go dormant again?"

He nodded again.

I looked into that serious face. "You said a sidhe comes into their power after a ritual. I had no ritual."

"The night you spent with the roane was your ritual."

I shook my head. "No, Doyle, we did nothing ritualistic that night."

"There are many rituals for awakening the power, Meredith. Combat, sacrifice, sex, and many more. It is not surprising that your power chose sex. You are descended from three different fertility deities."

"Five actually. But I still don't understand."

"Your roane was covered in Branwyn's Tears; for that one night he acted the part of a sidhe lover for you. He brought on your secondary powers."

"I knew it was magical, but I didn't know . . ." My voice trailed off. I frowned at him. "It seems like there should be more to it than just good sex."

"Why? It is sex that makes the miracle of life—what could be greater than that?"

"The magic healed Roane, gave him back his sealskin. I didn't try to heal him, because I didn't know I could."

Doyle sat down beside the bed, his long legs curled up against the dresser. "Healing one skinless roane is nothing. I have seen sidhe raise mountains from the sea, or flood entire cities, when they came into their power. You were lucky."

I was suddenly scared. "You mean my coming into my powers could have caused some great natural disaster?"

"Yes."

"You'd think someone would have warned me," I said.

"No one knew you were leaving us, so we could give you no parting advice. And no one knew that you had secondary powers, Meredith. The queen was convinced that if seven years with Griffin in your bed and years of duels had not awakened your powers then they were not there to waken."

"Why now?" I asked. "Why after all these years?"

"I do not know. All I know is that you are Princess of Flesh, and you have one more hand of power that has not manifested yet."

"It's rare for a sidhe to have more than one hand of power. Why would I have two?"

"Your hands had melted two of the metal bars on the bed. Two bars melted, one for each hand."

I stood and stepped away from him. "How did you know that?"

"I watched you sleep from the balcony. I saw the headboard."

"Why didn't you make yourself known to me?"

"At that point you were in what amounted to a drugged sleep. I doubt I could have wakened you."

"Why not the night you used the spiders? The night at Alistair Norton's?"

"You mean the human who was worshiping the sidhe."

That stopped me. I stared at him. "What are you talking about, Doyle? When did Norton worship the sidhe?"

"When he stole the power from the women using Branwyn's Tears," Doyle said.

"No, I was there. I was nearly a victim. There was no ceremony invoking the sidhe."

"Every schoolchild in this country is taught the one thing

that the sidhe were prohibited from doing when we were welcomed into this country."

"We could not set ourselves up as gods. We could not be worshiped. I got the lecture at home from Father, and at school in history class, government class."

"You are the only one of us ever educated with the common humans. I forget that sometimes. The queen was livid when she discovered Prince Essus had enrolled you in a public school."

"She tried to drown me when I was six, Doyle. She tried to drown me like a purebred puppy that came out with the wrong markings. I wouldn't think she'd have given a damn what school I went to."

"I don't think I've ever seen the queen so surprised as when Prince Essus took you, and his entourage, and set up housekeeping among the humans." He smiled, a brief flash of white in that dark face. "Once she realized that the prince would not stand for your mistreatment, then she began to try and lure him back to court. She offered him much, but he refused for ten years. Long enough for you to grow from child to woman out among the humans."

"If she was so upset, why did she allow so many of the Unseelie Court to visit us?"

"The queen, and the prince, feared that you would grow too human if you did not see your people. Though the queen did not approve of your father's choices for his entourage."

"You mean Keelin," I said.

He nodded. "The queen never understood why he insisted on choosing a fey who had no sidhe blood in her veins as your constant companion."

"Keelin is half brownie like my grandmother."

"And half goblin," Doyle said, "which you do not have in your background."

"The goblins are the foot soldiers of the Unseelie army. The sidhe declare war, but the goblins begin it."

"You're quoting your father now," Doyle said.

"Yes, I am." I was suddenly tired again. The short burst of humor, the amazing new possibilities of power, a return to the court—nothing could keep me from a bone-numbing weariness. But one thing I had to know. "You said Alistair Norton was worshiping the sidhe. What did you mean by that?"

"I meant that he used ritual to invoke the sidhe when he set up the circle of power around his bed. I recognized the symbols. You saw no ritual because even the most uneducated human would know that he was not allowed to call on sidhe power for magic."

"He did the preparation ritual before the women came," I said.

"Exactly," Doyle said.

"I saw a sidhe in the mirrors, but I did not see a face. Could you sense who it was?"

"No, but they were powerful enough that I could not break through. All I could send you was my animal, and my voice. It takes a great deal to bar me from a room."

"So one of the sidhe is allowing himself—"

"Or herself," Doyle said.

I nodded. "Or herself to be worshiped, and they gave Branwyn's Tears to a mortal to be used against other fey."

"Normally, humans of fey descent would not qualify for full fey status, but in this case, yes."

"To allow worship is a death sentence," I said.

"To allow the Tears to be used against another fey is to be condemned to torture for an indefinite period. Some would choose death over that."

"Have you told the queen?"

Doyle pushed himself to his feet. "I have told her of the sidhe who is allowing him or herself to be worshiped, and the Tears. I need to tell her that you have the hand of flesh, and you are blooded. She must also know that it is not Sholto who is the traitor, but one who spoke using the queen's own name."

I widened eyes at him. "Are you saying that she sent just you, alone, against Sholto and the entire sluagh, when she thought he had gone rogue?"

Doyle just looked at me.

"Nothing personal, but you needed backup."

"No, she sent me to fetch you home before Sholto left Saint Louis. I arrived the night that I sent the spiders to help you. It was the next day that Sholto began traveling this way."

"So someone found out the queen wanted me home, and within twenty-four hours they'd made a plan to have me killed."

"It would seem so," Doyle said.

"You haven't left the queen's side in—what? six hundred, eight hundred years, except for assassinations?"

"One thousand and twenty-three years to be exact."

"So if she doesn't mean you to kill me, then why send you? There are other of her Ravens that I trust more."

"Trust more, or like more?" Doyle asked.

I thought about that, then nodded. "All right, like more. This is the longest conversation we've ever had, Doyle. Why did she send you, her Darkness?"

"The queen wants you home, Meredith. But she feared you would not believe her. I am her token to you. Her Darkness sent with her personal weapon in hand, with her magic in my body, to prove that she is sincere."

"Why does she want me home, Doyle? She sent you before I came into my power—which was a surprise to all of us. So what changed her mind? Why am I suddenly worth keeping alive?"

"She never ordered your death."

"She never stopped anyone from trying either."

He gave a small bow. "That I cannot argue."

"Then what has changed?"

"I do not know why, Meredith, only that she wishes it."

"You never did ask enough questions," I said.

"And you, Princess, always asked too many."

"Maybe, but I want an answer to this question before I go back to court."

"Which question is that?"

I frowned at him. "Why the change of heart, Doyle? I need to know before I trust my life to the court again."

"If she will not share this information?"

I tried to think about giving up faerie forever because of one unanswered question. It was too big a topic for me to wrap my mind around. "I don't know, Doyle, I don't know. All I do know is that I'm tired."

"With your permission I will use the bathroom mirror to contact the queen and make my report."

I nodded. "Help yourself."

He gave as much of a bow as the crowded bedroom would allow and moved toward the bathroom door, which was around the corner, out of sight from where we stood.

"How did you know where the bathroom was?" I asked.

He glanced back at me, face pleasant, unreadable. "I've seen the rest of the apartment. Where else could it be?"

I looked at him and didn't believe him. Either it didn't show on my face, or he chose to ignore it, because he walked around the corner. I heard the bathroom door open and close.

I sat on the edge of the bed and tried to remember where I'd put the sleeping bags. Doyle had saved my life tonight—the least I could do was make him comfortable. For my life, I guess I could have offered him the bed, but I was achingly tired, and I wanted the bed. Besides, until I knew exactly why he'd saved me tonight I was holding off on the big gratitude. There are things worse than death at the Unseelie Court. Nerys was a perfect example. The queen's mark would not be violated by such a spell. So until I was certain down to the very fiber of my being that I was not being saved for some awful fate, I'd hold on to my gratitude. I found the sleeping bags in the small closet in the living room. I had them unrolled on the foot of the bed, airing, when I heard the shouting from the bathroom. Doyle's voice was raised in anger. The queen's Darkness and the queen were having a fight, or so it seemed. I wondered if he'd tell me what the fight was about, or if it would be just one more secret to keep.

Chapter 18

I WENT TO THE CLOSED BATHROOM DOOR. DOYLE'S RAISED voice was saying, "Please, my lady, do not make me do this."

I don't know what else I would have heard, because he came to the door then and opened it a crack. "Yes, Princess?"

"If you could stay in there a few minutes longer, I'm going to get dressed for bed."

He acknowledged it with a nod. He did not invite me in to see my aunt through the mirror. He did not try to explain the fight. He simply closed the door. I could hear their voices but faintly now. No more yelling. They didn't want me to know what the fight was about. I was guessing it had something to do with me. What did Doyle not want to do so badly that he'd argue with his queen?

He didn't mean to kill me, and, beyond that tonight, I wasn't sure I cared. I turned the overhead light off, and switched on the small Tiffany-shaded lamp beside the bed. The overhead light always seemed too bright for a bedroom. The fact that I was willing to turn off any light meant I was feeling better. Calmer at least.

My usual sleepwear runs high to lingerie. I like the feel of silk and satin against my skin. But it seemed almost cruel to Doyle.

It was the royal's privilege to sleep with her bodyguards, her Ravens, until one of them made her pregnant; then she wed that one and didn't sleep with the rest. Andais could have freed them to have other lovers, but she chose not to. Unless they slept with her, they slept with no one. They'd been sleeping with no one for a very long time.

I finally settled for a silk nightshirt that fell to my knees; it had short sleeves and revealed only a thin V of skin high up on my chest. It covered more than anything else in the drawer, but without a bra my breasts pressed against the thin material, showing my nipples like thumbs pressed against the thin cloth. The silk was a vibrant royal purple and looked very good against my skin and hair. I was trying not to flash Doyle, but I was vain enough not to want to look frumpy.

I stared at myself in the mirror. I looked like a woman waiting for her lover, except for the cuts. I raised my arms to the glass. Nerys's claws had traced my forearms in angry red lines. The gash on the left forearm was still seeping blood. Did it need stitches? I usually healed without needing them, but it should have stopped bleeding by now. I raised the nightshirt up enough to see the wound on my thigh. It was a puncture wound, very high up. She'd been trying to pierce the femoral artery. She'd meant to kill me, but I'd killed her instead. I still felt nothing about her death. It was a vast numb place. Maybe tomorrow I'd feel bad, or maybe I wouldn't. Sometimes you just stayed numb, because anything else was not helpful. Sanity relied on numbness, sometimes.

I stared at myself in the mirror, and even my face was empty. My eyes held that dull startled look that had more to do with shock than anything else. The last time I'd seen this look on my face had been after the last duel, when I knew finally that the duels would never stop until I was dead. The night I'd made my decision to run, to hide.

The invitation to return to faerie was only hours old, and already I looked like a shell-shock victim. I raised my arms again and stared at the claw marks. In a way I'd paid the price for my return to faerie. I'd paid in blood, flesh, pain: the coin of the Unseelie Court. The queen had invited me back and given me her promise of safety, but I knew her. She'd still want to punish me for running, for hiding, for defeating her best efforts at hunting me down. To say that my aunt is not a graceful loser is an understatement of universe-shattering proportions.

There was a knock on the bathroom door. "May I come out?" Doyle asked.

"I'm trying to decide that now," I said.

"Excuse me?" he asked.

"Fine, come out," I said.

Doyle had draped the straps of the sword sheath over his bare chest. The hilt rode upside down, slightly to one side of his ribs, like a gun in a shoulder holster. The straps seemed loose, as if he'd taken off something that had been helping hold it in place.

I'd never seen Doyle when he wasn't covered from neck to ankle. Even at high summer he rarely wore short sleeves, just lighter cloth. He had a silver ring in his left nipple. It was a startling thing against the utter blackness of his skin. The wound rode above the swell of his left pectoral muscle. The scarlet of the wound looked almost decorative against his chest, like some elaborate makeup meant to tease the eye.

"How badly are you hurt?" he asked.

"I could ask you the same thing."

"I carry no mortal blood, Princess. I will heal. I ask you again how badly are you injured?"

"I'm wondering if I need stitches on the arm, and . . ." I started to raise the nightshirt on the puncture wound, but stopped in midmotion. The sidhe are comfortable around nudity, but I'd always tried to be more circumspect around the guards.

"The puncture wound on my thigh, I'm wondering how deep it is." I let the purple silk fall back into place without pointing out the wound. It was very high up on my thigh and I was still not wearing underwear. I often didn't to bed. Habit. Now I wished I had put some on. Even though Doyle couldn't tell what I was or wasn't wearing under the nightshirt, I felt suddenly underdressed.

I'd have teased Jeremy, but I wouldn't have teased Uther, and I wouldn't tease Doyle, for very similar reasons. They were both cut off from that part of themselves. Uther because he'd been exiled and there were no women of his stature. Doyle on the whim of his queen.

He picked up the sleeping bags and laid them on the floor between the bed and the wall, then he sat on the end of the bed. "May I see the wound, Princess?"

I sat down on the edge of the bed beside him, smoothing the nightshirt down around me. I held my left arm out to him.

He used both his hands to raise the arm up, bending it at the elbow, so he could see the wound better. His fingers felt larger than they should have, more intimate than they were. "It is deep; some of the muscles are torn. It must hurt." He looked at me when he said the last.

"I can't seem to feel much of anything right now," I said.

He laid his hand on my forehead. His hand felt so warm, it was almost hot. "You are cool to the touch, Princess." He shook his head. "I should have noticed earlier. You are in shock. Not severe, but it was careless of me not to notice. You need healing and warmth."

I took my hand back from him. The feel of his fingers sliding along my skin as I drew away from him made me look away so he wouldn't see it in my face. "Since neither of us can heal by touch, I think I'll have to settle for some bandages and the warmth."

"I can heal by magic," he said.

I looked at him. His face was very careful, unreadable. "I've never seen you do it at court."

"It is a more . . . intimate method than the touch of hands. At court there are healers much more powerful than I. My own small abilities in the area of healing are not needed." He held his hands out toward me. "I can heal you, Princess, or would you prefer a trip to the emergency room and stitches? Either way the bleeding must be stopped."

Stitches are not my favorite thing. I laid my hand in his. He bent the arm at the elbow again, clasping his hand in my hand, entwining our fingers. My skin looked shockingly white against his darkness, like polished jet next to mother-of-pearl. He placed his other hand just in back of my elbow. My arm was held gently but firmly in place. I realized that I couldn't move away from him and I didn't know how his healing worked.

"Will it hurt?"

He looked at me around the edge of my arm. "It may, a little." He began to bend toward my arm as if to lay a kiss on the wound.

I put my free hand on his shoulder, stopping his forward movement. His skin was like warm silk. "Wait—how exactly are you going to heal me?"

He gave that small smile. "If you would wait but moments you would see."

"I don't like surprises," I said, hand still on his shoulder.

He smiled and shook his head. "Very well." But his hands stayed at my hand and arm. I was still being held, as if he were going to heal me whether I agreed or not. "Sholto told you that one of my names is Baron Sweet-tongue."

"I remember," I said.

"He implied that it was sexual, but it is not. I can heal your wound, but not with my hands."

I stared at him for a few heartbeats. "Are you saying you're going to lick the wound closed?"

"Yes."

I kept staring at him. "Some of the court dogs can do that, but I've never heard of a sidhe having the ability."

"As Sholto said, there are benefits to not being pure sidhe. He can regrow a severed body part, and I can lick your wound until it is healed."

I didn't try to keep the incredulity off my face. "If you were any other guard I'd accuse you of looking for an excuse to put your mouth on me."

He smiled, and this time it was brighter, more humor in it. "If my fellow Ravens were trying to trick you into this, it would not be your arm they were wanting to touch."

I had to smile. "You've made your point. All right, get the bleeding stopped if you can. I really don't want to go to the emergency room tonight." I dropped my arm from his shoulder. "Proceed."

He bent toward my arm, slowly, talking as he moved. "I will try to make it as painless as possible." His breath was almost burningly hot against my skin, then his tongue licked lightly over the wound.

I jumped.

He rolled his eyes up to me without moving his face back from my arm. "Did I hurt you, Princess?"

I shook my head, not sure I trusted my voice.

He bent back to the wound. He licked the length of the wound twice, very slowly, then his tongue slid inside the wound. The pain was sharp, immediate, and it brought a gasp to my throat.

He didn't pull away this time, but pressed his mouth closer to my skin. His eyes closed, as his tongue probed the wound, bringing small sharp pain sensations like tiny electric shocks. With every small pain things low in my body tightened and released. It was as if the nerves he touched were attached to other things that had nothing to do with my arm.

He began to lick the wound in long slow movements. His eyes were still closed, and I was near enough to see the black lashes, black on black against his cheeks. There was almost no pain now, just the sensation of his tongue sliding over me. The feel of his mouth against me sped my heart, made my breath catch in my throat. His earrings caught the light, reflecting it in silver glitter as if the curve of his ears had been set in silver. Warmth began to gather at the wound. It felt very like being healed by touch now. That growing warmth, the energy vibrating against my skin, inside my skin, was almost identical.

Doyle drew back from my arm, eyes half-closed, mouth slack. He looked like he was waking from a dream, or as if he'd been interrupted in more intimate things. He released my arm, slowly, almost reluctantly.

His voice came slow, hoarse. "It has been long since I have done this. I'd forgotten how it feels to heal."

I bent my arm back so I could see the wound, and there was no wound. I touched the skin with fingertips. The skin was smooth, untouched, still damp from Doyle's tongue, still warm to the touch as if some of that magic clung to the skin. "It's perfect; there's not even a scar."

"You sound surprised."

"Pleased, more like."

He gave a small bow, still sitting on the edge of the bed. "So happy to have been of service to my princess."

"I forgot the extra pillows." I stood, and started to move toward the closet. He grabbed my wrist.

"You are bleeding."

I glanced down at my arm, and it was still healed.

"Your leg, Princess."

I looked down and found blood trickling down my right leg. "Damn."

"Lie down on the bed and let me look at the wound." He still held my wrist and tried to pull me down on the bed.

I resisted, and he released me. "It should not still be bleeding, Princess Meredith. Let me heal it, as I did your arm."

"It's very high up on my thigh, Doyle."

"The hag was trying to pierce your femoral artery."

"Yes," I said.

"I must insist on seeing the wound, Princess. It is too vital an area to be ignored."

"It's very high up on my thigh," I said again.

"I understand that," he said. "Now please lie down and let me look at it."

"I'm not wearing anything under this shirt," I said.

"Oh," he said. Emotions played across his face so quickly I couldn't read them, like clouds passing over a field on a windy day. Finally, he said, "Perhaps you could put something on so that I might look at the wound."

"Good idea," I said. I opened the dresser drawer that held my unmentionables. The panties, like the sleepwear, run high to satin, silk, and lace. I finally picked a pair of plain black satin, no frills, no lace, no peek-a-boo panels. It was the closest to conservative that I owned.

I glanced back at Doyle. He had turned his back on me without being asked. I slipped the underwear on, made sure the shirt was in place, and said, "You can look now."

He turned, and his face was very solemn. "Most of the court ladies would not have thought to warn me. Some to tease, and some simply because it would not occur to them to tell me. Nudity is common enough in the courts. Why did you think to tell me?"

"Some of the guards tease, play slap and tickle, and I wouldn't have warned one of them. It would be just another part of the game. But you never play the game, Doyle. You are always apart from it. To have just lain down on the bed and spread would have been . . . cruel."

He nodded. "Yes, it would have been. So many of the court treat those of us who remain aloof like eunuchs, as if we feel nothing. But I would rather have no touch of soft flesh than to be teased up to that point, then have no release. That is worse than nothing at all to me."

"Is the queen still refusing to even allow you to touch yourselves?"

He looked down at the ground, and I realized I had overstepped polite questioning. "My apologies, Doyle, we are not close enough for such a question."

He spoke without looking up. "You are the most polite of all the Unseelie royals. The queen saw your . . . niceties as a weakness." He looked up at me, eyes searching my face. "But those of us in the Guard appreciated it. It was always a relief to be given guard duty over you, because we weren't afraid of you."

"I wasn't powerful enough for you to fear me," I said.

"No, Princess, I don't mean your magic. I mean we didn't fear your cruelty. Prince Cel has inherited his mother's . . . sense of humor."

"He's a sadist, you mean."

He nodded. "In every way. Now lie on the bed and let me look at your wound. If I let you bleed to death for modesty's sake, the queen might make me a eunuch."

"You are her Darkness, her right hand. She would not lose you over me."

"I think you undervalue yourself, and overvalue me." He held his hand out to me. "Please, Princess, lie down."

I took the offered hand and climbed onto the bed on my knees. "Would you, please, call me Meredith. It's been years since I heard princess this and princess that. I'll get my fill of it once I'm back in Cahokia. For tonight, let's drop the titles."

He gave a small bow at the neck. "As you wish, Meredith." I let him help me climb into the middle of the bed, though I didn't need the help. Partly because the older sidhe liked helping, and partly for the feel of his hand in mine.

I ended lying with my head cradled in the wealth of small pillows on the bed. Propped up I had a perfect view down the line of my body.

Doyle knelt to one side of my leg. "If you please, Princess."

"Meredith," I said.

He nodded. "If you please, Meredith."

I raised the dark purple silk until the wound showed. The puncture was high enough that black panties showed under the raised nightshirt.

He used his hands to examine the wound, pulling the skin, pressing on it. It hurt, and not a good kind of hurt, as if there was more damage than I'd realized. Blood flowed faster, but it certainly wasn't enough for an artery. I'd have bled to death long ago if the femoral had been punctured.

He raised up, hands in his lap. "The wound is very deep, and I think there is some muscle damage."

"It didn't hurt that much until you started touching it."

"If I do not heal it tonight, you'll be lame by tomorrow, and we'll be going to that emergency room. It might require surgery, stitching on the inside of your leg. Or I can heal it now."

"I vote for now," I said.

He gave his smile. "Good. I would hate to have to explain to the queen why I brought you home limping, when I could have healed you." He started to lean over my leg, then raised up. "This would be easier if I moved."

"You're the healer—do what you need to do," I said.

He moved between my legs, and I had to open them just to give him room for his knees. It took some maneuvering, and some "Excuse me, Princess"es, but he finally ended lying flat on his stomach, his hands cupping my thighs. His gazed moved up along my body until he met my eyes. Just staring down at him in this position made my pulse jump in my throat. I tried for it not to show on my face, and think I failed.

He blew his breath like a warm wind against the skin of my thigh. He looked at my face while he did it, and I realized it had been deliberate, and I don't think it had anything to do with healing me.

He raised back from my skin. "Forgive me, but it is not merely sex one misses, but the small intimacies. The look on a woman's face when she reacts to your touch." He flicked his tongue in a quick motion over my skin. "That small intake of breath as her body begins to rise to meet your touch."

He lay between my legs, staring up at me. I looked down the line of his body. His hair lay in a thick black rope across the bare skin of his back, trailing over the tight smoothness of his jeans. When I met his eyes again, they held that look that fills a man's eyes when he is sure that you will not tell him no, no matter what he asks. Doyle hadn't earned that look, not yet.

"You aren't supposed to tease, remember."

He rubbed his chin back and forth over my thigh as he spoke. "I normally don't allow myself to be maneuvered into such a compromising position, but I find that once I am here it is very difficult not take some advantage."

He bit my thigh, gently, and when that made me gasp, he set his teeth in my skin harder. It bowed my spine, made me cry out. When I could look again, he'd left a red imprint of his teeth in my thigh. It had been so long since I'd had a lover that not only would but wanted to leave my body marked.

His voice came purringly deep: "That was wonderful."

"Tease me and I'll tease back." I tried for it to be a warning, but my voice was too breathy.

"But you are all the way up there, and I am down here." His grip tightened on my thighs; the strength in his hands was immense. I understood what he was implying. He was strong enough to hold me in place with just his hands on my thighs. I could sit up, but I couldn't really get away. A tension in my body that I hadn't even known was there eased. I relaxed under his hands, settling back against the bed. There were things that I'd been missing that had little to do with orgasm. Doyle would never look up at me with slow horror on his face at something I'd asked him to do. He would never make me feel like a monster because of the things my body craved.

I worked the silk of the nightshirt out from under my back, then pulled it over my body, over my head. I raised up, sitting above him. That dark knowledge in his eyes was gone, chased away by sheer need. It was so raw on his face, I knew I'd taken the game too far. I held the nightshirt in front of my breasts, not sure how to apologize without making things more awkward than they already were.

"No," he said, "don't cover them. You surprised me, that's all."

"No, Doyle. We can't finish this, and for you, especially . . . I'm sorry." I started to slip the shirt back on.

His fingers tightened painfully around my thighs, fingertips digging into the skin. He made me gasp and look at him with the shirt only on my arms.

His voice was dark with command, a barely contained rage that made his eyes shine like black jewels. "No!"

That one word froze me where I was, left me staring down at him with wide eyes and my heart beating like a trapped thing in my throat.

"No," he said, voice only a breath less severe, "no, I want to see them. I'm going to make you writhe, my princess, and I want to watch your body while I do it."

I let the shirt fall to the bed and sat up, as close to him as I could get. His grip on my thighs had passed the point of pleasure and become simply pain, but that, too, under the right set of circumstances, was a kind of pleasure.

His fingers eased back just a little, and I saw that he'd left the marks of his fingernails in my thighs. The little half-moon marks filled with blood as I watched.

He started to move his hands out from under my thighs, but I shook my head no. "You're down there, and I'm up here, re-member."

He didn't argue, just settled his hands back around my thighs, not hurting this time, just solid enough that I couldn't move away. I ran my hands over my stomach, upward to cup my breasts, then lay down propped against the pillows so he could see me.

He stared at me for long seconds, as if he'd memorize the way my body lay among the dark-colored pillows, then his mouth settled against the wound. He licked it with thick, slow movements of his tongue. Then his mouth locked over the wound and he began to suck. He drew on the skin so tightly that it hurt, as if he were sucking some deep poison out of the wound.

The pain raised me up, and he rolled his eyes to me full of that dark knowledge that he hadn't earned. I laid back against the bed with the pressure of his mouth on my thigh, his strong fingers digging into my thighs hard enough that I knew to-morrow I'd be bruised. My skin had started to glow, glimmering in the soft bedroom light.

I stared down at him, but his eyes were turned downward, concentrating on his work. The warmth began to grow under the pressure of his mouth, to fill the wound like warm water poured down the hole in my skin.

Doyle began to glow. His bare skin shone like moonlight on a puddle of water at night. Except this moonlight was coming from inside him to shimmer in black shapes of light and dark underneath his skin.

The warmth of the healing beat against my thigh like a second pulse. His mouth locked against me, pulling at that pulse, as if he'd suck me clean and empty. A warmth grew in the center of my body, and I realized that it was my own power, but it had never been like this before.

The warmth in my thigh and the warmth in my body grew outward like two pools of heat, out and out, larger and larger until my body was eaten with heat, and my skin glowed white and pure with a dance underneath like water. The two powers flowed against each other, and for a heartbeat Doyle's healing warmth floated on the surface of my heat, then the two powers spilled into one another, merging into one rush of spine-bowing, skin-dancing, body-tightening magic.

Doyle raised his face up from my thigh. He cried out, "Meredith, no!"

But it was too late, the power poured through us both in a rush of warmth, of heat, that tightened things low in my body until there was no breath. Then the power spilled outward like a fist flinging open, straining for something it could not grasp. I cried out, and the power flowed out of me in a glow that left shadows in the room from my skin.

I saw Doyle as if through a haze. He was on his knees. He had one hand up as if to ward off a blow, then the power smashed into him. I saw his head snap back, his body raise high on his knees as if the power had arms to lift him. The dance of moonlight under his skin grew until I could see a nimbus of black light, shining like a dark rainbow around his body. He stayed for an impossible second lifted, straining, a shining thing, so beautiful that you could only cry, or go blind as you watched. Then a scream was torn from his mouth, half of pain, half of pleasure. He sagged onto the bed, catching himself with his arms. That wondrous glow began to fade as if his skin were absorbing the light, sucking it back into the depths from whence it came.

I sat up, reached for him with a hand that still held a hint of that soft white light.

He jerked back from me, fell off the bed in his haste, looked over the edge of it at me with wide, frightened eyes. "What have you done?"

"What's wrong, Doyle?"

"What's wrong?" He got to his feet, leaning against the wall suddenly as if his legs weren't quite steady. "I am not allowed a sexual release, Meredith. Not by my hand, or any-one else's."

"I never touched you there."

He closed his eyes and leaned his head back against the wall. He spoke without looking at me. "Your magic did. It ran through me like a sword." He opened his eyes, stared at me. "Do you understand now what you've done?"

I finally did. "You're saying that the queen will count this as sex."

"Yes."

"I never meant for it . . . My power has never been like this before."

"Was it like this the night you were with the roane?"

I thought about that for a moment, then frowned. "Yes, and no. It wasn't exactly like this, but—" I stopped in midsen-tence and stared at his chest.

My look must have been astonished, because it made him stare down at himself. "What? What do you see?"

"Your chest wound, it's gone." My voice was soft with amazement.

He ran his hands over his chest, searching the skin. "It's healed. I did not do this." He came to the edge of the bed. "Your arms."

I looked down and saw the claw marks were gone. My arms were healed. I ran my hands over my thighs, and they weren't healed. The nail marks, filled with their small bits of blood; the red marks of his teeth; the press of his mouth that had brought a red stain to my thigh where the wound had been. "Why is everything else healed but these marks?"

He shook his head. "I don't know."

I stared up at him. "You said that my initiation into power healed Roane, but what if it's not just that first flush of power. What if it's part of my newfound magic?"

I watched him try to make sense of it. "It could be, but healing by sex is not a gift of the Unseelie Court."

"It is of the Seelie Court," I said.

"You are of their bloodline," he said softly. "I must tell the queen."

"Tell her what?" I asked.

"Everything."

I crawled forward on the bed, still half-naked, reaching for him. He moved out of reach, clutching at the wall as if I'd threatened him. "No, Meredith, no more. The queen may forgive us because it was accidental, and she will be pleased that you have more powers. It may save us, but if you touch me again . . ." He shook his head. "She will not have pity on us if we come together again this night."

"I was just going to touch your arm, Doyle. I think we should talk before you go tattling to the queen."

He moved back to the edge of the wall, just before it turned the corner out of sight. "I have just had the first release in more centuries that you can imagine and you sit there like that . . ." He shook his head again. "You would just touch my arm, but my self-control is not limitless—we've proven that already. No, Meredith, one touch, and I might fall upon you and do what I've been wanting to do since I saw your breasts trembling above me."

"I can get dressed," I said.

"That would be good," he said, "but I am still going to tell her what happened."

"What does she do—take a sperm count? We didn't have sex. Why tell her?"

"She is the Queen of Air and Darkness; she will know. If we do not confess it, and then she finds out, the punishment will be a thousand times worse."

"Punishment? It was an accident."

"I know, and that may save us."

"You are not seriously saying that she will invoke the same penalty for this as if we had made deliberate love?"

"Death by torture," he said. "I hope not, but she is within her rights to call for it."

I shook my head. "No, she would not lose you after a thousand years for an accident."

"I hope not, Princess, I truly hope not." He started around the corner toward the bathroom.

"Doyle," I called.

He came back around the corner. "Yes, Princess?"

"If she tells you that we're going to be executed for this, there is one bright spot."

He put his head to one side in a birdlike movement, "And that would be?"

"We can have sex, real sex, flesh into flesh. If we're going to be executed for something, we might as well be guilty of it."

Emotions chased across his face—again I couldn't read them—then finally a smile. "I never thought I could face my queen with this news and have a divided mind on what I want her to say. You are a tempting thing, Meredith, a thing that a man might trade his life for."

"I don't want your life, Doyle, just your body."

That sent him laughing into the bathroom, which was better than crying. I had the nightshirt back on and was tucked under the covers by the time he came back out. He was solemn-faced, but said, "We are not going to be punished. Though she has made some hint that she would like to see you heal with this newfound power."

"I don't do her little public sex shows," I said.

"I know that, and so does she, but she is curious about it."

"Let her be curious. So we aren't going to be executed, either of us?"

"No," he said.

"Why don't you look happier?" I asked.

"I didn't bring a change of clothes."

It took me a second to realize what he meant. I dug him out a pair of men's silk boxers. They were a little snug through the hips, because he and Roane were not really the same size, but they would fit.

He took the boxers and went back into the bathroom. I thought he'd be quick and come back out to sleep, but I heard the shower turn on. I finally tossed down some pillows on top of the sleeping bags and turned over to try and sleep. I wasn't sure I would be able to sleep, but Doyle stayed in the bathroom a long time. The last thing I heard before sleep rolled over me was the sound of the blow dryer. I never heard him come out of the bathroom. I simply woke up the next day and he was standing over me with hot tea in one hand and our plane tickets in the other. I didn't know if Doyle had used the sleeping bags, or if he slept at all.

Chapter 19

DOYLE GRACIOUSLY LET ME TAKE THE WINDOW SEAT. HE SAT very straight in his chair, hands in a death grip on the arms, seat belt buckled. He closed his eyes when the plane took off. Normally, I like watching the ground get farther away, but today watching Doyle turn grey around the edges was much more fun.

"How can you possibly be afraid of flying?" I asked.

He kept his eyes closed, but answered me. "I am not afraid of flying. I am afraid of flying in airplanes." His voice sounded very reasonable, as if it all made perfect sense.

"So you could ride a flying steed and not be afraid?"

He nodded, finally opening his eyes as the plane leveled off. "I have ridden the beasts of the air many times."

"So why do planes bother you?"

He looked at me as if I should have known the answer. "It is the metal, Princess Meredith. I am not comfortable surrounded by so much manmade metal. It acts as a barrier between me and the earth, and I am a creature of the earth."

"As you said, Doyle, there are benefits to not being pure sidhe. I don't have a problem with metal."

He looked at me, turning just his head. "You can do major arcana within such a metal tomb?"

I nodded. "I've never found any magic that I can't perform just as well inside a metal tomb, as I can outside of one."

"That could be very useful, Princess."

The flight attendant, a tall leggy blonde wearing nearly perfect makeup, paused by Doyle's seat, bending over enough

216

to make sure he got a look at her cleavage, if he wanted it. She'd made sure he had a chance at a view every time she came by his seat. She'd come by three times in the last twenty minutes to ask if he wanted anything, anything at all. He declined. I asked for a red wine.

She'd brought my wine this time. Because it was first class it was actually served in a long-stemmed glass. The better to spill it all over yourself when the plane hit turbulence, which it did.

The plane bucked and swerved so badly that I gave the wine back to the flight attendant, and she gave me a handful of napkins for my hand.

Doyle closed his eyes again and kept repeating to all her questions, "No, thank you, I'm fine." She didn't actually offer to throw off her clothes and have sex on the floor of the plane, but the invitation was clear. If Doyle heard the invitation he managed to ignore it beautifully. I don't know if he actually didn't realize she was hitting on him, or if he was just accustomed to human women acting like fools. She finally got the hint and wandered off. She had to grip the backs of the seats as she moved down the plane, or she'd have fallen.

It was bad turbulence. Doyle looked greyish. I think it was his version of turning green. "Are you all right?"

He squeezed his eyes more tightly shut. "I will be fine once we are safely on the ground."

"Is there anything I can do to help the time pass quicker?"

He opened his eyes just a slit. "I think the stewardess made that offer already."

"Stewardess is a sexist term," I said. "It's flight attendant. So you did pick up on her hints."

"I don't think squeezing my thigh and brushing my shoulder with her breasts count as hints—more invitations."

"You ignored her beautifully."

"I have had much practice." The plane rocked violently enough that even I wasn't happy. Doyle squeezed his eyes shut again. "Do you really want to help this flight pass more quickly?"

"I owe you at least that much after you flashed your official Guard badge and we both got on the plane with our weapons. I know legally we're both allowed to carry in the U.S., but it doesn't usually go that smooth or that quick."

"It helped that the police escorted us to the gates, Princess." He'd been very carefully calling me Princess, or Princess Meredith, since I woke up this morning. We were no longer on a first-name basis.

"The cops seemed eager to get me on the plane."

"They feared you might get assassinated on their . . . turf. They did not want the responsibility for your safety."

"So that's how you got me on the plane armed."

He nodded, eyes still closed. "I told them that with only one bodyguard, it would be safer if you, yourself, were armed. Everyone agreed."

Sholto had dropped off the LadySmith 9 mm. I actually had an inner pants holster for it that fit nicely for a front cross-draw. I usually wore it at my back covered by a jacket, but the police had given me carte blanche to carry weapons, so I didn't have to worry about hiding it.

I had a ten-inch knife in a side sheath, the tip of which was tied around my leg with a leather thong for a fast draw, like an Old West gunfighter. The leather thong also made the sheath fit the movement of my leg better. Without a sheath tied off, you ended up having to move it every time you shifted position, or it tended to poke into your body or get caught on things.

I had a Spyerco folding knife clipped over the underwire of my bra. I always carried at least two blades at court, just a rule. The guns would only be allowed in certain parts of the sithen, the faerie mounds. But I'd be allowed to keep the knives. Before the banquet tonight, in my honor so Doyle informed me, I'd add more blades. A girl could never have too much jewelry or too much weaponry.

Doyle had Mortal Dread in the back sheath, the hilt sticking out from under his shoulder for a cross-draw like a gun shoulder holster. He had his own gym bag full of weapons. When I'd asked him why he hadn't used them against the sluagh, he'd said, "Nothing else I had with me would bring them true death. I wanted them to know that I was serious." Frankly, I've always found that blowing a hole bigger than a fist out someone's back lets them know you're serious. But many of the Guard feel that guns are inferior weapons. They carry them out among the humans, but guns are almost never used among ourselves, except in times of war. That Doyle had even packed a gun meant that things were bad, or maybe there'd been a policy change while I was away. If the other guards were carrying guns, then I'd know.

The plane dipped so suddenly that even I gasped. Doyle moaned. "Talk to me, Meredith."

"About what?"

"Anything," he said, voice tight.

"We could talk about last night," I said.

He opened his eyes just enough to glare at me, the plane took another dive, his eyes snapped shut, and he almost whispered, "Tell me a story."

"I'm not very good at stories."

"Please, Meredith."

He'd called me Meredith, an improvement. "I can tell you a story that you already know."

"Fine," he said.

"My grandfather on my mother's side is Uar the Cruel. Other than being a complete and utter bastard, he earned the name because he fathered three sons that were monsters even by fey standards. No blooded fey woman would sleep with him after the birth of his sons. He'd been told that he could father normal children if he found someone of fey blood who would willingly sleep with him."

I peered at Doyle's closed eyes and blank face. "Please continue," he said.

"Gran is half brownie and half human. She was willing to sleep with him, because she wanted more than anything to be a part of the Seelie Court." Silently, because it wasn't part of the story, I didn't blame Gran. She more than even myself understood what it was like to tread two very different worlds.

The plane had straightened but was still shuddering as wind buffeted it from every side. A rough flight. "Are you bored yet?" I asked.

"Anything you say will be most fascinating until we reach the ground in safety."

"You know, you're cute when you're scared."

He did the open eyes to slits, glare, close eyes again. "Please continue."

"Gran bore two beautiful twin girls. Uar's curse was ended, and Gran was one of the ladies of the court—Uar's wife, as a matter of fact, because she'd borne him children. To my knowledge, my grandfather never touched his 'wife' again. He was one of the fine and shining gentlemen. Gran was a little too common for him now that he was curse-free."

"He is a powerful warrior," Doyle said, eyes still closed.

"Who?"

"Uar."

"That's right; you must have fought against him in the wars in Europe."

"He was a very worthy opponent."

"Are you trying to make me feel better about him?"

The plane had actually flown straight and relatively smoothly for about three minutes. It was enough for Doyle to open his eyes completely. "You sounded very bitter just now."

"My grandfather beat my Gran for years. He thought if he hurt her enough he'd drive her away from court, because legally he couldn't divorce her without her permission. He couldn't put her aside because she'd given him children."

"Why did she not simply leave him?"

"Because if she were no longer Uar's wife she would no longer be welcome at court. They would never have allowed her to take her daughters with her. She stayed to make sure her children would be safe."

"The queen was most puzzled when your father invited

your mother's mother to accompany the two of you into exile."

"Gran was his lady of the house. She oversaw the household for him."

"She was a servant, then," Doyle said.

It was my turn to glare. "No, she was . . . she was his right hand. They raised me together for those ten years."

"When you left the court this last time, so did your grandmother. She opened a bed-and-breakfast."

"I've seen the write-ups in the magazines: Victoria, Good Housekeeping. Brownie's Bed-and-Breakfast, where you can be waited on, cooked for, by an ex-member of the royal court."

"Have you not spoken with her since you left three years ago?" he asked.

"I haven't contacted anyone, Doyle. It would have endangered them. I disappeared. That means I left everything and everyone behind."

"There were jewels, heirlooms, that were yours by right. The queen was amazed that you left with nothing but the clothes on your back."

"Any of the jewels would have been impossible to sell without it getting back to the courts; same with the heirlooms."

"You had money that your father had put away for you." He was watching me now, trying to understand, I think.

"I have been on my own for three years, a little over. I have taken nothing from anyone. I have been a woman on my own, free of obligation to anyone of the fey."

"Which means you can invoke virgin rights when you return to court."

I nodded. "Exactly." Virgin in the old Celtic ideal was a woman who stood on her own, owing nothing to anyone for a space of time. Three years was minimum for claiming it at court. To be virgin meant that I was outside any old feuds or grudges. I could not be forced to take sides on any issue, because I stood apart from all of it. It was a way of being in the court, without being of the court.

"Very good, Princess, very good. You know the law and

how to use it for your benefit. You are wise as well as polite, a true marvel for an Unseelie royal."

"Being virgin allowed me to make hotel reservations without risking the queen's anger," I said.

"She was puzzled as to why you did not wish to stay at the court. After all, you want to return to us, do you not?"

I nodded. "Yes, but I also want some distance until I see just how safe I'm going to be at court."

"Few would risk the queen's anger," he said.

I looked at him, searching his eyes so I would catch whatever he thought of my next words. "Prince Cel would risk her anger, because she's never seriously punished him for anything he's ever done."

Doyle's eyes tightened when I mentioned Cel's name, but nothing more. If I hadn't been watching for it, I wouldn't have noticed any reaction at all.

"Cel is her only heir, Doyle; she won't kill him. He knows that."

Doyle gave me empty eyes. "What the queen does, or does not do, with her son and heir, is not for me to question."

"Don't give the party line, Doyle, not to me. We all know what Cel is."

"A powerful sidhe prince who has the ear of the queen, his mother," Doyle said, and the tone in his voice was a warning to match the words.

"He has only one hand of power, and his other abilities are not that great."

"He is the Prince of Old Blood, and I for one would not want him using that ability on me on the dueling ground. He could bring every bleeding wound I have had in over a thousand years of battles on me at once."

"I didn't say it wasn't a frightening ability, Doyle. But there are others with more powerful magic, sidhe that can bring true death with a touch. I've seen your flame eat over a sidhe, seen it eat them alive."

"And you killed the last two sidhe that challenged you to a duel, Princess Meredith."

"I cheated," I said.

"No, you did not. You merely used tactics that they were not prepared for. It is the mark of a good soldier to use the weapons available to him or her."

We looked at each other. "Does anyone but the queen know that I have the hand of flesh now?"

"Sholto knows, and his sluagh. It will not be a secret by the time we land."

"It may frighten any would-be challengers," I said.

"To be trapped forever as a shapeless ball of flesh, never to die, never to age, merely to continue; oh, yes, Princess, I think they will be afraid. After Griffin . . . left you, many became your enemy, because they thought you powerless. They will all be remembering the insults they heaped upon you. They'll be wondering if you have come back holding a grudge."

"I'm invoking virgin rights—that means that I have a clean slate, and so do they. If I acknowledge an old vendetta, then I lose my status as a virgin, and I'll be sucked right back into the middle of all this crap." I shook my head. "No, I'll leave them alone if they leave me alone."

"You are wise beyond your years, Princess."

"I'm thirty-three, Doyle, that's not a child by human years."

He laughed, a small dark chuckle that made me think of what he'd looked like last night with half his clothes gone. I tried to keep the thought out of my face, and I must have succeeded, because his own expression didn't change. "I remember when Rome was merely a wide spot in the road, Princess. Thirty-three years is a child to me."

I let what I was thinking into my eyes. "I don't remember you treating me like a child last night."

He looked away, not meeting my eyes. "That was a mistake."

"If you say so." I looked out the window, watching the clouds. Doyle was determined to pretend that last night never happened. I was tired of trying to talk about it, when he so obviously didn't want to discuss it.

The flight attendant came back. This time she knelt, skirt

tight across her thighs. She smiled up at Doyle, magazines spread in a fan across one arm. "Would you like something to read?" She laid her free hand on his leg, slid her hand along the inside of his thigh.

Her hand was an inch from his groin when Doyle grabbed her wrist and moved her hand. "Madam, please."

She knelt closer to him, one hand on either of his knees, the magazines partially hiding what she was doing. She leaned in so that her breasts pressed against his legs. "Please," she whispered. "Please, it's been so long since I was with one of you."

That got my attention. "How long has it been?" I asked.

She blinked as if she couldn't quite concentrate on me with Doyle sitting so close. "Six weeks."

"Who was it?"

She shook her head. "I can keep a secret, just don't deny me." She looked up at Doyle. "Please, please."

She was elf-struck. If a sidhe has sex with a human and doesn't try to tone down the magic, they can turn the human into a sort of addict. Humans that are elf-struck can actually wither and die from want of the touch of sidhe flesh.

I leaned close to Doyle's ear, close enough that my lips brushed the edges of his earrings. I had a horrible urge to lick one of the earrings, but I didn't. It was just one of those wicked urges you get occasionally. I whispered, "Take her name and phone number. We'll need to report her to the Bureau of Human and Fey Affairs."

Doyle did what I asked.

The flight attendant had tears of gratitude shining in her eyes when Doyle took her name, number, and address. She actually kissed his hand and might have done more if the male flight attendant hadn't ushered her away.

"It's illegal to have sex with humans without protecting their minds," I said.

"Yes, it is," Doyle said.

"It would be interesting to know who her sidhe lover was."

"Lovers, I think," Doyle said.

"I wonder if she always flies the L.A. to St. Louis run?"

Doyle looked at me. "She might know who'd been flying back and forth to Los Angeles often enough to set up the cult that's worshiping them."

"One man doesn't constitute a cult," I said.

"You told me the woman mentioned a handful of others, some of them with ear implants, or perhaps even sidhe themselves."

"That's still not a cult—it's a wizard with followers, a sidhe-worshiping coven at best."

"Or a cult at worst. We have no idea how many people were involved, Princess, and the man who could have answered the question is dead."

"Funny how the police didn't mind me leaving the state with a murder investigation hanging over my head."

"I would not at all be surprised if your aunt, our queen, made some phone calls. She can be quite charming when she wants to be."

"And when that fails, she's scary as hell," I said.

He nodded. "That, too."

The male flight attendant took care of first class for the rest of the flight. The woman never came near us again, until we were getting off the plane. Then she took Doyle's hand, and said, voice urgent, "You will call me, won't you?"

Doyle kissed her hand. "Oh, yes, I will call, and you will answer every question that I put to you honestly, won't you?"

She nodded, tears trailing down her face. "Anything you want."

I had to drag Doyle away from her. I whispered, "I'd take a chaperone with me when you go to question her."

"I had not intended going alone," he said. He looked at me, our faces very close because we were whispering. "I learned very recently that I am not unaccessible to sexual advances." His look was very frank, open, the look I'd wanted on the plane. "I will have to be more careful in the future." With that he raised up, so that he was too tall for whispering, and began to walk down the narrow hallway toward the airport proper. I followed him.

We left the noise of engines behind and walked toward the sound of people.

Chapter 20

THE PEOPLE WERE A LARGE MURMUROUS NOISE THAT SWELLED toward me and over me, as if I were being swallowed in a sea of noise as I walked down the concourse. The crowd walked back and forth at the opening like bits of multicolored debris, a wall of people. Doyle walked just ahead of me like an advance guard, which was exactly what he was.

Our gate was in line with the broad hallway that led deeper into the airport. Doyle was at the opening of the concourse, standing to one side, waiting for me. Then through the crowd I saw a tall figure come striding toward us. Galen was dressed in layers of green and white: pale green sweater, paler green pants, and an ankle-length white duster coat floating out behind him like a cape. The sweater matched his hair, which fell in short curls to just below his ear, except for one long thin braid. His father had been a pixie, whom the queen had had killed for the audacious crime of seducing one of her handmaidens.

I don't believe the queen would have killed the pixie if she'd known he'd begotten a child. Children are precious, and anything that breeds, that passes the blood along, is worth keeping around.

I was happy to see him but knew if he was here, then a photographer wasn't far behind. Frankly, I'd been surprised we hadn't stepped out into a barrage of media. Princess Meredith had been missing for three years, and now she was coming home, alive, well. My face had been plastered across the supermarket tabloids for years; sightings of the Elven American Princess had rivaled Elvis sightings. I didn't know what had been done to save me from the media frenzy, but I was grateful.

I dropped my carry-on bag beside Doyle and ran to Galen. He swept me up in his arms and planted a kiss on my mouth. "Merry, good to see you, girl." His arms curved around my back, holding me a foot above the ground with ease.

I've never liked my feet dangling helplessly. I wrapped my legs around his waist, and he transferred his hands from my waist to my thighs to support me.

I'd been running into Galen's arms since I could remember. After my father's death he'd been my defender among the Unseelie more than once—though being a half-breed like myself, he didn't have much more clout than I did. What he did have was six feet of muscle and trained warrior to back up his threat.

Of course, when he swept me up in his arms at age seven, it was minus the kiss and other things. At just a little over a hundred, Galen was one of the youngest of Andais's royal guard. A mere seventy years between our ages—among the sidhe it was like growing up together.

The V neck of his sweater cut low over the swell of his chest, showing a curl of chest hair that was a darker green than his hair, almost black. The sweater was pettably soft, clinging to his body. His skin was white, but the sweater brought out the undercast of pale, pale green so that his skin was either pearl white or a dreamlike green depending on how the light hit it.

His eyes were a green the color of new spring grass, more human than the liquid emerald of my own. But the rest of him—the rest of him was too unique for words. I'd thought that since I was about fourteen, except he wasn't who my father had promised me to. Because Galen was too nice a guy. He didn't play politics well enough for my father to feel confident that Galen would live to see me grown. No, Galen spoke when silence would be wiser. It was one of the things I'd loved about him as a child and feared about him as I grew older.

He danced me around the hallway to some music that only he could hear, but I could almost hear it as I looked into his eyes, traced the curve of his lips with my gaze.

"I am glad to see you, Merry."

"I can tell," I said.

He laughed, and it was a very human laugh. Nothing but Galen's mirth to make it special, but that had always been special enough for me.

He leaned in close, whispering against my ear. "You cut your hair. Your beautiful hair."

I laid a gentle kiss on his cheek. "It'll grow back."

There were only a few reporters, because they hadn't had enough notice to plan a large-scale assault. But most of them had a camera. Pictures of sidhe royalty, especially if they were doing anything unusual, could always find a market. We let them snap their pictures because we couldn't stop them. Using magic against them was infringement on freedom of the press. So the Supreme Court had decreed. Reporters who routinely covered the sidhe were often psychics in their own right, or witches. They knew when you were using magic on them. All it took was one report and you could be in civil court. Let's hear it for the First Amendment.

The fey took two different tacks about the reporters. Some were very decorous in public, never giving anything of interest to the paparazzi. Galen and I were of the school that you give them something to photograph. Something unimportant so that they won't dig for more sensational stuff. Give them something positive, upbeat, and interesting. This was encouraged by Queen Andais. She'd been on a kick to give her court better, more upbeat publicity for the last thirty years or so. My lifetime. I'd been paraded with my father on spring outings. There'd been a public engagement ceremony between myself and Griffin. There was no private life if the queen decreed it public.

Someone cleared their throat and I looked past Galen to find Barinthus. If Galen looked unique, Barinthus looked alien. His hair was the color of the sea, the oceans. The turquoise of the Mediterranean; the deeper medium blue of the Pacific; a stormy greyish-blue like the ocean before a storm, sliding into a blue that was nearly black, where the water runs deep and thick like the blood of sleeping giants. The colors moved with every touch of light, melding into each other as if it wasn't hair at all. His skin was the alabaster white of my own. His eyes were blue, but the pupils were slits of black. I knew for a fact that he had a clear membrane like a second eyelid that came up over his eyes when he was underwater. When I was five he taught me to swim, and I'd loved the fact that he could blink twice with one eye.

He was taller than Galen, nearly seven feet tall, as befit a god. He was wearing a royal blue trench coat open over a black designer suit, but the shirt was blue silk with one of those high round collars that the designers are trying to sell so men don't have to wear ties anymore. Barinthus looked splendid in it all. He'd left his hair loose and flowing free around him like a second cloak. And I knew that someone else, probably my aunt, had picked his clothes for him. Left to his own devices Barinthus was a jeans-and-T-shirt—or less—man.

Galen and Barinthus had been two of the most frequent visitors to my father's house, out among the humans. Barinthus was a power among the sidhe; he was pure Old Court. The sidhe still whispered about the last duel he'd fought, long before I was born, in which a sidhe had drowned in a summer meadow miles from any water. Barinthus, like my father, never agreed to fight a duel unless mortality was invoked. Anything less was not worth his time.

Galen let me slide to the ground. I went to Barinthus, holding out both my hands in greeting. He drew his hands out of his coat pockets carefully, keeping them in loose fists until my own hands could be placed in his. He had webbing between his fingers, and he had been sensitive about it ever since a reporter in the fifties had called him "the fish man." Hard to believe that someone once worshiped as a sea god could be embarrassed by a twentieth-century hack, but there it was. Barinthus had never forgotten that little bit of publicity.

The webbing was completely retractable, just a thin extra line of skin between his fingers unless he chose to use it. Then he could expand the skin and swim like . . . like a, well, um, fish. Though this was not a compliment to be paid out loud, ever.

He took my hands in his and leaned down from his great height to plant a civilized but well-meant kiss on my cheek. I returned the favor. Barinthus liked to be civilized in public. His personal side was not for public consumption, and he had the power to make sure that even the queen herself couldn't change his mind. Gods, even fallen ones, should be treated with a certain respect. That reporter in the fifties, the one who had plastered the fish man headline along the worldwide news service, had died in a freak boating accident on the Mississippi that summer. The water just rose up and slapped the boat, eyewitnesses said. Strangest thing they'd ever seen.

The cameras kept taking pictures. We kept ignoring it. "It is good to have you back among us, Meredith."

"It's good to see you, too, Barinthus. I hope the court is safe enough for me to make this more than an extended visit."

The clear second eyelid blinked over his eyes. When he wasn't swimming, it was a sign of nervousness. "That you will have to discuss with your aunt."

I didn't like the sound of that. The reporter shoved a tiny tape recorder in my face. "Who are you?" That he had to ask meant he was on the job since I left home.

Galen moved in, smiling, charming. He opened his mouth to answer, but another voice filled the bustling hush. "Princess Meredith NicEssus, Child of Peace."

The man who'd spoken pushed away from the far windows where he'd been leaning.

"Jenkins, how unpleasant to see you," I said.

He was a tall thin man, though next to Barinthus he wasn't that tall. Jenkins had a permanent five-o'-clock shadow, so heavy that I'd asked him once why he didn't just grow a beard. He'd replied that his wife didn't like facial hair. I'd replied that I couldn't believe anyone would marry him. Jenkins had sold pictures of my father's hacked body. Not in the United States, of course, we're too civilized for that, but there are other countries, other newspapers, other magazines. People bought the pictures and published them. He was also the one who'd surprised me at the funeral and snapped pictures of me with tears trailing down my cheeks, my eyes so angry they had a glow to them. That one had been nominated for a prize of some kind. It lost, but my face and my father's dead body were worldwide news thanks to Jenkins. I still hated him for that.

"I heard a rumor that you'd be coming back for a visit. Are you staying the whole month until Halloween?" he asked.

"I can't believe that anyone would risk my aunt's displeasure talking to you," I said, ignoring his question. I'd had lots of practice ignoring reporter's questions.

He smiled. "You'd be surprised who talks to me and about what."

I didn't like the phrasing on that. It sounded vaguely threatening, vaguely personal. No, I didn't like it one little bit.

"Welcome home, Meredith," he said and gave a small but strangely stylish bow.

What I wanted to say to him wasn't fit for public consumption, but there were too many tape recorders. If Jenkins was here, then the television people couldn't be far behind. If he couldn't have an exclusive, he'd make sure there was a crowd.

I said nothing. I let it go. He'd been baiting me since I was a child. He was only about ten years older than I was, but he looked twenty years older, because I still looked like I was in my early twenties. Maybe I wasn't going to live forever, but I was going out well preserved. I think that really bothered Jenkins, covering people who either didn't age or aged more slowly than he did. There were moments when I was younger that it had been a comfort that he would probably die first.

"You still smell like an ashtray, Jenkins. Don't you know that smoking will shorten your life expectancy?"

His face went hard and thin with anger. He lowered his voice and whispered, "Still the little bitch of the west, heh, Merry."

"I've got a restraining order against you, Jenkins. Stay back fifty feet or I'll call the cops."

Barinthus came up to us and offered me his arm. He didn't have to say it. I knew better than to get into an insult match with a reporter in front of other reporters. The restraining order had been put in place after Jenkins plastered my picture all over the world. The court's attorneys had found several judges who thought that Jenkins had indeed exploited a minor and invaded my privacy. After that he was forbidden to speak with me and had to stay back fifty feet.

I think the only reason that Barinthus hadn't killed Jenkins for me was that the sidhe would have seen that as a weakness, too. I wasn't just sidhe royalty, I was two deaths away from the Unseelie throne. If I couldn't protect myself from over-zealous reporters, I didn't deserve to be in line for the throne. So he'd become my problem. The queen had forbidden any of us from harming the press after Barinthus's little boating accident. Unfortunately, the only thing that would have rid me of Barry Jenkins was his death. Anything short of that, and he'd just heal and crawl back after me.

I blew Jenkins a kiss and walked past him on Barinthus's arm. Galen trailed behind us fielding questions from the press. I caught parts of the story. Family reunion, home for the coming holidays, yadda-yadda-yadda. Barinthus and I outdistanced the reporters because they were hanging back with Galen. So I asked something serious. "Why has the queen suddenly forgiven me for running away from home?"

"Why does one usually call home the prodigal child?" he returned.

"No riddles, Barinthus, just tell me."

"She has told no one what she plans, but she was most insistent that you come home as an honored guest. She wants something from you, Meredith, something only you can give her, or do for her, or for the court."

"What could I possibly do that the rest of you can't?"

"If I knew I would tell you."

I leaned into Barinthus, running a hand down his arm and calling a spell. It was a small spell, like wrapping a piece of air around us so that noise bounced off. I didn't want to be overheard, and if we were being spied on by the sidhe no one would wonder at me doing it with the reporters around.

"What of Cel? Does he mean to kill me?"

"The queen has been most insistent, to everyone"—he emphasized the "everyone"—"that you are to be unmolested while at court. She wants you back among us, Meredith, and seems willing to enforce her wish with violence."

"Even against her son?" I asked.

"I don't know. But something has changed between her and her son. She is not happy with him, and no one knows quite why. I wish I had more concrete information for you, Meredith, but even the biggest gossips at court are lying low on this one. Everyone's afraid to anger either the queen or the prince." He touched my shoulder. "We are almost certainly being spied upon. They will be suspicious if we keep up the spell of confusion for our words."

I nodded and withdrew the spell, flinging it into the air with a thought. The noise closed around us, and I realized in the press of people that we'd been lucky not to be bumped into, which would have shattered the spell. Of course, I was walking with a seven-foot-tall blue-haired demi-god, which did tend to open a path for you. Some of the sidhe welcomed the faeriephiles, the groupies, but Barinthus was not one of those, and a mere glance from those eyes was enough to make almost anyone back up a step.

Barinthus continued in a voice that was a little too cheerful for his normal words: "We'll drive you from here to your grandmother's." He lowered his voice. "Though how you got the queen to agree to you visiting relatives before paying your respects to her, I do not know."

"I invoked virgin rights, which is why you're also taking me to my hotel to check in and get changed."

We were at the baggage carousel now, watching the empty silver of it glide around and around. "No one has invoked virgin rights among the sidhe in centuries."

"It doesn't matter how long it's been, Barinthus, it's still our law."

Barinthus smiled down at me. "You were always intelligent, even as a young child, but you have grown to be clever."

"And cautious, don't forget that, because without caution, all clever will do is get you killed."

"So cynical, so true. Have you really missed us, Meredith, or did you enjoy being free of all this?"

"Some of the politics I could do without, but—" I hugged his arm. "I've missed you, and Galen, and . . . home isn't something you can pick and choose, Barinthus. It is what it is."

He leaned down to whisper, "I want you home, but I fear for you here."

I looked into those wonderful eyes and smiled. "Me, too."

Galen came bounding up to us, putting an arm across my shoulders and the other around Barinthus's waist. "Just one big happy family."

Barinthus said, "Do not be flippant, Galen."

"Wow," Galen said, "the mood has plummeted. What were you two talking about behind my back?"

"Where's Doyle?" I asked.

Galen's smile wilted a little round the edges. "He's gone to report to the queen." His smile flashed back into place. "Your safety is now our concern." Something must have passed on my face, or Barinthus's, because Galen asked, "What is wrong?"

I glanced in the shiny mirrored surface in front of us. Jenkins was just outside the barrier for the carousel. He was staying back his fifty feet, more or less. Certainly far enough away that I couldn't have him arrested.

"Not here, Galen."

Galen glanced, too, and saw Jenkins. "He really hates you, doesn't he?"

"Yes," I said.

"I've never understood his animosity toward you," Barinthus said. "Even when you were a child, he seemed to despise you."

"It does seem to have become personal, doesn't it?"

"Do you know why it's so personal for him?" Galen asked,

and there was something in the way he asked it that made me look away, to avoid his eyes.

My aunt had decreed years before I was born that we could not use our darkest powers in front of a member of the press. I'd broken that rule only once, for Jenkins's personal edification. My only excuse was that I'd been eighteen when my father died. Eighteen when Jenkins plastered my pain across the media of the world. I'd pulled his darkest fears from his mind and paraded them before his eyes. I'd made him shriek and beg. I'd left him a quivering mass curled beside a lonely country road. For a few months he'd been kinder, gentler, then he'd come back with a vengeance. Meaner, harsher, more willing to do anything to get a story than he was before. He'd told me that the only way I could stop him was to kill him. I hadn't tamed him, I'd made him worse. Jenkins was what helped me learn the lesson that you either kill your enemies or you leave them the fuck alone.

My suitcase was one of the first to come sliding along the carousel. Galen picked it up. "Your chariot awaits, my lady."

I looked at him. If it had just been Galen, I might have believed it, but Barinthus wouldn't do the publicity stunts, and a chariot was definitely a stunt.

"Queen Andais sent her own personal car for you," Barinthus said.

I glanced from one to the other of them. "She sent the black coach of the wild hunt for me? Why?"

"Until dark this evening," Barinthus said, "it is merely a car, a limousine. And that your aunt offered it to you with me as your driver is a great honor that should not easily be dismissed."

I stepped in close to him and lowered my voice as if the waiting reporters could hear us. I couldn't keep calling magic to hide our words because, though I couldn't sense it, I couldn't be sure we weren't observed. "It's too great an honor, Barinthus. What's going on? I don't usually get the royal treatment from my relatives."

He looked down at me, silent so long I thought he wouldn't answer. "I do not know, Meredith," he said finally.

"We'll talk in the car," Galen said, smiling and waving for the reporters. He shepherded us out to the automatic doors. The limo was waiting like a sleek black shark. Even the windows were tinted black so that you could see nothing of what lay inside.

I stopped on the sidewalk. The two men walked past me, then stopped, looking back at me. "What's wrong?" Galen asked.

"Just wondering what might have crawled into the car while we were inside the airport."

They glanced at each other, then back to me. "The car was empty when we left it here," Galen said.

Barinthus was more practical. "I give my most solemn word that to my knowledge the car is empty."

I smiled at him, but it wasn't a happy smile. "You always were cautious."

"Let us say that I do not give my word on things that I cannot control."

"Like my aunt's whims," I said.

He gave a small bow that swirled his hair like a multihued curtain. "Indeed."

My aunt had chosen well. There were three times three times three royal bodyguards. Twenty-seven warriors dedicated to my aunt's every wish. Of those, the two I would have trusted most were standing beside me. Andais wanted me to feel secure. Why? My security or lack thereof had never interested her before. Barinthus's words came back to me. The queen wanted something from me, something only I could give her, or do for her, or for the court. The question was what was that one thing that only I could do? Off the top of my head, I couldn't think of a single thing that only I could give her.

"In the car, children," Galen said through smiling, gritted teeth. There was a television news van in the distance, caught in traffic but coming closer. If they pulled in and blocked our escape, which had happened in the past, we'd have other troubles than just my paranoia. No matter how well justified that paranoia happened to be.

Barinthus took keys out of his pocket and hit a button on the key chain. The trunk popped open with a hiss of escaping air like it was hermetically sealed. Galen put my suitcase in it and held his hand out for my carry-on bag.

I shook my head. "I'll keep this with me."

Galen didn't ask why—he knew, or could guess. I wouldn't have come home without more than the weapons I was carrying.

Barinthus held the rear door for me. "The news van will be here soon, Meredith. If we are to make a—how do they say?—clean getaway, we must do so now."

I took half a step toward that open door and stopped. The upholstery was black, everything was black. The car had too long a history not to ring every psychic bell I had. The power from that open door crept along my skin and raised the hair on my arms. It was the dark coach of the wild hunt, sometimes. Even if there were no tricks waiting inside it now, it was an object of wild power, and that power flowed over me.

"By the Lord and the Lady, Merry," Galen said. He moved past me and slid into the blackness of the car. He slid all the way in out of sight, then slid back out, holding his pale hand out to me. "It won't bite, Merry."

"Promise?" I said.

"Promise," he said, smiling.

I took his hand, and he drew me toward the open door. "Of course, I never promised that I wouldn't bite." He pulled me into the car, both of us laughing. It was good to be home.

Chapter 21

THE LEATHER OF THE UPHOLSTERY SIGHED WITH AN ALMOST human sound as I settled back against the seat. A panel of black glass blocked our view of Barinthus. It was like being in a black space capsule. There was a cloth-wrapped bottle of wine in a silver bucket in a small compartment across from us. Two crystal glasses sat in holes meant to cradle them, waiting to be filled. There was a small tray of crackers and what looked like caviar behind the wine.

"Did you do this?" I asked.

Galen shook his head. "I wish I had, though I'd have known to leave out the caviar. Peasant taste buds."

"You don't like it either," I said.

"But I'm a peasant, too."

I shook my head. "Never."

He gave me his smile, the one that warmed me down to my socks. Then the smile faded. "I peeked in back before we drove off." He shrugged at my look. "I agree that the queen is acting strangely. I wanted to make sure there were no surprises behind all that black glass."

"And?" I said.

He picked up the wine. "And this was not here."

"You're sure?" I asked.

He nodded, sweeping the cloth aside enough to read the label on the wine. He gave a low whistle. "It's from her private stock." He held the bottle carefully for me because it had been opened so it could breathe. "Would you care to try some thousand-year-old burgundy?"

I shook my head. "I'm not eating or drinking anything that this car happened to put out for us. Thanks anyway." I patted the car's leather seat. "No offense meant."

"It could be the queen's gift," Galen said.

"An even better reason not to drink it," I said. "Not until I find out what's going on."

Galen looked at me, nodding, and put the wine back in the bucket. "Good point."

We settled back into the leather seats. The silence seemed heavier than it should have, as if someone were listening. I always thought it was the car that was listening.

The Black Coach is one of the objects among the fey that has an energy, a life, of its own. It was not created by any fey or ancient god that we knew of. It has simply existed for as long as anyone among us can remember. Six thousand years and counting. Of course, then it had been a black chariot pulled by four black horses. The horses were not sidhe horses. They didn't seem to exist at all until after dark. Then they were things of blackness with empty eye sockets that filled with leprous flame when they were hooked to the chariot.

It was a coach—a coach and four—by the time I saw it. One day, no one remembers just when, the chariot had vanished and a large black coach had appeared. Only the horses had remained the same. The coach had changed when chariots were no longer in use. It had updated itself.

Then one night not even twenty years ago the Black Coach had vanished and the limo had appeared. The horses never returned, but I've seen what passes for an engine under the hood of this thing. I swear that it burns with the same sickly fire that filled those horses' eyes. The car doesn't take gasoline. I have no idea what it runs on, but I know that chariot or coach or car sometimes vanishes all by itself. It'll drive away into the night on business of its own. The Black Coach had been a death portent, warning of impending doom. There were beginning to be tales of a sinister black car sitting across from a person's home with its engine running and green fire dancing along its surface, and then doom would fall on that person. So, forgive me if I was just a tad nervous riding in its oh-so-soft leather seats.

I stared across the seats at Galen. I held my hand out to him. He smiled and wrapped his hand around mine. "Missed you," he said.

"Me, too."

He raised my hand to his lips and laid a gentle kiss across my knuckles. He pulled me toward him, and I didn't struggle. I moved across the leather seats into the circle of his arm. I loved the feel of his arm across my shoulders, wrapping me against his body. My head ended resting against the wonderful softness of the sweater, the firm swell of his chest underneath, and underneath that I could hear the beat of his heart like a thick clock.

I sighed and cuddled against him, wrapping my leg across his so that we were entwined. "You always did cuddle better than anyone else I know," I said.

"That's me—just a big, lovable teddy bear." There was something in his voice that made me look up.

"What's wrong?"

"You never told me you were leaving."

I sat up, his arm still across my shoulders, but the perfect comfort of a second before had been spoiled. Spoiled with accusations, with probably more to come.

"I couldn't risk telling anyone, Galen, you know that. If anyone had suspected that I was running away from the court, I'd have been stopped, or worse."

"Three years, Merry. Three years of not knowing if you were dead or alive."

I started to slide out from under his arm, but he tightened his grip, pulled me against him. "Please, Merry, just let me hold you, let me know you're real."

I let him hold me, but it wasn't comfortable now. No one else would question why I had told no one, why I had contacted no one. Barinthus, Gran, no one, no one but Galen. There were times when I understood why my father had not chosen Galen for my consort. He let emotion rule him, and that was a very dangerous thing.

I finally pulled away. "Galen, you know why I didn't contact you."

He wouldn't meet my eyes. I touched his chin and moved him to look at me. Those green eyes were hurt, holding emotion like a cup of water; you could see all the way to the bottom of Galen's eyes. He was miserably bad at court politics.

"If the queen had suspected that you knew where I was, or anything about it, she would have tortured you."

He grasped my hand, holding it against his face. "I would never have betrayed you."

"I know that, and do you think I could have lived with the thought of you being tortured endlessly while I was safe somewhere else? You had to know nothing, so there would be no reason for her to question you."

"I don't need you to protect me, Merry."

That made me smile. "We protect each other."

He smiled, because he could never go long between smiles. "You're the brains, and I'm the brawn."

I rose on my knees and kissed his forehead. "How have you stayed out of trouble without me to counsel you?"

He wrapped his arms around my waist, pulling me in against the line of his body. "With difficulty." He looked at me, frowning. "What's with the black turtleneck? I thought we both agreed never to wear black."

"It looks good with the charcoal grey dress pants and matching jacket," I said.

He rested his chin just above the swell of my breasts, and those honest green eyes wouldn't let me avoid the question.

"I'm here to get along if I can, Galen. If that means wearing black like most of the court, then I can do that." I smiled down at him. "Besides, I look good in black."

"You do, indeed." Those honest eyes held the first stirrings of that old feeling.

There'd been tension between us since I'd been old enough to realize what that strange feeling low in my body was. But no matter how much heat there was, there could never be anything between us. Not physically, at least. He, like so many others, was one of the queen's Ravens, and that meant he was hers and hers alone to command. Joining the Queen's Guard had been the only smart political move that Galen had ever made. He wasn't powerful magically, and he wasn't good at behind-the-scenes scheming; the only thing he really had was a strong body, a good arm, and the ability to make people smile. I meant that about the ability. He exuded cheer from his body like some women leave behind perfume. It was a wonderful ability, but like many of my own, not much help in a fight. As a member of the Queen's Ravens he had a measure of safety. You did not challenge them lightly to a duel, because you never knew if the queen would take it as a personal insult. If Galen had not been a guard he would probably have been dead long before I was born; yet the fact that he was a guard kept us eternally separated. Always wanting, never having. I'd been furious with my father for not letting me be with Galen. It had been the only serious disagreement we'd ever had. It took me years to see what my father had seen: that most of Galen's strengths are also his weaknesses. Bless his little heart, but he was very close to being a political liability.

Galen laid his cheek against the swell of my breasts and gave a small movement, rubbing against me. It made my breath stop for a second, then roll out in a sigh.

I traced my fingers down the side of his face, running a fingertip across the full soft mouth. "Galen . . ."

"Sshh," he said. He lifted me with his arms around my waist and brought me around in front of him. I ended with my knees on his thighs, staring down at him. My pulse was thudding so hard in my throat that it almost hurt.

He lowered his hands slowly down the line of my body, to end with his hands on my thighs. It reminded me forcibly of Doyle last night. Galen moved his hands so that my legs gradually parted, sliding me slowly down his body until I sat facing him, straddling him. I kept back from his body, putting just enough space between us that I wasn't actually riding him. I didn't want the feel of his body that intimately against me, not now.

His hands slid along my neck until he cradled the back of my head, long fingers sliding underneath my hair until the unbelievable warmth of his hands stroked against my skin.

Galen was one of the guards who believed that a little touch of flesh was better than nothing. We'd always danced the razor's edge with each other. "It's been a long time, Galen," I said.

"Ten years since I could hold you like this," he said. Seven years with Griffin, three years gone, and now Galen was trying to take up where we left off, as if nothing had changed.

"Galen, I don't think we should do this."

"Don't think," he said. He leaned in to me, lips so close that a sigh would have brought him to me, and power breathed from his mouth in a line of breath-stealing warmth.

"Don't, Galen." My voice sounded breathless, but I meant it. "Don't use magic."

He raised back enough to see my face. "We've always done it this way."

"Ten years ago," I said.

"What difference does that make?" he asked. His hands had slid under my jacket and were massaging along the muscles in my back.

Maybe ten years had not changed him, but it had changed me. "Galen, no."

He looked at me, clearly puzzled. "Why not?"

I wasn't sure how to explain without hurting him. I was hoping the queen would give me permission to choose a guard as consort again, as she had when she'd given my father permission to choose Griffin. If I let things go back as they were with Galen, he would assume he would be the choice. I loved him, I would probably always love him, but I couldn't afford to make him my consort. I needed someone who would help me politically and magically. Galen was not that person. My consort would no longer have the protection of the queen once he left the Guard. My threat was not enough to keep Galen safe, and his own threat was less, because he was less ruthless than I was. The day Galen became my consort would be the day I signed his death warrant. But I'd never be able to explain all that to him. He'd never accept how terribly dangerous he was to me, and to himself.

I'd grown up, and I was finally my father's daughter. Some choices you make with your heart, some with your head, but when in doubt choose head over heart—it will keep you alive.

I knelt over him, starting to move off his lap. His arms locked behind my back. He looked so hurt, so lost. "You really mean it."

I nodded. I watched his eyes try to make sense of it. Finally he asked, "Why?"

I touched his face, brushed my fingers through the edge of his curls. "Oh, Galen."

His eyes held sorrow now the way they could hold happiness, or puzzlement, or any emotion that he was feeling. He was the world's worst actor. "A kiss, Merry, to welcome you home."

"We had a kiss in the airport," I said.

"No, a real kiss, just once more. Please, Merry."

I should have said no, made him let me go, but I couldn't. I couldn't say no to the look in his eyes, and truthfully if I was never going to let myself be with him again, I wanted a last kiss.

He raised his face to mine, and I lowered my mouth to his. His lips were so soft. My hands found the curve of his face and cradled him as we kissed. His hands kneaded at my back, spilled lightly over my buttocks, slid along my thighs. He pulled my legs gently so that I slid down the line of his body again. This time he made sure there was no space between us. I could feel him pressed tight and hard against his pants, against me.

The feel of him pressed against me tore my mouth from his, brought a gasp from my throat. His hands spilled down my body, cupping my buttocks, pressing me harder against him. "Can we get rid of the gun? It's digging into me."

"The only way to get rid of the gun is to take off the belt," I said, and my voice held things that the words didn't.

"I know," he said.

I opened my mouth to say no, but that wasn't what came out. It was like a series of decisions: each time I should have said no, I should have stopped, and each time I didn't stop. We ended stretched across the long leather seat with most of our clothes and all of our weapons scattered on the floor.

My hands glided over the smooth expanse of Galen's chest. The thin braid of green hair trailed across his shoulder, curling across the dark skin of his nipple. I traced my hand across the line of hair that ran down the center of his stomach to vanish into his pants. I couldn't remember how we'd gotten here like this. I was wearing nothing but my bra and panties. I didn't remember taking off my pants. It was as if for minutes I was losing time, then I'd wake up and we'd be further along.

His pants were unzipped. I caught a glimpse of green bikini briefs. I wanted to plunge my hand down the front of his body. I wanted it so badly that I could feel him in my hand as if I were already holding him.

Neither of us had used power—it was just the feel of skin on skin, our bodies touching. We'd gone further than this years ago. But something was wrong. I just couldn't remember what.

Galen leaned over, kissing my stomach. He licked a thick wet line down my body. I couldn't think, and I needed to think.

His tongue played along the edge of my panties, his face burying against the lace, moving it aside with his chin and mouth, working lower.

I grabbed a handful of his hair and pulled his face up, away from my body. "No, Galen."

He spilled his hands up my body, forced his fingers under the wire of my bra, lifted it, exposed my breasts. "Say, yes, Merry, please say yes." He rolled his hands over my breasts, kneading them, massaging them.

I couldn't think, couldn't remember why we shouldn't be doing this. "I can't think," I said out loud.

"Don't think," Galen said. He lowered his face to my breasts, kissed them gently, licked the nipples.

I put a hand on his chest and pushed him away. He stayed over me, an arm on either side, his legs out behind him, half on top of mine. "Something's wrong. We shouldn't be doing this."

"Nothing's wrong, Merry." He tried to lower his face back to my breasts, but I kept both hands on his chest, kept him pushed away from me.

"Yes, there is."

"What?" he asked.

"That's just it, I can't remember. I can't remember, Galen, do you understand? I can't remember. I should be able to remember."

He frowned down at me. "There is something." He shook his head. "I can't remember."

"Why are we in the back of this car?" I asked.

Galen eased back off of me, sitting with his pants still undone, hands in his lap. "You're going to see your grandmother."

I slid my bra back in place and sat up, moving to my side of the car. "That's right."

"What just happened?" he asked.

"It's a spell, I think," I said.

"We didn't drink the wine or eat the food."

I looked at the black interior of the car. "It's here somewhere." I began running my hands along the edge of the seat. "Someone put it in the car, and it wasn't the car."

Galen ran his hands over the ceiling, searching. "If we had made love . . ."

"My aunt would have had us executed." I didn't tell him about Doyle, but I doubted seriously if the queen would let me defile two of her guards in as many days without being punished for it.

I found a lump under the black cloth of the floorboard. I raised it gently, not wanting to hurt the car. What I found was a woven cord tied with a silver ring. The ring was the queen's ring—one of the magical items that the fey were allowed to take away from Europe during the great exodus. The ring was a thing of great power, which is what had allowed the cord's magic to work without touching either of our skins or being invoked.

I held the thing up so he could see it. "I found it, and it's wearing her ring."

Galen's eyes widened. "She never lets that ring off her hand." He took the cord from me, touching the different-colored strands. "Red for lust, orange for reckless love, but why the green? That's usually reserved for finding a monogamous partner. You'd never mix those three colors."

"Even for Andais this is psychotic. Why invite me home to be an honored guest, but set me up for execution on the way to the court? It makes absolutely no sense."

"No one could have gotten that ring without her permission, Merry."

Something white was sticking out from between the seat and the back. I moved closer to it and found it was half an envelope. "This wasn't there before," I said.

"No, it wasn't," Galen said. He picked his sweater up off the floor and slipped it on.

I pulled at the envelope, and it felt as if something was pushing from the other end; it was a flexing, as if of muscle. It brought my pulse in my throat, but I took the envelope. It had my name written across it in beautiful handwriting—the queen's handwriting.

I showed it to Galen as he continued to dress. "You'd better open it," he said.

I turned it over and found her seal set in black wax, unbroken. I broke the seal and pulled out a single sheet of thick white stationery.

"What does it say?" Galen asked.

I read it aloud to him. " 'To Princess Meredith NicEssus. Take this ring as a gift and a token of things to come. I want to see it on your hand when we meet.' She even signed her name." I looked at Galen. "This makes less and less sense."

"Look," he said.

I looked where he was pointing, and there was a small velvet bag sticking out of the seat now. It had not been there when I took the envelope out of the seat.

"What is going on?"

Galen pulled the bag into sight, carefully. It was very small, and the only thing in it was a piece of black silk. "Let me see the ring," he said.

I slipped the silver ring off the cord, holding it in the palm of my hand. The cold metal grew warm against my hand. I waited tensely for it to grow hot, but it was just a slight pulsing warmth. Either it was part of the ring's enchantment or . . . I held the ring out to Galen. "Hold it in the palm of your hand; see what you feel."

He took the ring tentatively between two fingers and laid it in his opposite hand. The heavy octagonal ring sat in his palm gleaming softly.

We sat and stared at the ring for a few seconds. Nothing happened. "Is it warm?" I asked.

Galen looked up at me, eyebrows raised. "Warm? No, is it supposed to be?"

"Not for you, apparently."

He wrapped the ring in the bit of silk and slipped it into the small velvet bag. It fit perfectly, but there was no room for the heavy cord. He looked at me. "I don't think the queen did the spell. I think she put this ring in here for you as a gift, just like the note says."

"Then someone else added the spell," I said.

He nodded. "It was a very subtle spell, Merry. We almost didn't notice it."

"Yes, I almost thought it was me making up my mind. If it had been some outrageous lust spell we'd have noticed something wrong much sooner." There weren't that many people in the Unseelie Court who were capable of such a sophisticated love spell. Love wasn't our specialty; lust was.

Galen echoed my thoughts. "There are only three, maybe five people in the entire court that could do such a spell. If you'd asked me, I'd have said none of them would willingly hurt you. They may not all like you, but they aren't your enemies."

"Or they weren't three years ago," I said. "People change their minds, new alliances form."

"I haven't noticed anything that different," Galen said.

I had to smile. "You say that like it's a big surprise that you wouldn't notice political wheeling and dealing behind the scenes."

"All right, all right, I'm not a political animal, but Barinthus is, and he never mentioned any change of heart this severe among the neutral parties at court."

I held my hand out for the ring. Galen handed me the bag. I took the ring out and laid it on my palm. Even before the ring touched my skin I could feel the small warmth. I wrapped my hand around the ring, squeezing it in my fist, and the warmth grew. The ring, my aunt's ring, the queen's ring, answered to my flesh. Would that please our queen or anger her? If she didn't want the ring to acknowledge me, why would she have given it to me?

"You look pleased," Galen said. "Why? You've just been the victim of an assassination attempt—you do remember that part, right?" He was studying my face, as if trying to read my expression.

"The ring is warm to my touch, Galen. It's a relic of power and it knows me." The seat underneath me twitched. It made me jump. "Did you feel that?"

Galen nodded. "Yes."

The overhead light flashed on, and I jumped again. "Did you do that?" I asked.

"No."

"Me, either," I said.

This time I watched the leather seat push out the object. It was like watching something alive twitching. It was tiny, silver, a piece of jewelry. I was almost afraid to touch it, but the seat kept moving until the item lay bare to the light, and I could see at a glance that it was a cuff link.

Galen picked it up. His face darkened, and he held it out to me. The cuff link had the letter "C" in lovely flowing lines. "The queen had cuff links made for all the guards about a year ago. They have our first initials on them."

"So you're saying a guard put the spell in the car and tried to bury the letter and the bag in the seats."

Galen nodded. "And the car kept the cuff link until it showed it to you."

"Th ... thanks, car," I whispered. Thankfully, the car didn't seem to acknowledge the greeting. My nerves were grateful for that. But I knew that it had me. I could feel it watching me, like the sensation of eyes staring at the back of your head, and when you turn around there is someone watching.

"When you said all the guards, did you mean the prince's guards, too?" I asked.

Galen nodded. "She liked the look of the female guards in men's shirts, said it was stylish."

"That adds what, five, six more to the list of possible suspects?"

"Six."

"How long has it been known that the queen was going to send the Black Coach to meet me at the airport?"

"Barinthus and I only found out two hours ago."

"They had to act quickly. Maybe the love spell wasn't intended for me. Maybe it was just something they had lying about for some other purpose."

"We're lucky it wasn't meant especially for us. We might not have come to our senses in time if it had been."

I put the ring back in the velvet bag and picked up my turtleneck from the floor. For some reason I couldn't define, I wanted to be dressed before I put the ring on. I looked up at the car's black ceiling. "Is that all you have to show me, car?"

The overhead light went out.

I jumped, even though I'd hoped it would happen.

"Shit," Galen said. He backed away from me, or from the darkened light. He stared at me, eyes very wide. "I've never ridden in the car with the queen, but I've heard . . ."

"That if it answers to anyone," I said, "it answers to her."

"And now you," he said softly.

I shook my head. "The Black Coach is wild magic; I am not so presumptuous as to assume I have control over it. The car hears my voice. If there is more to it than that . . ." I shrugged. "Time will tell."

"You haven't been on the ground in Saint Louis an hour, Merry, and there's been one attempt on your life. It's worse than when you left."

"When did you become a pessimist, Galen?"

"When you left the court," he replied.

There was a sorrowful look on his face. I touched his cheek. "Oh, Galen, I have missed you."

"But you've missed the court more." He pressed my hand against his cheek. "I can see it in your eyes, Merry. The old ambition rising."

I drew my hand away from him. "I'm not ambitious in the way that Cel is. I just want to be able to walk the court in relative safety, and unfortunately that is going to take some political maneuvering." I laid the velvet bag in my lap and slipped on the turtleneck. I scrambled into my pants, fitting the gun and the knives back in place. I slipped the suit jacket over everything.

"Your lipstick is gone," Galen said.

"Actually you seem to be wearing most of it," I said.

We used the mirror in my purse to reapply my lipstick, and wipe it off of his mouth with a Kleenex. I ran a brush through my hair, and I was dressed. I couldn't put it off any longer.

I held the ring up in the dimness. It was too large for my ring finger, so I slipped the ring on my first finger. I'd put it on my right hand without thinking about it. The ring was warm against my skin like a comforting touch, a reminder that it was there, waiting for me to figure out what to do with it. Or, maybe, for it to figure out what to do with me. But I trusted my own magic sense. The ring wasn't actively evil, though that didn't mean that accidents couldn't happen. Magic is like any tool: it has to be treated with respect, or it can turn on you. Most magic isn't overtly harmful any more than a buzz saw is harmful, but they can both kill you.

I tried to take the ring off, and it wouldn't come off. My heart beat a little faster; my breath caught in my throat. I started pulling at it sort of desperately, then stopped myself. I took a few deep calming breaths. The ring was a gift from the queen—just seeing it on my hand would make some people treat me with more respect. The ring, like the car, had its own agenda. It wanted to stay on my finger, and there it would stay until it wanted to leave, or until I figured out how to take it off. It wasn't hurting me. There was no need to panic.

I held my hand out to Galen. "It won't come off."

"It was the same on the queen's hand once," he said, and I knew he meant that to be comforting. He brought my hand to his face and kissed it lightly. When his hands brushed the ring, there was a shock of something like electricity, but it wasn't that. It was magic.

Galen let me go and scooted away from me to the far side of the seat. "I'd like to know if Barinthus's touch makes the ring jump like that."

"So would I," I said.

Barinthus's voice came over the intercom. "We'll be at your grandmother's in about five minutes."

"Thanks, Barinthus," I said. I wondered what he was going to say when he saw the ring. Barinthus had been my father's closest adviser, his friend. He was Barinthus Kingmaker, and after my father's death he became my friend and adviser. Some at court called him Queenmaker, but only behind his back, never to his face. Barinthus was one of the few at court who could have defeated my would-be assassins with magic. But if he had stepped in and destroyed my enemies, I would have lost what little credibility I had among the sidhe. Barinthus had had to watch helplessly while I defended myself, though he had counseled me to be ruthless. Sometimes it's not how much power you wield, but what you are willing to do with that power. "Make your enemies fear you, Meredith," he had said, and I had done my best. But I would never be as frightening as Barinthus. He could destroy entire armies with a thought. It meant that his enemies gave him a wide berth.

It also meant that if you were going to swim with sharks, a six-thousand-year-old ex-god was a good swimming partner. I loved Galen, but I worried about him as an ally. I worried that being my friend would get him killed. I didn't worry about Barinthus. I figured that if anyone buried anyone, it would be him, burying me.

Chapter 22

GRAN HAD TAKEN THE ROOMS AT THE VERY TOP OF THE HOUSE
for herself. In olden times when this Victorian monstrosity
was new, the rooms would have been servant quarters. They
would have been frigid in the winter and broiling in the
summer. But air-conditioning and central heating are mar-
velous things. She'd knocked down some of the walls so that
there was a cozy parlor area with a small full bathroom to one
side, a small room, just for the hell of it, beside it, and a large
bedroom that was all hers on the other side of the parlor.

The parlor was done in shades of white, cream, pink, and
rose. We sat on a stiff-backed love seat done in a cabbage-
rose print with more lace-edged pillows than I knew what to
do with. I'd made a little mound of them to one side like an
impromptu mountain of flowers and lace.

We were drinking tea from a flowered tea set. My second
cup of tea complete with dainty saucer was floating from the
small coffee table toward my hand. The trick to catching
something that is being levitated to you is to simply hold still.
Don't grab at it, or you'll spill it. Wait, and if the person doing
the levitating is good, the cup or whatever will touch your
hand, then you grab it. Sometimes, I think my first lesson in
patience was waiting for a cup to float to my hand.

I'd been concentrating very hard on the moment. Concentrating on not spilling the tea, on how to get a sugar cube out
of a floating sugar bowl. Concentrating on simply being with
my grandmother after three years. But the back of my mind
was crowded with questions. Who had tried to kill us in the
car? Was it Cel? Why did the queen want me home so badly?

255

What did she want from me? They call horse racing the sport of kings, but that's not the true sport of kings. The true sport is survival and ambition.

Gran's voice brought me back to the present with a jolt that made me jump. The levitating tea cup moved a little away, like a spaceship adjusting for docking. "Sorry, Gran, I didn't hear you."

"Dearie, your nerves are wound so tight, they're like to snap."

"I can't help it."

"I do na think that the queen would drag you back just to watch your enemies kill you."

"If she was ruled by logic, I'd agree, but we both know her too well for that."

Gran sighed. She was even tinier than I was, inches under five feet. I remembered a time when she'd seemed huge, and I'd believed that nothing could harm me when I was in her arms. Gran's long wavy brown hair spilled around her delicate body like a silken curtain—but it didn't hide her face. Her skin was brown like a nut and somewhat wrinkled, and it wasn't age. Her eyes were large, and brown like her hair, with lovely lashes. But she had no nose and very little mouth. It was almost as if her face were a brown skull. You could see the dual holes where the nose should be, as if the nose were cut away, but this was the face she was born with. Her mother, my great-grandmother, thought she was beautiful. Her human father, my great-grandfather, had told her as a little girl that of course she was beautiful. She looked just like her mother, the woman he loved.

I'd have liked to have met my great-grandfather, but he was pure human and lived in the 1600s. It was a few centuries before my time. I would have been able to meet my great-grandmother if she hadn't gotten herself killed in one of the great wars between human and fey in Europe. Killed for a war that, as a brownie, she had no reason to fight. But if you refuse a call to battle, then it's treason. Treason is an executable offense.

The sidhe leaders get you coming and going.

The china saucer touched my hand, and I carefully uncurled my fingers and took it out of the air. It would have been easier to put my entire hand under the saucer to cradle it, but that was not ladylike. I'd learned to drink tea to rules of etiquette that were a hundred years or more out of date. The next dangerous point with a hot beverage being levitated is that when the person takes the levitation away, the cup gets heavier. Almost everyone sloshes a little tea over the side the first few times. No shame in it.

I didn't slosh any tea. Gran and I had had our first tea party when I was five.

"I wish I knew what to tell you about the queen, child, but I don't. The best I can do is feed you. Have some pasties, dear. I know they're a little heavy for tea time, but they're your favorites."

"Mutton filling?" I asked.

"With turnips and potatoes, just the way you like it."

I smiled. "They'll have food tonight at the banquet."

"But will you want to eat it?" she asked.

She had a point. I picked up one of the meat-filled pastries. A small plate floated underneath the little handheld pie. "What do you think about the ring?"

"Nothing."

"What do you mean, nothing?"

"I mean, dearie, that I don't have enough information to even hazard a guess."

"Was it Cel that tried to kill me and Galen? I think I'm most angry about the fact that whoever put the spell in the car was willing to sacrifice Galen to get to me, as if Galen had no importance." The pastie smelled wonderful, but suddenly I just wasn't hungry. The tea I'd drunk was sloshing around in my stomach like it might come back up. I was never good at eating when I was nervous. I laid the pie on the floating plate, and the plate floated back to the table.

Gran gripped my hand. She'd painted her fingernails a deep rich burgundy that was almost the same color as her skin. "I don't know high magic, Merry; my magic is more innate ability. But if the assassin meant it as a death sentence, why the green cord? The color of faithfulness, of a fruitful family life. Why add that?"

"The only thing I can come up with is that they had the spell for some other purpose and used it for this at the last moment. Because what other reason could the spell have been there for?"

"I do na know, dearie; I wish I did," Gran said.

I held my hand up so that the ring glistened in the thick autumn sunlight. "Whoever put the spell in the car used this ring to fuel the magic. They knew the ring would be there. Who would the queen trust with such information?"

"The list is small for those that she trusts, but the list is long for those she knows are too afraid of her to go against her wishes. She could have given the ring and the note to anyone, and trusted that they would do as she asked with it. It would ne'r occur to her that her guard would disobey her." She squeezed my hand. "You're obviously not going to eat these good pasties. I'm going to send them downstairs. My guests will certainly appreciate them."

"I'm sorry, Gran. I just can't eat when I'm nervous."

"I'm not offended, Merry, just practical." She gestured, and the door opened to the small hallway and the stairs beyond. The plates with food began trooping out the door.

"What purpose would it serve to have Galen and me executed?" I asked.

The plates were still making their uneven dance out the door, but she turned to me without missing a beat or spilling anything. "You might rather ask what purpose would it serve if the queen's ring were found wrapped around a love spell designed for you."

"But it wasn't designed for me. It could have been anyone in the backseat of the car."

"I don't think so," Gran said. She took my hand and traced the silver band. It didn't respond to her touch as it had to Galen's. "This is the queen's ring, and you are the queen's blood. But for an accident of birth order, Essus might have been king. You would already be queen, and not Andais. It would be your cousin Cel who was second in line to the throne, and not you."

"Father never approved of how Andais ran the court."

"I know there were those who urged him to kill his sister and take the throne," Gran said.

I didn't try and hide the surprise. "I didn't think that was commonly known."

"Why do you think he was killed, Merry? Someone got nervous that Essus might take the advice and start a civil war."

I gripped her hand. "Do you know who ordered him killed?"

She shook her head. "If I did, child, I would have told you by now. I was not a part of either court's machinations. I was tolerated, nothing much more."

"Father did more than tolerate you," I said.

"Ah, that he did. He gave me the great gift of being allowed to watch you grow from child to woman. I will always be grateful for that."

I smiled. "So will I."

Gran sat up straighter, hands clasped in her lap—a sure sign she was uncomfortable. "If your mother could only have seen his goodness, but she was blinded by the fact that he was Unseelie. I knew it would come to grief allowing herself to be part of a peace treaty. King Taranis used Besaba as chattel. It wasn't right."

"Mother wanted to wed a prince of the Seelie Court. None of them would touch her, because no matter how tall and beautiful she was, they were afraid to take her to their beds. Afraid they'd mingle their so pure blood with hers. They wouldn't sully themselves with her, not after her twin sister, Eluned, got pregnant after just one night with Artagan, trapping him in a marriage."

Gran nodded. "Your mother always thought that Eluned had ruined her chances for a Seelie marriage."

"She did," I said. "Especially after their daughter was born, and she . . ." I looked at Gran's face. "Looked like you." I reached out to her as I said it.

She took my hand. "I know what the Seelie think of my looks, child. I know what my other granddaughter thinks of the family likeness."

"Mother went with my father because King Taranis promised her a royal lover when she returned. Three years among the unclean, unholy, Unseelie Court, and she could come back and claim a Seelie lover. I don't think she expected to get pregnant in the first year."

"Which made the temporary arrangement permanent," Gran said.

I nodded. "That's why I'm Besaba's Bane at the Seelie Court. My birth tied her to the Unseelie Court. She always resented me for that."

Gran shook her head. "Your mother is my daughter and I love her, but she is very . . . confused at times about who she loves and why."

I was actually thinking that maybe my mother loved no one but her own ambition, but I didn't say it out loud. Gran was, after all, her mother.

The afternoon sun was low and heavy. "I need to check into my hotel and get dressed for the festivities."

Gran touched my arm. "You should be staying here."

"No, and you know why."

"I've put wards on my house and my grounds."

"Wards that can withstand the Queen of Air and Darkness? Or whoever else may be trying to kill me? I don't think so." I hugged Gran, and her thin arms wrapped around me, pressing me against her with a strength that should never have been held in such a delicate body.

"Have a care tonight, Merry. I could not bear to lose you."

I stroked a hand through that wonderful hair and saw over her shoulder a photograph. It was a picture of her and Uar the Cruel, her one-time husband. He was tall and muscular. They'd had to sit him in a chair and had her stand beside him. She had a hand on his shoulder. His hair fell around him like golden waves. His suit was black with a white shirt, nothing remarkable. Nothing remarkable but his face. He was . . . very fair of face. His eyes were circles of blue within blue. He was outwardly everything a woman, fey or human, could want. But he wasn't called "the cruel" just because he'd fathered three monstrous sons.

He'd beaten my grandmother because she was ugly. Because she wasn't royal. Because she bore him twin daughters, and that meant that unless she agreed to end it, their marriage was forever. With Gran and Uar, they weren't kidding about forever.

She had only granted him a fey version of a divorce three years ago when I left the court. I'd wondered at the time if Gran had given him the divorce in exchange for him intervening on my behalf with Andais. He was powerful, and Andais respected that power. I'm not saying Uar threatened her. No, that would have been unwise. But he might have suggested that they let me go my own way for a time.

I'd never asked. I drew away from her and looked into those large brown eyes, so like my mother's. "Why did you grant him the divorce three years ago? Why then?"

"Because it was time, child, time to let him go."

"He didn't talk to Andais on my behalf, did he? That wasn't the price of his freedom from you, was it?"

She laughed loud and long. "Child, child, do you really think that old stuffed bucket would talk to the Queen of Air and Darkness? He's still not recovered from the embarrassment that his three sons were kicked out of his court and forced to become Andais's people."

I nodded. "My cousins are really not that bad. Modern surgical gloves are so thin it's almost like wearing nothing at all. They don't accidentally poison people by their touch anymore."

Gran hugged me again. "But poison coming from your hands does prevent you from being a blooded royal guard, doesn't it?"

"Well . . . yeah. But as long as you avoid the blood royal, there are women who are willing."

"In the Unseelie court I could believe it."

I looked at her.

She had the grace to look embarrassed. "I'm sorry, Merry. That was quite uncalled for on my part. I apologize. I should know better than most that there isn't that much to choose from between the two courts."

"I need to get to the hotel, Gran."

She walked me to the door, arm around my waist. "You be careful tonight, child, very careful."

"I will be." We stood staring at each other for a second or two, but what could we say. What can you ever say? "I love you, Gran."

"And I you, child." There were tears in those lovely brown eyes. She kissed me with those thin lips that had always touched me with more gentleness and love than my mother's beautiful face or lily white hands. Her tears were hot against my cheek. Her hands clung to me as I began to walk down the stairs. We tore away from each other, fingertips trembling in a last touch.

I glanced back many times to watch that small brown figure at the top of the stairs. They say not to look back, but if you're not sure what lies ahead, what else is there but looking back?

Chapter 23

THE HOTEL HAD ALL THE CHARM OF A FRESHLY OPENED BOX OF Kleenex. Functional, somewhat decorative, but it was still a generic hotel with all the sameness that that implied.

We stepped through the lobby doors, Barinthus and Galen carrying my suitcases. I had the carry-on bag. I preferred to carry my own weapons, not that I thought I'd be able to get them out in time to use them if the gun and knife failed me, but it was good to have them close.

I'd been on the ground in St. Louis only for a few hours, and there'd already been an attempt on my life, and Galen's. It was not a comforting trend. The trend went downhill when I saw who was waiting in the lobby.

Barry Jenkins had beat us to the hotel. I'd made reservations in the name of Merry Gentry. It was not an alias I'd ever used in St. Louis. Which meant Jenkins knew it was me. Damn.

He'd make sure that the rest of the newshounds found me. And nothing I could say would help. If I asked him to keep it quiet, he'd just enjoy it more.

Galen touched my arm gently. He'd seen Jenkins, too. He led me to the desk as if afraid of what I'd do, because there was something in Jenkins's face as he rose from the comfortable lobby chair—something personal. He'd hurt me if he could. Oh, I don't mean he'd shoot me or stab me, but if something he could write could hurt me, he'd be happy to print it.

The woman behind the desk was smiling up at Barinthus. She had a good smile and had turned it up to about 100 watts, but Barinthus was all business. I'd never seen him be other than business. He never teased or tested the limits of the geas that the queen had placed upon him. He seemed simply to accept.

The woman's hand brushed mine as I took my key. I had a vivid glimpse of what she was thinking: Barinthus lying on white sheets, with all that multihued hair spread around his naked body like a bed of silk.

My fist clenched at not just the image but the strength of her lust. I could feel her body clenched tight as my fist. She watched Barinthus with hungry eyes, and I spoke without thinking, using words to acknowledge and break the connection with the girl.

I leaned in close, and said, "The picture you have in your mind of him nude."

She started to protest, then let her words die, eyes large, licking her lower lip. She finally just nodded.

"You're not doing him justice."

Her eyes got even bigger, and she stared at Barinthus as he stood by the elevators.

I was still picking up her emotions. It happened sometimes, like picking up random bits of television or radio signal. But my bandwidth was narrow: lust images, mostly. Random lust images, and only from humans—I'd never gotten a flash from any other fey. I never understood why. "Want me to ask him to take off his coat so you can see better?"

That made her blush, and the image she'd built up in her mind crumbled under her embarrassment. Her mind was just a series of jumbles now. I was freed from her thoughts, her emotions.

I'd been told by one of the old fertility gods at the Seelie Court that being able to see other people's lust images was a useful tool if you were seeking priests and priestesses for your temple. People with strong lust could be used in ceremonies, the sexual energy harnessed and magnified so that their lust could be imparted to others. It had once been assumed that lust equated fertility. Unfortunately, not.

If lust equaled reproduction, the fey would have populated the world by now, or so the old stories go. The desk clerk would be so disappointed to discover that Barinthus was celibate. If he'd been staying in the hotel, I might have warned him about her. She struck me as the type who just might surprise him in his room after hours. But Barinthus would be back at the mound by nightfall. No worries.

Jenkins was now standing by the elevators, leaning his back against the wall, smiling. He was trying to talk to Barinthus as Galen and I walked up to them. Barinthus was ignoring him as only a deity can: with a total disregard, as if Jenkins's voice was the buzzing of some unimportant insect. It was beyond disdain. It was as if, for Barinthus, the reporter truly did not exist.

This was an ability I lacked, and envied.

"Well, Meredith, fancy meeting you here." Jenkins managed to make his voice both cheerful and cruel.

I tried ignoring him as Barinthus was, but knew that if the elevator didn't come soon, I'd lose.

"Merry Gentry, couldn't you do better than that? The gentry has been a euphemism for the fey for centuries."

Maybe he was still guessing, but I didn't think so. I had an idea. I turned to him, smiling sweetly. "Do you really think I'd use such an obvious pseudonym if I cared a tinker's dam whether someone found out?"

Doubt crossed his face. He straightened, moving within touching distance of me. "You mean you don't care if I print your alias?"

"Barry, I don't care what you print, but I'd say you're less than two feet away from me." I looked at the lobby. "In fact I don't think there's anywhere in this lobby that is more than fifty feet away from me." I turned to Galen. "Can you please have the desk clerk call the police"—I looked at Jenkins—"and tell them I'm being harassed?"

"My pleasure," Galen said. He walked back toward the desk.

Barinthus and I stood there with my luggage.

Jenkins looked from me to Galen. "They won't do anything to me."

"We'll see, won't we?" I said.

Galen was speaking with the same desk clerk who had eyed Barinthus. Was she picturing Galen naked now? It was good to be across the lobby and out of accidental touching range. Maybe being able to sense people's lust at random intervals was useful for picking out priestesses for your temple, but since I didn't have a temple, it was just irritating.

Jenkins was staring at me. "I'm so glad you're home, Meredith, so very, very glad." The words were mild, but the tone was pure venom. His hatred of me was an almost touchable thing.

He and I watched the desk clerk use the phone. Two young men, one with a badge that said "Asst. Manager," the other with a badge that just said his name, walked very purposefully toward us.

"I think, Barry, that you're about to get your walking papers. Enjoy waiting for the police."

"No court order is going to keep me away from you, Meredith. My hands itch when I'm near a story. The bigger the story, the more they itch. I'm just about to scratch my skin off every time I'm near you, Meredith. Something big is coming and it revolves around you."

"Gee, Barry, when did you become a prophet?"

"One afternoon by a quiet country road," he said. He leaned in so close I could smell his aftershave under the odor of cigarettes. "I had what you might call an epiphany, and I've had the gift ever since."

The hotel men were almost upon us. Jenkins leaned in close enough that from a distance it must have looked like a kiss. He whispered, "Those that the gods would destroy they first make mad."

The men grabbed his arms and pulled him away from me. Jenkins didn't struggle. He went quietly.

Galen said, "They'll hold him in the manager's office until the police come. They won't arrest him, Merry, you know that."

"No, Missouri doesn't have stalker laws yet." I had an

amusing idea. If I could get Jenkins to follow me out to California, the laws are different. There are very strict stalker laws in L.A. county. If Jenkins made too big a pest of himself, maybe I'd see if he'd follow me somewhere where he could get jail time for what he'd just done. He'd forced a kiss on me in public—or so I could claim—in front of impartial witnesses. Under the right set of laws, that made him a very bad boy.

The elevator doors opened. Great, now that I didn't need the rescue. The elevator doors closed, leaving us alone in a mirrored box. We all watched our own reflections, but Galen spoke. "Jenkins never learns. You'd think after what you did to him, he'd be afraid of you."

I watched my reflection show surprise, eyes widening. By the time I recovered, it was too late. "That was a guess," I said.

"But a good one," Galen said.

"What did you do to him, Meredith?" Barinthus said. "You know the rules."

"I know the rules," I said.

I started to step into the hallway, but Galen stopped me, a hand on my shoulder. "We're the bodyguards. Let one of us go first."

"Sorry, I've gotten out of the habit," I said.

Barinthus said, "Get back into the habit, quickly. I don't want you hurt because you didn't hide behind us. It's our job to take the risks and keep you safe." He pressed the "hold door open" button.

"I know that, Barinthus."

"And yet you would have stepped into the hall," he said.

Galen very cautiously peeked out of the elevator, then stepped into the hallway. "Clear." He swept a low bow. The small braid spilled over his shoulder to touch the floor. I remembered when his hair spilled like a green waterfall to pool onto the floor. There was a part of me that thought that was what a man's hair should look like. Long enough to drag the floor. Long enough to cover my body in a silken sheet when we made love. I'd mourned when he cut it, but it hadn't been any of my business.

"Get up, Galen." I started walking down the hallway, key in hand.

He stood and half ran, half danced down the hallway to get ahead of me. "Oh, no, my lady. I must needs open the lock."

"Stop it, Galen. I mean it."

Barinthus just followed us quietly, suitcase in hand, like a father watching grown children misbehave. No, no, he was ignoring us the way he'd ignored Jenkins, almost. I glanced back at him and could read nothing on that pale face. He was self-contained, unreadable. There had been a time when he'd smiled more, laughed more, hadn't there? I remembered his arms lifting me from the water with a great shout of laughter, his hair floating around his body like a slow cloud. I'd swum in that cloud, wrapped it around tiny hands. We'd laughed together. The first time I swam in the Pacific Ocean I thought of Barinthus. I wanted to show him this vast new ocean. To my knowledge he'd never seen it.

Galen was waiting in front of the door. I stopped and waited for Barinthus to catch up with me. "You seem solemn today, Barinthus."

He looked at me with those eyes, and the invisible eyelid flicked over them. Nervous. He was nervous. Was he afraid for me? He'd been pleased about the ring, displeased about the spell in the car. But not too displeased, not too distressed, as if it were all normal business. In a way it was. "What's wrong, Barinthus? What haven't you told me?"

"Trust me, Meredith."

I took his free hand in mine, fingers sliding around his. My hand was lost in his. "I do trust you, Barinthus."

He held my hand delicately as if afraid I would break. "Meredith, little Meredith." His face softened as he spoke. "You were always a mixture of directness, coyness, and tenderness."

"I'm not as tender as I used to be, Barinthus."

He nodded. "The world does tend to beat such things out of you, unfortunately." He brought my hand to his lips and laid a gentle kiss against my fingers. His lips brushed the ring and sent a tingling wave through both of us.

He looked solemn again, face closing down, as he dropped my hand.

"What, Barinthus? What?" I grabbed his arm.

He shook his head. "It has been a very long time since that ring has come to life in such a manner."

"What does the ring have to do with anything?" I asked.

"It had become just another piece of metal, and now it lives again."

"And?" I asked.

He looked past me to Galen. "Let's get her to the room. The queen does not like to be kept waiting."

Galen took the key from me and unlocked the door. He checked the room for spells and hidden dangers while Barinthus and I waited in the hall.

"Tell me what it means that the ring reacts to you and Galen, but not my grandmother."

He sighed. "The queen once used the ring to choose her consorts."

I raised eyebrows at him. "Which means, what?"

"It reacts to men that the ring deems worthy of you."

I stared up at him, searching that handsome, exotic face. "What does that mean, worthy of me?"

"The queen is the only one who knows the complete powers of the ring. I know only that it has been centuries since the ring has been alive on her hand. That it lives for you is both good and dangerous. The queen might be jealous that the ring is yours now."

"She gave it to me—why would she be jealous?"

"Because she is the Queen of Air and Darkness." He said it as if that explained it all. In a way it did, in a way did not. Like so much about our queen, it was a paradox.

Galen came to the door. "All clear."

Barinthus walked past him, forcing Galen to step back out of the way of the big man and the suitcase. "What's his problem?" Galen asked.

"The ring, I think." I stepped into the room. It was a typical box room done in shades of blue.

Barinthus had put the suitcase on one of the dark blue bedspreads. "Please make haste, Meredith. Galen and I still have to dress for dinner."

I looked at him standing in the blue-on-blue room. He matched the decor. If the room had been green, Galen would have matched. You could color code your bodyguards to your room. I laughed.

"What?" Barinthus asked.

I motioned at him. "You match the room."

He looked around as if he'd just noticed the blue print wallpaper, the dark blue bedspreads, the powder blue carpet. "So I do. Now, please, get dressed." He unzipped the suitcase to emphasize the request, though it had the taste of an order, no matter how it was worded.

"Is there a deadline I'm not aware of?" I asked.

Galen sat down on the other bed. "I agree with the big guy on this one. The queen's planning a welcome home event for you, and she won't like waiting for us to get dressed, and if we're not dressed in the outfits she had made for us, she'll be angry with us."

"Are the two of you going to be in trouble?" I asked.

"Not if you hurry," Galen said.

I went into the bathroom with the carry-on bag. I'd packed my outfit for tonight in the bag just in case the suitcase went missing. I didn't want to have to do emergency shopping for an outfit that would meet with my aunt's approval for court fashion. Slacks were not appropriate dinner wear for women. Sexist, but true. Dinner was formal attire, always. If you didn't want to dress up, you could eat in your room.

I slipped into black satin and lace panties. The bra was underwire, firm hold with lace. The hose were black and thigh high. The old human saying about wearing clean underwear in case you get hit by a bus applied to the Unseelie Court, sort of. Here you wore nice underwear because the queen might see it. Though truthfully I liked knowing that everything I wore was pretty, even the things that touched my skin where no one else would see.

I darkened the eye shadow and mascara to shades of grey and white. I applied enough eyeliner that my eyes stood out in shocking relief, like emeralds and gold set in ebony. I chose a shade of lipstick that was a dark, dark wine burgundy.

I had two Spyderco folding knives. I flipped one of them open. It was a six-inch blade, long, slender, gleaming silver, but it was steel—their military model. Steel or iron was what you needed against my relatives. The other knife was much smaller—a Delica. Each knife had a clip-on so you just slipped them over your clothing. I checked both knives for ease of release, then closed them, and put them on. The Delica fit down the center of the bra on the underwire. I slipped a black garter over my left leg, not to hold up the hose—they didn't need it—but to hold the military blade.

I slipped the dress out of the garment bag. The dress was a deep rich burgundy. It had just enough strap to hide the bra. The bodice was satin, tight and fitted; the rest of the dress was a softer, more natural-looking cloth, falling in a soft, clinging line to the floor. The matching jacket was made of the same soft burgundy cloth except for the satin lapels.

I had an ankle holster complete with a Beretta Tomcat, their newest .32 auto pistol. The thing weighed nearly a pound. There were guns out there that were smaller, but if I had to shoot someone tonight, I wanted more than a .22 backing me up. The real trouble with ankle holsters is that they make you walk funny. There is a tendency to drag the foot that the holster's on, to widen your step in an odd little movement. The added problem was I was wearing hose, and the chances of not snagging them on the holster as I walked were pretty much nil. But it was the only place I could think to hide a gun that wasn't obvious just by glancing at me. I'd sacrifice the hose to keep the gun.

I walked back and forth in the burgundy high heels. They were only two-inch heels. The better to move quickly in, and with a skirt this long most people wouldn't be noticing how high, or how low, my heels were. I'd had the shop where I bought the dress hem it for the shoes. At five foot even, you don't buy off-the-rack formals, wear two-inch heels, and not have to hem the dress.

I added the jewelry last. The necklace was antique metal darkened until it was almost black, with only hidden glimpses of the true silver color. The stones were garnets. I purposefully hadn't cleaned the metal so that it would keep that dark color. I thought the stain set the garnets off nicely.

I'd gone to the trouble of curling under the ends of my hair so that it brushed my shoulders. It gleamed a red so dark it was the color of the garnets. The burgundy dress brought out a matching burgundy sheen in my hair.

My aunt might let me keep my weapons or she might not. I probably wouldn't be challenged to a duel my first night back with a special request from the queen herself for my presence, but . . . it was always better to be armed. There are things at the court that aren't royal and don't fight duels. They are the things that have always been of the Host—the monsters of our race, our kind—and they do not reason as we do. Sometimes, for no reason that anyone can explain, one of the monsters will attack. People can die before it can be stopped.

So why keep such unstable horrors around? Because the only rule that has always been in the Unseelie Court is that all are welcome. No one, nothing, may be turned away. We are the dark dumping ground of nightmares too wicked, too twisted, for the light of the Seelie Court. So it is, so it has always been, so it will always be. Though being accepted into the court doesn't mean you're accepted as one of the sidhe. Sholto and I both could attest to that.

I looked in the mirror one more time, added a touch more lip pencil, and that was it. I put the lip pencil in the small beaded purse that matched the dress. What did the queen want of me? Why had she insisted I come home? Why now? I let out a long breath, watching the satin across my chest rise and fall. Everything about me gleamed: my skin, my eyes, my hair, the deep gleam of the garnets at my throat. I looked lovely. Even I could admit that. The only thing that said I was not pure sidhe was my height. I was just too short to be one of them.

I added a small brush to the lipstick in my small purse, then had to decide whether I was going to take more makeup to use to freshen up throughout the evening or a small sleek canister of mace. I chose the mace. If you have a choice between extra makeup or extra weapons, always take the weapons. Just the fact that you're debating between those two choices proves that you're going to need the weapons more.

Chapter 24

THE SITHIN, THE FAERIE MOUNDS, ROSE OUT OF THE DYING light, small mountains of velvet against an orange melt of sky. The moon was already high, smooth and shining silver. I took several deep breaths of the chill, crisp air. Sometimes in California you'd wake to a morning where the air felt like autumn. You'd wear pants and a light sweater before noon. Some leaves would fall to the ground sporadically, with no pattern to it, and there would be small pools of dried brown leaves that on certain mornings would dance in a dry skittering dance, pushed by a wind that felt like October. Then by noon you'd need to switch to shorts, and it would feel like June.

But this was the real thing. The air was chill, but not quite cold. The wind that trailed at our backs smelled like dried cornfields and the dark, crisp scent of dying leaves.

If I could have come home to October and seen only the people I wanted to see, I'd have enjoyed it. Fall was my favorite time of year, October my favorite month.

I stopped on the path, and the men stopped with me. Barinthus looked down at me, eyebrows raised. Galen asked, "What's wrong?"

"Nothing," I said, "absolutely nothing." I took another deep breath of the autumn air. "The air never smells like this in California."

"You always did love October," Barinthus said.

Galen grinned. "I took you and Keelin trick o' treating almost every year until you got too old for it."

I shook my head. "I didn't get too old for it. My own glamour just got powerful enough to hide what I was. Keelin and I went alone when I was fifteen."

"You had enough glamour at fifteen to hide Keelin from the sight of mortals?" Barinthus asked.

I looked at him, nodding. "Yes."

He opened his mouth as if to speak, but we were interrupted. A smooth male voice said, "Well, isn't this touching?"

The voice whirled us all around to face a spot farther down the path. Galen moved in front of me, putting me behind the shield of his body. Barinthus was searching the darkness behind us for others. The near darkness spread behind us empty, but what was in front was enough.

My cousin Cel stood in the middle of the path. He wore his midnight hair like a long straight cloak so that it was hard to tell where hair ended and his black duster coat began. He was dressed all in black except for a gleam of white shirt that shone like a star among all the blackness.

He wasn't alone. Standing to one side of him, ready to move in front of him if the need arose was Siobhan, the captain of his guard and his favorite assassin. She was small, not much taller than me, but I'd seen her pick up a Volkswagen and crush someone with it. Her hair shone white in the dark, but I knew the hair was white and silvery grey, like spiderwebs. Her skin was a pale, dull white, not the shining white of Cel's and mine. Her eyes were a dull grey, filmed over like the blind eyes of a dead fish. She was wearing black armor, her helmet tucked under one arm. It was a bad sign that Siobhan was in full battle armor.

"Full body armor, Siobhan," Galen said. "What's the occasion?"

"Preparation is all in battle, Galen." Her voice matched the rest of her, a dry whispering sibilance.

"Are we about to do battle?" Galen asked.

Cel laughed, and it was the same laugh that had helped make my childhood hellish. "No battle tonight, Galen, just Siobhan's paranoia. She feared that Meredith would have gained powers in her trip to the lands of the west. I see that Siobhan's fears were groundless."

Barinthus put his hands on my shoulders, pulling me against him. "Why are you here, Cel? The queen sent us to bring Meredith to her presence."

Cel glided down the path, tugging on the leash that went from his hand to a small figure crouched at his feet. The figure had been hidden behind the sweep of Cel's coat and Siobhan's body. At first I didn't realize who it was.

The figure unfolded from the ground to a crouch that put her head no taller than Cel's lower chest. She was brown of skin as Gran, but the hair on her head was thick and fell in straight brown folds to her ankles. She looked human or close to it in the near dark, but I knew that in good light one would see that her skin was covered in thick, soft, downy hair. Her face was flat and featureless, like something half-formed and never finished. Her thin, delicate body held several extra arms and one extra set of legs, so that she moved in a strange rocking motion. Clothing could hide the extra appendages but not the movement of her walk.

Keelin's father had been a durig, a goblin of a very dark sense of humor—the kind of humor that could get a human killed. Her mother had been a brownie. Keelin had been chosen as my companion almost from birth. It had been my father's choice, and I had never had cause to complain of it. We'd been best friends growing up. Maybe it was the brownie blood that we both carried. Whatever caused it, there had been an instant connection between us. We'd been friends since the first time I looked into her brown eyes.

Seeing Keelin on the end of Cel's leash left me wordless. There were a variety of ways to end up as Cel's "pet." One was to be punished by the queen and given to Cel. The other was to volunteer. It had always amazed me how many of the lesser fey women would allow Cel to abuse them in the most base manner possible, because if they got pregnant they would be members of the court. Just like my Gran.

Though Gran would have put an iron spike through my

grandfather's heart before she let him treat her like an abused dog.

I stepped away from Barinthus until his hands fell away and I stood alone on the path. Galen and Barinthus stood behind me, one to either side like good royal guards. "Keelin," I said, "what are you doing . . . here?" It wasn't exactly the question I wanted to ask. My voice sounded calm, reasonable, ordinary. What I wanted to do was shout—scream.

Cel drew her to him, stroking her hair, pressing her face against his chest. His hand slid down her shoulder, lower and lower, until he cupped one of her breasts, kneading it.

Keelin turned her head so her hair hid her face from me. The sun was almost down, true dark only minutes away; she was just a thicker shadow against Cel's darkness.

"Keelin, Keelin, talk to me."

"She wants to be part of the court," Cel said. "My pleasure in her makes her part of all the festivities." He pulled her closer into his body, his hand sliding out of sight down the round neck of her dress. "If she gets with child, she will be a princess, and her babe heir to the throne. Her child could push you back to fourth from the throne instead of third," he said, voice smooth and even as he reached farther and farther down her body.

I took a step forward, hand half reaching. "Keelin . . ."

"Merry," she said, turning to face me for a moment, her voice the same small sweet sound it had always been.

"No, no, my pet," Cel said. "Don't speak. I will speak for us." Keelin fell silent, hiding her face again.

I stood there, and until Barinthus touched my shoulder and made me jump, I didn't realize my hands were in tight fists. I was shaking again, but not from fear, from anger.

"The queen put a geas on us all not to tell you, Merry. I should have warned you anyway," Galen said, moving up on the other side. It was almost as if the two of them expected to have to grab me and keep me from doing something foolish. But I wasn't going to be foolish—that's what Cel wanted. He'd come here to show off Keelin, to enrage me, with Siobhan at his back to kill me. I'm sure he could have concocted some story about me attacking him and his guard having to defend him. The queen had believed thinner stories than that over the years. He had every reason to be confident where the queen was concerned. I could be calm, because I could do nothing here and now but die. Cel, I might have considered taking on. He was one of the few people that I would use the hand of flesh on, and not lose sleep over it. But Siobhan, she was different. She would kill me.

"How long has Keelin been with him?" I asked.

Cel started to answer, and I raised a hand. "No, don't speak, cousin. I asked the question of Galen."

Cel smiled at me, a flash of white in the moonlit dark. Strangely, he stayed silent. I hadn't really expected him to, but I also knew that if I had to hear his voice one more time, I was going to start screaming just to drown out his voice.

"Answer me, Galen."

"Almost since you left."

My chest was tight, eyes hot. This was my punishment. My punishment for escaping the court. Even though I hadn't told Keelin that I was leaving, even though she was innocent, they'd hurt her to hurt me. Cel had kept her as a pet for nearly three years waiting for me to come home. Enjoying himself no doubt, and if there was a child, all the better. But it wasn't a desire for children that had motivated the choice of Keelin. I looked into Cel's smug face, and even by moonlight I could read his expression. She'd been chosen out of revenge to punish me. And I'd been thousands of miles away, unknowing.

Cel and my aunt had waited patiently to show me their surprise. Three years of Keelin's torment and no one told me. My aunt knew me better than I'd thought, because the knowledge that Keelin had suffered the entire time I'd been gone would eat at me. And if she held out Keelin's freedom to me as a prize for whatever it was she wanted from me, she might have me. I needed to speak with Keelin alone.

As much as I hated Cel, this was one of the very few ways that Keelin could enter the court. She'd been one of my ladies in waiting—my companion. But being my friend and my servant had allowed her to see the inner workings of the court. I'd known she had a great hunger to be accepted in that darkling throng, hunger enough, maybe, to endure Cel and resent if I put a stop to it. Just because I saw it as a rescue didn't mean Keelin would. Until I knew exactly how she felt, I could do nothing.

Cel's hand finally slid back into sight. Seeing his pale hand on Keelin's shoulder instead of deep in her dress made it easier to just stand and watch. "The queen has sent me to escort my fair cousin to her private chambers. The two of you have an appointment at the throne room."

"I am aware of what I am expected to do," Barinthus said.

"How can we trust you not to harm her?" Galen asked.

"Me? Harm my fair cousin?" Cel laughed again.

"We shall not leave." Barinthus's voice was very low and steady. You had to know his voice well to hear the anger in it.

"You fear that I will harm her, too, Barinthus?"

"No," Barinthus said. "I am afraid she will harm you, Prince Cel. The life of her only heir means a great deal to our queen."

Cel laughed loud and long. He laughed until either tears actually crept from his eyes, or he merely pretended to wipe them away. "You mean, Barinthus, that you're afraid she will try to harm me, and I will put her in her place."

Barinthus leaned over me and whispered, "You cannot afford to appear weak before Cel. I did not expect him to meet us. It is a bold move. If you have gained power in the lands to the west, show it now, Meredith."

I turned, staring up into his face. He was so close to me that his hair trailed against my cheek, smelling of the ocean and something herbal and clean. I whispered back to him, "If I show him my powers now, it will take away all element of surprise later on."

His voice was the soft murmur of water over round stones. He was using his own power to quietly make sure that Cel could not overhear us. "If Cel insists that we leave and we refuse, it will go badly for us."

"Since when has the Queen's Guard answered to her son?" I asked.

"Since the queen has decreed it so."

Cel called to us, "I order you, Barinthus, and you, Galen, to go to your overdue appointment. We will escort my cousin to the queen's presence."

"Make him afraid of you, Meredith," Barinthus said. "Make him wish for us to remain. Cel would have access to his mother's ring."

I stared up at him. I didn't bother to ask if Barinthus really thought that Cel had tried to kill me in the car. If he didn't believe it possible, he wouldn't have said it.

"I gave you both a direct order," Cel said. His voice rose, riding on the growing wind.

The wind picked up, rushing through the men's long coats, whispering in the dried leaves of the trees at the edge of the field to our left. I turned to those whispering trees. I could almost understand the wind and the trees, almost hear the trees sighing of winter's coming and the long cold wait ahead. The wind rushed and hurried, sending a small herd of newly fallen leaves skittering down the rock path past Cel and his women, to brush up against my feet and legs. The wind picked the leaves up in a swirl like tiny hands playing against my legs. The leaves were carried up and past us in a sudden burst of sweet autumn wind. I closed my eyes and breathed in that wind.

I stepped away from the men at my back, a few steps closer to Cel, but it wasn't him I was moving toward. It was the call of the land. The land was happy that I was back, and in a way that it had never done before, the power in that land welcomed me.

I spread my arms to either side and opened myself to the night. I felt the wind blow not against my body but through it, as if I were the trees above, not an obstacle to the wind but part of it. I felt the movement of the night, the rushing, hurrying, pulse of it all. Underneath my feet the ground went down and down below me to unimaginable depths, and I could feel them all, and for a moment I felt the world turning under my feet. I felt that slow, ponderous swing around the sun. I stood with my feet planted solidly like the roots of a tree going down and down to cool living earth. But that was all that was solid about me. The wind swept through me as if I were not there, and I knew I could have wrapped the night around me and walked invisible among the mortals. But it wasn't mortals I was dealing with.

I opened my eyes with a smile. The anger, the confusion, it was all gone, washed away in the wind that smelled like dried leaves and somehow spicy, as if I could smell things on the wind that were only half remembered or half dreamed. It was a wild night, and there was wild magic to be had from it, if you could ken to it. Earth magic can be ripped from the world by someone powerful enough to do it, but the Earth is a stubborn thing and resents being used. You always pay for force against the elements. But on some nights, or even days, the Earth offers herself up like a woman willing her lover to come to her arms.

I accepted her invitation. I left my barriers down and felt the wind blow little bits of me like dust upon the night, but for every bit that left more was pouring in. I gave of myself to the night and the night filled me, the earth beneath my feet embraced me, sliding up through the soles of my feet, up, up like a tree is fed, deep and quiet and cool.

For a moment I wasn't sure if I wanted to move my feet enough to walk, afraid to break that contact. The wind swirled around me, chasing my hair across my face, bringing the scent of burned leaves, and I laughed. I walked down the stone path and with each slap of my heels the Earth moved with me. I moved through the night as if I were swimming, swimming on currents of power. I walked toward my cousin, smiling.

Siobhan stepped in front of him. Her cobweb hair vanished under the unrelieved black of her helmet. Only her white hands showed like ghosts floating in the dark. She could injure or kill with a touch of that pallid skin.

Barinthus came up behind me. I knew without seeing that he reached for me—I could feel him moving through the power at my back. I could almost see him standing there as if I had other eyes. All the magic I'd ever possessed had been very personal. This was not personal. I felt how tiny I was, how vast the world, but it wasn't a lonely feeling. I felt for that moment embraced, whole. Wanted.

Barinthus's hand fell back without touching me. His voice hissed and slurred like water over sand. "If I'd known you could do this, I would not have feared for you."

I laughed, and the sound was joyous, free. I opened further, like a door thrown wide open. No, as if the door, the wall it sat on, and the house it was held inside of, melted into the power.

Barinthus caught his breath sharply. "By the Earth's grace, what have you done, Merry?" He never used my nickname.

"Sharing," I whispered.

Galen came up to us, and the power opened to him without any thought from me. The three of us stood there filled with the night. It was a generous power, a laughing, welcoming presence.

The power moved outward from me, or maybe I moved forward through something that was always there, but tonight I could sense it. Siobhan moved forward, and the power did not fill her. The power rejected her. Siobhan's magic was an insult to the Earth and that slow cycle of life because Siobhan stole that life, rushed death to the door of someone or something before their time. For the first time I understood that somehow Siobhan stood outside the cycle—that she was a thing of death that still moved as if it lived, but the Earth did not know her.

The power would have welcomed Cel, but he thought that first brush was my doing and he guarded himself against it. I felt his shields crash into place, holding him behind the metaphysical walls, safe and unable to share in the bounty offered.

But Keelin did not close herself away from it. Perhaps she didn't have shields enough to build her walls, or perhaps she didn't wish to. But I felt her in the power, felt her open to it, and heard her voice spill out in a sigh that mingled with the wind.

Keelin walked to the end of her leash, raising each of her four arms wide to the welcoming night.

Cel jerked her back by the leather leash. She stumbled, and I felt her spirit crumble.

I reached a hand toward her, and the power, though it wasn't mine to control, spilled outward, surrounded Keelin. It pushed at Cel like water pushes at a rock in the center of a stream, something to go around, to ignore. The push made him stumble back, the leash fell from his hand. His pale face raised to the rising moon, and stark terror showed on that handsome face.

The sight pleased me, and it was a petty pleasure. The generous run of power flexed around me like a mother's hand tugging on the arm of a naughty child. There was no place for pettiness in the midst of such . . . life.

Keelin stood in the center of the path, arms wide, head thrown back so that the moonlight shone full upon her half-formed face. It was a rare and treasured moment for Keelin to show her face clearly in any light.

Siobhan came for me in a dark flash of white hands and the dark gleam of armor. I reacted without thought, pushing my hand forward as if that great sluggish power would respond to my gesture. But it did.

Siobhan stopped as if she'd come against a wall. Her white hands glowed with a pale flame that was not flame at all. Her power flared against something that not even I could see. But I felt her coldness trying to eat the warm, moving night, and she had no power here. If she had been among the truly living, if her touch had brought ordinary death, the Earth would not have stopped her. The power was more neutral than that. It loved me in a way, welcomed me back, but it would welcome my decaying body to its warm, worm-filled embrace just as readily. It would take my spirit on the wind and send it elsewhere.

But Siobhan's magic was not natural, and she could not pass. Understanding even that much might—might give me the key to her destruction. But it was going to take someone more adept at offensive spells than I to unravel the key.

There was movement beyond our little group. Cel and Siobhan turned to see this latest threat, and when they saw it was Doyle, their bodies didn't relax. The prince and heir to the dark throne and his personal guard were afraid of the queen's Darkness. That was interesting. Three years ago Cel had not feared Doyle. He had feared no one except his mother. Even there he did not fear death, because he was all she had to pass her blood along. Her only child. Her only heir. No one challenged Cel to a duel, ever, because you dared not win, and to lose might mean your own death. He'd passed through the last three centuries untouched, unchallenged, unafraid, until now.

Now I saw, almost felt, Cel's unease. He was afraid. Why?

Doyle was dressed in a black, hooded cape that swept around his ankles and hid all of him. His face was so dark that the whites of his eyes seemed to float in the black circle of his hood. "What goes on here, Prince Cel?"

Cel moved off the path so he could keep Doyle and the rest of us in sight. Siobhan moved with him. Keelin remained on the path, but the power was folding away, as if the power moved on the wind and was sweeping past us to travel elsewhere. It gave a last cool, spice-laden caress and slipped away.

I was suddenly solid once more inside my own skin. There was a price for all magic, but not this. It had offered itself to me. I had not asked. Maybe that was why I felt strong and whole instead of exhausted.

Keelin came down the path toward me, her primary hands held out toward me. She must have felt renewed as I did, because she was smiling and that awful pinched fear was gone, washed away in the sweet wind.

I took her hands in mine. We kissed each other twice on both cheeks, then I drew her into the circle of my arms and she hugged me across the shoulders with her upper arms, around the waist with the smaller lower ones. We held each other so tightly that I could feel the press of her small breasts, all four of them. The thought came: Had Cel enjoyed being with someone with that many breasts? An image came on the heels of the thought. I squeezed my eyes tight as if I could rid myself of the image.

I ran my hand down her back through her thick, furlike hair and realized I was already crying.

Keelin's sweet almost birdlike voice was comforting me. "It's all right, Merry. It's all right."

I shook my head and pulled back so I could see her face. "It's not all right."

She touched my face, catching my tears on her fingers. She couldn't cry. Some trick of genetics had left her without tear ducts. "You always cried my tears for me, but don't cry now."

"How can I not?" I glanced back at Cel who was talking in low whispers to Doyle. Siobhan was looking at me, staring at me. I could feel her dead gaze through the helmet she wore, even if I couldn't see her eyes. She would not forget that I had used magic against her and won, or rather not lost. She would neither forget nor forgive it.

But that was a problem for another night. I turned back to Keelin. One disaster at a time, please. My hands went to the hardened leather collar around her neck.

She touched my wrists. "What are you doing, Merry?"

"Taking this off of you."

She pulled my hands down, gently. "No."

I shook my head. "How can you . . . How could you?"

"Don't cry again," Keelin said. "You know why I did it. I only have a few more weeks, just until Samhain. Three years to the day. If I'm not with child, then I am free of him. If I am with child, he'll have to treat me as a wife should be treated, or not touch me at all."

She was so calm about it, a terrible, solid calm, as if it were quite . . . ordinary. "I do not understand this," I said.

"I know. But you've always been of royal blood, Merry." She reached up a free hand to touch my lips before I could protest, her other hands still holding my hands. "I know you have been treated like a poor relation, Merry, but you are a part of them. Their blood flows in your veins, and they . . ." She hung her head, dropping her hand from my mouth, but gripped my hands all the tighter. "You are a member of the club, Merry. You're inside the great house, while we wait outside in the cold and the snow with our faces pressed to the glass."

I looked away from those tender brown eyes. "You're using my own metaphor against me."

She touched my face with her left upper hand, her dominant hand. "I heard you use it often enough as we were growing up."

"If I had asked, would you have come with me?"

She smiled, but even by moonlight it was bitter. "Unless you could be with me every hour of the day or night, you couldn't use your glamour to protect me." She shook her head. "I am far too hideous for human eyes."

"You are not—"

She stopped me this time with only a glance. "I am like you, Merry. I am neither durig nor brownie."

"What of Kurag? He cared for you."

She lowered her face. "It is true that among a certain type of goblin I am considered quite striking. Having extra limbs, especially extra breasts is a mark of great beauty among them."

I smiled. "I remember the year you took me to the Goblin's Ball. They considered me plain."

Keelin smiled but shook her head. "But they all tried to dance with you, ugly or not." She looked up, gathering my gaze into hers. "They all wanted to touch the skin of a blooded royal princess, because they knew that short of rape it was as close as they would ever get to that sweet body of yours."

I didn't know how to react to the bitterness in her voice.

"It's not your fault that you look as you do, and I look as I do. It's no one's fault. We are what we are. Through you I saw the court and all the gleaming throng. I couldn't go back to Kurag and his goblins after the life you'd shown me. I would have been content to stand behind your chair at banquets for the rest of my days, but to have it suddenly gone . . ." She dropped my hands and moved back from me. "I could not bear to lose everything when you left." She laughed; the laughter was still birdlike, but it was mocking now, and I heard Cel's echo in it. "Besides, Cel likes a four-breasted woman and says he's never slept with anyone that could wrap two sets of legs around his white body."

Keelin made a small dry sobbing sound, and I knew that she was crying. Simply because she had no tears didn't mean she could not weep.

She turned and walked back toward Cel. I let her go. She blamed me for showing her the moon when she could not have it. Maybe Keelin was right. Maybe I had used her ill, but I had not meant to. Of course, not meaning to did not make it hurt less.

I took some very slow deep breaths of the autumn air, trying not to cry again. The air was still as sweet as before, but some of the pleasure had gone out of it.

"I am sorry, Meredith," Barinthus said.

"Don't be sorry for me, Barinthus, I'm not the one at the end of Cel's leash."

Galen touched my shoulder, and started to hug me, but I held him away with one arm. "Don't, please. If you comfort me, I'll cry."

He gave a quick smile. "I'll try to remember that for future reference."

Doyle glided toward us. He'd pushed the cloak hood back, but it was almost impossible to tell where his black hair ended and the black cloak began. What I could see was that the front part of his hair had been gathered in a small bun in the center of his head, leaving his exotic pointed ears bare. The silver earrings gleamed in the moonlight. He'd changed some of them to larger hoops so that they brushed together as he moved, making a small chiming music. When he was standing in front of us, I could see that he had hoops graced by feathers so long they brushed his shoulders.

"Barinthus, Galen, I believe our prince gave you orders."

Barinthus moved forward to stand towering over the

smaller man. If Doyle was intimidated by the other's sheer physical presence, it didn't show. "Prince Cel said he would escort Meredith to the queen. I thought that unwise."

Doyle nodded. "I will escort Meredith to the queen." He looked past Barinthus to me. It was hard to tell in the dark, but I think he gave that small, small smile of his. "I believe that our royal prince has had quite enough of his cousin for one meeting. I did not know you could call the Earth."

"I did not call it. It offered itself to me," I said.

I heard him draw a long breath and let it out. "Ah, that is different. In some ways not as powerful as those who can wrest the Earth from her course. In some ways more unsettling, because the land welcomed you home. It acknowledges you. Interesting."

He turned back to Barinthus. "I believe you are wanted elsewhere, both of you." His voice was very quiet, but underneath the ordinary words was something dark and threatening. Doyle had always been able to control his men with his voice, inflicting the mildest words with the most ominous threats.

"Do I have your word that she will come to no harm?" Barinthus asked.

Galen moved up beside Barinthus. He touched the taller man's arm. Asking such a thing was almost the same as questioning orders. That could get you flayed alive.

"Barinthus," Galen said.

"I give you my word that she will arrive in the queen's presence unharmed."

"That is not what I asked," Barinthus said.

Doyle stepped close enough to Barinthus that his cloak mingled with the taller man's coat. "Have a care, sea god, that you do not ask more than you should."

"Which means that you fear for her safety at the queen's hand, as do I," Barinthus said, voice neutral.

Doyle raised a hand that was outlined with green fire. I was walking toward them before I had time to think of anything good to say when I got there.

Barinthus kept his attention on Doyle and that burning hand, but Doyle watched me stride toward them. Galen stood near them, obviously unsure what to do. He started to reach for me, to stop me, I think.

"Stand aside, Galen. I don't plan to do anything foolish."

He hesitated, then stepped back and left me to face the other two men. The fire on Doyle's hand painted them both with greenish-yellow light shadows. Doyle's eyes didn't so much reflect the fire as seem to burn in sympathy with it. This close I could feel not just his power like a march of insects down my skin, but the slow rise of Barinthus's power like the sea pulling toward the shore.

I shook my head. "Stop it, both of you."

"What did you say?" Doyle asked.

I pushed Barinthus back, hard enough for him to stumble. Maybe I couldn't lift small cars and beat people to death with them, but I could put my fist through a car door, all the way through, and not break my hand. I pushed him again and again, until there was enough distance that I wasn't afraid they were about to come to blows.

"You have been ordered once by the royal heir, and once by the captain of your guard. Obey your orders and go. Doyle has given you his word that I will come to the queen in safety."

Barinthus looked at me. His face was neutral, but his eyes were not. Doyle had always been one of the obstacles between the queen and an untimely death. For a moment I wondered if Barinthus was looking for an excuse to try the queen's Darkness. If so, I wasn't going to give it to him. To kill Doyle would be the beginning of a revolution. I stared into Barinthus's face and tried to understand what he was thinking. Had it been the land's welcome to me? Or was there some new tension between the two men, that I had not been told about? It didn't matter.

"No," I said. I kept our gazes locked, and said again, "No."

Barinthus looked past me to set those eyes on Doyle.

Doyle turned his free hand so that it came together with the burning one to form a single wick of both hands.

I stepped between him and Barinthus. "Stop the theatrics, Doyle. I'm coming."

I could feel the two of them watching each other like a weight pressing in the air. There'd always been tension between them, but not like this.

I walked to Doyle until the colored fire cast sickly shadows on my face and clothes. I stood close enough that I could feel that the fire gave nothing, no heat, no life, nothing, but it was not illusion. I'd seen what Doyle's fire could do. As with Siobhan's hands, it could kill.

I had to do something to break the tension between them. I'd seen too many duels start over less. Too much blood, too much death over such stupid things.

I touched each of Doyle's elbows and moved my hands slowly up his forearms. "Seeing Keelin has taken some of the heart from me, as Andais knew it would, so take me to her." My hands slid slowly up his arms, and I realized that his black skin was bare; he was wearing short sleeves under that long cloak.

"The land welcomes you, little one, and you grow bold," Doyle said.

"That wasn't bold, Doyle." My hands were almost at his wrists, almost inside the sickly flames. There was no heat to warn me off, only my own memories of watching a man writhe and die covered in crawling green flame. "This—is bold." I did two things simultaneously. I brought my hands sliding upward into where the flame was and blew a breath out like blowing out a candle.

The flames vanished as if I'd snuffed them out, which I had not. Doyle had killed them a fraction of a heartbeat before my skin touched them.

I was close enough that by moonlight I could see he was shaken, frightened at what I'd almost done. "You are mad."

"You gave your word I would reach the queen unharmed. You always keep your word, Doyle."

"You trusted me to not harm you."

"I trusted your sense of honor, yes."

He glanced back at Cel and Siobhan. Keelin had joined them again. Cel was staring at us. There was a look on his face that said he almost believed I'd done exactly what it looked like I'd done—blown out Doyle's flame.

I kept one hand on Doyle's wrist and blew my cousin a kiss with my free hand.

He actually jumped as if that windblown kiss had struck him. Keelin had cuddled close to him and was staring back at me with what I knew now were not entirely friendly eyes.

Siobhan stepped in front of them, and this time she drew her sword in a shining line of cold steel. I knew the handle was carved bone, and the armor was bronze; but for killing we used steel or iron. She had a bronze short sword at her side, but she'd drawn the steel blade that rested against her back. For defense she'd have drawn the bronze, but she had drawn steel. She drew to kill. Nice to know she was being honest.

Doyle grabbed me by both arms and turned me to face him. "I do not want to fight Siobhan tonight because you have frightened your cousin."

His fingers dug into my skin and I knew I'd be bruised, but I laughed. And it had a bitter edge that reminded me of someone—someone with tearless brown eyes. "Don't forget I've frightened Siobhan, too. That's much more impressive than frightening Cel."

He shook me once, hard. "And more dangerous." He let me go so suddenly I stumbled, nearly falling. Only his hand on my elbow saved me from a fall.

He looked behind me. "Barinthus, Galen, go, now!" There was real anger in his voice, and he rarely let such raw emotion show through. I was unsettling everyone, and a small dark part of me was pleased.

Doyle kept his grip on my arm and began leading me up the path.

I didn't look back to see Barinthus and Galen going, or to give Siobhan another worry. It wasn't caution. I didn't want to see Keelin holding Cel in her arms again.

I stumbled, and Doyle had to catch me again. "You're going too fast for the shoes I'm wearing," I said. Truthfully it was the ankle holster combined with the long hem. But I'd blame it on the shoes if I could. I was walking beside the person who'd take the gun away if he found it.

He slowed. "You should have worn something more sensible."

"I've seen the queen force sidhe to strip and go naked to the banquet when she didn't like their clothes. So forgive me, but I want her to like the outfit." I knew I couldn't break his grip on my elbow without an actual fight. Even then I might lose. I tried reason. "Give me your arm, Doyle; escort me like a princess, not a prisoner."

He slowed further, looking at me out of the corners of his eyes. "Are you quite through with your own theatrics, Princess Meredith?"

"Quite through," I said.

He stopped and offered me his arm. I slipped my arm under and over his to rest my hand lightly on his wrist. I could feel the small hairs on his arm under my fingers.

"A little cold for short sleeves, isn't it?" I asked.

He glanced at me, gaze traveling down my body. "Well, at least you chose well for yourself."

I put my free hand on top of the hand I had resting on his arm, giving a sort of double hug, but nothing that wasn't allowed. "Do you like it?"

He looked down at my hand. He stopped walking and grabbed my right hand, and the moment his skin touched the ring it flared to life, washing us both with that electric dance. Whatever magic was in the ring, it recognized Doyle as it had recognized Barinthus and Galen.

He jerked his hand back as if it had hurt, rubbing it. "Where did you get that ring?" His voice sounded strained.

"It was left in the car for me."

He shook his head. "I knew it had gone missing, but I did not expect to find it on your hand." He looked at me, and if it had been anyone else, I'd have said he was afraid. The look vanished as I was still trying to puzzle it out. His face became smooth and dark and unreadable. He gave a formal bow and offered me his arm as any gentleman would.

I took his arm, encircling it with both my hands, but as my right hand rested on top of my left, it didn't touch his skin. I thought about touching him accidently on purpose, but I didn't know exactly what the ring did. I didn't know what it was for, and until I did, it was probably not a good idea to keep invoking its magic.

We walked down the path arm in arm, at a sedate but steady pace. My heels made a sharp sound on the stones. Doyle paced beside me silent as a shadow; only the solidness of his arm, the sweep of his cloak against my body let me know he was there. I knew that if I let go of his arm, he could melt into the darkness that was his namesake—I would never see the blow that killed me unless he wished it. No, unless my aunt wished it.

I would have liked to fill the silence with talk, but Doyle had never been much for small talk, and tonight neither was I.

Chapter 25

THE STONE PATH MET THE MAIN AVENUE, WHICH WAS WIDE enough for a cart and horse or a small car, if cars had been allowed, which they were not. Once upon a time, so I was told, there had hung torches, then lanterns, to light the avenue. Modern fire laws frowned on all-night torches, so now the poles that rested every eighteen feet or so held will-o'-the-wisps. One of the craftsfolk had fashioned wooden and glass cages for the lights. The lights were palest blue, ghostly white, a yellow so pale it was almost another shade of white, and a green leeched to a dim color, barely distinguishable from the faint glow of the yellow lights. It was like walking through pools of colored phantoms as we passed from one dim light to the next.

When Jefferson had invited the fey into this country, he'd also offered them land of their choice. They'd chosen the mounds at Cahokia. There are tales whispered on long winter nights about what lived in the mounds before we came. What we . . . evicted from the mounds. The things that lived inside the land were chased away or destroyed, but magic is a hardier thing. There was a feel to the place as you walked down the avenue with the great hulking mounds to either side. The largest mound in the city proper was at the end of the avenue. I went to Washington, D.C., during college, and when I came home it was almost unnerving how forcibly the mound city reminded me of being in Washington, standing on the plaza surrounded by those monuments to American glory. Now, walking down the center and only street, I had the sense of great time passing. This place had once been a great city as

Washington was now, a center of culture and power, and now it lay quiet, cleansed of its original inhabitants. The humans had thought the mounds were empty when they offered them up to us, just bones and some pots buried here and there. But the magic had still been there, deep and slumbering. It had fought and then embraced the fey. The conquering or winning over of that alien magic had been one of the last times the two courts worked together against a common foe.

Of course, the very last time had been World War II. Hitler had at first embraced the fey of Europe. He'd wanted to add them to the genetic mix of his master race. Then he'd met a few of the less human members of the fey. Among ourselves there is a class structure as rigid and unbreakable as it is foolish; the Seelie Court especially looks down on those who do not look like blood. Hitler mistook this arrogance for lack of caring. But it was like a family with siblings. Among themselves they could fight and beat each other bloody, but let anyone turn on one of them and they became a united force against the common enemy.

Hitler used the wizards he'd gathered to trap and destroy the lesser fey. His fey allies didn't desert him. They turned on him without warning. Humans would have felt the need to distance themselves from him, to warn him of their change of heart, or maybe that was an American ideal. It certainly wasn't a fey ideal. The allies found Hitler and all the wizards hanging up by their feet in his underground bunker. They never found his mistress, Eva Braun. Every once in a while the tabloids say that Hitler's grandson has been found.

None of my direct relatives were involved in Hitler's death, so I don't know for sure, but I suspect strongly that something simply ate her.

My father had gotten two silver stars in the war. He'd been a spy. I never remembered being particularly proud of the medals, mainly because my father never seemed to care about them. But when he died, he left them to me in their satin-lined box. I'd carried them around in a carved wooden box along with the rest of my childhood treasures: colored bird feathers, rocks that sparkled in the sun, the tiny plastic ballerinas that had graced my sixth-birthday cake, a dried bit of lavender, a toy cat with fake jewel eyes, and two silver stars given to my dead father. Now the medals were back in their satin box in a drawer in my dresser. The rest of my "treasures" were scattered to the winds.

"Your thoughts are far away, Meredith," Doyle said.

I was still walking at his side, hands on his arm, but for a moment only my body had been there. It startled me to realize how far away I'd been.

"I'm sorry, Doyle, were you speaking to me?" I shook my head.

"What were you thinking about so very hard?" he asked. The lights played over his face, painting colored shadows against his black skin. It was almost as if his skin reflected the lights like carved and polished wood. I was touching his arm, so I could feel the warmth, the muscles underneath, the softness of his skin. His skin felt like anyone's skin, but light didn't reflect off skin, not like that.

"I was thinking about my father," I said.

"What of him?" Doyle turned his head to look at me as we walked. The long feathers brushed his neck, mingling with the spill of black hair that was only partially trapped down the back of the cloak. I realized that except for the small knot that captured the front pieces of his hair, the rest of his hair was spilling out underneath the cloak, loose.

"I was thinking about his medals that he won in World War II."

He kept walking but turned his face full to me, never missing a step. He looked bemused. "Why would you be thinking of that now?"

I shook my head. "I don't know. Thinking about faded glory, I guess. The mounds remind me of the plaza in Washington, D.C. All that energy and purpose. It must have been like that here once."

Doyle looked up at the mounds. "And now it is quiet, almost deserted."

I smiled. "I know better than that. There's hundreds, thousands under our feet."

"But yet the comparison of the two cities saddens you. Why?"

I looked up at him, and he looked down at me. We were standing in a pool of yellow light, but there were pinpricks of every color of will-o'-the-wisp in his eyes, swirling like a tiny cloud of colored fireflies. Except the colors in his eyes were rich and pure, not ghostly, and there were reds and purples and colors that shone nowhere near us.

I closed my eyes, suddenly dizzy and nauseated. I answered with my eyes still shut. "Sad to think that Washington may someday be a tired ruin. Sad to know that the glory days passed this place by long before we arrived." I opened my eyes and looked up at him. His eyes were just black mirrors once more. "Sad to think that the fey's glory days are passed and us being here in this place is proof of that."

"Would you prefer that we be out among the humans, working with them, mating with them like the fey that stayed behind in Europe? They are no longer fey, just another minority."

"Am I just a part of the minority, Doyle?"

A look passed over his face, some serious thought that I couldn't read. I'd never been around a man whose face reflected so many emotions, and yet been able to read so few of them. "You are Meredith, Princess of Flesh, and as sidhe as I am. That I will stake my oath on."

"I take that as a great compliment coming from you, Doyle. I know how much store you set by your oath."

His head cocked to one side, studying me. The movement pulled some of his hair farther out of his cloak to fold under but not fall free as he straightened his neck. "I have felt your power, Princess, I cannot deny it."

"I've never seen your hair when it wasn't braided or tied in a club. I've never seen it loose," I said.

"Do you like it?"

I hadn't expected him to ask my opinion. I'd never heard him ask anyone's opinion of anything. "I think so, but I'd need to see the hair without the cloak to be sure."

"Easily done," he said, and undid the cloak at his neck. He let the cloak slide off his shoulders, spilling it over one arm.

He was wearing what looked like a leather-and-metal harness from the waist up, though if it had been meant to be armor, it would have covered more. The colored lights played over the muscles in his body as if he were indeed carved of some black marble. His waist and hips were slender, long legs encased in leather. The pants clung to him and spilled into black boots that came up over his knees where the loose tops of the leather were held in place by straps with small silver buckles. The buckles were echoed in the straps that covered his upper body. The silver glittered against the blackness of him. His hair hung like a second black cloak boiling in the wind, tangling in long strands around his ankles and calves. The wind sent the feathers that edged his face across his mouth.

"My, look what you're not wearing," I said, trying for flippant and failing.

The wind rushed past us, flinging my hair back from my face. It rustled the tall dried grass in the near field, and beyond that I could hear the cornstalks whispering to each other. The wind blew down the avenue, channeled between the mounds so that it swirled around us like eager hands. It was an echo of that welcoming Earth magic that had greeted me when I first stepped on sidhe land tonight.

"Do you like my hair unbound, Princess?"

"What?" I said.

"You said you needed to see it without the cloak. Do you like it?"

I nodded, wordlessly. Oh, yes, I liked it.

Doyle stared at me, and all I could see were his eyes. The rest of his face was lost to the wind and the feathers and the dark. I shook my head and looked away.

"That's twice you've tried to bespell me with your eyes, Doyle. What's going on?"

"The queen wanted me to test you with my eyes. She has always said they were my best feature."

I let my gaze linger over the strong curves of his body. The wind gusted, and he was suddenly caught in a cloud of his own hair, black and soft, with the near-bare flesh almost lost, black on black.

My gaze rose up to meet his eyes once more. "If my aunt thinks that your eyes are your best feature, then . . ." I shook my head and let out a breath. "Let's just say she and I must have different criteria."

He laughed. Doyle laughed. I'd heard him laugh in L.A., but not like this. This was a rumbling belly laugh, like a peal of thunder. It was a good laugh, hearty and deep. It echoed off the mounds and filled the windy night with a joyous sound. So why was my heart thudding in my throat until I couldn't breathe? My fingertips tingled with the shock of it. Doyle did not laugh, not like that, not ever.

The wind died. The laughter stopped, but the glow of it stayed in his face, making him smile wide enough to show perfect white teeth.

Doyle slipped the cloak back over his shoulders. If he had been cold in the October night without it, he never showed a sign of it. He left the cloak flipped back over one shoulder and offered me his bare arm. He was flirting with me.

I frowned at him. "I thought we had our little talk, and we were going to pretend last night never happened."

"I have not mentioned it," he said, voice very bland.

"You're flirting," I said.

"If it were Galen standing here, you would not hesitate." The humor was fading to a dim glow that filled his eyes. He was still amused with me, and I didn't know why.

"Galen and I have been teasing each other ever since I hit puberty. I've never seen you tease anyone, Doyle, until last night."

"There are wonders yet to behold tonight, Meredith. Wonders much more surprising than me with my hair loose and no shirt on a cold October evening." Now there was that note to his voice that so many of the old ones had, a condescending tone that said I was a child and no matter how old I got to be, I would still be a child compared to them, a foolish child.

Doyle had been condescending to me before. It was almost

comforting. "What could be more wondrous than the queen's Darkness flirting with another woman?"

He shook his head, still offering me his hand. "I think the queen will have news that will make anything I could say seem tame."

"What news, Doyle?" I asked.

"That is the queen's pleasure to tell, not mine."

"Then stop hinting," I said. "It isn't like you."

He shook his head, and a smile crept across his face. "No, I suppose it isn't. After the queen gives you her news, I will explain the change in my behavior." His face sobered, slowly, almost its usual ebony mask. "Is that fair enough?"

I looked at him, studying his face until every vestige of humor faded away. I nodded. "I suppose so."

He offered me his arm.

"Put the body away and I'll take the arm," I said.

"Why does it bother you so much to see me like this?"

"You were adamant that last night never happened, never to be spoken of again, now suddenly you're back to flirting. What's changed?"

"If I said the ring upon your finger, would you understand?"

"No," I said.

He smiled, gently this time, almost his usual slight twitch of lips. He flipped the cloak back over his shoulder so that his hand was all that showed out of that thick cloth. "Better?"

I nodded. "Yes, thank you."

"Now, take my arm, Princess, and allow me the pleasure of escorting you before our queen." His voice was flat, unemotional, empty of meaning. I'd almost have preferred to hear the thick emotion of the moment before. Now his words just sat there. They could have meant many things or nothing at all. The words without emotion to color them were almost useless.

"Do you have a tone of voice somewhere between utter emptiness and joyous condescension?" I asked.

That tiny smile quirked his lips. "I will try to find a . . . middle ground between the two."

I slid my arms carefully around his arm, the cloak bunched between our bodies. "Thank you," I said.

"You are welcome." The voice was still empty, but there was the faintest hint of warmth in it.

Doyle had said he'd try to find a middle ground, and he was already working on it. How terribly prompt of him.

Chapter 26

THE STONE ROAD ENDED ABRUPTLY IN THE GRASS. THE ROAD, like the paths, stops short of any mound. We stood at the end of the road and there was nothing but grass beyond. Grass trampled down by many feet, but trampled down evenly so that no one way was more traveled than any other. One of our old nicknames is "the hidden ones." We may be a tourist attraction now, but old habits die hard.

Sometimes fey-watchers will camp outside the area, using binoculars, and see nothing for days, nights. If anyone was watching in the chill dark, they were about to see "something."

I didn't try to find the doorway. Doyle would get us inside without any effort from me. The door rotated on some schedule of its own, or perhaps the queen's schedule. Whatever caused it to move, sometimes the door faced the road and sometimes it did not. As a teenager, if I wanted to sneak out at night and come home late, I could only hope that the door hadn't moved while I was out. The small magic needed to search for the opening would alert the guards within, and the jig, as they say, would be up. I'd thought more than once as a teenager that that damned door moved on purpose.

Doyle led me out onto the grass. My heels sank in the soft earth, and I was forced to walk almost tiptoe to keep the heels free of dirt. The gun in its ankle holster made it a very awkward way to walk. I was glad I hadn't chosen higher heels.

As Doyle led me away from the avenue and the ghostly lights, the darkness seemed thicker than it had before. The lights had been dim, but any light gives the darkness weight and substance. I clung a little harder to Doyle's arm as we left the light behind us and walked into the star-filled dark.

Doyle must have noticed because he offered, "Do you wish a light?"

"I can conjure my own will-o'-the-wisp, thank you very much. My eyes will adjust in a minute."

He shrugged, and I could feel the movement as his arm raised in my grasp. "As you like." His voice had fallen into its usual neutral tone. Either he was having trouble finding a middle ground for his voice, or it was simply habit. I was betting the latter.

By the time Doyle stopped halfway around the mound, my eyes had adjusted to the dim, cold light of stars, and the rising moon.

Doyle stared at the earth. His magic gave a small warm breath along my body as he concentrated on the mound. I stared up at the grass-covered earth. Without some effort of concentration this grassy spot looked just like every other grassy spot.

The wind blew through the grass like fingers ruffling a box of lace. The night was full of the dry rustling of autumn grass, but faintly, oh so faintly, you could hear music on the wind. Not enough to recognize the tune or even be a hundred percent sure that you'd heard anything but the wind, but that phantom music was a hint you were standing near the entrance. Sort of like a spectral doorbell or a magical game of "hot and cold." No music meant you were cold.

Doyle drew his arm out of my hold and passed his hand over the grass of the mound. I was never sure whether the grass melted away or the door appeared over the grass and the grass was still there underneath the door in some metaphysical space. However it worked, a rounded doorway appeared in the side of the mound. The doorway was exactly the right size to admit us both. Light filled the opening. If needed, the doorway could be big enough to have a tank driven through, as if the doorway sensed how big it needed to be.

The light appeared brighter than I knew it was because my eyes were accustomed to the dark now. The light was white but not harsh, a soft white light that breathed from the doorway like a luminous fog.

"After you, my princess," Doyle said, bowing as he said it.

I wanted to come back to court, but looking at that glowing hill I was reminded that a hole in the ground is a hole in the ground whether it be a sithen or a grave. I don't know why I suddenly thought of that particular analogy. Maybe it was the assassination attempt. Maybe it was just nerves. I went through the door.

I stood in a huge stone hallway large enough for that tank to have driven through comfortably or for a small giant to pass without bumping his head. The hallway was always large no matter how small the doorway happened to be. Doyle joined me and the doorway vanished behind him. Just another grey stone wall. Just as the outside of the mound hid its entrance, so the inside did as well. If the queen wished it, the door wouldn't appear from this side at all. It was very easy to go from guest to prisoner here. The thought was less than comforting.

The white light that filled the hallway was sourceless, coming from everywhere and nowhere. The grey stone looked like granite, which means it wasn't native to St. Louis. If you want stone here it's red or reddish tan, not grey. Even our stone is imported from some alien shore.

I'm told once upon a time there were entire worlds under the ground. Meadows and orchards and a sun and moon of our very own. I've seen the dying orchards and flower gardens with a few straggling blossoms, but no underground moon or sun. The rooms are bigger and more square than they should be, and the blueprint of the interior seems to change at random, sometimes with you walking through it, like walking through a fun house made of stone instead of mirrors. But there are no meadows, or none that I've seen. I'm more than willing to believe that the others are keeping secrets from me. That wouldn't surprise me in the least, but to my knowledge there are no worlds under the ground, just stone and rooms.

Doyle offered me his arm, very formally. I took his arm lightly, out of habit mostly.

There was a sharp bend to the corridor. I heard footsteps coming toward us. Doyle pulled gently on my arm. I stopped and looked at him. "What is it?" I asked.

Doyle led me back down the corridor. I walked backward with him, and he stopped abruptly. He grabbed a handful of my dress and raised the skirt enough to bare my ankles, and the gun. "It wasn't your heels setting you off balance on the stones, Princess." He sounded angry with me.

"I'm allowed weapons."

"No guns inside the mound," he said.

"Since when?"

"Since you killed Bleddyn with one."

We looked at each other for a frozen second, then I tried to move away, but his hand closed over my wrist.

With footsteps coming ever closer, Doyle jerked me off balance so that I fell against him. He pinned me to his body with an arm across my back. He opened his mouth to speak, and the footsteps turned the corner.

We were left standing in full sight, Doyle pinning me to his body, the other hand on my wrist. It looked like an interrupted fight or the beginning of one.

The two men that stepped around the corner fanned out so that they covered as much of the corridor as possible with space to spare for fighting.

I looked up into Doyle's face and tried to put the request into one glance. I begged him with my eyes not to tell about the gun and not to take it.

He put his mouth against my cheek, and whispered, "You will not need it."

I just looked up at him. "Will you give me your oath on that?"

The anger tightened the muscles in his jaw, thrummed down his arms. "I will not give my oath on the queen's whim."

"Then let me keep the gun," I whispered.

He moved to stand between me and the other guards. He still had the grip on my arm. All the others could see was the sweep of Doyle's cape.

"What's wrong, Doyle?" one of the men asked.

"Nothing," he said. But he forced my other hand behind my back until he could grip both my wrists in one of his hands. His hands were not that large, and to get a firm grip meant my wrists were ground together, bruising. I'd have struggled more if I'd thought I could get away, but even if I escaped Doyle, he'd seen the gun. There was nothing I could do about it, so I didn't struggle. But I was not happy.

Doyle used his other arm to pick me up and lower me to the ground in a sitting position. Except for my wrists it was all done gently enough. He knelt, his cloaked back still hiding us from the other men. As his hand hovered over my leg, moving toward the gun, I thought about kicking him, being difficult, but there was no point. He could have crushed my wrists with no effort. I might get the gun back tonight. If he crushed my arms, my options were over. He slid the gun out of the ankle holster. I sat on the floor and let him do it. I stayed passive in his grip, let him move my body as he wanted. Only my eyes weren't passive—I couldn't keep the anger out of them. No, I wanted him to see the anger.

He let me go and slid the gun behind his own back, though the leather pants were tight enough that it couldn't have been comfortable. I hoped it dug into his back until he bled.

He took one of my hands, helping me stand. Then he turned with a flourish of his cape to present me to the other guards, one hand holding mine as if we were about to make a grand entrance down a long marble staircase. It was an odd gesture for the grey hallway and what had just happened. I realized that Doyle was uneasy about the gun or his choice of taking it, or maybe wondering if I had other weapons. He was ill at ease and he was covering.

"A small disagreement, nothing more," he said.

"A disagreement about what?" The voice belonged to Frost, Doyle's second in command. Other than the fact that they were both tall, physically they were almost opposites. The hair that fell in a glimmering curtain to Frost's ankles was silver, a shimmering metallic silver like Christmas tree tinsel. The skin was as white as my own. The eyes were a soft

grey like a winter sky before a storm. His face was angular
and arrogantly handsome. His shoulders were a touch broader
than Doyle's, but other than that they were both very alike and
very unalike.

He wore a silver jerkin that hit him just above the knees to
meet the silver cloth of his pants, tucked into silver boots. The
jeweled belt at his waist was silver studded with pearls and
diamonds. It matched the heavy necklace that graced his
chest. He gleamed as if he'd been carved all of one great silver piece, more statue than man. But the sword at his side with
its silver-and-bone hilt was real enough, and if you could see
one weapon, there'd be more because he was Frost. The queen
called him her Killing Frost. If he'd ever had another name I
did not know it. He wasn't wearing any magical or bespelled
weapons—for Frost it was almost the same thing as being
unarmed.

He stared at me with those grey eyes, clearly suspicious.

I found my voice, anything to fill the silence. Distraction
was what was needed. I let go of Doyle's hand and took a step
forward. Frost was vain about his appearance and his clothes.
"Frost, what a bold fashion statement." My voice came out
strong, somewhere between teasing and mockery.

His fingers went to the edge of the tunic before he could
stop himself. He frowned at me. "Princess Meredith, a pleasure as always." A slight change in tone made mockery of his
polite words.

I didn't care. He wasn't wondering about what Doyle was
hiding. That was all I had wanted to accomplish.

"What about me?" Rhys said.

I turned to find my third-favorite guard. I didn't trust him
as I did Barinthus or Galen. There was something weak about
Rhys, a sense that he wouldn't exactly die for your honor, but
right up to that point you could depend on him.

He put his cape and the waist-length spill of white wavy
hair over one arm so I'd have an unobstructed view of his
body. Rhys was a full half foot under six feet, short for a
guard. To my knowledge he was full-blooded court. He just

happened to be short. His body was encased in a white body-suit so tight that you knew at a glance that there was nothing under it but him. There was white-on-white embroidery on the cloth edging the round collar and the slight flare of the long sleeves, and encircling the cutout over his stomach, which revealed his cobblestone abs like a woman showing off her cleavage.

He let the cape and his hair fall back into place. He smiled his full cupid-bow lips at me. They matched the round boyishly handsome face and the one pale blue eye. His eye was a tricircle of blue; cornflower blue around the pupil, sky blue, then a circle of winter sky. The other eye was lost forever under a furrow of scars. Claw marks cut across the upper right quarter of his face. One single claw mark parted an inch from the rest, cutting across otherwise perfect skin to cross from his upper right forehead to cut down the bridge of his nose and the lower left cheek. He'd told me a dozen different stories about how he lost his eye. Great battles, giants, I think I remember a dragon or two. I think it was the scars that made him work so very hard on his body. He was small, but every inch of him was muscled.

I shook my head. "I don't know whether you look like the top of a pornographic wedding cake or a superhero. You could be Ab Boy, or Abdominal Man." I grinned happily.

"A thousand sit-ups a day does wonders for your abs," he said, running a hand over them.

"Everyone needs a hobby, I guess."

"Where is your sword?" Doyle asked.

Rhys looked at him. "The same place yours is. The queen says we do not need them tonight."

Doyle glanced at Frost. "What of you, Frost?"

Rhys answered with a quick smile that made his lovely blue eye gleam. "The queen's weaning him a weapon at a time. She's decreed he has to be unarmed by the time she dresses to go to the throne room."

"I do not think it wise to have her entire guard unarmed," Frost said.

"Nor I," Doyle said, "but she is the queen and we will follow her orders."

Frost's handsome face closed down into tight lines. If he'd been human, he'd have had frown wrinkles by now, but his face was unlined and always would be.

"Frost's clothes are fine for a welcome home banquet, but why are you and Rhys dressed so . . ." I spread my hands helplessly trying to find a phrase that wasn't an insult.

"The queen designed my outfit personally," Rhys said.

"It's lovely," I said.

He grinned. "Just keep saying that as you meet the rest of the guard tonight."

My eyes widened. "Oh, please. She isn't taking hormones again, is she?"

Rhys nodded. "Baby hormones and her sex drive goes into overtime." He looked down at his clothes. "A shame to be dressed up with no place to go."

"Very punny," I said.

He looked up at me with a genuinely unhappy face. He hadn't meant the play on words to be funny. His sad face made the smile fade from mine.

"The queen is our sovereign. She knows best," Frost said.

I laughed before I could stop myself.

The look on Frost's face when he turned made me regret the laugh. I saw those grey eyes unguarded for a split second, and what I saw in them was pain. I watched him rebuild his walls, watched his eyes close down, so that nothing showed again. But I'd seen what lay beyond his careful facade, his expensive clothes, his fastidious attention to detail—his rigorous morality and his arrogance. Some of it was real, but some of it was a mask to keep things locked away.

I'd never liked Frost, but having that one glimpse meant I couldn't dislike him anymore. Damn.

"We will speak no more of this," he said. He turned and moved down the hallway, back the way they'd come. "The queen awaits your presence." He walked away without looking back to see if we were following.

Rhys came up beside me. He slid an arm across my shoulders and hugged me. "I'm glad you're back."

I leaned into him briefly. "Thanks, Rhys."

He gave me a small shake. "I missed you, Green-eyes."

Rhys even more than Galen spoke modern English. He loved slang. His favorite author was Dashiell Hammett; his favorite movie, The Maltese Falcon with Humphrey Bogart. Rhys had a house outside the mound city. He had electricity and a television set. I'd spent quite a few weekends at his house. He'd introduced me to old films, and when I was sixteen we'd gone to a film noir festival at the Tivoli in St. Louis. He'd dressed in a fedora and a trench coat. He'd even found me period clothes so I could hang on his arm like a femme fatale.

Rhys had made it clear on that trip that he thought of me as more than a little sister. Nothing we could get killed over, but enough that it was a real date. After that, my aunt made sure we didn't spend much time together. Galen and I teased each other unmercifully in a very sexual way, but the queen seemed to trust Galen, as did I. Neither of us quite trusted Rhys.

Rhys offered me his arm.

Doyle stepped up to my other side. I thought he would offer his own arm so that I would be wedged between them. Instead, he said, "Go down the hallway and wait for us."

Frost would have argued or even refused, but not Rhys. "You are the captain of the Guard," he said. It was the answer of a good soldier. He walked around the corner and Doyle moved, moving me with him, a hand on my arm, to watch him move far enough away not to overhear us. Then Doyle edged us back, out of sight of Rhys.

His hand tightened on my upper arm. "What else are you carrying?"

"You trust me to just tell you?" I asked.

"If you give me your word, I will take it," he said.

"I left in danger of my life, Doyle. I need to be able to protect myself."

His hand tightened, and he gave a small shake. "It is my job to protect the court, especially the queen."

"And it's my job to protect myself," I said.

He lowered his voice even further. "No, that is my job. The job of all the Guard."

I shook my head. "No, you are the Queen's Guard. The King's Guard protects Cel. There is no Guard for the princess, Doyle. I was raised very aware of that."

"You always had your contingent of bodyguards, as did your father."

"And look how much that helped him," I said.

He grabbed my other arm, drawing me to tiptoe. "I want you to survive, Meredith. Take what she gives you tonight. Do not try to harm her."

"Or what? You'll kill me?"

His hands relaxed, and he set me down flat-footed on the stones. "Give me your word that that was your only weapon and I will believe you."

Staring up into his so sincere face, I couldn't do it. I couldn't lie to him, not if I had to give my word about it. I looked at the floor, then back up at his face. "Ferghus's Balls."

He smiled. "I take it that means you have other weapons."

"Yes, but I can't be here unarmed, Doyle. I can't."

"You will have one of us with you at all times tonight—that I can guarantee."

"The queen has been very careful tonight, Doyle. I may not like Frost, but to an extent I trust him. She's made sure every guard I meet is one I either trust or like, but there are twenty-seven queen's guardsmen, another twenty-seven king's guardsmen. I trust maybe half a dozen of them, ten at the outside. The rest of them frighten me, or have in the past actively hurt me. I am not walking around here unarmed."

"You know I can take them from you," he said.

I nodded. "I know."

"Tell me what you have, Meredith. We'll go from there."

I told him everything I was carrying. I half expected him to insist on searching me himself, but he didn't. He took me at my word. It made me glad I hadn't held anything back.

"Understand this, Meredith. I am the queen's bodyguard before I am yours. If you try to harm her, I will take action."

"Am I allowed to defend myself?" I asked.

He thought about that for a moment. "I . . . I would not have you killed simply because you stayed your hand for fear of me. You are mortal and our queen is not. You are the more fragile of the two." He licked his lips, shook his head. "Let us hope that it does not come down to a choice between the two of you. I do not think that she plans you violence tonight."

"What my dear aunt plans and what comes to pass isn't always the same thing. We all know that."

He shook his head again. "Perhaps." He offered me his arm. "Shall we go?"

I took his arm lightly, and he led me around the corner to the patiently waiting Rhys. Rhys watched us walk toward him, and there was a seriousness to his face that I didn't like. He was thinking about something.

"You'll hurt yourself thinking that hard, Rhys," I said.

He smiled, lowering his eye, but when his gaze came back up it was still serious. "What are you up to, Merry?"

The question startled me. I didn't try to keep the surprise off my face. "My only plan for the evening is to survive and not get hurt. That's all."

His eyes narrowed. "I believe you." But his voice sounded uncertain, as if he really wasn't sure he believed me at all. Then he smiled, and said, "I offered her my arm first, Doyle. You're cutting in on my action."

Doyle started to say something, but I got there first. "I've got two arms, Rhys."

His smile widened to a grin. He offered me his arm, and I took it. As I slid my hand over his sleeve, I realized it was my right—the one the ring was on. But the ring didn't react to Rhys. It lay quiet, just a pretty piece of silver.

Rhys saw it, eyes widening. "That's . . ."

"Yes, it is," Doyle said, quietly.

"But . . ." Rhys began.

"Yes," Doyle said.

"What?" I asked.

"All in the queen's good time," Doyle said.

"Mysteries make my head hurt," I said.

Rhys did his best Bogart impression. "Then buy a bottle of aspirin, baby, because the night is young."

I looked at him. "Bogart never said that in a movie."

"No," Rhys said in his normal voice. "I was ad-libbing."

I gave his arm a little squeeze. "I think I missed you."

"I know I missed you. No one else at court knows what the hell film noir means."

"I most certainly do," said Doyle.

We both looked at him.

"It means dark film, correct?"

Rhys and I looked at each other and started to laugh. We walked down the hallway to the echoes of our own laughter. Doyle didn't join in. He kept saying things like, "It means dark film, doesn't it?"

It made the last few yards to my aunt's private chambers almost fun.

Chapter 27

ONCE THE DOUBLE DOORS OPENED, THE STONE CHANGED. MY
aunt's chamber, my queen's chamber, was formed of black
stone. A shiny, nearly glasslike stone that looked as if it
should shatter at a heavy touch. You could strike it with steel
and all you got were colored sparks. It looked like obsidian,
but it was infinitely stronger.

Frost stood as close to the door leading into the room as he
could, and as far away from the queen. He stood very straight,
a shining silver figure in all that blackness, but there was
something about the way he held himself that said he was
near the door for a reason—a quick getaway, maybe.

The bed was against the far wall, though it was so covered
in sheets, blankets, and even furs that it was hard to say whether
it was a bed or merely a gigantic pile of covers. There was a
man in the bed, a young man. His hair was summer blond, cut
long on top and short halfway down, a skater's cut. His body
was tanned a soft gold from the summer or maybe a tanning
bed. One slender arm was flung outward into space, hand limp.
He seemed deeply asleep and terribly young. If he was under
eighteen, it was illegal in any state, because my aunt was fey
and the humans didn't trust us with their children.

The queen rose from the far side of him, emerging slowly
from the nest of covers and a spill of black fur that was only a
little blacker than the hair that swept back from her pale face.
She'd pulled the hair atop her head until it seemed to form a
black crown, except for three long curls trailing down her
back. The bodice of the dress looked very much like a black

vinyl merry widow with two thin lines of sheer black cloth that graced her white shoulders more than covered them. The skirt was full and thick, spilling behind her in a short train; it looked like shiny leather but moved like cloth. Her arms were encased in leather gloves that went the entire length of her arm. Her lips were red, her eye makeup dark and perfect. Her eyes were three different shades of grey, from charcoal, to storm cloud, to a pale winter's sky. The last color was a grey so pale that it looked white. Set in the dark makeup, her eyes were extraordinary.

Once upon a time, the queen had been able to dress herself in spiderwebs, darkness, shadows—bits and pieces of things she governed over would form clothing at her will. But now she was stuck with designer clothes and her own personal tailor. It was just one more sign of how far we'd fallen in power. My uncle, the king of the Seelie Court, could still clothe himself in light and illusion. Some thought it proved the Seelie Court was stronger than the Unseelie Court. Anyone who thought that was careful not to say it in front of Aunt Andais.

Her standing had revealed a second man, though he was sidhe and not mortal. It was Eamon, the royal consort. His hair was black and fell in soft, thick waves around his white face. His eyes were heavy-lidded either from sleep . . . or other things.

Frost and Rhys hurried to the queen's side. They each took a leather-clad hand. They braced her at hand and elbow and lifted her over the blond man. The black skirt swirled around her, giving a glimpse of layers of black petticoats, and a pair of black patent leather sandals that left most of her foot bare. As they lifted her and set her gracefully on the floor, I half expected music to begin and dancers to appear from nowhere. My aunt was certainly capable of the illusion.

I dropped to one knee, and my dress had enough give to make the gesture look graceful. The material would spring back into place once I stood, which was one of the reasons I'd chosen it. The garter was pressed in outline against the material, but all you could tell under the burgundy cloth was that I was wearing at least one garter—the knife didn't show. I didn't bow my head yet. The queen was putting on a show. She wanted to be watched.

Queen Andais was a tall woman even by today's standards: six feet. Her skin glowed like polished alabaster. The perfect black line of eyebrows and the thick black of her lashes were an almost startling contrast.

I bowed my head at last because it was expected. I kept my head bowed low so that all I could see was the floor and my own leg. I heard her skirt slither across the floor. Her heels made sharp sounds as they passed from throw rug to stone floor. Why she didn't get wall-to-wall carpet escaped me. The petti-coats crinkled and hissed together as she walked toward me, and I knew they were crinoline, scratchy and uncomfortable next to the skin.

Finally, a spill of black skirt showed on the floor at my foot. Her voice was a low, rich contralto. "Greetings, Princess Mere-dith NicEssus, Child of Peace, Besaba's Bane, my brother's child."

I kept my head bowed, and would until told otherwise. She had not called me niece, though she had acknowledged our kinship. It was a slight insult not to name my familial rela-tionship to her, but until she named me niece I couldn't name her my aunt. "Greetings, Queen Andais, Queen of Air and Darkness, Lover of White Flesh, Sister of Essus, my father. I have come from the lands to the west at your request. What would you have of me?"

"I've never understood how you do that," she said.

I kept my gaze on the floor. "What, my queen?"

"How you can say exactly the right words with exactly the right tone of voice and still sound insincere, as if you find it all terribly, terribly tiresome."

"My apologies if I offend you, my queen." That was as safe an answer to the charge as I could make because I did find it all terribly, terribly tiresome. I just hadn't meant for it to show so clearly in my voice. I stayed kneeling, head bowed, waiting for her to tell me I could stand. Even two-inch heels were not meant for prolonged kneeling in this position. They made it hard not to wobble. If Andais wished, she could leave me just as I was for hours, until my entire leg fell asleep except for a point of agony on the knee where nearly all my weight rested. My record for kneeling had been six hours after I'd broken curfew when I was seventeen. It would have been longer, but I either fell asleep or fainted, I really wasn't sure which.

"You cut your hair," she said.

I was starting to memorize the texture of the floor. "Yes, my queen."

"Why did you cut it?"

"Having hair nearly to your ankles marks you as high court sidhe. I've been passing as human."

I felt her lean over me, her hand lifting my hair, running her fingers through it. "So you sacrificed your hair."

"It is much easier to care for at this length," I said, voice as neutral as I could make it.

"Get up, niece of mine."

I rose slowly, carefully in the high heels. "Thank you, Aunt Andais." Standing, I was woefully short compared to her tall slender presence. With the heels she was over a foot taller than me. Most of the time I'm not that aware that I'm short, but my aunt tried to make me aware of it. She tried to make me feel small.

I looked up at her and fought not to shake my head and sigh. Next to Cel, Andais was my least favorite part of the Unseelie Court. I looked up at her with calm eyes and fought very hard not to sigh out loud.

"Am I boring you?" she asked.

"No, Aunt Andais, of course not." My expression had not betrayed me. I'd had years to practice the polite blank expression. But Andais had had centuries to perfect her study of people. She couldn't truly read our minds, but her awareness of the slightest change in body language, breath, was almost as good as true telepathy.

Andais stared down at me, a small frown forming between

her perfect brows. "Eamon, take our pet and have him dress you for the banquet, in the other room."

The royal consort pulled a purple brocade robe from the tangle of bed clothes, slipping it over his body before he climbed out of the bed. The sash had been tied behind the back of the robe so it no longer closed over his body. His hair fell in a tangle of black waves nearly to his ankles. The dark purple of the robe didn't so much hide his body as act as a frame for the pale glimpses you got as he moved across the floor.

He gave a small nod as he passed me. I nodded back. He laid a gentle kiss on Andais's cheek and walked toward the small door that led into the smaller bedroom and bathroom beyond. One modern convenience that the court had adopted was indoor plumbing.

The blonde sat on the edge of the bed, naked as well. He stood stretching his body in a long tanned line of flesh. His eyes flicked to me as he did it. When he realized I was watching, he smiled. The smile was predatory, lascivious, aggressive. The human "pets" always misunderstood the casual nudity of the guards.

The blonde stalked toward us putting a swing in his step. The pun was intended. It wasn't the nudity that made me uncomfortable. It was the look in his eyes.

"I take it he's new," I said.

Andais watched the man with cool eyes. He had to be very new not to realize what that look meant. She was not happy with him, not happy at all.

"Tell him what you think of his display, niece." Her voice was very quiet, but there was an undertone to it that you could almost taste on your tongue like something bitter in among the sweet.

I looked him over from his bare feet to his fresh haircut and every inch in between. He grinned as I did it, drifting closer to me, as if the look were an invitation. I decided to take the smile out of his step.

"He's young, he's pretty, but Eamon is better endowed."

That stopped the mortal and made him frown, the smile returning to his face but uncertain now.

"I don't believe he knows what 'endowed' means," Andais said.

I looked at her. "You never did choose them for their intellect," I said.

"One does not talk to one's pet, Meredith. You should know that by now."

"If I want a pet, I'll get a dog. This . . ." I motioned at the man, "is a little too high-maintenance for me."

The man was frowning, looking from one to the other of us, obviously not happy and also confused. Andais had broken one of my cardinal rules for sex. No matter how careful you are, you can end up pregnant. That's what sex is designed to do, after all. So, never sleep with someone who's mean or stupid, and ugly is a judgment call, because all three may breed true. The blonde was cute but not cute enough to make up for the frowning puzzlement on his face.

"Go with Eamon. Help him dress for the banquet," Andais said.

"May I come to the ball tonight, my lady?" he asked.

"No," she said. She turned back to me as if he ceased to exist.

He looked at me again, and there was a sullen anger there. He knew I'd insulted him but wasn't quite sure how. The look made me shiver. There were people at court a lot less pretty than her new "pet" that I'd have slept with first.

"You disapprove," she said.

"It would be presumptuous of me to approve or disapprove of the actions of my queen," I said.

She laughed. "There you go again, saying exactly what you should say but making it sound like an insult all the same."

"Forgive me," I said and started to drop back to one knee.

She stopped me with a hand on my arm. "Don't, Meredith, don't. The night will not last forever, and you are staying at a hotel tonight. So we haven't much time." She withdrew her hand without hurting me. "We certainly don't have time to play games, do we?"

I looked at her, studied her smiling face, and tried to decide if she were sincere or if it was a trap of some kind. I finally said, "If you wish to play games, my queen, then I am honored to be included. If there is business to be done, then I am honored to be included in that, as well, Aunt Andais."

She laughed again. "Oh, good girl, to remind me that you are my niece, my blood kin. You fear my mood, distrust it, so you remind me of your value to me. Very good."

It didn't seem to be a question, so I said nothing because she was absolutely right.

She looked at my face, but said, "Frost."

He came to her, head bowed. "My queen."

"Go to your room and change into the clothes that I had made for you to wear tonight."

He dropped to one knee. "The clothes did not . . . fit, my queen."

I watched the light die in her eyes, leaving them as cold and empty as a white winter sky. "Yes," she said, "they did. They were literally tailor-made for you." She grabbed a handful of his silver hair and jerked his face up to meet her gaze. "Why are you not wearing them?"

He licked his lips. "My queen, I found the other clothing uncomfortable."

She put her head to one side the way a crow looks at a hanging man's eyes before it plucks them out. "Uncomfortable, uncomfortable. Do you hear that, Meredith? He found the clothes I had made for him uncomfortable." She pulled his head backward until his neck was a long exposed line of flesh. I could see the pulse in his neck jump against his skin.

"I heard you, Aunt Andais," I said, and this time my voice was as neutral as I could make it, bland and empty as a new penny. Someone was about to get hurt, and I didn't want it to be me. Frost was a fool. I'd have worn the clothes.

"What do you think we should do with our disobedient Frost?" she asked.

"Have him go to his room and change into the clothes," I said.

She pulled his head back until his spine bowed and I knew she could snap his neck with just a little more pressure. "That is hardly punishment enough, niece. He disobeyed a direct order of mine. That is not allowed."

I tried to think of something Andais would find amusing, but wouldn't actually be painful for Frost. My mind went blank. I'd never been good at this particular game. Then I had an idea.

"You said we wouldn't be playing any more games tonight, Aunt Andais. The night is short."

She released Frost so abruptly that he fell to the floor on all fours. He stayed kneeling, head bowed, silver hair hiding his face like a convenient curtain.

"So I did," Andais said. "Doyle."

Doyle came to her side, bowing his head. "M'lady?"

She looked at him, and the look was enough. He dropped to the floor onto one knee. The cloak spilled out around him like black water. He stayed kneeling beside Frost, so close their bodies nearly touched.

She put a hand on both their heads, a light touch this time. "Such a pretty pair, don't you think?"

"Yes," I said.

"Yes, what?" she said.

"Yes, they are a pretty pair, Aunt Andais," I said.

She nodded as if pleased. "I charge you, Doyle, to take Frost to his room and see that he puts on the clothes I had made for him. Bring him to the banquet in those clothes or deliver him over to Ezekial for torture."

"As m'lady wishes, so shall it be done," Doyle said. He stood, drawing Frost to his feet, a hand on the taller man's arm.

They both began to back toward the door, heads bowed. Doyle flashed me a look as they moved away. He might have been apologizing for leaving me with her, without him, or warning against something. I couldn't decipher the look. But he left the room with my gun still in his waistband. I'd have liked to have had the gun.

Rhys moved so he'd be by the door like a good guard.

Andais watched him move the way cats watch birds, but what she said was mild enough, "Wait outside the door, Rhys. I wish to speak with my niece in private."

The surprise showed on his face. He glanced at me, the look on his face almost asking my permission.

"Do as you are told—or do you wish to join the others in Ezekial's workplace?"

Rhys bowed his head. "No, my lady. I will do as I am told."

"Get out," she said.

He left with one more quick glance for me, but he closed the door behind him. The room was suddenly very, very quiet. The sound of my aunt's dress moving along the floor was loud in the stillness, like the dry rustling scales of some great serpent. She walked to the far end of the room where steps led to a heavy black curtain. She flicked the curtain aside to reveal a heavy wooden table with a carved chair at one side and a backless stool at the other. There was a chess game laid out on the round table, the heavy pieces worn smooth from centuries of hands shifting them across the marble surface. There were literally grooves worn in the marble board like paths worn by tramping feet.

Against the rounded wall of the large alcove was a wooden gun case full of rifles and handguns. There were two crossbows on the wall above the gun case. I knew the arrows were underneath in the closed doors of the bottom of the case, along with the ammunition. There was a morning star like a heavy spiked ball on a chain and a mace mounted to one side of the gun case. They were crossed like the crossed swords on the other side of the case. A huge shield with Andais's livery of raven, owl, and red rose on its surface was underneath the mace and morning star. Eamon's shield was underneath the crossed swords. There were chains in the wall set for wrist and ankle on either side. There were hooks above the chains where a whip lay coiled like a waiting snake. A smaller whip hung above the right-hand side's chains. I would have called it a cat-o'-nine-tails, but it had many more tails than that, each one weighted with a small iron ball or a steel hook.

"I see your hobbies haven't changed," I said. I tried for neutral, but my voice betrayed me. Sometimes when she swept back that curtain, you played chess. Sometimes, you didn't.

"Come, Meredith, sit. Let us talk." She sat in the high-backed chair, spilling the train of her dress over one arm so it wouldn't wrinkle. She motioned me to the stool. "Sit down, Niece. I won't bite." She smiled, then gave an abrupt laugh. "Not yet, anyway."

It was as close as I was going to get to a promise that she wouldn't hurt me—yet. I perched on the high, backless stool, the heels of my shoes through one of the spindles to help keep my balance. Sometimes, I think Andais won chess matches simply because the other person's back gave out.

I touched the edge of the heavy marble board. "My father taught me to play chess on the twin of this board," I said.

"You do not have to remind me, yet again, that you are my brother's daughter. I mean you no harm tonight."

I caressed the board and glanced up at her, meeting those pleasant unreliable eyes. "Perhaps I would be less cautious if you didn't say things like 'I mean you no harm tonight.' Perhaps, if you simply said you meant me no harm." I made it half question, half statement.

"Oh, no, Meredith. To say that would be too close to lying, and we do not lie, not outright. We may talk until you think that black is white and the moon is made of green cheese, but we do not lie."

I said, as evenly as I could, "So you do mean me harm, just not tonight."

"I will not harm you if you don't force it upon me."

I looked at her then, frowning. "I don't understand, Aunt Andais."

"Have you ever wondered why I made my beautiful men celibate?"

The question was so unexpected that I simply stared at her for a second or two. I finally closed my mouth and found my voice. "Yes, Aunt, I have wondered." Actually it had been the great debate for centuries: why had she done it?

"For centuries the men of our court spread their seed far and wide. There were many half-breeds but fewer and fewer full-blooded fey. So I forced them to conserve their energies."

I looked at her. "Then why not allow them access to the women of the high court?"

She settled back against her chair, leather-clad hands caressing the carved arms. "Because I wanted my bloodline to continue, not theirs. There was a time when I would have preferred you dead than risk you inheriting my throne."

I met her pale eyes. "Yes, Aunt Andais."

"Yes, what?"

"Yes, I knew."

"I saw the mongrels taking over the entire court. The humans had chased us underground and now their very blood was corrupting our court. We were being outbred by them."

"It is my understanding, Aunt, that humans have always outbred us. Something to do with the fact that they're mortal."

"Essus told me that you were his daughter. That he loved you. He also told me that you would make a fine queen someday. I laughed at him." She watched my face. "I am not laughing now, Niece."

I blinked at her. "I don't understand, Aunt."

"You have Essus's blood in your veins. The blood of my family. I would rather have some of my blood continue than none of it. I want our bloodline to continue, Meredith."

"I'm not sure what you mean by 'ours', Aunt?" Though I had a frightening feeling that I did.

"Ours, ours, Meredith, yours, mine, Cel's."

The addition of my cousin in the mix made my stomach clench tight. It was not unknown among the fey to marry close relatives. If that was what she had in mind, I was in very deep trouble. Sex was not a fate worse than death. Sex with my cousin Cel just might be.

I looked down at the chess pieces because I didn't trust myself to guard my expression. I would *not* sleep with Cel.

"I want our bloodline to continue, Meredith, at any cost."

I finally looked up, face blank. "What would that cost be, Aunt Andais?"

"Nothing so unpleasant as you seem to be thinking. Really, Meredith, I am not your enemy."

"If I may be so bold, my aunt, neither are you my friend."

She nodded. "That is very true. You mean nothing to me but a vessel to continue our line with."

I couldn't keep the smile off my face.

"Was that funny?" she asked.

"No, Aunt Andais, it was most certainly not funny."

"Fine, let me speak plainly. I gave you the ring on your finger from my own hand."

I stared at her. Her face seemed innocent of evil intent. She really didn't seem to know anything about the assassination attempt in the car. "The gift is most appreciated," I said, but even to me the words sounded less than sincere.

Either she didn't hear it or she ignored it. "Galen and Barinthus told me the ring lives once more upon your hand. I am more pleased by that than you can know, Meredith."

"Why?" I asked.

"Because if the ring had remained quiet on your hand it would mean you were barren. That the ring lives is a sign that you are fruitful."

"Why does it react to everyone that I touch?"

"Who else has it reacted to besides Galen and Barinthus?" she asked.

"Doyle, Frost."

"Not Rhys?" she asked.

I shook my head. "No."

"Did you touch the silver to his bare skin?"

I started to say yes, then thought about it. "I don't think so. I think I touched only his clothing."

"It must be bare skin," Andais said. "Even a small piece of cloth may stop it." She leaned forward, placing her hands on the tabletop, picking up a captured rook, turning it in her gloved hands. If it had been anyone else, I'd have said she was nervous.

"I am going to rescind my geas of celibacy for my Guard."

"My lady," I said, voice soft with the breath I'd taken. "That is wonderful news." I had better adjectives, but I stopped with wonderful. It was never good to appear too pleased in front of the queen. Though in my head, I wondered why she was telling me first.

"The geas will be lifted for you and you alone, Meredith." She concentrated on the chess piece, not meeting my eyes.

"Excuse me, my lady?" I didn't even try to keep the shock off my face.

She looked up. "I want our bloodline to continue, Meredith. The ring reacts to the guards that are still able to father children. If the ring remains quiet, then do not bother with them. But if the ring reacts, then you may sleep with them. I want you to pick several of the Guard to sleep with. I don't really care who, but within three years I want a child from you, a child of the blood." She set the chess piece down with a thick scraping sound and met my eyes.

I licked my lips and tried to think of a polite way to ask questions. "This is a most generous offer, my queen, but when you say several, what exactly do you mean?"

"I mean that you should pick more than two; three or more at a time."

I stayed quiet for a few seconds, because again I was left with needing information and not wanting to be rude. "Three at a time in what way, my lady?"

She frowned at me. "Oh, Danu's titties, just ask your questions, Meredith!"

"Fine," I said, "when you say three or more at one time, do you mean literally in the bed with me at one time, or just like dating three of them at the same time."

"Any way you wish to interpret it," she said. "Take them into your bed one at a time, or all together, as long as you take them."

"Why must it be three or more at once?"

"Is it such an awful prospect to choose among some of the most beautiful men in the world? To bear a child to one of them and continue our line? How is this so terrible?"

I looked at her, trying to read that beautiful face, and failing. "I approve of letting the men out of their celibacy, but Auntie dearest, do not make me their only avenue. I beg you. They will fall upon each other like starving wolves, not because I am such a prize but because anyone is better than no one."

"That is why I am insisting that you sleep with more than one at a time. You must sleep with most of them before making your choice. That way they'll all feel they've had a chance. Otherwise, you are right. There will be duels until no one is left standing. Make them work at seducing you instead of killing each other."

"I like sex, my queen, and I have no designs upon monogamy, but there are some among your Guard that I can't even speak a civil word to, and sex is a step up from polite small talk."

"I will make you my heir," she said, voice very quiet.

I stared at her so careful, unreadable face. I didn't trust what I'd heard. "Could you repeat that, please, my queen?"

"I will make you my heir," she said.

I stared at her. "And what does my cousin Cel think of that?"

"Whichever one of you gives me a child first, that one shall inherit my throne. Does that not sweeten the pot?"

I stood up, too abruptly, and the stool clanged to the floor. I stared at her for a space of heartbeats. I wasn't sure what to say, because it didn't seem real. "May I humbly point out, Aunt Andais, that I am mortal and you are not. You will surely outlive me by centuries. Even if I bore a child, I would never see the throne."

"I will step down," she said.

Now I knew she was toying with me. It was all some game. It had to be. "You once told my father that being queen was your entire existence. That you loved being queen more than you loved anyone or anything."

"My, you do have a long memory for eavesdropped conversations."

"You always spoke freely in front of me, Aunt, as if I were

one of your dogs. You nearly drowned me when I was six. Now you're telling me that you would abdicate the throne for me. What in the land of the blessed could have changed your mind so completely?"

"Do you remember what Essus's answer to me was that night?" she asked.

I shook my head. "No, my queen."

"Essus said, 'Even if Merry never takes the throne she will be more queen than Cel will ever be a king.' "

"You hit him that night," I said. "I never remembered why."

Andais nodded. "That was why."

"So you're unhappy with your son."

"That is my business," she said.

"If I let you elevate me to coheir with Cel, it will become my business." I had the cuff link in my purse. I thought about showing it to her, but I didn't. Andais had lived in denial of what Cel was, and what he was capable of, for centuries. You spoke against Cel to the queen at your peril. Besides, the cuff link could belong to one of the guards, though I couldn't fathom why, without Cel's urging, any of the guard would want me dead.

"What do you want, Meredith? What do you want that I can give you that would be worth you doing what I ask?"

She was offering me the throne. Barinthus would be so pleased. Was I pleased? "Are you so sure that the court will accept me as queen?"

"I will announce you Princess of Flesh tonight. They will be impressed."

"If they believe it," I said.

"They will if I tell them to," she said.

I looked at her, studied her face. She believed what she said. Andais overestimated herself. But such absolute arrogance was typical of the sidhe.

"Come home, Meredith, you don't belong out there among the humans."

"As you reminded me so very often, Aunt, I am part human."

"Three years ago you were content, happy. You had no plans

to leave us." She settled back in her chair, watching me, letting me stand over her. "I know what Griffin did."

I met her pale gaze for a heartbeat, but couldn't sustain the look. It wasn't pity in her glance. It was the coldness in it, as if she simply wanted to see my reaction, nothing more.

"Do you really think I left the court because of Griffin?" I didn't try and keep the astonishment out of my voice. She couldn't honestly believe I'd left the court over a broken heart.

"The last fight the two of you had was very public."

"I remember the fight, Auntie dearest, but that is not why I left the court. I left because I wasn't going to survive the next duel."

She ignored me. In that moment I realized that she would never believe the worst of her son, not unless forced to beyond any shadow of doubt. I couldn't give her that absolute proof, and without it, I couldn't tell her my suspicions, not without risking myself.

She kept talking about Griffin as if he were the true reason I'd left. "But it was Griffin who began that fight. He, the one who was demanding to know why he wasn't in your bed, in your heart, as before. You'd been chasing him around the court for nights, and now he pursued you. How did you effect such a quick change in him?"

"I refused him my bed." I met her eyes, but there was no amusement in them, just a steady intensity.

"And that was enough to make him pursue you in public like an enraged fishwife?"

"I think he truly believed that I'd forgive him. That I would punish him for a while and then take him back. That last night he finally believed that I meant what I said."

"What did you say?" she asked.

"That he would never be with me again this side of the grave."

Andais looked at me very steadily. "Do you still love him?"

I shook my head. "No."

"But you still have feelings for him." It was not a question.

I shook my head. "Feelings, yes, but nothing good."

"If you still want Griffin, you may have him for another year. If at that time you are not with child, I would ask that you choose someone else."

"I don't want Griffin, not anymore."

"I hear a regret in your voice, Meredith. Are you sure that he is not what you want?"

I sighed, and leaned my hands against the tabletop, staring down at them. I felt hunched and tired. I'd tried very hard not to think about Griff and the fact that I'd see him tonight. "If he could feel for me what I felt for him, if he could truly be as in love with me as I was with him, then I would want him, but he can't. He can't be other than what he is, and neither can I." I looked at her across the small table.

"You may include him in the contest to win your heart, or you may exclude him from the running. It is your decision."

I nodded and stood up straight, no hunching like some kind of wounded rabbit. "Thank you for that, Auntie dearest."

"Why does that fall from your lips like the vilest of insults."

"I mean no insult."

She waved me to silence. "Do not bother, Meredith. There is little affection lost between us. We both know that." She looked me up and down. "Your clothing is acceptable, though not what I would have chosen."

I smiled, but it wasn't a happy smile. "If I'd known I was going to be named heir tonight, I'd have worn the Tommy Hilfiger original."

She laughed and stood with a swish of skirts. "You can purchase an entire new wardrobe, if you like. Or you can have the court tailors design one for you."

"I'm fine as I am," I said. "But thank you for the offer."

"You are an independent thing, Meredith. I've never liked that about you."

"I know," I said.

"If Doyle had told you in the western lands what I planned for you tonight, would you have come willingly, or would you have tried to run?"

I stared at her. "You're naming me heir. You're letting me date the Guard. It's not a fate worse than death, Aunt Andais. Or is there something else you haven't told me about tonight?"

"Pick up the stool, Meredith. Let's leave the room neat, shall we?" She glided down the stone steps to walk toward the door in the opposite wall.

I picked up the stool, but didn't like that she hadn't answered my question. There was more to come.

I called after her before she got to the small door. "Aunt Andais?"

She turned. "Yes, Niece." There was a faintly amused, condescending look on her face.

"If the lust charm that you placed in the car had worked and Galen and I had made love, would you have still killed him and me?"

She blinked, the slight smile fading from her face. "Lust charm? What are you talking about?"

I told her.

She shook her head. "It was not my spell."

I held my hand up so the silver ring glinted. "But the spell used your ring to power itself."

"I give you my word, Meredith, I did not put a spell of any kind in the coach. I merely left the ring in there for you to find, that was all."

"Did you leave the ring, or did you give it to someone to put in the coach?" I asked.

She would not meet my eyes. "I put it there." And I knew she'd lied.

"Does anyone else know that you plan to rescind the order of celibacy where I'm concerned?"

She shook her head, one long black curl sliding over her shoulder. "Eamon knows, but that is all, and he knows how to keep his own counsel."

I nodded. "Yes, he does." My aunt and I looked at each other from across the room, and I watched the idea form in her eyes and spill across her face.

"Someone tried to assassinate you," she said.

I nodded. "If Galen and I had made love and you hadn't lifted the geas, you could have killed me for it. Galen's fate seems to be incidental to it all."

Anger played across her face like candlelight inside glass.

"You know who did it," I said.

"I do not, but I do know who knew that you were going to be named coheir."

"Cel," I said.

"I had to prepare him," she said.

"Yes," I said.

"He did not do this," she said, and for the first time there was something in her voice—the same protest you'll hear in any mother's voice when defending her child.

I simply looked at her and kept my face blank. It was the best I could do, because I knew Cel. He would not simply give up his birthright on the whim of his mother, queen or no.

"What did Cel do to anger you?" I asked.

"I tell you, as I told him, I am not angry with him." But there was too much protest to her voice. For the first time tonight Andais was on the defensive. I liked it.

"Cel didn't believe that, did he?"

"He knows what my motives are," she said.

"Would you care to share those motives with me?" I asked.

She smiled, and it was the first genuine smile I'd seen on her tonight. An almost embarrassed movement of lips. She wagged a gloved finger at me. "No, my motives are my own. I want you to choose someone for your bed tonight. Take them back to the hotel with you, I don't care who, but I want it to begin tonight." The smile was gone. She was her royal self once more, unreadable, self-contained, mysterious and absolutely obvious all at the same time.

"You never have understood me, Aunt."

"And what, pray, does that mean?"

"It means, Auntie dearest, that if you had left off that last order, I would probably have taken someone to my bed tonight. But being commanded to do it makes me feel like a royal whore. I don't like it."

She settled her skirts so the train glided behind her and walked toward me. As she moved, her power began to unfold, flitting around the room like invisible sparks to bite along my skin. The first two times I jumped, then I stood there and let her power eat over my skin. I was wearing steel, but a few knives had never been enough for me to withstand her magic. It had to be my own newfound powers that kept it from being so much worse.

Her eyes narrowed as she came to stand in front of me. With me standing on the small raised platform, we were eye-to-eye. Her magic pushed out from her like a moving wall of force. I had to brace my feet as if I were standing against wind. The small burning bites had turned into a constant ache like standing just inside an oven, not quite touching the glowing surface, but knowing that one tiny shove and your skin would burn and crisp.

"Doyle said your powers had grown, but I didn't quite believe it. But there you stand before me, and I must accept that you are true sidhe, at last." She put her foot on the lowest step. "But never forget that I am queen here, Meredith, not you. No matter how powerful you become, you will never rival me."

"I would never presume otherwise, my lady," I said. My voice was just a touch shaky.

Her magic pushed at me. I couldn't draw a good breath. My eyes blinked as if I were looking into the sun. I fought to stand and not to give ground. "My lady, tell me what you wish me to do and I will do it. I have not offered challenge in any way."

She came up another step, and this time I did give ground. I did not want her to touch me. "Simply by standing in the face of my power you challenge me."

"If you wish me to kneel, I will kneel. Tell me what you want, my queen, and I will give it to you." I did not want to get into a contest of magic with her. I would lose. I knew that. It left me with nothing to prove.

"Make the ring have life on my finger, Niece."

I didn't know what to say to that. I finally held my hand out to her. "Do you want the ring back?"

"More than you will ever know, but it is yours now, Niece. I wish you joy of it." That last sounded more like a curse than a blessing.

I went to the far edge of the table, gripping it to steady myself against the growing pressure of her magic. "What do you want from me?"

She never answered me. Andais made a gesture with both hands toward me and that pressure became a force that shoved me backward. I was airborne for a second until my back met the wall, and my head hit a heartbeat later. I kept my feet through a shower of grey and white flowers on the edge of my vision.

When my vision cleared, Andais was standing in front of me with a knife in her hand. She pressed the tip of it against the small hollow at the base of my throat, pressed the tip of the blade until I felt it bite into my skin. She put her finger against the wound and came away with a trembling drop of my blood clinging to her leather-clad finger. She held her finger upside down so the drop fell quivering to the floor.

"Know this, niece of mine. Your blood is my blood, and that is the only reason I care what happens to you. I do not care if you like what I have planned for you or not. I need you to continue our bloodline, but if you will not help do that, then I do not need you." She withdrew the knife very slowly, drawing it back an inch or two. She laid the flat of the blade against my face, the point dangerously close to my eye.

I could taste my pulse on my tongue, and I'd forgotten to breathe. Looking into her face, I knew that she would kill me, just like that.

"That which is not useful to me is discarded, Meredith." She pressed the flat of the blade into my flesh so that when I blinked the tip of the knife brushed my eyelashes. "You will pick someone to sleep with tonight. I don't care who. Since you have invoked virgin rights, you are free to go back to Los Angeles, but you will have to pick some of my Guard to take with you. So look at them tonight, Meredith, with those emerald-green-and-gold eyes of yours, those Seelie eyes of yours, and choose." She put her face next to mine, so close that she could have kissed me. She whispered the last words into my mouth. "Fuck one of them tonight, Meredith, because if you don't, tomorrow night you will entertain the court with a group of my choosing."

She smiled, and it was the smile that touched her face when she had thought of something wicked, and painful. "At least one that you choose must be enough my creature to spy for me against you. If you go back to Los Angeles."

My voice came out the barest of whispers. "Must I sleep with your spy?"

"Yes," she said. The blade point moved a fraction closer, so close it blurred in my vision, and I fought not to blink, because if I did the point would pierce my eyelid. "Is that all right with you, Niece? Is it all right with you that I make you sleep with my spy?"

I said the only thing I could say. "Yes, Aunt Andais."

"You'll choose your little harem tonight at the banquet?"

My eyes weren't fluttering. They were twitching with the need to blink. "Yes, Aunt Andais."

"You'll sleep with someone tonight before you fly back to your western lands?"

I widened my eyes and concentrated on her face, on looking at her face. The knife was a blur of steel taking up most of my right eye's vision, but I could still see, still see her face looming above me like a painted moon.

"Yes," I whispered.

She drew the knife from my face and said, "There. Was that so difficult?"

I sagged against the wall, eyes shut. I kept them closed because I couldn't keep the rage out of them, and I didn't want Andais to see it. I wanted out of this room, just out of this room, and away from her.

"I'll call Rhys to escort you to the banquet. You look a bit shaken." She laughed.

I opened my eyes, blinking to clear the tears that had gathered from being forced not to blink. She was walking down the steps.

"I'll send Rhys to you, though perhaps with the spell in the coach you might need another guard. I will think on who to send to your side." She was nearly to the outer door when she turned and said, "And who shall my spy be? I shall try to pick someone beautiful, someone who is good in bed, so that the chore may not be too onerous."

"I don't sleep with stupid men or mean-spirited ones," I said.

"The first does not limit the field too terribly much but the last . . . someone generous of spirit, that is a tall order." Her smile brightened—obviously she'd thought of someone. "He might do."

"Who?" I asked.

"Don't you love surprises, Meredith?"

"Not particularly."

"Well, I do. I like surprises a great deal. He will be my treat to you. He's scrumptious in bed, or was sixty—or is it ninety years?—ago. Yes, I think he'll do nicely."

I didn't bother to ask who again. "How can you be sure that he'll spy for you once he's in Los Angeles?"

She paused with her hand on the door handle. "Because he knows me, Meredith. He knows what I'm capable of, both of pleasure and of pain." With that she swung open the double doors and had Rhys come back in the room.

He glanced from her to me. His eyes widened just a touch, but that was all. His face was carefully blank as he walked to me and offered me his arm. I took it gratefully. It seemed to take a very long time to walk across that floor to the open door. I wanted to run to it and keep running. Rhys patted my hand, as if he felt the tension in my body. I knew he'd seen the small wound on my neck. He could make his own guesses as to how it got there.

We made it to the door, then out into the hallway beyond. My shoulders relaxed just a touch.

Andais called after us, "Have fun, children. We'll see you at the banquet." She closed the doors behind us with a sharp bang that made me jump.

Rhys started to stop. "Are you all right?"

I clutched his arm and pulled him into a walk again. "Get me away from here, Rhys. Just get me away from here."

He didn't ask questions. He just led me down the hallway away from there.

Chapter 28

WE WALKED BACK THE WAY WE HAD COME, BUT THE HALL WAS straight now and narrower—a different hallway altogether. I glanced behind us, and there was no double door. The queen's rooms were elsewhere. For a moment I was safe. I started to shiver and couldn't stop.

Rhys hugged me with both his arms, pressing me to his chest. I sank against him, arms sliding around his waist, under his cloak. He stroked my hair from my face. "Your skin is cold to the touch. What did she do, Merry?" He raised my head back, gently, so he could see my face while I clung to him. "Talk to me," he said, voice soft.

I shook my head. "She offered me everything, Rhys, everything a little sidhe could want. The trouble is, I don't trust it."

"What are you talking about?" he asked.

I pulled away from him then. "This." I touched my throat where the blood was drying. "I am mortal, Rhys. Just because I'm offered the moon doesn't mean I'll survive to put it in my pocket."

There was a look on his face that was gentle, but I was also suddenly aware of how very much older he was than I. His face was still young, but the look in his eye was not. "Is that the worst of the injuries?"

I nodded.

He reached out and touched the spot of blood. It didn't even hurt when he touched it. It really wasn't much of a wound. It was so hard to explain that what was hurting didn't show on my skin. The queen was living in denial about what Cel was, but I wasn't. He'd never share the throne with me:

One of us would have to be dead before the other sat on the throne.

"Did she threaten you?" Rhys asked.

I nodded again.

"You look totally spooked, Merry. What did she say to you in there?"

I stared at him and didn't want to tell him. It was as if saying it out loud would make it more real. But it was more than that. It was the fact that if Rhys knew, he wouldn't be totally displeased. "It's sort of good news, bad news," I said.

"What's the good news?"

I told him about being named coheir.

He hugged me tight and hard. "That's wonderful news, Merry. What could possibly be bad news after that?"

I pulled back from the hug. "Do you really think Cel will let me live long enough to displace him? He was behind the attempts on my life three years ago, and he didn't have nearly this good a reason for wanting me dead."

The smile faded from his face. "You bear the queen's mark now—even Cel would not dare kill you. It's death by the queen's mercy if anyone harms you now."

"She stood in there and told me that I left the court because of Griffin. I tried to tell her that I hadn't left because of a broken heart, that I'd left because of the duels." I shook my head. "She talked over me, Rhys, like I wasn't saying anything. She is in very major denial, and I don't think my death would change that."

"You mean her baby boy would never do such a thing," he said.

"Exactly. Besides do you really think he'd risk his own lily-white neck? He'll have someone else do it if he can—then they'll be the ones in danger, not him."

"It's our job to protect you, Merry. We're good at our job."

I laughed, but it wasn't a good laugh, more stress than humor. "Aunt Andais has changed your job description, Rhys."

"What do you mean?"

"Let's walk while I tell you. I feel the need for more distance between myself and our queen."

He offered me his arm again. "As my lady wishes." He smiled when he said it, and I went to him, but I slid my arm around his waist instead of taking his arm. He stiffened, surprised for a second, then slid his arm across my shoulders. We walked down the hallway, arms wrapped around each other. I was still cold, as if some inner warmth had been extinguished.

There are men that I can't walk arm in arm with, as if our bodies have different rhythms. Rhys and I moved down the hallway like two halves of a whole. I realized that I simply couldn't believe that I had permission to touch him. It didn't seem real to suddenly be given the keys to the kingdom.

Rhys stopped, turning me in his arms, until he could rub his hands up and down my arms. "You're still shivering."

"Not as badly as before," I said.

He planted a soft kiss on my forehead. "Come on, honey bun, tell me what the Wicked Witch of the East did to you?"

I smiled. "Honey bun?"

He grinned. "Honey bear? Honey child? Snookums?"

I laughed. "Worse and worse."

His smile faded. He glanced at the ring lying against the whiteness of his sleeve. "Doyle said the ring came to life for him. Is that true?"

I glanced at the heavy silver octagonal band and nodded. "It lies quiet against my arm."

I looked up into his face. He looked . . . forlorn. "The queen used to let the ring choose her consort," he said.

"It's reacted to almost every guard I've touched tonight."

"Except me." His voice was so thick with regret that I couldn't let it stand.

"It has to touch bare skin," I said.

He started to reach for my hand and the ring. I pulled away from him. "Please don't."

"What's wrong, Merry?" he asked.

The light had faded to a dim twilight glow. Cobwebs draped the hallway like great shining silver curtains. Pale white spiders larger than my two hands together hid in the webs like round bloated ghosts.

"Because even at sixteen I was the one who said stop. You should have known better."

"A little slap and tickle and I'm exiled from the game forever. Baby, that is cruel."

"No, it's practical. I don't want to end my life nailed to a Saint Andrew's cross." Of course, now that didn't apply. I could tell Rhys and we could do it up against a wall right this minute, and there would be no penalties. Or so Andais said. But I didn't trust my aunt. She'd told only me that the celibacy had been lifted. I only had her word that Eamon knew, and he was her consort, her creature. What if I threw Rhys up against a wall, and then she changed her mind? It wasn't going to be real, to be safe, until she announced it in public. Then, and only then, would I really believe it.

A large white spider came to the edge of the webbing. The head was at least three inches across. I was going to have to pass right under the thing.

"You see one mortal woman tortured to death for seducing a guard and you remember it for the rest of your life. Long memory," Rhys said.

"I saw what she had her pet torturer do to the guard who transgressed, Rhys. I think your memory is too short." I stopped him, pulling on his arm, just short of the heavy-bodied spider. I could call will-o'-the-wisps, but the spiders weren't impressed by them.

"Can you call something stronger than a will-o'-the-wisp?" I asked. I stared at that waiting spider, its body bigger around than my fist. The spider webs above my head seemed suddenly heavier, weighed down with the round bloated bodies like a net full of fish about to spill on my head.

Rhys looked at me, face puzzled, then he looked up as if just seeing the thick webs, the scurrying sense of movement. "You never did like the spiders."

"No," I said, "I never did like the spiders."

Rhys moved toward the spider that seemed to be lying in wait for me. He left me standing in the middle of the hall, listening to the heavy scurrying and watching the webs waver above my head. He did nothing that I could see. He simply touched a finger to the spider's abdomen. The spider started to scurry away, then it stopped abruptly, and started to shake, legs spasming frantically. It writhed and jerked, tearing a partial hole in the webbing, and it dangled helplessly half in and half out of the webbing.

I could hear dozens of the things running for safety in a soft clattering retreat. The webs swayed like an upside-down ocean with the rush of their flight. Lord and Lady, there had to be hundreds of them.

The spider's white body began to shrivel, falling in upon itself as if some great hand were crushing it. That fat white body turned to a black dry husk until I wouldn't have been sure what it was if I hadn't seen it alive.

There was no sense of movement in the spiderwebs now. The hallway was utterly still except for Rhys's smiling figure. The dim, dim light seemed to collect around his white curls and the white suit until he glowed against the grey cobwebs and the greyer stone. He was smiling at me, cheerful, normal for him.

"Good enough?" he asked.

I nodded. "I only saw you do that once before and that was in battle, but that was when your life was in danger."

"Do you mourn the insect?"

"It's an arachnid, not an insect, and no, I don't mourn it. I've never had the right kind of power to walk safely through this place." But . . . I'd really meant for him to call fire to his hands, or brighter lights, and frighten them away. I hadn't meant for him to . . .

He held his hand out to me, still smiling.

I stared at the black husk swaying gently in the webbing as our movement caused tiny air currents to pass through the hallway.

Rhys's smile didn't change, but his eyes grew gentle. "I am a death god, or was once, Merry. What did you think I was going to do, light a match and yell boo?"

"No, but . . ." I stared at his offered hand. I stared at it for longer than was polite. But finally, tentatively, I reached toward him. Our fingertips touched, and his breath came out with a sigh.

He gazed down at the silver band on my hand. His gaze came up to meet mine. "Merry, may I, please?"

I looked into his pale blue eye. "Why is it so important to you?" I wondered if the rumor had already spread about what she planned to announce tonight.

"We're all hoping she called you back to choose another would-be consort for yourself. I'm assuming that if the ring doesn't recognize someone, they're out of the running."

"That's closer than you know," I said.

"Then may I?" he asked.

He tried to keep the eagerness off his face, but failed. I guess I couldn't blame him. It was going to be like this all night once word got out. No, it was going to be worse, much worse.

I nodded.

He began to bring my hand to his lips as he spoke. "You know I would never willingly hurt you, Merry." He kissed my hand, and his lips brushed the ring. It quickened—that was the only word I had for it. It flared through me, through us both. The sensation seemed to squeeze my heart, chase it into my throat like a trapped thing.

Rhys stayed bent over my hand, but I heard him breathe out an "Oh, yes." He raised up, and his eye looked unfocused.

It was the strongest reaction yet, and that sort of worried me. Did the strength of the reaction say something about how strong the man's virility was, sort of a supernatural sperm count? Nothing personal to Rhys, but if I had to sleep with anyone tonight, it was probably going to be Galen. The ring could pulse away to its carved little heart. *I* would decide who shared my bed. Until Auntie dearest sent her spy to me, of course. I pushed that thought away—I couldn't deal with it right now. There were sidhe in her Guard that I'd sooner kill than kiss, let alone anything more.

Rhys wrapped his fingers through mine, pressing the palm of his hand against the ring. The second pulse was stronger, bringing an involuntary gasp from my throat. It felt like things deep inside my body were being caressed. Things that no hand should ever touch—but power . . . power wasn't constrained by the bounds of flesh.

"Oh, I like it," Rhys said.

I pulled my hand out of his. "Don't do that again."

"It felt good and you know it."

I looked into his eager face, and said, "She doesn't just want me to find another fiancé. She wants me to have sex with several or all of the Guard that this ring recognizes. It's a race to see who gives her an heir of the blood royal first. Cel, or me."

He stared at me, studying my face, as if trying to read my expression. "I know you wouldn't make a joke of this, but it seems too good to be true."

It made me feel better that Rhys didn't trust it either. "Exactly. Right now she's told me the celibacy is off for little ol' me, but I have no witnesses. I think she's sincere, but until she announces it in full court, I'll just pretend that sex is still taboo."

He nodded. "What's a few hours more of waiting after a thousand years?"

I raised eyebrows at him. "I can't do everybody tonight, Rhys, so it's going to be more than a few hours wait."

"As long as I'm first in line, what does it matter?" He tried to make it a joke, but I didn't laugh.

"I'm afraid that this is exactly how everyone else is going to feel. There's only one of me, and what, twenty-seven of you?"

"Do you have to sleep with all of us?"

"She didn't say so, but she *is* going to insist on me sleeping with her spy, whoever he turns out to be."

"You hate some of the Guard, Merry, and they hate you back. She cannot expect you to take them to your bed. Lord and Lady, if one that you hated got you pregnant . . ." He didn't finish the thought.

"I'd be trapped into marriage with a man I despised, and he would be king."

Rhys blinked at me, the white eye-patch catching the light as he moved his head. "I hadn't thought about that. Truthfully all I was seeing was the sex, but you're right—one of us is going to be king."

I glanced up at the grey sheet of webs. They were empty, but . . . "Should we be talking about this here with this above us?"

He looked up at the spiderwebs. "Good point." He offered me his arm. "May I escort you to the banquet, my lady?"

I slid my hand over his arm. "With pleasure."

He patted my hand. "I hope so, Merry, I certainly do hope so."

I laughed, and the sound echoed strangely in the hallway, making the cobwebs drift and float. It was almost as if the ceiling stretched far, far overhead into some vast darkness that only the spiderwebs hid from our view. My laughter faded, long before we stepped out from under the webs.

"Thank you, Rhys, for understanding why I'm afraid, instead of just concentrating on the fact that you may be about to end several hundred years of celibacy."

He pressed my left hand to his lips. "I live only to serve under you, or above you, or any way you want me."

I punched him in the shoulder. "Stop it."

He grinned.

"Rhys isn't the name of any known death god. I researched you in college, and you weren't there."

He was suddenly very busy staring down the ever-narrowing hallway. "Rhys is my name now, Merry. It doesn't matter who I was before."

"Of course it matters," I said.

"Why?" he asked, and suddenly he was all serious, asking a very grown-up question.

Watching him glow white and shining in the grey light, I didn't feel grownup. I felt tired. But there was a weight to his gaze, a demand in his face, that I had to answer.

"I just want to know who I'm dealing with, Rhys."

"You've known me all your life, Merry."

"Then tell me," I said.

"I don't want to talk about the long-ago days, Merry."

"What if I invited you into my bed? Would you tell me all your secrets then?"

He studied my face. "You're teasing me."

I touched the scarred edge of his face, tracing with my fingers from the roughened skin to pass a fingertip over the full softness of his lips. "No teasing, Rhys. You're beautiful. You've been a friend to me for years. You protected me when I was younger. It would be poor repayment if I left you celibate when I could put an end to it—besides the fact that running my mouth down that washboard stomach of yours has been a recurring sexual fantasy."

"Funny, I've had the same fantasy," he said. He wiggled his eyebrows at me and did a miserably bad Groucho Marx impression. "Maybe you can come up to my place and look at my etchings."

I smiled and shook my head. "Don't you watch any movies made after color came into the cinema?"

"Not often." He held out his hand, and I took it. We walked down the hallway hand in hand, and it was companionable. Of all the guards I liked, I'd have thought Rhys would have been the most obnoxious about the possibility of sex. But he'd been the perfect gentlemen. Proof once again that I didn't really understand men.

Chapter 29

THE DOORS AT THE END OF THE HALLWAY WERE SMALL TO-
night: man height. Sometimes the doors were big enough for
an elephant to pass through. They were a pale grey with gold
edgings, very Louis the something. I didn't bother asking
Rhys if the queen had redecorated. The sithen, like the Black
Coach, did its own redecorating.

Rhys opened the elegant double doors, but we never got to
step into the room beyond because Frost stopped us. It wasn't
that he was physically blocking the door—though he was.
He'd changed into the queen's outfit, and the sight of him in it
stopped me cold. I think Rhys stopped moving because I did.

The shirt was completely see-through, to the point where I
wasn't sure if the cloth was actually white, or if it was clear
and it was his skin that made it look white. The shirt was cut
like a second skin to his chest, but the sleeves had a large puff
of diaphanous material, cut tight just above the bend of his
elbow by a broad appliqué of glittering silver. The rest of the
sleeves fell in a long full tube like a crystal morning glory.
The thread that kept the shirt together was silver and gleamed
at every seam. The pants were silver satin cut so low around
the waist that his hip bones showed through the cloth of his
shirt. If he'd tried to wear underwear they would have shown
at the waist of the pants. The only thing that kept the pants up
was that they were unbelievably tight. A series of white
strings over the groin, like the ties on the back of a merry
widow, took the place of a zipper.

His hair had been divided into three sections. The upper
part was pulled up through a white carved piece of bone so

347

that the silver hair fell like the water of some fountain around his head. The second section of hair was simply pulled back on either side and held in place with bone barrettes. The lower section hung loose and free, but so little was left that it was like a thin silver veil emphasizing his body instead of hiding it.

"Frost, you're almost too beautiful to be real."

"She treats us like dolls to be dressed at her whim." It was the closest thing to an overt critisim of the queen that I'd ever heard him say.

"I like it, Frost," Rhys said. "It's you."

He scowled at Rhys. "It is not me."

I'd never seen the tall guard so angry about something so small. "It's just clothes, Frost. It won't hurt you to wear them with grace. Showing your displeasure in them *could* hurt you, very much."

"I have obeyed my queen."

"If she knows how much you hate the clothes she'll order more of the same for you. You know that."

The scowl deepened until he managed to put lines across that perfect face. Then a scream came from the room behind him. Even wordless, I recognized that voice. It was Galen.

I stepped forward. Frost stood his ground.

"Get out of my way, Frost," I said.

"The prince has ordered this punishment, but has graciously allowed privacy. No one may enter until it is complete."

I stared up at Frost. I couldn't fight my way past him, and I wasn't going to kill him. It used up my options.

"Merry is being named coheir tonight," Rhys said.

Frost's eyes flicked from one to the other of us. "I do not believe it."

Galen screamed again, and the sound raised the flesh on my arms, clenched my hands into fists. "I will be coheir to-night, Frost."

He shook his head. "That changes nothing."

"What if she told you that our celibacy will be lifted for Merry, and Merry alone?" Rhys asked.

Frost managed to look arrogant and disbelieving. " 'What if' is not a game I will play with you."

Galen gave another sharp scream. The queen's Ravens do not scream easily. I moved toward Frost, and he tensed. I think he was expecting a fight.

I ran my fingers lightly over the front of his shirt. He jumped as if I'd hurt him. "The queen will announce tonight that I am to have my pick of the Guards. She's ordered me to sleep with one of you tonight, or tomorrow I will have a star-ring role in one of her little orgies." I wrapped my arms around his waist, pressing myself lightly against his body. "Trust me, Frost, I will have one of you tonight, and to-morrow, and the night after that. It would be a shame if you were not among those I bedded."

The arrogance was gone, replaced by something eager and afraid. I didn't understand the fear, but the eagerness, that I understood. He looked to Rhys. "Your oath that this is true."

"You have it," Rhys said. "Let her pass, Frost."

He stared down at me. He still hadn't touched me back—my caress had been like a kiss against unresponsive lips—but he moved out of the way, sliding from the circle of my arms. He watched me like you'd watch a coiled rattlesnake, no sud-den movements, and no trust that it wouldn't bite you anyway. He was afraid of what was happening in that room.

I walked past him. I felt Rhys at my back, but all I could see was what lay in the center of the room. There was a small water garden in the center of the room, with a large decora-tive rock in the center of it. Stepping-stones led to the rock, in which were embedded permanent chains. Galen was chained to the rock. His body was almost lost to sight under the slowly fanning butterfly wings of the demi-fey. They looked like true butterflies on the edge of a puddle, sipping liquid, wings mov-ing slowly to the rhythm of their feeding. But they weren't sipping water, they were drinking his blood.

He screamed again, and it sent me rushing forward. Doyle was suddenly in front of me. He must have been guarding the other doors. "You cannot stop them once they have begun to feed."

"Why is he screaming? It shouldn't hurt that much." I tried to get past him, and he grabbed my arm.

"No, Meredith, no."

Galen shrieked long and loud, his body arching against the chains. The movement dislodged some of the demi-fey, and I glimpsed why he was screaming. His groin was a bloody mess. They were taking flesh as well as blood.

Rhys hissed, "Bloody beasts."

Doyle tightened his grip on my arm.

"They're mutilating him," I protested.

"He will heal."

I tried to pull away but his fingers were like something welded to my skin. "Doyle, please?"

"I am sorry, Princess."

Galen shrieked, and the rock strained under the pull of his body, but the chains held. "This is excessive and you know it."

"The prince is within his rights to punish Galen for disobeying him." He tried to pull me farther away, as if that would make it better.

"No, Doyle, if Galen has to endure it, I won't look away. Now let go of me."

"You promise not to do anything rash?"

"My word," I said.

He released me, and when I touched his shoulder, he moved to one side so my view was unobstructed. The wings were every color of the rainbow, and some that the rainbow could only dream of—huge wings bigger than my hands flexing slowly in and out above brief glimpses of Galen's nearly nude body. His pants were down around his ankles, and there was no other clothing that I could see. There was a terrible beauty to the scene, like a very pretty slice of hell.

One set of wings was larger than the others, like huge pale swallow-tailed kites. It was Queen Niceven herself feasting just above his groin. I had an idea. "Queen Niceven," I said, "it does not become a queen to do the dirty work of a prince."

She raised her small pale face and hissed at me, her lips and chin red with Galen's blood, the front of her white gown splattered with crimson.

I held up the hand with the ring on it. "I am to be named co-heir tonight."

"What is that to me?" Her voice was like evil bells, sweet and disturbing.

"A queen deserves better than the blood of a sidhe lord."

She watched me with tiny pale eyes. She was all leprous in her paleness, like a tiny ghost. "What do you offer that is more tender than this?"

"Not more tender, but more powerful. The blood of a sidhe princess for the queen of the demi-fey."

She stared at me, one dainty hand wiping at the blood on her mouth. She rose on huge luna-moth wings to fly toward me. The others continued to feed. Niceven hovered in front of my face, her wings making a small current of air against my skin. "You would take his place?"

Doyle said, "No, Princess."

I silenced him with a gesture. "I offer Queen Niceven of the demi-fey my blood. The blood of a sidhe princess is too fine a prize to be shared."

Frost and Rhys moved up beside Doyle. They watched us as if they'd never seen such a show before.

Niceven licked her lips with a tiny tongue like the petal of a flower. "You would let me take blood from you?"

I held up a finger to her. "Let him go, and you may pierce my skin and drink."

"Prince Cel petitioned that we ruin this one's manhood."

"As Doyle said, it will heal. Why would the prince ask a favor of the demi-fey for something that is not permanent damage?"

She hovered near my finger for all the world like a butterfly inspecting a flower. "That, you have to ask Prince Cel." She turned her gaze from my finger to my face. "You should have heard what he wanted us to do at first. Wanted us to ruin him for life, but the queen does not allow her lovers to be damaged goods." Niceven hovered close to my face, her tiny hand touching the tip of my nose. "Prince Cel reminded me that he will be king someday." She touched my lips lightly with those diminutive fingers. "I reminded him that he does not rule here yet, and that I would not risk Queen Andais's anger for him."

"What did he say to that?"

"He took the compromise. We taste royal blood and flesh, both precious, and for tonight this one will be useless in the queen's bed." She frowned, arms crossing over her tiny chest. "I do not know why he is jealous of this one and not the others."

"It is not the queen's bed he was trying to keep Galen out of," I said.

She cocked her head to one side, long spiderweb hair trailing around her. "You?"

I waggled the ring at her. "I have been ordered to sleep with a guard tonight."

"And this one would have been your choice?"

I nodded.

Niceven smiled. "Cel is jealous of you."

"Not in the way you mean, Queen Niceven. Do we have a bargain, my blood for your sweet mouth, and Galen goes free?"

She stayed hovering near my face for a few seconds more, then nodded. "We have a bargain. Extend your arm and give me a place to land."

"Free Galen first, then by all means feed."

"As you like." She flew back to the others, and whatever she said to them scattered them ceilingward in a bright colored cloud. Galen's pale, pale green skin was covered in tiny red bites; thin lines of blood began to trail across his skin like an invisible red pen trying to connect the dots.

"Unchain him and see to his wounds," I said. Rhys and Frost moved to obey me. Only Doyle stayed nearby as if he didn't trust one of us, or any of us.

I extended my arm outward, my hand cupping slightly upward. Niceven landed on my forearm. She was heavier than she appeared, but still light and strangely brittle, as if her tiny bare feet were made of dried bones. She wrapped both her hands around my index finger, then lowered her face toward my fingertip as if she meant to bestow a kiss. Tiny razor teeth bit into my finger. The pain was sharp and immediate. Her tiny petal tongue began to lap the blood tickling against my skin. She curved her body around my hand until every inch of her small being was insinuated against my skin. It was a strangely sexual movement, as if she gained more than mere blood from the feeding.

The rest of the demi-fey hovered in the air around me like colored wind, moving gently. Their tiny mouths were blood-stained, miniature hands red with Galen's blood. Niceven caressed my hand with her hands, her bare feet; a tiny knee beat against my palm.

She raised her head and took a breath. "I am full of flesh and blood from your lover. I can hold no more." She sat up in my hand, her head resting against my finger. "I would give much for a longer drink someday, Princess Meredith. You taste of high magic, and sex." She stood and slowly lifted herself from my hand with slow beats of her wings. She hovered near my face just looking at me, as if she saw something I did not, or was trying to find something in me that was not there. Finally, she nodded, and said, "We will see you at the banquet, Princess." With that she rose higher into the air, the others following her in a multi-colored cloud. The huge doors at the end of the room opened without anyone touching them, and once the bright flying crowd had vanished inside, the doors closed slowly behind them.

A small sound brought my attention back to the room. Galen was leaning up against the far wall, his pants in place though not fastened. Rhys was dabbing at the small bites with a bottle of clear liquid, until Galen's naked upper body gleamed in the lights.

He gazed up at me. "Is it true about the celibacy being lifted?"

"It's true," I said, and crouched on my heels by him.

He smiled, but it left his eyes pain-filled. "I won't be much use to you tonight."

"There will be other nights," I said.

The smile widened, but he winced as Rhys cleaned more of

the wounds. "Why did Cel care if I in particular came to your bed?"

"I think Cel believes that if I cannot sleep with you tonight, that I will sleep alone."

Galen looked at me.

I didn't wait for him to say something that would make all this even more uncomfortable. "I don't know if you heard what I told the others, but if I don't have sex tonight with someone of my choosing, tomorrow I entertain the court with a group of the queen's choosing."

"You'll have to take someone to your bed tonight, Merry."

"I know." I touched his face and found it cool to the touch and lightly dewed with sweat. He'd lost a lot of blood, nothing fatal for a sidhe, but he would be weak tonight for many things, not just for sex.

"If this was your punishment for disobeying Cel, then what was Barinthus's punishment?"

"He was forbidden to attend tonight's banquet," Frost said.

I raised my eyebrows at that. "Galen gets cut up and Barinthus just misses supper?"

"Cel is afraid of Barinthus, but he does not fear Galen," Frost said.

"I'm just too nice a guy."

"Yes," Frost said, "you are."

"That was supposed to be a joke," Galen said.

"Unfortunately," Doyle said, "it isn't funny."

"We can't keep the queen waiting," Rhys said. "Can you walk?"

"Get me on my feet and I'll walk." Doyle and Frost helped him stand.

He moved slowly, arthritically, as if things hurt a great deal, but by the time they'd helped him to the far doors, he was moving on his own power. He was healing before our eyes, his skin absorbing the bites. It was like watching reverse film of flowers blooming.

The oil helped speed the process, but mostly it was just his own body. The amazing flesh machine of a sidhe warrior. Within hours the bites would be healed; within days the rest of the damage would be gone as well. In a few days Galen and I could finally quench the heat between us. But for tonight there would have to be someone else. I looked at the other three guards in an almost proprietary way, like going into your kitchen and knowing the shelves are well stocked with your favorite things. None of them was a fate worse than torture. It was just a question of which one. How do you decide between one perfect flower and another if love is not an issue? I didn't have the faintest idea. Maybe I could toss a coin.

Chapter 30

THE DOORS THAT OPEN FROM THE FOUNTAIN OF PAIN LEAD TO A large antechamber. It is a dark room. The sourceless white light seemed very dim and very grey here. Something crunched under my feet, and I looked down to find leaves. Dried leaves everywhere. I looked up and found that the vines that entwined above our heads were dry and lifeless. The leaves had folded in upon themselves or dropped completely.

I touched the vines near the door and there was no sense of life to them. I turned to Doyle. "The roses are dead." I whispered it as if it were some great secret.

He nodded.

"They have been dying for years, Meredith," Frost said.

"Dying, Frost, but not dead." The roses were a last defense for the court. If enemies penetrated this far, the roses would come to life and kill them, or try to, either by strangling or by the thorns. The newer, lower growth had thorns like any other climbing rose, but there were vines deep in the tangle that held thorns the size of small daggers. But they weren't merely a defense. They were a symbol that there had once been magical gardens under the ground. The fruiting vines and trees had died first, so I'm told, then the herbs, and now the last of the flowers.

I searched the vines with my eyes for any sign of life. They were dry and lifeless. I sent a flash of power into the vines and felt an answering pulse of power, strong still, but faint, nothing like the warm pressing presence it should have been. I touched the nearest vines gently with my fingers. The thorns were small here, but dry, like straight pins.

"Stop petting the roses," Frost said. "We have more pressing problems."

I turned to him, hand still on the roses. "If the roses die, truly die, do you understand what this means?"

"Most likely, better than you do," he said, "but I also understand that we can do nothing for the roses or the fact that the sidhe's power is dying. But if we are careful, we may save ourselves this night."

"Without our magic we are not sidhe," I said. I pulled my hand back without looking, spearing my finger on the thorns. I jerked back, which broke a thorn off in my skin. The small dark thorn was easy to see and easy to remove with an edge of fingernail. It didn't even hurt that much, just a small dot of crimson on my finger.

"How bad is it?" Rhys asked.

"Not bad," I said.

A thick, dry hiss ran through the room like some great serpent gliding through the dark. The sound came from above us, and we all looked upward. A shudder ran through the vines, and dried leaves fell like a crumbling rain onto the floor, catching in our hair, our clothes.

"What's happening?" I asked.

Doyle answered, "I don't know."

"Then shouldn't we get to the other room?" Rhys said. His hand went for a sword that was not there. But his other hand went for my arm, and he pulled me toward the closest door, back into the hallway. None of them were armed, unless Doyle still had my gun. And somehow I didn't think a gun was what we needed.

The others closed around me like a wall of flesh. Rhys's hand touched the door handle, and vines spilled over the door like dry rushing water. He jumped back, pushing me away from the door and the reaching vines. Doyle grabbed my other arm, and we were suddenly running for the far door. They were moving too fast for my high heels. I stumbled, but their hands kept me upright and moving, my feet barely touching the floor. Frost was ahead of us, going for the doors. He called back, "Hurry!"

Rhys muttered under his breath, "We are."

I glanced back to see Galen. He was facing away from me, guarding my back with nothing in his hands but his own skin. But the thorns were not touching him. There was a sense of movement everywhere like a nest of snakes, but the thin, dry tendrils dangled above me like an octopus—reaching just for me. As Doyle and Rhys carried me farther into the room, the thorns receded behind me and fell above my head, brushing my hair, pulling at us. When Doyle turned his head to look upward, I caught a scarlet flash on his face, fresh blood.

The thorns wrapped in my hair, trying to pull me away. I screamed, jerking my head down. Rhys grabbed the handful of my hair and together we pulled it free of the thorns, leaving strands of hair behind.

Frost had the far doors open. There was a glimpse of brighter lights and faces turned toward us, some human, some not. Frost was yelling, "A sword, give me a sword!"

A guard started to move forward, hand on his sword. I heard a voice yell, "No! Keep your sword." It was Cel's voice.

Doyle barked out an order: "Sithney, give us your sword!"

The guard at the door started to lift his sword from its sheath. Frost held his hand out for it. The vines poured over the opening in a dry rushing wave. There was a moment when Frost could have dived through the door, could have saved himself, but he turned back into the room. The door vanished behind a reaching, slashing wave of thorns.

Rhys and Doyle took me to the floor. Doyle pushed Rhys on top of me. I was suddenly under a pile of bodies. Rhys hair spilled past my face like curly silk. I had a glimpse through his hair and someone's arm of a black cloak. I was pressed so hard against the floor I not only couldn't move, I could barely breathe.

If it had been anyone but Doyle and Frost on top, I'd have been waiting for screams. Instead, I waited for the pile to grow lighter as the men were dragged away by the thorns. But the pile didn't grow lighter.

I lay flat on my stomach, pressed to the cool stone floor,

staring out through Rhys's hair. The arm that was braced outside the curtain was bare of cloth, and slightly less purely white, so it was Galen.

My blood had been pounding in my ears until all I could hear was the beat of my own body. But minutes passed and nothing happened. My pulse quieted. I pressed my hands to the stones underneath me. The grey stone was almost as smooth as marble, worn away from centuries of passing feet. I could hear Rhys's breathing next to my ear. The shift of cloth as someone above us moved. But over all was the sound of the thorns, a low continuous murmur like the sound of the sea.

Rhys whispered against my hair, "May I have a kiss before I die?"

"We don't seem to be dying," I said.

"Easy for you to say. You're on the bottom of the pile." This from Galen.

"What's happening up there? I can't see a thing," I said.

"Be happy you cannot," Frost said.

"What is happening?" I asked again, putting more force into my voice.

"Nothing," Doyle's deep voice rumbled down through the pile of men, as if the other bodies carried the low tone of his words like a tuning fork straight down my spine. "And I find that surprising," he said.

"You sound disappointed," Galen said.

"Not disappointed," Doyle said, "curious."

Doyle's cloak slid out of sight, the weight above me was suddenly less.

"Doyle!" I shouted.

"Have no fear, Princess. I am fine," he said.

The pressure above me lightened once more, but not by much. It took me a few seconds to figure out that Frost was raising up, but not moving his body from the pile. "This is singular," he said.

Galen's arm vanished from my sight. "What is it doing?" he asked.

I couldn't hear anyone walking around, but I could see Galen to one side, kneeling. I parted Rhys's hair from my face like two edges of a curtain. Frost was kneeling beside Galen. Doyle was the only one standing alone on the other side of us. I could see his black cloak.

Rhys raised upward, bracing with his arms like half a push-up. "Strange," he said.

That was it. I had to see. "Get off of me, Rhys. I want to see."

He lowered his head over my face so he was looking at me upside down, still supporting his upper body with his arms, but pinning my lower body with his. Under other circumstances I'd have said he was doing it on purpose. But the material of my dress was thin enough and his clothing light enough that I could tell he wasn't happy to see me. Staring into his tri-blue eye from inches away but upside down was almost dizzying, and somehow strangely intimate.

"I'm the last body between you and the great bad thing," he said. "I'll move when Doyle tells me to move."

Watching his small round mouth move upside down made my head hurt. I closed my eyes. "Don't talk upside down," I said.

"Of course," Rhys said, "you could just look up." He drew his face back, pulling back until he was on all fours above me like a mare shielding her foal.

I stayed flat on the ground but craned my neck backward. All I could see was the snaking tendrils of the roses. They hung above us like thin, fuzzy, brown ropes waving gently back and forth almost as if there was wind, but there was no wind, and the fuzziness was thorns.

"Other than the fact that the roses are alive again, what am I supposed to be seeing?"

Doyle answered, "It is only the small thorns that are reaching for you, Merry."

"And?" I said.

His black cloak came closer as he stood above us. "It means I don't believe the roses mean you harm."

"What else could they want?" I asked. It should have felt silly talking from the ground with Rhys perched over me on all fours. But it didn't. I wanted something, someone, between me and the rustling of the thorns.

"I believe, I think, it may want a drink of royal blood," Doyle said.

"What do you mean a drink?" Galen asked it before I could. He sat back on the floor, moving so I could see most of his upper body. Blood had dried in spots and small trails down his upper body, but the bites were almost gone, leaving only the blood as proof that he'd been injured. The front of his pants was blood-soaked, but he moved better, less pain-filled. Everything was healing.

I would not heal if the thorns tore into my body. I'd simply die.

"The roses once drank from the queen every time she passed this way," Doyle said.

"That was centuries ago," Frost said, "before we ever dreamed of traveling to the lands to the west."

I propped myself up on my elbows. "I have passed under the roses a thousand times in my life, and they've never reacted to me, not even when they still had a few blooms left."

"You have come into your power, Meredith. The land recognized that when it welcomed you tonight," Doyle said.

"What do you mean the land welcomed her?" Frost asked. Doyle told him.

Rhys bent over to stare into my face again in that awkward upside-down movement. "Cool," he said.

It made me smile, but I pushed his head up out of my face anyway. "The land recognizes me as a power now."

"Not merely the land," Doyle said. He sat down on the far side of me from Galen, spreading the black cloak around his body in a familiar gesture, as if he wore a lot of ankle-length cloaks. He did.

I could see his face now. He looked thoughtful, as if contemplating some weighty philosophy.

"This is all fascinating," Rhys said; "but we can discuss whether Merry is the chosen whatever, later. We need to get her out of here before the roses try to eat her."

Doyle looked at me, dark face impassive. "Without swords we have very little chance of making either door with Merry alive. We would survive the roses' worst attentions, but she would not. Since it is her safety that is paramount and not our own, we must think of a way out of this that does not require violence. If you offer the roses violence, they will return the favor." He waved his hand upward, vaguely including the trailing vines. "They seem to be quite patient with us, so I suggest we use their patience to think."

"The land has never welcomed Cel, nor have the roses reached for him," Frost said. He crawled around me to sit near Doyle. He didn't seem to trust the roses' patience as much as Doyle did. I agreed with Frost on this one. I had never seen the roses move before, not so much as a twitch. I'd heard the stories, but never thought to see the reality of it for myself. I'd often wished to see the room covered in sweet fragrant roses. Be careful what you wish for. Of course, there were no blooms, just thorns. That wasn't exactly what I'd wished for.

"Just because you put a crown on someone's head doesn't make them fit to rule," Doyle said. "In olden days it was the magic, the land, that chose our queen or king. If the magic rejected them, if the land didn't accept them, then bloodline or no bloodline, a new heir had to be chosen."

I was suddenly very aware of all of them looking at me. I looked from one to the other of them. They had almost identical expressions on their faces and I was half afraid I knew what they were thinking. The target on my back just kept getting bigger and bigger. "I am not the heir apparent."

"The queen will make you so, tonight," Doyle said.

I looked into his dark face and tried to read those raven-black eyes. "What do you want of me, Doyle?"

"First, let us see what happens when Rhys opens the way for the thorns. If they react violently, then we will go no farther. Eventually, the other guards will rescue us."

Rhys asked, "Do you want me to move now?"

Doyle nodded. "Please."

I wrapped a hand around both of Rhys's arms, keeping him above me. "What happens if the roses pour over me and try tearing me limb from limb?"

"Then we throw ourselves on your body and let the thorns rend us before they touch your white flesh." Doyle's voice was bland, empty of meaning, but still interested. It was the voice he used in public at court when he didn't want anyone to guess his motives. A voice honed by centuries of answering to royals that were often not quite sane.

"Why is that less than comforting?" I asked.

Rhys flipped his head upside down to peer into my face again. "How do you think I feel? I'll be sacrificing all this toned and muscled flesh just when I thought someone else might get to appreciate it."

It made me smile.

He smiled at me upside down like the Cheshire cat. "If you'll let go of my arms," he said, "I promise to throw myself on top of you at the first hint of danger." His smile widened to a grin. "In fact, with your permission I'll throw myself on top of your body at every opportunity."

It was almost impossible not to smile at him. If I was about to be torn limb from limb, I might as well go smiling as frowning. I let go of his arms. "Get off of me, Rhys."

He kissed me lightly on the forehead and stood.

I was left lying on the floor all by myself. I rolled onto one side, gazing upward. The men had all gotten to their feet. They stood above me, but only Rhys was looking at me. The others were looking up at the thorns.

The thorns swayed gently above us as if they were dancing to some music that we could not hear.

"They don't seem to be doing anything," I said.

"Try standing." Doyle held his hand down to me.

I looked at that perfectly black hand with its pale almost milky-white nails. I looked from the hand to Rhys. "You'll throw yourself on top of me at the first hint of danger?"

"Quick as a little bunny," he said.

I caught Galen giving Rhys a look. It was not a friendly look. "I heard that about you," Galen said. "That you were quick."

"If you want on bottom next time, help yourself," Rhys said. "I'm more of an on-top man myself." His teasing had a bite to it, and he didn't look happy either.

"Children," Doyle said, a soft warning in his voice.

I sighed. "The proclamation hasn't even been formally announced and the bickering has already begun. And Rhys and Galen are two of the more reasonable ones."

Doyle made a small bow, putting his hand just inches above me. "Let us take our problems one at a time, Princess. To do it any other way is to be overwhelmed."

I stared into his dark eyes and slid my hand into his. His grip was firm and unbelievably strong as he lifted me to my feet almost faster than I could stand. It left me off center and wobbling, forced to catch his hand tight to keep from falling. His other hand came out to catch my arm. For a moment it was very close to an embrace. I glanced up at him. There was no hint on his face that he'd done it deliberately.

The thorns gave a furious hiss above our heads. I was suddenly looking upward, hands on Doyle's arms, but not for support—I was frightened.

"Perhaps you should give us the knives you carry before we go farther?" he said.

I glanced at him. "How much farther are we going?"

"The roses desire a drink of your blood. They must touch you at the wrist or elsewhere, but usually the wrist," he said.

I did not like the sound of that. "I don't remember offering to donate blood again."

"The knives first, Meredith, please," he asked.

I looked up at the quivering thorns. One thin strand seemed lower than the rest now. I let go of Doyle and reached a hand inside my bodice for the knife within the bra. I brought it out, flicking it open. Frost looked surprised and not happy about it. Rhys looked surprised but pleased.

"I did not know that you could hide such a weapon under such a small piece of clothing," Frost said.

"Maybe we won't have to do nearly as much protecting as I thought," Rhys said.

Galen knew me well enough to know I always went armed at court.

I handed the knife to Doyle and raised my skirt. By the time the skirt was to my knees I could feel the men's attention like a weight on my skin. I looked up at them. Frost looked away as if embarrassed. But the others either looked at my leg, or my face. I know they'd seen more skin than this on longer legs. "If you keep watching me this closely, you're going to make me self-conscious."

"My apologies," Doyle said.

"Why the sudden attention, gentlemen? You've seen the court ladies in much less than this." I kept lifting the skirt until I bared the garter. They watched each movement the way that cats watch birds in a cage.

"But the court ladies are off limits to us. You are not," Doyle said.

Ah. I lifted the knife, hilt and all, from around the garter. I let the skirt fall back into place and watched their eyes following the movement of the cloth. I enjoy being noticed by men, but this level of scrutiny was almost unnerving. If I survived the night, I'd have a talk with them about it. But as Doyle said, one problem at a time or you are overwhelmed. "Who gets this knife?"

Three pale hands reached out for it. I looked at Doyle. He was, after all, captain of the Guard. He nodded, as if he approved of my looking to him for the choice rather than making it myself. I knew who I liked the best of the three, but I wasn't sure who was the best with a blade.

"Give it to Frost," Doyle said.

I handed the knife to him handle first. He took it with a small bow. I noticed for the first time that there were faint blood stains on his pretty shirt. He'd been pressed against Galen's back wounds. He'd need to soak the shirt or the bloodstains would set.

"I realize that Frost is worth a stare or two tonight, Meredith, but you are stalling," Doyle said.

I nodded. "I suppose I am." I looked up at the dangling thorns. My stomach was tight, my hands cold. I was afraid.

"Hold your wrist out to the vine that is the lowest. We will protect you to the last breath in our bodies. You know that."

I nodded. "I know that." I did know that. I even believed it, but still . . . I watched the thorns and my gaze slid upward into the dimness. Vines as wide as my leg twisted and turned upon themselves like a knot of sea serpents. Some of the thorns were as big as my hand, catching the light in a dull black gleam.

I brought my gaze back down to the thin tiny thorns on the vines directly over my head. They were small, but there were a lot of them, like a bristling armor of tiny pins.

I took a deep breath and blew it out. I started raising my hand slowly upward, hand balled into a tight fist. My hand was barely even with my forehead when the vine poured downward like a snake down a hole. The brown thing wrapped around my wrist, and the thorns set in my skin like hooks in a fish's mouth. The pain was sharp and immediate, coming a second before the first trickle of blood slid onto my wrist. The blood tickled down my skin like tiny fingers caressing the skin. A fine crimson rain began to glide down my wrist, thick and slow.

Galen hovered by me, hands fluttering around me as if he wanted to touch me but was afraid to. "Isn't that enough?" he asked.

"Apparently not," Doyle said.

I looked where his gaze was fixed and found a second thin tendril hanging above my head. It stopped as the first one had stopped—waiting. Waiting for my invitation to come closer.

I looked at Doyle. "You must be joking."

"It has been long since it fed, Meredith."

"You've endured more pain than a few thorns," Rhys said.

"You even enjoyed it," Galen said.

"The context was different," I said.

"The context is everything," he said, softly. There was something in his voice, but I didn't have time to decipher it.

"I would give my wrist in your place, but I am not heir," Doyle said.

"Neither yet am I."

The vine moved lower, tickling against my hair like a lover trying to caress his way to the promised land. I offered my other arm, fist closed. The vine wrapped around my wrist with an eager speed. The thorns sank into my flesh. The vine pulled tight. It brought a gasp from my throat. Rhys was right.

I'd endured greater pain, but every pain is singular, a unique torture. The vines pulled themselves taut, raising my hands tight above my head. There were so many thorns that it felt like some small animal was trying to bite through my wrists.

Blood ran down my arms in a fine, continuous rain. I'd been able to feel each individual line of blood at first, but my skin grew dead to so much sensation. The pain in my wrists drew all my attention. The vines raised me up on tiptoe, until their grip was all that kept me from falling. The sharp biting pain began to fade into a burning. It wasn't poison. It was just my body reacting to the damage.

I heard Galen's voice as if from a distance. "That's enough, Doyle." It wasn't until he spoke that I realized I'd closed my eyes. Closed my eyes and given myself to the pain, because only by embracing it could I rise above it, travel through it, to the place where there was no pain and I floated on a sea of blackness. His voice brought me back, wrenched into the kiss of thorns and the spill of my own blood. My body jerked with the suddenness of it, and the thorns answered that movement by jerking me into the air, free of ground.

I cried out.

Someone grabbed my legs, supporting my weight. I blinked down to find Galen holding me. "It's enough, Doyle," he said.

"They never drank so long from the queen," Frost said. He'd moved up to us, my knife in his hand.

"If we cut the vines, they will attack us," Doyle said.

"We have to do something," Rhys said.

Doyle nodded.

The sleeves of my jacket were blood-soaked. I thought vaguely that I wished I'd worn black. It didn't show blood as badly. The thought made me giggle. The grey light seemed to be swimming around us. I was dizzy, light-headed. I wanted the blood loss stopped before I got nauseated. There was nothing like nausea induced by blood loss. You felt too weak to move and still wanted to spill your stomach onto the floor. My fear was fading into a light, almost shining, sensation, as if the world were edged with fog.

I was perilously close to passing out. I'd had enough of the thorns. I tried to say "enough," but no sound came out. I concentrated on my lips and they moved, forming the word, but there was no sound.

Then there was a sound, but it wasn't my voice. The vines hissed and shivered above me. I looked upward, my head falling back bonelessly. The vines rolled above me like a black sea made of rope. The thorns around my wrist pulled upward with a sharp hiss. Only Galen's arms on my legs kept me from being lifted into the nest of thorns. The vines at my wrists pulled, and Galen held, and my wrists bled.

I screamed. I screamed one word: "Enough!"

The vines shuddered, trembling against my skin. The room was suddenly thick with falling leaves. A dry brown snow filled the air. There was a crisp sharp smell like autumn leaves, and under that, like a second wave of scent, was the rich smell of fresh earth.

The thorns lowered me toward the ground. Galen cradled me, picking me up in his arms as the vines let me down, slowly. Both Galen's arms and the vines themselves seemed strangely gentle, if teeth could be gentle while they tried to bite your arm off.

The sound of the door banging back against the wall was the first hint I had that the vines had pulled back from the door.

Galen was holding me in his arms with the vines still pulling my wrists above my head when we all turned to the spill of light from the open doors.

The light seemed brilliant, dazzling, with an edge of soft mist. I knew the light only appeared bright after the dimness, and I thought the edge of mist was just my ruined vision—until a woman stepped out of that light with smoke rising from her fingertips as if each pale yellow finger were a snuffed-out candle.

Fflur moved into the room dressed in a gown of unrelieved black that made her yellow skin the bright color of daffodils. Her yellow hair fanned around her dress like a shining cloak twisting in a wind of her own power.

The guards spilled out to either side of her. A handful had weapons; the rest came into the room bare-handed. There were twenty-seven men in the Queen's Guard and the same number of women in the King's Guard, which now answered to Cel because there was no king. Fifty-four warriors, and less than thirty came through the doors.

Even through the faintness I tried to memorize each face, tried to remember who came to our aid and who stayed behind in safety. Any guard that hadn't come through those doors had lost any chance they had at my body. But I couldn't focus on all the faces. A flood of new forms swept in behind the Guard, most of them shorter and much less human.

The goblins had come.

The goblins were not Cel's creatures. That was my last thought before darkness spilled over my vision and ate the mist across my eyes. I sank into that blissful darkness like a stone thrown in deep water that could only fall and fall because there was no bottom.

Chapter 31

THERE WAS A LIGHT IN THE DARKNESS. A PINPOINT OF WHITE-ness that floated toward me, growing larger and larger. And I could see that it wasn't light but white flames. A ball of white fire swept through the darkness, swept toward me, and I could not escape it because I had no body. I was just something floating in the cool dark. The fire washed over me and I had a body. I had bones and muscles and skin and a voice. The heat ate over my skin, and I felt my muscles cooking, popping from the heat. The fire ate into my bones, filled my veins with molten metal, and began to peel me apart from the inside out.

I woke shrieking.

Galen was bending over me. His face was all that kept me from total panic. He was cradling my head and upper body against my thighs, stroking my forehead, smoothing my hair back from my face. "It's all right, Merry. It's all right." His eyes glittered with unshed tears, gleaming like green glass.

Fflur leaned over me. "Poor greeting I bring, Princess Mere-dith, but answer to our queen, I must." Translated, that meant she had called me out of the darkness, forced me awake, and at the queen's bidding. Fflur was one of those who tried very hard to live as if the year had never gone to four digits. Her ta-pestries had been displayed in the St. Louis Art Museum. They'd been photographed and written up in at least two major magazines. Fflur had refused to look at the articles, and under no circumstances could she be persuaded to go to the museum. She'd turned down interviews from television, news-paper, and the aforementioned magazines.

It took two tries to get my voice to work in something other than a scream. "Did you clear the door of roses?"

"I did," she said.

I tried to smile at her and didn't quite make it. "You risked much to aid me, Fflur. You have no apologies to make."

She glanced up and around at the crowding faces. She placed a fingertip on my forehead, and thought one word: "Later." She wanted to speak to me later, but wanted no one to know. She was a healer, among other talents. She could have checked my health with the same gesture, so no one was the wiser.

I didn't even dare risk a nod. The best I could do was stare into her black eyes, a startling contrast to all that yellow, so that they looked like the eyes of a doll. I looked into her eyes and tried to tell her with a glance that I'd understood. I hadn't even seen the throne room yet and I was already neck deep and rising in court intrigue. Typical.

My aunt knelt beside me in a cloud of leather and vinyl. She took my right hand in hers, petting it, getting blood all over her leather gloves. "Doyle tells me that you pricked your finger on a thorn, and the roses sprang to life."

I looked up at her, tried to read her face, and failed. My wrists ached with a sharp burning that seemed to go all the way down to the bone. Her fingers kept playing over the fresh wounds, and every time the leather passed over it, it made me twitch. "I pricked my finger, yes. What caused the roses to come to life is anyone's guess."

She cradled my hand in both of hers, gently now, gazing down at the wounds with a look of . . . wonderment on her face. "I had given up hope of our roses. One more loss in a sea of loss." She smiled, and it seemed genuine, but I'd seen her use the same smile while torturing someone in her bed-chamber. Just because the smile was real didn't mean you could trust it.

"I'm glad you're pleased," I said, my voice as empty as I could make it.

She laughed then, pressing her hands together over the wounds. I was suddenly very aware of every seam in the leather gloves as they pressed into my flesh. She pressed with a slow steady pressure until I made a small pain sound. That seemed to make her happy, and she let me go. She stood with a swish of skirts.

"When Fflur has bound your wounds, you may join us in the throne room. I am eager for your presence at my side." She turned and the crowd parted before her, forming a tunnel of light that led into the throne room beyond. Eamon moved from the crowd like a black leather shadow to take her arm.

A small goblin with a ring of eyes like a necklace across its forehead knelt beside me, crowding the edge of Fflur's black skirts. The goblin's eyes flicked to me, flicked to her, to me, to her, but what it was really looking at was the blood. It was a small goblin, barely two feet tall. The ring of eyes marked it as handsome among the goblins. They literally called such a marking a "necklace of eyes," and said it in tones that humans reserved for large breasts or a tight ass.

The queen could think what she wanted about the roses. I didn't believe that one drop of my blood had inspired the dying roses. I did believe that my royal blood had saved me, but the initial attack . . . I suspected another spell, hidden somewhere in the thorns. It was doable if someone were powerful enough.

I had enemies. What I needed were friends—allies.

I let my hand slide down my hip as if I were faint. The fresh wound was only inches from the little goblin's mouth. He darted forward and licked a rough tongue like a cat's across the wound. It brought a small sound from my throat, and he cringed.

Galen swung at him the way you'd chase an unwanted dog away. But Fflur grabbed the goblin by the scruff of the neck. "Greedy gut, what mean you with such impertinence?" She started to cast him away.

I stopped her. "No, he has tasted my blood uninvited. I demand recompense for such abuse."

"Recompense?" Galen made it a question.

Fflur kept her grip on the little goblin. His row of eyes flicked back and forth. "Meant nothin' by it. Sorry, so sorry."

He had two main arms and two tiny useless-looking ones. All four arms writhed, clasping and unclasping tiny clawed fingers.

Frost took the goblin from Fflur, raising the small figure in two hands, skyward. His hands were empty of my knife. I'd have to remember to ask for it back. But at the moment I had other business.

"I need to bind the wounds," Fflur said, "or you will lose more blood. I have given you some of my strength, but you did not find it pleasant and would find it less so a second time."

I shook my head. "Not yet."

"Merry," Galen said, "let her treat your wounds."

I looked at his face so full of concern. He'd been raised in the court as had I. He should have known that now was not a time to tend our wounds. Now was a time for action. I looked into his face. Not at his handsome, open face, or his pale green curls, or the way his laugh made his entire face glow—I looked at him as my father must have looked at him once when he decided to give me to someone else. I didn't have time to explain things that Galen should already have been thinking of. I searched the crowd peering down at me like gawkers at a car wreck, simply better dressed and more exotic. "Where is Doyle?"

There was movement in the crowd to my right. Doyle stepped forward. He looked very tall from where I lay on the floor. A black-cloaked pillar to loom above me. Only the peacock-feathered earrings framing his face softened the unrelieved intimidation of his figure. The look on his face, the set of his shoulders under the cloak, all of it was the old Doyle. The queen's Darkness stood beside me, and the colorful feathers looked out of place. He'd been dressed for a party and found himself in the middle of a fight. His expression told nothing, but the very lack of expression said he was not happy.

I suddenly felt six again and vaguely frightened of this tall dark man who had stood at my aunt's side. But he wasn't at her side now. He was at mine. I settled back in Galen's lap and found comfort in his touch, but it was Doyle I turned to for help.

"Bring Kurag to me if he wishes to ransom this thief," I said.

Doyle arched a line of black eyebrow. "Thief?"

"He drank my blood without invitation. The only greater theft among the goblins is a theft of flesh."

Rhys knelt on the other side of me. "I heard that goblins lose a lot of flesh during sex."

"Only if it's agreed on beforehand," I said.

Galen leaned over me, whispering against my skin. "If you are so weakened by blood loss that you can't bed anyone tonight . . ." He touched his lips to my face, "I don't think I could stand to watch you in one of her sex shows. You must be well enough to bed someone tonight, Merry. Let Fflur bind your wounds."

His face loomed at the corner of my eye like a pale blur, his lips like a pink cloud next to my cheek. It wasn't that he was wrong. It was that he wasn't thinking far enough ahead. "I have better use for my blood than soaking into bandages."

"What are you talking about?" Galen asked.

Doyle answered, "The goblins consider anything that comes from the body more valuable than jewels or weapons."

Galen stared up at him. He reached down toward my wrist. I felt his chest move against my head as he sighed. "And what does that have to do with Merry?" But there was something in his voice that said he knew the answer.

Doyle's dark eyes went from me to Galen. He stared at the younger guard. "You are too young to remember the goblin wars."

"So is Merry," Galen said.

Those black eyes turned back to me. "Young, but she knows her history." He flicked his gaze back to Galen. "Do you know your history, young Raven?"

Galen nodded. He pulled me farther into his lap, away from Fflur, away from everyone. He held me against him, holding my arms close so that my blood stained his skin. "I remember my history. I just don't like it."

"I'll be all right, Galen," I said.

He stared down at me, nodding, but not like he believed me. "Fetch me Kurag," I said to Doyle.

He looked at the waiting crowd. "Sithney, Nicca, fetch the goblin king."

Sithney turned with a swirl of long brown hair. I didn't see Nicca's dark purple hair; the pale flash of his lilac skin would have been noticeable among the white and black skin of the court. But if Doyle called him, he was there.

The crowd parted and Kurag came forward with his queen at his side. The goblins, like all of the sidhe, considered the royal consort to be a member in arms, not someone to be hidden away in safety. She had so many eyes scattered across her face that she looked like a spider done large. The wide, lipless mouth held fangs large enough to make any spider proud. Some goblins held venom in their bodies. I was betting that Kurag's new queen was one of those. The eyes, the poison, and a nest of arms around her body like a collection of snakes, made her almost the perfection of goblin beauty, though she could only boast one set of strong bowed legs. Extra legs were the rarest beauty among the goblins. Keelin did not appreciate her good fortune.

There was an air of contentment about the goblin queen that said here was a woman who understood her worth and had made it work for her. That nest of arms clung to Kurag's body, stroking, caressing. One pair of arms had slid between his legs stroking both shaft and balls through his thin pants. The fact that she felt compelled to do something so overtly sexual when introduced to me was a sign that she considered me a rival.

My father had felt it important that I know the goblin court well. We'd visited their court many times, as they had visited our home. He had said, "The goblins do most of the fighting in our wars. They are the backbone of our armies, not the sidhe." This had been true since the last goblin war, when we'd made a treaty that had lasted between us. Kurag had been so comfortable with my father that he had asked for my hand as consort. The rest of the sidhe were mortally offended.

Some talked of going to war over the insult. The goblins considered his desire for such a human-looking bride to be the height of perversity and talked behind his back of finding a new king. But other goblins saw the benefit to sidhe blood in a queen. It took some very serious diplomacy to keep us from either war or my wedding a goblin. It was soon after that that my engagement to Griffin was announced.

Kurag loomed over me. His skin was a shade of yellow similar to Fflur's skin. But where hers was smooth like the perfection of aged ivory, Kurag's skin was covered in warts and lumps. Each imperfection in his skin was a beauty mark. One large lump on his right shoulder spouted an eye. A wandering eye, the goblins called it, because it wandered away from the face. I'd loved the eye when I was a child. Loved the way it moved independently of his face, the three eyes that graced his broad, strong features. The eye on his shoulder was the color of violets, with long black lashes. There was a mouth just above his right nipple that had full red lips and tiny white teeth. A thin pink tongue would lick those lips, and air breathed from that mouth. If you put a feather in front of that second mouth it would blow the feather upward, again and again. While my father and Kurag talked, I entertained myself with watching that eye, and that mouth, and the two thin arms that poked awkwardly from Kurag's right side on either side of his ribs. We played cards, that eye, that mouth, and those arms. I thought Kurag very clever to be able to concentrate on such disparate things all at once.

What I hadn't known until I was a teenager was that there were two thin legs below Kurag's belt on the right side, complete with a small but completely functional penis. A goblin's idea of courtship was crude. Sexual prowess counted for a great deal among them. When I'd seemed unenthusiastic about Kurag's proposal, he'd dropped his pants and shown off both his own equipment and that of his parasitic twin. I was sixteen and I still remember the dawning horror of the realization that there was another being trapped within Kurag's body. Another being with enough mind to play card games with a child while Kurag paid no attention. There was an entire person trapped inside there. An entire person who, if genetics had been kinder, might have matched that lovely lavender eye.

I had never been comfortable around Kurag after that. It hadn't been the proposal or the sight of his rather formidable manhood come to full quivering attention. It had been the sight of that second penis, large and swollen, independent of Kurag and eager for me. When I had turned them down, for "them" it was, that one lavender eye had shed a single tear.

I had had nightmares for weeks. Extra limbs were dandy, but entire extra people in pieces trapped inside someone else . . . there were no words for that kind of horror. The second mouth could breathe, so it obviously had access to the lungs, but it lacked vocal cords. I wasn't sure if that was a blessing or one last curse.

"Kurag, Goblin King, greetings. Twin of Kurag, Goblin King's Flesh, greetings as well." The thin arms on the side of the king's bare chest waved at me. I had greeted both of them from the night I realized that the person with whom I'd been playing cards and stupid games like feather-blowing had actually not been Kurag at all. To my knowledge I was the only one who ever greeted both of them.

"Meredith, Sidhe Princess, greetings from both of us." His orange eyes stared down at me, the largest one perched like a cyclops eye slightly above and in the middle of the other two. The look he gave me was the look any man would give a woman he desired. A look so bald-faced, so obvious, that I felt Galen's body stiffen. Rhys rose to his feet to stand beside Doyle.

"You honor me with your attentions, King Kurag," I said. It was an insult among the goblins if the men did not leer at your woman. It implied that she was ugly and infertile, unworthy of lust.

The queen kept her hands on Kurag, but moved one hand to his side where I knew the other set of genitalia hung. Her maze of eyes glared at me, as her hands worked them. Kurag's breath came out in a rush from both mouths.

If we didn't hurry, we'd be here when the queen brought him, them, to a climax. The goblins saw nothing wrong with public sex. It was a mark of prowess among the men to be brought many times at one banquet, and the woman that could do it was prized. Of course, the goblin male who could sustain a female's attentions for a lengthy time was prized among the females. If a goblin had any sex problems like premature ejaculation or impotency or, for a female, frigidness, then everyone knew it. Nothing was hidden.

Kurag's eyes went to Frost and the small goblin in the guard's grasp. For all the goblin king's attention, his queen might have been in another room.

"Why do you hold one of my men?"

"This is not a battlefield, and I am not carrion," I said.

Kurag blinked. The eye on his shoulder blinked a second or two later than the three main eyes. He turned to the little goblin. "What have you done?"

The little goblin babbled, "Nothing, nothing."

Kurag turned back to me. "Tell me, Merry. This one lies like he breathes."

"He drank my blood without my permission."

The eyes blinked again. "That is a grave charge."

"I want recompense for the stolen blood."

Kurag drew a large knife from his belt. "Do you want his blood?"

"He drank from a royal princess of the high court of the sidhe. Do you really think his lowly blood is a fair trade for that?"

Kurag looked down at me. "What would be a fair trade?" He sounded suspicious.

"Your blood for mine," I said.

Kurag pushed his queen's hands away from his body. She made a small cry, and he was forced to shove her hard enough for her to fall on her butt to the ground. He never looked at her to see how she had fallen, or if she was all right.

"Sharing blood means something among the goblins, Princess."

"I know what it means," I said.

Kurag stared at me with his yellow eyes. "I could simply wait until you have lost enough blood to be carrion," he said.

His queen crowded next to him. "I could speed the process along." She held up a knife that was longer than my forearm. The blade gleamed dully in the light.

Kurag turned on her with a snarl. "This is not your concern!"

"You would share blood with her, who is not a queen. It is my business!" She stabbed the knife straight up toward his body. The knife was a blur of silver, the movement almost too quick to follow with the eye.

Kurag had time only to sweep an arm in an effort to keep the blade from his body. The blade opened his arm in a splash of crimson. His other main arm hit her full in the face. There was a sharp crunch of breaking bone, and she sat down on her butt for a second time. Her nose had exploded like a ripe tomato. Two of the teeth between her fangs had broken off. If there was blood coming from her mouth, it was lost in the blood gushing from her nose. The eye nearest the nose had spilled from its cracked socket and lay on her cheek like a balloon on a string.

Kurag trapped her knife under his foot. He hit her again, and this time she fell over on her side and lay still. There had been more than one reason that I did not want to marry Kurag.

He bent over the fallen queen. His thick fingers checked to see that she was still breathing, that her heart still beat. He nodded to himself and scooped her up in his arms. He cradled her gently, tenderly. He barked out an order, and a huge goblin squeezed through the crowd.

"Take her back to our hill. See her wounds are tended. If she dies, I will have your head on a pike."

The goblin's eyes flashed up to the king's face, then down. But there had been that one moment of pure fear on the goblin's face. The king had beaten the queen, nearly killed her, but it would be the goblin guard's fault if she died. That way the king would be blameless and would be able to find a new queen all the quicker. If he had outright killed her in

front of so many royal witnesses, he could have been forced
to give up either his throne or his life. But she had been very
much alive when he'd lifted her tenderly into the arms of the
redcap. The king's hands were metaphorically clean if she
died now.

Though it was doubtful the goblin queen would die. Goblins were a tough lot.

A second goblin guard, shorter and more barrel-chested
than the first, took the queen's knife from Kurag and followed
the first goblin guard back through the crowd. Kurag would
be within his rights to have both of them killed if the queen
died. One of the things that most royals learn early is how to
spread the blame. Spread the blame and keep your head. It
was like a complicated game with the Red Queen from *Alice
in Wonderland*. Say the wrong thing, don't say the right thing,
and it could be off with your head. Metaphorically speaking,
or not so metaphorically speaking.

Kurag turned back to me. "My queen has saved us the
trouble of opening my vein."

"Then let's get on with it. I'm wasting blood," I said.

Galen still had his hands over my wrists, and I realized he
was holding pressure on my wounds.

I looked up at him. "Galen, it's all right." He kept his hands
tight around my wrists. "Galen, please, let me go."

He stared down at me, opened his mouth as if to say something, then closed it and slowly moved his hands back from
my wrists. His hands came away stained with my blood. But
the pressure he'd applied had slowed the bleeding, or maybe it
was just Galen's touch. Maybe it wasn't just my imagination
that made his hands a cool, soothing presence.

He helped me to my feet. I had to push his hands away so I
could stand alone. I spread my legs to get as good a balance
on the heels as I could, and faced Kurag.

Standing, I came almost up to his sternum. His shoulders
were nearly as wide as I was tall. Most of the sidhe were tall,
but the larger goblins were truly bulky.

Fflur had moved to one side of me to join Galen, Doyle,

and Rhys at my back. Frost stood to one side, with the little goblin dangling from his hands. There was a press of bodies all around us: sidhe, goblin, and others. But I had eyes only for the goblin king.

"Though I do offer you my apologies for my man's rudeness," Kurag said, "I cannot offer you my blood without gaining in return."

I held my right hand out to him, and my left hand to the red mouth on his chest. "Drink then, Kurag, Goblin King." I raised my right wrist as close to his main mouth as I could reach. Reaching so far above my head left me faintly dizzy. I pressed my left wrist to the open mouth on his chest, and it was those lips that closed around my wrist first, that tongue that worked over the wound to get it to bleed afresh. The tongue in that mouth felt soft and human, not at all like the little goblin's harsh cat tongue.

Kurag bowed his head over my wrist, careful not to use his hands to hold the wound close to him. To use his hands would have been rude and taken as a sexual overture. His tongue was rough like sandpaper, even rougher than the little goblin's had been. It abraded the wound and brought a soft gasp from my throat. The mouth in his chest had already formed a seal over the wounds, sucking like a baby with a bottle. Kurag's tongue lingered until the blood flowed fresh and easy. When he wrapped his lips around my wound, his mouth took in almost all of my wrist. His teeth pressed against my flesh painfully as the suction grew. The smaller mouth in his chest was much more polite.

Kurag's mouth worked at my wrist, lips in a tight seal. Just as I grew accustomed to his sucking, his teeth grazed the wound, his tongue flicking in a sharp painful movement. He was staying at the wound a long time. It was sort of like a beer-chugging contest: you took as much in at a time as you could manage without throwing up.

But finally, finally, Kurag drew his head back from my wrist. I drew my left hand from his chest. The lips placed a light kiss against my wrist as I pulled away.

Kurag stretched his thin lips in a smile, showing the yellowed teeth stained with blood. "Do better if you can, Princess, though I've always found the sidhe a little too prissy for good tongue action."

"You must be entertaining the wrong sidhe, Kurag. I've found them all . . ." I lowered my voice to a husky whisper and put a look in my eyes to match. ". . . Orally talented."

Kurag chuckled, low and evil, but appreciative.

I swayed slightly, but I kept my feet and that was all that was required. But I was going to need to sit down soon, before I fell down. "My turn," I said.

Kurag's grin widened. "Suck me, sweet Merry, suck me hard."

I'd have shaken my head if I hadn't been convinced that it would make the dizziness worse. "You never change, Kurag," I said.

"Why should I?" he said. "No female I've bedded in over eight hundred years has ever gone away wanting."

"Just bleeding," I said.

He blinked, then laughed again. "If there ain't blood, what's the point?"

I tried not to smile and failed. "Big talk for a goblin who hasn't offered up his blood yet."

He held his arm out to me. Blood flowed down it in a thick red wash. The wound he offered in front of my face was deeper than it had looked, a red gaping thing like a third mouth.

"Your queen meant to kill you," I said.

He looked down at the wound, still grinning. "Aye, she did."

"You sound pleased," I said.

"And you, Princess, sound like you're delaying the moment when you must place that clean white mouth on my body."

"Sidhe blood may be sweet," Galen said, "but goblin blood is bitter." It was an old saying among us. It was also untrue.

"As long as the blood is red, it all tastes pretty much the same," I said. I lowered my mouth to the open wound. I couldn't come close to wrapping my mouth around Kurag's arm, as he had mine. But the taking of his blood had to be more than a mere kiss of my lips. To treat the blood-taking as less than the passionate sharing it was meant to be, the honor it was meant to be, was an insult.

There's an art to sucking blood from a wound that's bleeding this deeply. You have to start slowly, work into it. I licked the skin near the shallowest end of the wound with long sure strokes of my tongue. One of the tricks to drinking a lot of blood is to swallow often. The other trick is to concentrate on each task separately. I concentrated on how rough Kurag's skin was, on the large roughened lump that edged the wound like a knot in the skin. I paid attention to that knot, rolling it around in my mouth for a second, which was more than I had to do, but I was working my courage up for the wound. I like a little blood, a little pain, but this wound was deep and fresh and a little too much of a good thing.

I gave two more quick licks to the shallow end of the wound and then locked my mouth over it. The blood flowed too quickly and I was forced to swallow convulsively, breathing through my nose, and still there was too much of the sweet metallic liquid. Too much to breathe around, too much to swallow. I fought the urge to gag and tried to concentrate on something else, anything else. The edges of the wound were very clean and smooth. By that alone I knew how sharp the knife had been. It would have helped if I could have touched my hands to him, had some other sensory input. I was aware that my hands were straining in the air as if trying to find something to hold on to. But I couldn't help it. I had to do something.

A hand brushed my fingertips, and I grabbed that hand tight in my own, squeezing it. My other hand swept the air until it, too, was taken. I thought it was Galen, for the smooth perfection of the tops of his hands, but the palm and fingers were calloused from sword and shield—too rough for Galen's. These were hands that had been training in weaponry for longer than Galen had been alive. Those hands held mine, responding to my pressure, squeezing as I clung to the feel of them.

My mouth stayed against Kurag's arm, but my attention was in my hands and the strength that was holding me. I could feel the pull of his arms as he forced my hands behind my back and slightly up, just this side of pain. It was perfectly distracting and exactly what I needed.

I pulled away from the wound with a gasp, finally able to draw a good breath. I started to gag, but the hands jerked my arms upward, and I gasped again instead. The moment passed and I was all right. I wasn't going to embarrass myself by throwing up all that good blood.

The hands eased my arms back from the pain; now they were just something to hang on to.

"Hmm," Kurag said, "that was well done, Merry. You are indeed your father's daughter."

"High praise indeed coming from you, Kurag." I stepped back from him and stumbled. The hands steadied me, allowing me to lean back against the chest that went with them. I knew who it was before I turned my head to see. Doyle stared down at me as I leaned against his body, hands still clinging to him.

I mouthed the words, "Thank you," to him.

He gave a small nod of his head. He made no move to let me go, and I made no move to leave the press of his body. I was terribly afraid if I did step away from him or let go of his hands, I would fall. But it was also in that moment I felt safe. I knew that if I fell, he would catch me.

"My blood is in your body and yours in mine, Kurag," I said. "Blood kin we are until the next moon."

Kurag nodded. "Your enemies, my enemies. Your beloved, my beloved." He took a step closer, looming over me, even over Doyle. "We are blood allies for a moon's space of time, if . . ."

I stared up at him. "What do you mean if? The ritual is complete."

Kurag raised his three eyes and stared at Doyle. "Your Darkness knows what I mean."

"He is still the queen's Darkness," I said.

Kurag's eyes flicked down to me, then back to Doyle. "It's not the queen's hands he's holding."

I started to pull away from Doyle, but he tightened his grip on my hands. I forced myself to relax against his body. "It's none of your business what Doyle holds of mine, Kurag."

Kurag's eyes narrowed. "Is he your new consort? I heard rumor that that was why you were coming back to the court, to choose a new consort."

I wrapped Doyle's hands around my waist. "I have no consort." I leaned more solidly into Doyle's arms. He stiffened for a second, and then I felt his body relax one muscle at a time until he rested like a heavy warmth around me. "But you might say I'm shopping around."

"Good, good," Kurag said.

I felt Doyle tense, though I doubt anyone watching could have told a difference. I was missing something here. But what?

"No consort means I can demand one more thing or the alliance is broken."

"Do not do this, Kurag," Doyle said.

"I invoke the right of flesh," Kurag said.

"He has taken your blood under false pretenses," Frost said. "He knows who your enemies are, and the goblin king fears them."

"Do you call Kurag, Goblin King, a coward?" Kurag asked.

Frost tucked the little goblin he was holding under one arm, leaving his other hand free, but still bare of weapon. "Yes, I name you coward, if you hide behind flesh."

"What is the right of flesh?" I asked. I started to step away from Doyle, but his arms tightened. I looked up at him. "What is going on, Doyle?"

"Kurag is trying to hide his cowardice behind a very old ritual."

Kurag grinned at them both. Call anyone a coward at any of the courts and you ended up fighting a duel. Kurag was being much too reasonable. "I fear no sidhe," he said. "I invoke flesh not to avoid her enemies, Guardsmen, but to truly join my flesh with hers."

"You are already wed," Frost said. "Adultery is a crime among the sidhe."

"But not among the goblins," Kurag said. "So my marital status makes no difference here, only hers."

I pushed away from Doyle. The movement was too sudden. I swayed, and Fflur's hand on my elbow saved me from falling. "I am going to bind your wrists now," she said.

I couldn't really argue. "Thank you," I said to her. As she began to dress my wrists I turned back to the men. "Someone, please, explain what he is talking about."

"Glad to," Kurag said. "If your enemy is mine and I must help you defend yourself against powerful forces, then my beloved must truly be your beloved. We will share flesh as we shared blood."

"You mean sex?" Galen asked.

Kurag nodded. "Yes, sex."

I said, "No."

Galen said, "Oh, no."

"No flesh sharing, no alliance," Kurag said.

"Among the sidhe," Doyle said, "your marriage vows are still sacred. Meredith can no more help you cheat on your wife than she could cheat on her own husband. The rule of flesh only works if both parties are unjoined."

Kurag scowled. "You would not lie outright. Damn." He looked at me. "You always escape me, Merry."

"Only because you always resort to trickery to try and get in my pants."

A servant had come with a bowl of clean water, holding it for Fflur as she washed my wrists. She popped open a bottle of antiseptic and drenched both of my wrists with it. The reddish liquid fell into the water, floating on the surface like drops of new blood.

"I made you a valid offer of marriage once," Kurag said.

"I was sixteen," I said. "You scared the shit out of me." Fflur patted my wrists dry.

"Just too much man for you, aren't I?"

"The two of you together are too much man for me, Kurag, you're right," I said.

His hand went to his side where the extra genitalia lay. One heavy stroke and there was a bulge under the pants in a place where most men didn't have to worry about it.

"Flesh has been invoked," Kurag said, still stroking his side. "It cannot be undone, until it is answered."

I looked to Doyle. "What does he mean?"

Doyle shook his head. "I'm not sure."

A second servant brought up a tray of medical supplies and held it while Fflur started binding clean white gauze around my wrists. The servant acted as a sort of nurse, giving her scissors and tape as she needed it.

"I know what Kurag is doing," Frost said. "He is still trying to run from your enemies."

Kurag turned on Frost like a large, broad storm. "Merry needs every strong arm she can muster at her back. That is lucky for you, Killing Frost."

"Will you honor your alliance then and be one of the strong arms at her back?" Frost said.

"Truth," Kurag said. "If I cannot have sex with our Merry, then I would rather not honor the alliance." His lopsided multi-eyed face suddenly seemed serious, even intelligent. I realized for the first time that Kurag was neither as stupid as he acted, nor as ruled by his glands as he pretended to be. There was a moment of absolute shrewdness in those three yellow eyes. A look so intent, so different than a moment ago, that it made me step back, as if he'd tried to strike me. Because underneath that so serious look was something else—fear.

What was happening in the courts that Kurag, the goblin king, was afraid?

"If you do not honor your alliance," Frost said, "then all the court will know you for an honorless coward. Your word will never be trusted again."

Kurag looked around at the crowd. Some had gone with the queen like a brightly colored train of toadies, but many had remained behind. To watch. To listen. To spy?

The goblin king did a slow circle of the waiting faces, then came back to me. "I have invoked flesh. Share flesh with one of my goblins, one of my unwed goblins, and I will honor this alliance of blood."

Galen stepped up next to me. "Merry is a princess of the sidhe, second in line to this throne. Sidhe princesses do not sleep with goblins." There was a force in his voice, a heat. Anger.

I touched his shoulder. "It's all right, Galen."

He turned to me. "No, it's not. How dare he make such a demand."

There was a low angry murmur that swept through the sidhe in the room. The small knot of goblins that he'd been allowed to bring into our hill closed at his back.

Doyle moved up at my back. He whispered, "This could go badly."

I glanced at him. "What do you expect me do?"

"Be a princess and a future queen," he said.

Galen caught part of that. He turned on Doyle. "What are you asking her to do?"

"The same thing she is doing with us at Queen Andais's request," Doyle said. He stared at me. "I would not ask if the sacrifice were not worth the goal."

"No!" Galen said.

Doyle stared at Galen then. "Which do you value more, her virtue, or her life?"

Galen glared at him, tension running through his body like a near-visible current of anger. Finally, he said, "Her life," but it was spat out as if it were something bitter.

If I had the goblins as allies, then if Cel did manage to kill me, he'd have a blood feud with Kurag and his court. It would make Cel, or anyone else, hesitate. I needed this alliance. "One of your goblins' flesh in my body, I take it," I said.

Kurag smiled. "His flesh in your sweet body. Let your flesh and his be one, and all the goblin nation will be your allies."

"Whose flesh will I be sharing?" I asked.

Kurag looked thoughtful. The eye on his shoulder went wide, and the two thin arms on his side gestured wildly, pointing.

Kurag turned to the circle of goblins and began to move through them, following the small arms of his twin. I couldn't see who he finally stopped at. He walked back out of the tightly packed knot of goblins and it wasn't until the small goblin stepped out from behind him that I could see him at all.

He was only four feet tall with pale skin like gleaming mother-of-pearl. I knew sidhe skin when I saw it. His hair curled over his neck, black and thick, but cut short of his shoulders. His face was strangely triangular with huge almond-shaped eyes that were a solid sapphire blue with a line of black pupil like a stripe in the center of all that blue. He was wearing nothing but a silver-edged loincloth, which in a goblin meant that there was something of a deformity on the bare spots. They did not hide deformities, but saw them as a sign of honor.

He walked toward me over the stone like a tiny perfect male doll. If there was a deformity I couldn't see it. Except for his size and the eyes, he could have been of the court.

"This is Kitto," Kurag said. "His mother was a sidhe lady raped in the last goblin war." Which made Kitto nearly two thousand years old. He certainly didn't look it.

"Greetings, Kitto," I said.

"Greetings, Princess." There was a strange sibilance to his words, as if he had trouble forming the words. His lips were full and pink and shaped like a perfect cupid's bow, but those pretty lips barely moved when he spoke, as if there was something in his mouth that he didn't want me to see.

"Before you agree," Kurag said, "see the whole show."

Kitto turned his back and showed why he was wearing the loincloth. There was a spread of shining iridescent scales starting at the base of his hairline and descending down his back to the base of his spine. His butt was small and tight and perfect, but the glittering scales told me why his eyes had elliptical pupils and why he had trouble with his "sss."

"Snake goblin," I said.

Kitto turned back to face me. He nodded.

"Open your mouth, Kitto. Let me see it all," I said.

He looked at the floor for a moment, then rolled his strange eyes up at me. He opened his mouth in a wide yawn, flashing dainty fangs. His tongue flicked out like a red ribbon with a dab of black on the end of each point. "Ssatissfffied?" he asked.

I nodded. "Yes."

"You can't," Rhys said. He'd been so quiet I'd almost forgotten he was with us.

"It's my choice," I said.

Rhys touched my shoulder, took me to one side. "Take a good look at the scar across my face. I know I've told you a thousand heroic stories about how I got this, but the truth is the queen punished me. She gave me to the goblins for a night of sport. I thought, why not, free sex even if it is with goblins." He blinked his one good eye. "A goblin's idea of sex is more violent than you can imagine, Merry." He traced the length of the scar with his fingertip, and the look in his eye was distant, remembering.

I touched the scar where it ended on his cheek, catching his hand in mine. "A goblin did this to you during sex?"

He nodded.

"Oh, Rhys," I said, voice soft.

He patted my hand and shook his head. "No pity. I just want you to understand what you're agreeing to."

"I understand, Rhys. Thank you for telling me." I patted his cheek, squeezed his hand, and walked past him back to the waiting goblins. I was walking straight and upright, but there was a little turning inside my head that made me want badly to hold on to something. But when you're negotiating a war treaty, you need to look strong, or at least not like you're about to faint dead away.

"Kitto's flesh in my body, right?" I asked.

Kurag nodded, and he looked pleased with himself, as if he knew he'd already won.

"I agree to take Kitto's flesh into my body."

"Agreed?" Kurag said, surprise dripping from his voice. "You would agree to share flesh with a goblin?"

I nodded. "I agree, on one condition."

His eyes narrowed. "What condition?"

"If the alliance between us is a season long," I said.

I felt Doyle step closer to me. The ripple of surprise spread through the room in whispers and small movements.

"A season," Kurag said. "No, too long."

"Eleven moons from now," I said.

He shook his head. "Two moons."

"Ten," I said.

"Three."

"Be reasonable," I said.

"Five," he said.

"Eight," I countered.

He grinned. "Six."

"Done," I said.

Kurag stared at me for a heartbeat or two. "Done." He said it softly, as if even at the moment he spoke he was sure it was the wrong thing to do.

I raised my voice so it would carry throughout the room, standing with feet braced wide apart. It must have looked like an aggressive stance, but I wasn't trying for aggressive. I was trying not to let my body sway to the swirling inside my head. "The alliance is forged."

Kurag raised his own voice. "Forged only after you share flesh with my goblin."

I held my hand out to Kitto. He laid his hand on top of mine, a light touch of smooth flesh. I raised his hand up to my face. I tried to bend down and kiss the back of his hand, but the room swam. I had to straighten up and raise his hand with both of mine, spreading the small perfect fingers wide. I'd never held a man's hand that was smaller than my own. Sucking a finger would have been the most sexual thing I could do, but I'd sucked the last piece of flesh I wanted tonight. I laid a gentle but full kiss on his open palm. I didn't leave a lipstick print behind, which meant I'd worn it all off sucking on Kurag's arm.

Kitto's strange eyes widened.

I raised my mouth away from his hand, slowly, so that I rolled my eyes at Kurag as I came up over the goblin's hand, as if it were a fan. "We'll get around to sharing flesh, Kurag, don't worry. Now join me, Kitto. The queen awaits me and all my men."

Kitto darted a glance at Kurag, then back to me. "I am honored."

I looked up at the tall king. "Remember this, Kurag, as I share flesh with Kitto in the nights to come: that it was your own lust and cowardice that gave him to me, and me to him."

Kurag's face changed from yellow to a dark orange. His great hands balled into fists. "Bitch," he said.

"I spent many a night at your court, Kurag. I know that to have me share myself with another sidhe is nothing to you. For only sharing flesh with a goblin is true sex to you. Anything less is merely foreplay. And you have given me over to another goblin, Kurag. The next time you try and trick me into your bed, think where your trickery has gotten you and me."

I felt my strength ebb as I finished the speech. I stumbled, just a step. Strong hands caught me at both arms—Doyle on one side, Galen on the other. I looked from one to the other of them and managed to whisper, "I need to sit down, soon."

Doyle nodded. Galen kept his arm at my elbow and slid his other arm around my waist. Doyle's hold stayed on my arm but became firm as stone. I let go with my upper body, letting them take most of my weight while to other eyes I appeared to be standing just fine. I'd perfected this particular technique many times being dragged by the Guard before my aunt, when she demanded I stay on my feet and I couldn't do it alone. Some of the guards would help you pull the trick off. Some would not. Walking was going to be interesting.

Doyle and Galen turned me toward the open doors. One high heel scraped loudly on the stones. I had to do better than that. I concentrated on picking my feet up just enough to walk, but Galen and Doyle were holding me up. The world narrowed down to me putting one foot in front of the other. Gods, but I wanted to go home. But the queen was waiting, and being kept waiting wasn't one of her strong suits.

I caught a glimpse of Kitto moving just behind us and to one side. According to goblin etiquette, he was my consort, my boy-toy. Yes, he could hurt me during sex, but only if I were stupid enough to get into bed with him without negotiating a contract of what was and was not acceptable. Rhys's injuries could have been saved if he'd known goblins, but most of the sidhe simply saw them as barbarians, savages. Most did not study the law of savages, but my father had.

Of course, I wasn't planning on having sex of any kind with the goblin. I was planning to share flesh with him—literally. The goblins loved flesh better than blood or sex. To share flesh meant both sex and the greater gift of an allowed bite that would leave a scar until your lover died. It was a way of marking your lover, showing that they'd been with a goblin. Many goblins had special scar patterns that they used for all their lovers so that people would see their conquests at a glance.

But whatever I had to do to cement the bargain, I had the goblins as my allies for the next six months. My allies, not Cel's, not even the queen's. If there was a war between now and six months from now, the queen would have to negotiate with me if she wished the goblins to fight on her behalf. That was worth a little blood, and maybe even a pound of flesh, if I didn't have to lose it all at once.

Chapter 32

A DIP LAY IN THE STONES JUST INSIDE THE DOOR. A PLACE where feet have turned for thousands of years, pivoting on their heels to mount the low dais to either side of the room. I could have walked this floor in the absolute dark, but tonight I tripped on the small depression in the floor. Sandwiched between two guards, I should have been solid as inside a wall, but my ankle twisted and threw me so violently into Doyle that it brought Galen with me. Doyle caught us for an instant, then we were all in a heap on the floor.

Kitto was there first, offering a hand to Galen. I caught the look on Galen's face as he stared at that small hand, but he took it. He allowed the goblin to help him to his feet. There were other guards who would have spit on the hand instead of taking it.

It was Frost, one hand holding my knife, who took my hand and raised me to my feet. He wasn't looking at me. He was searching the area for threats. It had been subtle. If the spell had been a little less vicious, I might have chalked it up to blood-loss-induced clumsiness on my part, but the spell had been too large, too much. You did not bring down two of the royal guard in an unceremonious heap because the woman in the middle tripped.

Frost's hand forced me to take my full weight on my own two feet, and one of my feet wasn't up to it. Pain shot through my left ankle. I gasped, going to one foot. Frost had to catch me around the waist, lifting me completely off the ground, pressed against his body, encircled in his arm. He was still searching for the attack—the attack that wasn't coming, not here, not now.

Rhys was moving around the floor, checking for other traps. None of us moved very much until he nodded, still crouched on the floor.

Doyle was on his feet. He hadn't taken out the other knife. He met my eyes. "How badly are you hurt, Princess?"

"Twisted ankle, maybe the knee, too. Frost swept me off my feet before I could tell."

That earned me a glance from Frost. "I can put you down, Princess."

"I'd rather you carry me to a chair."

He looked at Doyle. "It's not a matter for knives, is it?" He sounded almost wistful.

"No," Doyle said.

Frost snapped the blade closed one-handed. To my knowledge he'd never handled a folding knife of any sort, but he made the gesture look smooth and practiced. He slid the blade into the back of his waistband and scooped me up in his arms.

"What chair would you prefer?" he asked.

"This one," the queen said. She was standing in front of her throne on the far raised dais. Her throne rose above everyone else's, as befit her position. But there were two smaller thrones on the dais just below her own, reserved for the consort and the heir, usually. Tonight, Eamon was standing at her side, his chair empty.

Cel was sitting in the other small throne. Siobhan was at his back. Keelin was at his feet on a small cushioned stool, like a lap dog. Cel was looking at his mother, and there was something very close to panic on his face.

Rozenwyn moved up beside Siobhan. She was Cel's second in command, Frost's equivalent. Her cotton-candy hair was piled in a crown of braids atop her head, like a bowl woven of pink Easter grass. Her skin was the color of spring lilacs, her eyes molten gold. I'd thought her lovely when I was small, until she made it clear that I was lesser than she. It was

Rozenwyn's hand-shaped scar across my ribs, she who had almost crushed my heart.

Cel stood so violently that it slid Keelin down the steps with the leash straining between them. He never looked at her as she got to her feet. "Mother, you cannot do this."

She looked at him, hand still guiding us toward Eamon's empty chair. "Oh, but I can, Son. Or have you forgotten that I am still queen here?" There was an edge to her voice such that, if it had been anyone but Cel, they'd have thrown themselves down on the floor in an abject bow, waiting for the blow to fall. But it was Cel, and she'd always been soft with him.

"I know who rules here now," Cel said. "What I am concerned with is who shall rule after."

"That, too, is my concern," she said, still in that so calm, so dangerous voice. "I wonder who could have set such a powerful spell just inside the throne room without anyone else noticing it." She looked around the huge room, settling her gaze on each face in its small throne. There were sixteen chairs on each side of the room on raised daises. Smaller chairs clustered around them, but the main chairs held the heads of each royal family. She studied them, especially the ones nearest the doors. "I don't see how anyone could have worked such a spell and had no one notice it."

I looked at the sidhe nearest the doors and they avoided my gaze. They knew. They had seen. And they had done nothing.

"Such a powerful spell," Andais continued. "If my niece had not been supported by two guards she might have fallen and broken her neck." Frost was still standing with me in his arms but had made no move to come closer. "Bring her, Frost. Let her sit beside me as she is meant to," Andais said.

Frost carried me forward. Doyle and Galen bracketed him, one right, the other left. Rhys and Kitto came like a rear guard.

Frost went to both knees on the bottom step that led up to the throne. He knelt with me in his arms as if it were no strain, as if he could have stayed like that all night, and there would have been no tremble in his arms. I wondered briefly if his knees ever fell asleep from being forced to kneel too long.

The others dropped to their knees a little behind and to either side of us. Kitto didn't just go to his knees, he flattened himself to the floor, facedown, arms and legs outstretched like some kind of religious penitent. I hadn't fully appreciated his problem until then. There were very specific types of bows and curtseys that you gave depending on your rank and the rank of the person being met. Kitto was not royal even among the goblins. If he had been, Kurag would have mentioned it. It had been a double insult to give me a goblin that was also a commoner. Kitto was not allowed to touch the steps except with express invitation. Only members of other sidhe royal houses were allowed to go to both knees in the throne room, without bowing the body in any way.

Kitto didn't know what the protocol was, so he'd taken the absolute lowest road. I knew in that instant that he'd cooperate with taking flesh instead of sex. He was more interested in staying alive than in any false sense of pride.

"Come, sit, Meredith. Let us make this announcement before another trap is sprung." She glanced at Cel when she said that last. He was my bet for the spell, too, but only because he was always one of my first choices when something nasty happened to me in the court. Andais had always looked the other way for Cel's sake. Something had happened between them, something that had changed Andais's attitude toward her only son. What had he done to turn her from him?

Frost stood in one easy motion and carried me up the steps. I could feel his legs push us upward as he carried me. He laid me gently in the chair, sliding his hands out from under my body. He went down on one knee in front of me, cradling my left foot in his lap.

I looked out into the room. I'd never been allowed on the dais. I'd never seen the view from up here. It wasn't so very high, or so very grand, but there was a sense of rightness to it.

"Bring a stool for Meredith to prop her ankle upon. When I have made my announcements, then Fflur may attend her."

She seemed to be speaking to no one in particular, but a small cushioned footstool floated toward us. I looked out of the corner of my eyes, deliberately not looking directly at the floating stool. A pale wisp of a shape showed like a white shadow holding the small stool in slender ghostly hands. The white lady set the stool beside Frost's leg. I felt that pressure as if the weight of thunder filled a small piece of air. It was the feel of a ghost standing far too close. I didn't have to see her to know she was there now. Then the pressure eased, and I knew she'd floated away.

Frost lifted my foot onto the much lower stool. I swallowed a gasp at the movement, but the pain had helped clear my head. I didn't feel faint anymore. It was the third attempt on my life in a single night. Someone was very determined.

Frost moved to stand behind my chair as Siobhan shadowed Cel, as Eamon had moved back to stand by the queen.

Andais stared out over the assembled nobles. The goblins and lesser folk, those invited at all, had spilled back in to fill the long ornate tables to either side of the room. But even Kurag did not have a throne to sit upon in this room. He was just one of the rabble here.

"Let it be known that Princess Meredith NicEssus, daughter of my brother, is now my heir."

A gasp ran through the room from mouth to mouth like a wind, until there was nothing but silence. A silence so thick that the white ladies rose into the air like half-seen clouds and began to dance on the tension of it.

Cel was on his feet. "Mother."

"Meredith has come into her power at last. She bears the hand of flesh as did her father before her."

Cel was still standing. "My cousin must have used the hand in mortal combat, and have been blooded in front of at least two sidhe witnesses." He sat down looking confident again.

The queen gave him a look so cold that his confidence faded from his face, leaving him unsure. "You speak as though I do not know the laws of my own kingdom, my son. All has been accomplished according to our traditions. Sholto!" she called.

Sholto stood from his big chair near the door. Black Agnes was on one side of him, Segna the Gold on the other. Night-flyers hung from the ceiling like great bats. Other creatures of the sluagh filled in around him. Gethin waved at me.

"Yes, Queen Andais," Sholto said. His hair was tied back from a face that was as handsome, as arrogant as any in the room.

"Tell the court what you have told me."

Sholto told of Nerys's attack on me, though not why she'd done it. He told an edited version of the events, but there was enough. He did not mention Doyle, though, and I found it a strange thing to leave out.

The queen stood. "Meredith is equal to Cel, my own son, in all things. But as I have only one throne for them to inherit, it will go to the one who is with child first. If Cel makes one of the court women with child within three years, then he will be your king. If Meredith is with child first, then she will be your queen. To ensure that Meredith has her choice of the court's men, I have lifted my Guard's celibacy geas for her and her alone."

The ghosts whirled overhead like happy clouds, and the silence deepened as if we were all sitting at the bottom of some deep, shining well. The looks on the men's faces ran from surprise to disdain to shock, and some went straight to lust. But in the end almost every male face turned to me.

"She is free to choose any among you." Andais sat down on her throne, spreading her skirts out around her. "In fact, I believe she has already begun the selection." She turned those pale grey eyes to me. "Haven't you, Niece?"

I nodded.

"Then bring them forth, let them sit at your side."

"No," Cel said, "she must have two sidhe witnesses. Sholto is only one."

Doyle spoke, still kneeling. "I am the other."

Cel slowly sat back down on his own throne. Even he would not be so bold as to question Doyle's word. Cel stared at me, and the hate in his eyes was hot enough to burn along my skin.

I turned from his hatred to gaze at the men who were still kneeling at the foot of the dais. I held my hands out to them. Galen, Doyle, and Rhys rose and walked up the steps toward me. Doyle kissed my hand and took up his post beside Frost at my back. Galen and Rhys sat by my legs, the way Keelin sat beside Cel. It was a little subservient for my taste, but I wasn't sure what else to do. Kitto stayed pressed to the floor, motionless.

I turned to my aunt. "Queen Andais, this is Kitto, a goblin. He is part of my bargain with Kurag, Goblin King, to bind an alliance between the goblin kingdom and myself for six months."

Andais's eyes raised upward. "You have been a very busy girl tonight, Meredith."

"I felt the need of powerful allies, my queen," I said. My eyes strayed to Cel even though I tried not to look at him.

"You must tell me later how you managed to get six months out of Kurag, but for now, call your goblin."

"Kitto," I said, holding my hand outward, "rise and come to my hand."

He raised his face without moving his body. The movement looked almost painful in its awkwardness. His eyes flicked to the queen, then back to me. I nodded. "It's all right, Kitto."

He looked back to the queen. She shook her head. "Get up off the ground, boy, so a doctor may attend your mistress's wounds."

Kitto rose to all fours. When no one shouted at him, he came to his knees, then to one knee, then very carefully to his feet. He came up the steps too quickly, almost a run, and sat down at my feet with something like relief on his face.

"Fflur, attend the princess," Andais said.

Fflur came up the steps with two white ladies on either side of her. The one holding the tray of bandages was the more solid of the two. She looked almost alive in a white, transparent sort of way. The other spirit was utterly invisible, holding a small closed box in midair as if aided by brownie magic, but no brownies worked magic here. Nothing that Earthly haunted the Unseelie Court.

Fflur removed my shoe and rotated my foot, which made me scoot around in my chair. I managed not to say "ow, ow, ow," but I wanted to. Thankfully it was just the ankle. Everything else was working.

"You need to remove your stocking so I can bind the ankle," she said.

I started to work the skirt up and fish for the band of my thigh-highs, but Galen put his hands over mine and stopped me. "Allow me," he said. He was not coming to my bed tonight, but the look in his eyes, the hush in his voice, the weight of his hands against mine over my thigh was like a promise for the future.

Rhys laid a hand on my other knee. "Why do you get to remove her stocking?"

Galen looked at him. "Because I thought of it first."

Rhys smiled and shook his head. "Good answer."

Galen smiled back at him. That smile that made his entire face glow as if someone had lit a candle behind his skin. He turned that shining face to me, and the humor in his eyes slid away, changing to something darker and more serious.

He was kneeling in front of me, on the far side of the injured leg, with Rhys next to the other leg. His hands had my hands trapped against my thigh. He raised my hands in his, gently kissing the back of each hand as he laid it on the arm of the throne. He pressed my fingers against the wood, as if telling me silently not to move my hands.

Because of the way my leg was propped on the stool, Galen was kneeling to one side, giving a full view to most of the room. He pushed the long skirt up, baring my leg, and the garter. He slid the garter down my leg and slipped it over his arm. His fingertips touched the hose just above my knee, sliding along the sleek fabric until both his hands pressed against my leg, coming to rest midthigh, like a hot weight against my skin. He met my eyes, and the look on his face made my heart race.

He lowered his eyes to watch his hands slide slowly up my leg. His fingers moved under the edge of my skirt, then his hands slid out of sight, almost to their wrists, as his fingertips found the top of the hose.

His hands seemed larger than they were, pressed under my skirt. When his fingertips moved past the elastic band onto my bare skin, it brought an involuntary jerk.

His eyes went back to my face, as if asking if I wanted him to stop. The answer was both no and yes. The feel of his hands on my body, the knowledge that we didn't have to stop, was intoxicating, exhilarating; if we'd been alone, and he completely healed, I would have thrown caution and all my clothes to the wind. But we were surrounded by nearly a hundred people, and that was a little too much audience for me.

I had to close my eyes before I could shake my head no.

His fingers moved ever so slightly upward, one fingertip caressing the edge of the hollow in the very upper line of my inner thigh. It brought my breath in a quick shaking sigh.

I opened my eyes and looked at him. This time I had the face to go with the head shake. Not here. Not now.

Galen smiled, but it was a private smile. The kind of smile a man gives you when he's sure of you and knows that only a little privacy stands between him and your body.

He folded his fingers over the edge of the elastic band and started rolling the hose down my leg, carefully, slowly.

A voice came from behind us, "The princess seems to have already made her choice." It was Conri, never one of my favorite people. He stood tall, dark, handsome with eyes like melted tricolored gold. "With all due respect, Your Highness, you give us a promise of flesh, then we are forced to sit and watch while another claims that prize."

"Meredith does seem to have been a busy little bee among all you lovely flowers," Andais said. She laughed, and the sound was derisive, joyous, cruel, and somehow intimate. It made a flush creep up my face as Galen slid the hose down my leg and off my foot.

He moved to one side, letting Fflur kneel over my ankle. He raised the hose to his face, brushing the sheer, black cloth against his mouth, as he stared at Conri.

Conri had never been my friend. He was one of Cel's childhood friends, a loyal supporter of the one true heir.

I watched the rage in his gold eyes, the jealousy, not of me as a person, but me as the only female they had access to. You could feel the tension in the room, growing, swelling, like the pressure before a storm. The white ladies always seemed to respond to great tension or great change in the court. The ghosts whirled around the edges of the room, swinging in a spectral dance above the floor. The more excited the ladies became, the more agitated they were—and the greater the events unfolding. They were like prophets that only predicted seconds ahead.

What can you do with seconds of warning? Sometimes much. Sometimes nothing. The trick was that you had to see the danger coming to stop it. Seconds to see it and stop it, and I was too slow, too late, again.

Conri's voice bellowed out, "I challenge Galen to death."

Galen started to stand and I caught his arm. "What do you hope to gain from his death, Conri?"

"To take his place at your side."

I laughed. I couldn't help it. The look of sullen rage on Conri's face at my laughter was chilling. I pulled Galen back down to kneel at my side. Fflur chose that moment to tighten the bandages, and I had to breathe out before I could speak.

"Is Galen Greenhair a coward then?" Conri scoffed. He had moved from his chair, off the dais, to the floor.

I patted Galen's arm, keeping him with me. "You never did have a sense of humor, Conri," I said.

His eyes narrowed. "What are you talking about?"

"Ask me why I laughed."

He stared at me for a second or two, then he nodded. "Fine, why did you laugh?"

"Because you and I are not friends. We are very close to enemies. I don't sleep with people I don't like, and I don't like you."

He looked puzzled.

I sighed. "I mean that if you kill Galen, that won't get you a place in my bed. I don't like you, Conri. You don't like me. I won't sleep with you under any circumstance. So sit down, shut up, and let someone talk who has a chance in hell of sharing my bed."

Conri was left standing, open-mouthed, and lost as to what to do. He was one of the most courtwise of all the guards. He sucked up to Cel expertly. He flattered the queen within an inch of propriety. He knew which nobles to treat well and which he could ignore or even treat badly. I'd fallen into the last category, because you couldn't be Cel's friend and be mine. Cel wouldn't allow it. I watched Conri's face as he realized that he hadn't been quite as courtwise as he thought he had. I enjoyed his embarrassment.

But he rallied. "My challenge stands. If I cannot share your bed, then I don't want Galen to have you either."

My hand tightened on Galen's arm. "Why fight if you know you don't get the prize?" I asked.

Conri smiled, and it wasn't pleasant. "Because his death will cause you pain, and that will be almost as sweet as your body next to mine."

Galen rose, sliding away from my grip on his arm. He started down the steps, and I was afraid for him. Conri was a cruel, brown-nosing bastard, but he was also one of the best swordsmen in the court.

I stood, hopping because I couldn't bear weight on my left foot. Rhys caught me or I might have fallen. "I am still the reason for this duel, Conri."

Conri nodded, watching Galen walk toward him. "Indeed, you are, Princess. Know that when I kill him, I did it all for spite of you."

Then I had one of those moments of desperate inspiration, a brilliant idea born of panic.

"You cannot challenge a royal consort to a death duel, Conri," I said.

"He is not a royal consort until you are pregnant," Conri said.

"But if I am actively trying to have a child with him, then he is my royal consort, because we have no way of knowing if I am with child at this second."

Conri turned to me, shocked. "You have not—I mean—"

The queen laughed again. "Oh, Meredith, you have been a busy, busy little bee." She stood. "If there is even a remote chance that Galen could have fathered a child upon my niece, then he is indeed a royal consort until proven otherwise. If you slew him and she was with child, and you had deprived this court of a fertile royal pair, I would see your head rotting in a jar on a shelf in my room."

"I don't believe it," Cel said. "They have not had sex tonight."

Andais turned to him. "And was there not a lust spell in the car when they were alone in the back of it?"

The blood drained from Conri's face in a wash, leaving him pasty and sickly looking. The look on his face was enough. The lust spell had been his doing. Though few sidhe in this room would doubt who had told him to do it.

"Meredith is not the only one who has been a very busy bee tonight." Her voice was warm with the beginnings of a really fine rage.

Cel sat up very straight and still managed to sink back into his chair. Siobhan moved from behind his chair to his side, not quite putting herself between the prince and the queen. But the gesture looked like what it was. Siobhan had stated her loyalties before the entire court. Andais would not forget it or forgive it.

Rozenwyn hesitated, not quite following her captain's lead. She eventually drifted up beside Siobhan, but her reluctance at having to choose between queen and prince showed. Rozenwyn's loyalty was mainly to Rozenwyn.

Eamon moved up beside the queen, and Doyle moved a step closer to the queen as if he wasn't sure where he should be standing. I'd never before seen him unsure where his duty lay. I saw the queen search his face, and I think his hesitation hurt her. He'd been her bodyguard for a thousand years, her right hand, her Darkness. Now he stood unsure if he should leave my side to go to hers.

"Enough of this," Andais said. The rage burned through those simple words. "I see you have made yet another conquest, Meredith. My Darkness has not hesitated in over a thousand years of service, but there he stands practically dancing from foot to foot wondering whom he should protect if all goes badly." The look she gave me made me grip Rhys's hand tight.

"Be glad that you are blood of my blood, Meredith. For anyone else to have divided the loyalties of my most trusted would be death."

It was almost as if she were jealous, but in all the years that I'd been old enough to notice, she'd never treated Doyle as anything but a servant, a guard. She'd never treated him as a man. He'd never in over a thousand years been one of her chosen lovers. But now, she was jealous.

The look on Doyle's face was soft, puzzled, full of wonderment. I realized in that moment that he'd loved her once, but no longer, and it hadn't been my doing. Andais had thrown him away by simply not paying any attention to him at all. It was too intimate a moment for such a public display.

Among humans some of us would have looked away, given them an illusion of privacy, but that wasn't the sidhe way. We stared, we watched every nuance cross their faces, and in the end, mere minutes, Doyle stepped back to stand with me, his hand on my shoulder. It was not a particularly intimate gesture, especially after the show Galen had put on, but from Doyle, in such a moment, it was intimate. He, like Siobhan, had shown his loyalty, burned his bridges.

I'd known that Doyle would keep me alive at the expense of his own life because the queen ordered it. Now I knew he'd keep me alive because if I died now, the queen would never trust him again. He would never again be *her* Darkness. He was mine, for better or worse. It gave a whole new meaning to "till death do us part." My death would almost surely mean his now.

I kept my eyes on my aunt but raised my voice for the entire room. "They are all my royal consorts."

Protests spread throughout the room, male voices raised: "You couldn't have slept with all of them!" And: "Whore!" I think that was a woman.

I raised my hand in a gesture that I'd seen my aunt use time and again. The room didn't grow totally quiet, but it was close enough for me to continue. "My aunt in her wisdom foresaw the duels that might be fought. That dangling any woman before the Guard could lead to great bloodshed. We could lose the best and brightest of us all."

A female voice cried out, "As if you are such a prize!"

I laughed, hand digging into Rhys's shoulder for support as if he were a cane. Kitto moved up and offered his hand to my free hand. I took the extra support gratefully. The ankle was beginning to ache hanging down at my side.

"I know that was you, Dilys. No, I am not such a prize, but I am female, and I am available to them, and no one else is. That makes me the prize whether any of us likes it or not. But my aunt foresaw the problem."

"Yes," Andais said. "I have ordered Meredith to choose not one among you, or four, or five, but many. She is to treat you all as her own personal . . . harem."

"Are we allowed to refuse if she chooses us?" I looked out into the crowd but couldn't see who had asked.

"You are free to refuse," Andais said. "But which of you would refuse the chance to be the next king? If she is with your child, then it will not be royal consort but monarch."

Galen and Conri were still standing about three yards apart, staring at each other.

"We all know who she wants to be her king. She has made that abundantly clear tonight," Conri said.

"All I've made clear," I said, "is that I won't be sleeping with you, Conri. The rest, as they say, is up for grabs."

"You won't be making Galen your royal consort," Cel said,

and his voice held satisfaction. "If you are with child, it will be his last."

I looked at him, trying to understand this level of animosity, and failing. "I bargained with Queen Niceven before the damage was too great."

"What did you have to offer Niceven?"

The tiny queen rose above the crowd where her miniature throne sat on a shelf, like a doll house, with her court surrounding her. "Blood, Prince Cel. Not the blood of a lowly lord, but the blood of a princess."

"We all carry the coin of the Unseelie Court in our veins, Cousin," I said.

Siobhan stepped in to try and save him, guarded him with her words as she would guard him with her sword. "What if it is the goblin that makes her with child?" Siobhan asked that.

The queen turned to her. "Then it is the goblin that will be king."

There was a shocked ripple through the court. Murmurs, curses, exclamations of horror. "We will never serve a goblin king," Conri said. Others echoed him.

"To refuse the chosen of the queen is treason," Andais said. "Deliver yourself to the Hallway of Mortality, Conri. I think you are overdue for a lesson in what disobedience will gain you."

He stood there staring at her, then his eyes flicked to Cel, and that was a mistake.

Andais stomped her foot. "I am queen here! Do not look to my son. Go to Ezekial's tender care, Conri. Go now or face worse."

Conri gave a low bow and kept the bow all the way out of the room, through the still-open doors. It was the only thing he could do. To have argued further could have earned him a beheading.

Sholto's voice came loud in the tense silence. "Ask Conri who ordered him to place the lust spell in the Black Coach."

Andais turned to Sholto like a storm about to break on the shore. Sitting next to her I could feel her magic gathering, prickling along my skin. It raised goose bumps on Galen's bare back.

"I will punish Conri, do not fear," she said.

"But not Conri's master," Sholto said.

The court held its collective breath, because Sholto was finally saying what everyone knew to be true. For years Cel had ordered things done; his toadies had suffered when caught, but never him.

"That is my business," Andais said, but there was the faintest hint of panic in her voice.

"Who was it told me that Your Majesty wished the sluagh to travel to the western lands and kill Princess Meredith?" Sholto asked.

"Don't," the queen said, but her voice was soft, like a dreamer trying to convince herself that a nightmare is not real.

"Don't what, Your Majesty?" Sholto asked.

Doyle spoke next. "Who had access to Branwyn's Tears and allowed mortals to use it against other fey?"

The thick silence was filled with dancing ghosts, whirling fast and faster. Faces were turned to the dais, some pale, some eager, some frightened, but all waiting. Waiting to see what the queen would do at last.

But it was Cel who spoke next. He leaned across and hissed at me, "Isn't it your turn next, Cousin?" His voice held such hatred.

I realized he thought I'd seen him in Los Angeles, but like Sholto I'd only been waiting for the perfect moment to reveal him. I drew a breath, but Andais gripped my arm. She leaned in to me, whispering, "Do not tell about his worshipers."

She knew. She knew that Cel had let humans worship him. It left me speechless. Unsaid between us was the knowledge that to protect her son she had risked all of us. Because if it could be proven in human courts that any sidhe had allowed themselves to be worshiped on American soil, we would be expelled. Not just the sidhe, but all fey.

I stared into those triple-grey eyes and saw not the terrifying Queen of Air and Darkness but a mother afraid for her only child. She had always loved Cel too much.

I whispered back to her. "The worshiping must cease."

"It has, you have my word."

"He must be punished," I said.

"But not for that," she whispered.

I thought about that for a second or two, while her hand gripped the blood-soaked cloth of my sleeve. "Then he must be punished for giving the Tears to a mortal."

Her hand tightened on my arm until it hurt. If her eyes hadn't held such fear I'd have thought she was threatening me. "I will punish him for trying to kill you."

I shook my head. "No, I want him to be punished for giving Branwyn's Tears to a mortal."

"That is a death sentence," she said.

"There are two punishments possible, my queen. I'll agree he keeps his life, but I want the full sentence allowed for the torture."

She pulled back from me, pale, her eyes suddenly tired. The torture was very specific for the crime. You were stripped naked and chained in a dark room, then covered with the Tears. Your body would be full of burning need, magical lust, but left untouched, unfinished, unrelieved. It is said that it can drive a sidhe mad. But it was the best, or the worst, I could do.

"Six months is too long," she said. "His mind would not survive it." It was the first time I'd ever heard her admit that Cel was weak, or at least not strong.

We bargained much as Kurag and I had, and ended with three months. "Three months, my queen, but if I or my people are harmed in any way during that time, then Cel forfeits his life."

She turned and stared at her son, who was watching us closely, wondering what we were saying. She finally turned back to me. "Agreed."

Andais pushed herself to her feet, slowly, almost as if her age were showing. She would never have an old body, but inside the years still passed. She announced in a clear, cold voice Cel's crime, and his punishment.

He stood. "I will not submit to this."

She turned on him, lashing out with her magic, pushing him into his chair, pressing on his chest with invisible hands of power until he could not draw breath to speak.

Siobhan made some small movement: Doyle and Frost moved between her and the queen.

"You are a fool, Cel," Andais said. "I have saved your life this night. Do not make me regret what I have done." She released him suddenly, and he slid to the floor, near where Keelin still crouched.

Andais turned back to the court. "Meredith will take whom she pleases with her tonight to her hotel. She is my heir. The land welcomed her at her return tonight. The ring on her finger is alive and full of magic once more. You have seen the roses, watched them come to life for the first time in decades. All these wonders and still you question my choice. Have a care that you do not question yourselves to death." With that she sat down and motioned for everyone else to sit down. We all sat down.

The white ladies began to bring in the small individual tables that sat in front of the thrones. The meal began to float in on ghostly hands.

Galen joined us again at the side of the dais. Conri was already being punished and missing the banquet, but not Cel. He and his would be allowed to enjoy the banquet before his sentence was carried out. Unseelie etiquette, if you were prince.

The queen began to eat. The rest of us ate. The queen took her first sip of wine. We drank.

She paused in sipping her soup and looked at me. It was not an angry look, more puzzled, but it certainly wasn't a happy look. She leaned in very close to me, close enough that her lips brushed my ear. "Fuck one of them tonight, Meredith, or you will be joining Cel."

I drew back enough to see her face. She'd known all along that Galen and I hadn't made love. But she'd helped me save him from Conri's challenge, and for that I was grateful. Still, Andais did nothing without a motive, and I had to wonder why this act of mercy? I would have loved to ask her, but the queen's mercy is a fragile thing like a bubble floating on the air. If you poked at it too much it would simply burst and cease to be. I would not prod this piece of kindness. I would simply accept it.

Chapter 33

WE WERE BACK IN THE BLACK COACH WHEN THE DARKNESS still pressed against the sky, but there was a feel of dawn on the air, almost like the taste of salt in the air near the sea. You couldn't see it, but all the same you knew it was there. Dawn was coming, and I for one was glad. There were things in the Unseelie Court that could not come out in the light of day, things that Cel could send after me, though Doyle thought it doubtful that the prince would try anything else tonight. But technically Cel's punishment wouldn't begin until tomorrow night, so the three months had not yet begun. Which meant that when the men went to pack, they'd gotten all their weapons. Frost practically clanked when he walked. The others were a little more subtle, but not by much.

Frost's great sword Geamhradh Po'g—Winter Kiss—was propped between him and the car door. Even strapped to his back, the sword was too long to wear sitting in a car. It wasn't a killing weapon like Mortal Dread, but it could steal a fey's passion, leaving them cold and barren as a winter snow. There had been a time when to be passionless, without his or her spark, would have frightened a fey more than death.

Doyle drove and Rhys rode in front with him. Doyle had ordered Rhys to ride in back with the rest of us, but Frost had insisted that he be allowed in the back. That had been . . . odd.

Now he sat in the far corner of the seat, pressed against the door, spine stiff, all that silver hair shimmering in the dimness. Galen sat on the other side. Most of his wounds were almost healed, and the ones that weren't were hidden under fresh jeans. He'd put on a white tank top underneath a pale green dress shirt. The shirt was tucked into his jeans but un-buttoned so the heavy ribbed material of the tank top showed. The only thing that remained of the court was the knee-high boots of soft, soft hide, dyed a deep forest green. The braid that decorated the tops of the boots dangled down in two beaded strings, making them look very Native American. The brown leather jacket that he'd had for years was folded across his knees.

There was room on the seat for Kitto, but he had curled himself into a corner of the floorboard, hugging his knees tight to his chest. Galen had loaned him a long-sleeved dress shirt to cover the metallic thong he was wearing. The shirt was huge on him, white sleeves flapping down over his hands. All I could see were his small bare feet sticking out from under the cloth. He looked about eight, huddled there in the dark.

To questions like, "Are you all right? Are you sure?," he answered, "Yes, Mistress." That seemed to be his answer to everything, but it was obvious that he was miserable for some reason. I gave up trying to pry information from him. I was tired, and my ankle ached. No, my foot and my leg ached all the way up to my knee. Rhys and Galen had taken turns holding ice on my ankle during the after-dinner entertain-ment. The dance that was supposed to help me choose among the men had been a bust because I couldn't dance. Even without the ankle I felt unwell and achingly tired.

I leaned against Galen's shoulder, half dozing. He raised his arm to put it over my shoulders but stopped in midmotion. "Ouch," he said.

"The bites still hurt?" I asked.

He nodded and slowly lowered his arm. "Yeah."

"I am not wounded." Frost's voice turned us to him.

"What?" I asked.

"I am not wounded," he said.

I stared at him. His face was its usual arrogant perfection, from impossibly high cheekbones to the strong jaw with its hint of dimple. It was a face that should have gone with a straight, thin line of lips. Instead, the lips were full, sensual.

The dimple and the mouth saved his face from being utterly stern. At that moment his face was set in as harsh a line as I'd ever seen it, his back very straight, one hand gripping the door handle so tightly that you could see the strain in his arm. He had looked at me to make the offer, but now he turned, giving me only his profile.

I watched him sitting there and realized that the Killing Frost was nervous. Nervous of me. There was something fragile in the way he held himself, as if it had cost him dearly to offer me his shoulder to lean against.

I glanced back at Galen. He raised his eyebrows, tried to shrug, and stopped in midmotion. He settled for a shake of his head. Nice to know that Galen didn't know what was going on either.

I wasn't comfortable enough with Frost to tuck my head against his shoulder, but . . . but he could have gone out the door, saved himself when the thorns attacked, but he hadn't. He had stayed with us, with me. I had no illusions that Frost had been harboring some deep love for me in secret all these years. That just wasn't true. But the geas had been lifted, and if I said yes, sex was a possibility for Frost for the first time in a very long time. He'd insisted on riding in back with me, and now he'd offered his shoulder for me to lean upon. Frost in his own way was trying to court me.

It was kind of awkwardly sweet. But Frost was not sweet. He was arrogant and full of pride. It must have cost him dearly to make even such a small overture. If I turned down the offer, would he ever risk himself again? Would he ever offer himself to me in even a small way again?

I couldn't crush him like that, and even as I thought it, I knew how much Frost would hate that what prompted me to scoot across the car seat wasn't lust or his physical beauty, but something very close to pity.

I slid across the seat, and he raised his arm, so I could slide underneath. He was a little taller than Galen, so it really wasn't his shoulder I laid my head against, but the upper swell of his chest.

The sheer material of his shirt was scratchy against my cheek, and I just couldn't relax. I'd never been this close to Frost, and it was . . . awkward. It was like we couldn't get comfortable together. He felt it, too, because we both kept making small adjustments. He moved his hand from my back to my waist. I tried my head higher on his chest, lower on his chest. I tried snuggling my body closer to him, and farther away. Nothing worked.

I finally laughed. He stiffened, arm tense against my back. I heard him swallow. Goddess, he was nervous.

I started to go up on my knees beside him but remembered my ankle and could only tuck one foot underneath me, carefully so the high heel didn't snag either my one remaining thigh-high or the satin of my panties.

Frost was giving me just his profile again. I touched his chin and turned him to face me. From inches away, even in the dark, I saw the pain in his eyes. Someone, somewhere, had done him a hurt. It was there, naked and still bleeding in his eyes.

I felt my face soften, the laughter sliding away. "The reason I laughed," I said, "was because—"

"I know why you laughed," he said and pulled away from me. He tucked himself against the car door, though he stayed upright and stiff. It reminded me of how Kitto was huddling on the floorboard.

I touched his shoulder gently. That thin veil of hair had fallen across his shoulders. It was like touching silk. The color of his hair was so harshly metallic that I hadn't expected it to be so soft. It was softer than Galen's curls. A totally different texture.

He was watching me pet his hair.

I looked up at him. "It's just that we're at that awkward first-date phase. We've never held hands or hugged or kissed, and we don't know how to be comfortable with each other yet. Galen and I took care of all the little preliminaries years ago."

He turned away from me, sliding his hair out of my hands, though I don't think he meant to. He stared stolidly out the window, though it acted as a black mirror showing his face to me like one of the white ladies of the court. "How does one overcome this awkwardness?"

"You must have dated once," I said.

He shook his head. "It has been over eight hundred years for me, Meredith."

"Eight hundred," I said. "I thought it was a thousand since the geas went into effect."

He nodded without turning around, staring at his reflection in the window. "I was her chosen consort eight hundred years ago. I serviced her for my three times nine years, then she chose someone else." There was the slightest hesitation in his voice when he said the last.

"I didn't know," I said.

"Me, either," Galen said.

Frost just stared out the window as if fascinated by the reflection in his own grey eyes. "I was like Galen for the first two hundred years, teasing the court women. Then she chose me, and when she cast me aside, it was so much harder to abstain. The memory of her body, of what we . . ." His voice trailed away. "So I do nothing. I touch no one. I have touched no one in over eight hundred years. I have kissed no one. Held no one's hand." He pressed his forehead against the glass. "I don't know how to stop."

I raised up on one knee until my face floated beside his in the window. I rested my chin on his shoulder, a hand on either side of him. "You mean you don't know how to start," I said.

He raised his face and looked at my reflection beside his. "Yes," he whispered.

I slid my arms across his shoulders, hugged the feel of him against my body. I wanted to say I was sorry that she'd done that to him. I wanted to voice my pity but knew that if he once smelled pity that it would be over. He might never open himself up to me again.

I rubbed my cheek against the unbelievable softness of his hair. "It's all right, Frost. It's going to be all right."

He rested his head against my cheek, and I felt his shoulders relax in the curve of my arms. I wrapped my hands across his chest, one hand grasping my other wrist. Slowly, tentatively, he slid his hands over mine, and when I didn't move or tense, he held my hands, pressed them against his chest.

His palms were sweating, oh, so slightly. His heart beat so hard I could feel it pulsing against my hands. I touched my lips to his cheek, almost too light to be called a kiss.

His breath ran out in a long sigh that made his chest rise and fall under my hands. He turned his head, and that one small movement put our faces close, so close. I looked into his eyes, caressed his face with my gaze, as if I'd memorize it, and in a way that was what I was doing. This was the first caress, the first kiss. It would never come again, never be this new again.

Frost could have closed that small distance with his lips, but he didn't. His eyes studied my face as I studied his, but he made no move to finish it. I was the one who leaned into him, closed the distance between our mouths. I kissed him, soft. His lips were utterly still against mine; only his half-parted mouth and the frantic beat of his heart let me know that he wanted this. I started to pull back, and his hand slid up my arm until he cradled the back of my head. He balled his hand into my hair, squeezing, feeling the thick hair as I'd felt the silk of his earlier. His eyes were just a little wide, flashing white. He lowered my face back to his mouth. We kissed, and this time he kissed me back. His lips pressed against my mouth. He turned his shoulders into me, so that I half spilled across one broad shoulder.

I opened my mouth to the press of his lips, flicking my tongue, a small wet touch. His mouth opened to me, and the kiss grew. His hand stayed in my hair, but the other hand swept around my waist and spilled me into his lap. He kissed me as if he would eat me from the mouth down. I could feel the muscles in his neck working under my hands as he kissed me with lips and tongue, as if his mouth had parts I'd never felt before. I turned in his arms, sitting more solidly in his lap. It brought a sound low in his throat, and his hands were at my waist lifting me upward so that my legs swung to either side of his, and I was suddenly kneeling with a leg on either side of him with the kiss in one unbroken wet line. My bad ankle brushed the seat and I had to come up for a complete breath.

Frost pressed his face against my upper chest. His breathing came in ragged gasps. I held his face against me, arms around his shoulders. I was blinking as if I'd been asleep.

Galen was nearly open-mouthed. I'd been afraid he'd be jealous, but he was too astonished to be jealous. That made two of us who were astonished. I could hardly believe that it was Frost I held in my arms, that it was Frost whose mouth seemed to leave a memory like a burn against my mouth.

Kitto looked at me with his huge blue eyes, and the look on his face wasn't astonished. It was heated. I remembered that he didn't know that he wasn't getting real sex tonight.

Galen recovered first. He applauded and said with an edge of nervous laughter in his voice, "On a scale of one to ten, I give it a twelve and all I was doing was watching."

Frost hugged me to him, still breathing as if he'd run a long way. He spoke with an edge of gasping to it, as if he hadn't quite recovered. "I thought I'd forgotten how to do that."

I laughed then, a low, rich sound, the kind of laughter that will turn a man's head in a bar, but this wasn't pretend. My body was still pulsing with too much blood, too much heat. I held Frost against my body. The weight of his face on my upper chest, his mouth leaning downward so the heat of his breath seemed to burn through the thin cloth of my shirt, and I more than half wanted his mouth to go lower, kissing across my breasts.

I found my voice. "Trust me, Frost, you haven't forgotten a thing." I laughed again. "And if you ever kissed better than this, I'm not sure I'd survive it."

"I'd like to be jealous," Galen said. "I was all set to be jealous, but damn, Frost, can you just teach me how to do it?"

Frost raised his head up so he could see my face, and the look on his face was full of a shining pleasure with an edge of something dark and satisfied in his eyes. It changed his face into something more . . . human, but no less perfect.

His voice was soft, low, intimate, as he said, "And that was just the touch of my flesh. No power, no magic."

I stared down into his eyes and swallowed. Suddenly, I was the one who was nervous. "It was magical, Frost, all on its own." My voice sounded breathy.

He blushed, a pale pink flush from his throat to his forehead. It was perfect. I kissed him on the forehead and let him help me bring my injured ankle back over his lap. I sat back down on the seat with Frost's arm around my shoulders. My body fit in the curve of his arm as if I'd always been there.

"See, all comfy," I said.

"Yes," he said, and even that one word held a warmth that made my stomach and lower things clench.

"You need to prop that foot up," Galen said. "I volunteer my lap." He patted his leg.

I stretched my legs out, and he put my feet on his legs. But it was awkward with me sitting up against Frost. "My back doesn't bend that way," I said.

"If you don't elevate the ankle, it's going to swell," Galen said. "Keep your feet in my lap and lie down. I'm sure Frost won't mind if you put your head in his lap." That last came out with a nice edge of sarcasm.

"No," Frost said, "I don't mind." If he got the sarcasm, it didn't show in his voice.

I laid down, keeping a hand on my skirt so it didn't slide up; with my legs elevated in Galen's lap I was very glad for the long skirt, which made it all more modest. I was tired enough that modest was just about the right speed.

I rested my head on Frost's thigh, my temple cradled against his stomach. His hand slid across my stomach until his fingers touched my hand, and we held hands as I gazed up at his face. The look was almost too intimate. I moved my head to one side, cheek resting full against his thigh. His free hand played with the hair on the side of my face, fingers gently pulling.

"Can I take off your other shoe?" Galen asked.

I looked down the length of my body at him. "Why?"

He raised his hips slightly, and I felt the stiletto heel press into flesh that was far too soft to be thigh. He kept himself pressed against the sharp heel, his gaze like a weight on my face. "The heel's a little sharp," he said.

"Then stop pressing yourself against it," I said.

"It still hurts to move around, Merry," he said.

"I'm sorry, Galen, you can take the shoe off."

His smile flashed. He slipped the shoe off my foot, holding it up, shaking his head. "I like the way you look in heels, but flats might have saved your ankle."

"She's lucky that was all that twisted," Frost said. "It was a powerful, if poorly constructed, spell."

I nodded, my head snuggling against the bend of his leg. "Yes, it was like shooting at squirrels with buckshot. You'll kill them, but there isn't much left to eat."

"Cel has power but very little control," Frost said.

"Are we sure it was Cel?" Galen asked.

We both looked at him. "Aren't you?" I asked.

"I'm just saying we shouldn't put everything at Cel's door. He's your enemy, but he may not be the only one. I don't want us to be looking so hard in Cel's direction that we miss something important."

"Well said," Frost said.

"Gee, Galen, that was almost like a smart thing to say," I said.

Galen slapped the top of my foot gently. "Compliments like that will get you nowhere near my body."

I thought briefly of pressing my foot into his groin and kneading, to prove that I was already close to his body, but I didn't. He was hurt and it would just pain him to no purpose.

Kitto was watching us all with an intense blue stare. There was something in his face, the way he held himself so attentive, that I was betting he'd be able to repeat everything we'd done, everything we'd said. Would he tell Kurag? How much "mine" was he?

He caught me looking at him, and his eyes stared into mine. The look was not fearful. It was bold, expectant. He'd been more relaxed since I'd kissed Frost, though I wasn't sure why.

My stare seemed to make Kitto grow more bold. He crept forward, toward me. His eyes flicked to Galen, then to Frost, but he knelt on the floorboard, legs straddling the hump in the middle.

He spoke very carefully, keeping his mouth as closed as he could to hide the fangs and the forked tongue. "You have fucked the green-haired sidhe tonight."

I started to protest, but Galen touched my leg, squeezing slightly. He was right. We didn't know how much we could trust the goblin.

"You have kissed—" The "s" in kiss was the first sibilance he'd allowed in the speech, and it made him hesitate. He started over. "You have kissed the silver-haired sidhe tonight. I would ask permission to uphold the goblin's honor in this matter. Until we share flesh, the treaty between you and my king is not finalized."

"Hold your tongue, goblin," Frost said.

"No," I said, "it's all right, Frost. Kitto's actually being very polite for a goblin. Their culture is very bold when it comes to sex. Besides, he's right. If anything happens to Kitto before we can share flesh, the goblins are free of the treaty."

Kitto bowed until his forehead touched the seat, hair brushing along Frost's hand where he still held mine. He rubbed his head against the seat, along the line of my body like a cat.

I tapped his head. "Don't get any ideas about doing it in the car. I'm not into group sex."

He raised up slowly, those drowning blue eyes staring at me. "When we get to the hotel?" He made it a question.

"She's injured," Galen said. "I think it can wait."

"No," I said. "We need the goblins."

I could feel Galen tense just through the hand on my leg. "I don't like it."

"You don't have to like it, Galen, just acknowledge the practicality of it."

"I do not like the thought of the goblin touching you, either," Frost said, "but it would be a simple thing to assassinate the goblin. They are easier to kill than a sidhe, if you use magic."

I looked at Kitto's delicate body. I knew he could trade blows with almost anything and limp away, but magic . . . That wasn't a goblin's strong point.

I was tired, so tired. But I'd worked hard for the alliance with the goblins. I wasn't going to lose it now through squeamishness. The question was what piece of my body was I willing to let him sink those fangs into? I wasn't going to lose a pound of flesh, but a bite, which Kitto was within his rights to take. Where would you want someone to take a bite of you?

Chapter 34

I COULDN'T WALK BECAUSE OF MY ANKLE. DOYLE CARRIED ME into the hotel lobby. Kitto stayed very close to me. Rhys had made a nasty comment on the way inside. If Rhys continued to carry a grudge against all goblins, it was going to make things harder than they already were. I didn't need harder. I needed something to be easier.

What was waiting in the lobby was not easier.

Griffin was sitting in one of the overstuffed chairs, long legs stretched out so that the back of his head rested against the back of the chair. His eyes were closed when we entered, as if he were asleep. His thick wavy copper-colored hair spilled just to his shoulders. I remembered when it had hit his ankles, and I'd mourned when he cut it. I'd avoided searching the crowd for him tonight. A glance was enough to prove that that deep, nearly auburn, red hair wasn't in the room. Why was he here? Why hadn't he been at the banquet?

I watched him with his line of black lashes closed on the pale face. He was wasting glamour to pass for human. But even dulled by his own magic, he was a shining thing. He was dressed in jeans with the bottoms of cowboy boots showing, a white dress shirt, buttoned up, and a jean jacket with leather touches at shoulder and arm. I waited for my chest to tighten, my breath to catch, at the sight of him. Because he wasn't asleep. He was posing so that I could get the full effect. But my chest was just fine. My breath didn't catch.

Doyle had stopped with me in his arms just short of the imitation Oriental rug that the chairs sat upon. I stared down at Griffin from Doyle's arms and was empty. Seven years of my life and I could look at him now and feel nothing but an aching emptiness. A wistful sort of sadness that I had wasted all that time, all that energy, on this man. I'd been afraid to see him again, afraid that all those old feelings would come flooding back, or that I'd be furious with him. But there was nothing. I would always have sweet memories of his body and less sweet memories of his betrayal, but the man that sat so carefully posed was not my love anymore. The realization was both a profound relief and a great sorrow.

He opened his eyes slowly, that smile curling his lips. The smile made my chest hurt, because once I had believed that that special smile was meant just for me. The look in his honey-brown eyes was familiar as well. Too familiar. He looked at me as if I'd never gone away. He looked at me with the same surety that Galen had had earlier. His eyes filled with a knowledge of my body and the promise that he would have access to it soon.

That killed any kindness I might still have felt for him.

The silence had gone on a little too long, but I didn't feel the need to break it. I knew if I simply said nothing, Griffin would break first. He'd always been fond of the sound of his own voice.

He stood in one fluid motion, slouching just a touch so he didn't look his six feet three. He flashed me the full smile, the one that made his eyes crinkle and showed that flash of dimple in one cheek.

I stared at him, face immobile. It helped that I was so tired I could barely think, but it was more than that. I felt empty inside and I let it show in my face. I let him see that he meant nothing to me, though knowing Griffin, he wouldn't believe it.

He stepped forward, one hand outstretched as if he'd take my hand. I stared at him until his hand dropped away, and for the first time he looked uncomfortable.

His gaze slid over all of us, then came back to rest on me. "The queen insisted I not be there tonight. She thought it might upset you." The surety was sinking away from his eyes, leaving him anxious. "What did I miss tonight?"

"What are you doing here, Griffin?" I said. My voice was as empty as my heart.

He shifted from one foot to the other. It was obvious that this reunion wasn't going the way he'd planned. "The queen said she'd lifted the geas on the Guard for you." His eyes flicked to Doyle, to the others. He frowned at the goblin. He didn't like any of this. He didn't like me in someone else's arms. There was a small flare of satisfaction. Petty, but true.

"How does the geas being lifted for me and me alone answer my question, Griffin?"

He frowned at me.

"Why are you here?" I asked.

"The queen said she told you that she'd be sending one guard of her choosing along." He tried the smile again, and it faded as I stared at him.

"Are you trying to tell me that the queen has sent you as her spy?"

His face raised, that smooth chin jutting out. It was a sure sign that he wasn't happy. "I thought you'd be pleased, Merry. There are a lot of guards that would be worse to share your bed with."

I shook my head, leaned my face against Doyle's shoulder. "I am too tired for this."

"What do you want us to do, Meredith?" Doyle asked.

Griffin's eyes hardened, and I knew that Doyle had used my first name deliberately—not a title, but my name.

It made me smile. "Take me up to the room and contact the queen. I will not be forced to share a bed with him again, not for any reason."

Griffin took a step toward us, hand stroking my hair. Doyle moved me out of his reach with a turn of his shoulders.

"She was my consort for seven years," Griffin said, and there was anger in his voice now.

"Then you should have valued her as the precious gift she is."

"Go away, Griffin," I said. "I'll get the queen to send someone else."

He moved in front of Doyle, blocking our way to the elevators. "Merry, Merry, don't you—"

"Feel anything?" I finished for him. "I feel like getting out of this lobby before we attract a crowd."

He looked toward the desk; the late-night attendant was giving us all her attention. A man had come and joined her, as if they were afraid there'd be trouble.

"I am here at the queen's orders. Only she can send me away, not you."

I stared into his angry eyes and laughed. "Fine, fine, let's all troop up to the room and call her from there."

"Are you sure?" Doyle said. "If you wish him to stay in the lobby, we can make it so." There was the faintest edge to his words, and I realized that Doyle wanted to hurt Griffin, wanted an excuse to punish him. I don't think it was personal over me. I think it was more that Griffin had had what they all wanted, access to a woman that adored him, and he'd thrown it away while all they could do was watch.

Frost moved up at Doyle's back. Kitto followed him. Rhys moved in from the other side, and Galen began to edge around to come at Griffin from the back.

Griffin was suddenly tense. His hand went to the edge of his belt and started to slide out of sight under the jacket.

Doyle said, "If your hand goes out of sight, I'll assume you mean us harm. You don't want me to assume that, Griffin."

Griffin tried to keep them all in sight, but he'd allowed them to flank him. You couldn't look at every side of a circle. It was too careless for words, and Griffin was many things, but not careless. For the first time I wondered if he had truly felt distress at our breakup, enough distress to make him careless, enough distress to get him hurt or even dead.

The idea was sort of amusing in a sociopathic sort of way, but I didn't want him dead. I just wanted him away from me.

"As amusing as it would be to watch you beat the shit out of each other, let's not and just say we did."

"What are your orders?" Doyle asked.

"Everybody upstairs, contact the queen, clean up a little, then we'll see."

"As you like, Princess," Doyle said. He carried me toward the elevators. The others came behind, forming a sort of half-circular net to sweep Griffin at our backs. Without being told, Rhys and Galen took up posts to either side of Griffin as we entered the elevator.

Doyle stood to one side, back to the mirrored walls so he could see both Griffin and the closed doors. Frost mirrored him on the other side of the doors. Kitto kept eyeing Griffin as if he'd never seen him before.

Griffin leaned his shoulders against the wall, arms crossed on his chest, ankles crossed, the picture of casual ease. But his eyes weren't casual. There was a stiffness to his shoulders that no amount of pretense could hide.

I looked at him between Galen and Rhys. He was the taller by three inches and a lot more than that for Rhys.

He caught me watching and he threw off his glamour, slowly, like a striptease. I'd seen him do it nude too many times to count. It was like watching a light spread from under his skin, his feet first always, then up the muscled ridge of his calves, to the strong thighs, up, up his body until every inch of him glowed like polished alabaster with a candle inside it, so bright that there were almost shadows cast from the glow of his skin.

The memory of his body nude and shining was burned on the inside of my head, and closing my eyes didn't help. It had been too dear a memory for too long. I opened my eyes and watched his copper-red hair glow as if it had thin metallic wire running through it. The thick, large waves in his hair crackled and moved with his power. The eyes weren't honey-brown. They were tricolored: brown around the pupil, liquid gold, then a burnished bronze. The sight of him all aglow did make me catch my breath. He would always be beautiful. No amount of hatred could take that away from him.

But beauty wasn't enough, not enough by half.

No one said a word until the elevator stopped. Then Galen grabbed Griffin's arm, and Rhys checked the hallway before Doyle carried me out.

"Why the caution?" Griffin asked. "What happened tonight?"

Rhys checked the door, then took the key card from me and opened the door. He checked the room while we all waited out in the hall. If Doyle's arms were getting tired from lugging me around, it didn't show.

"The room's clear," Rhys said. He took Griffin's other arm, and they escorted him into the room. The rest of us followed.

Doyle laid me on the bed, so I was sitting against the headboard. He took a pillow out from the blue covers and propped it under my ankle. He took off his cloak and laid it at the foot of the bed. He was still wearing the leather and metal-studded harness across his bare chest; the silver earrings still glittered in his curved ears; the peacock feathers still brushed his shoulders. It occurred to me for the first time that I'd never seen Doyle any different than he was right now. Oh the clothes, but I wasn't sure if he was using glamour or not. Doyle didn't try to be other than what he was.

I looked at Griffin still glowing, still beautiful. Galen and Rhys had made him sit in a chair. Galen leaned on the small table by the chair. Rhys leaned against the wall. None of them were glowing, but I knew that Galen, at least, wasn't trying to pass for human.

Kitto climbed onto the bed curling beside me, one hand sliding across my waist, dangerously close to my lap. But he didn't try to take advantage. He curled his face against my hip and seemed content, as if he meant to sleep.

Frost sat down on the far side of the bed, legs still on the floor, but not leaving the bed to just the goblin. He crossed his hands over his chest just below the blood stains. He sat there tall and straight and heart-stoppingly handsome, but he didn't glow the way Griffin glowed.

I had a sudden revelation. Griffin hadn't removed glamour. He'd added it. All those times that I thought he was throwing off all trickery, he was actually wrapping himself in the greatest trick of all. Most sidhe couldn't use glamour to make themselves look better to other sidhe. You could try it, but it was wasted effort. Even with me having come into my power he glowed, but now I could see it for what it truly was—a lie.

I closed my eyes, leaning my head back against the wall. "Drop the glamour, Griffin. Just sit there like a good little boy." My voice sounded tired even to me.

"He is very good at it," Doyle said. "Maybe the best I've ever seen."

I opened my eyes and looked at Doyle. "Glad to know the show wasn't just for my benefit. I was feeling pretty stupid."

Doyle glanced at the rest of the room. "Gentlemen?"

"He glows," Galen said.

"Like a lightning bug in June," Rhys said.

Frost nodded.

I touched Kitto's hair. "Do you see him?" I asked.

Kitto raised his head, eyes half-closed. "All the sidhe are beautiful to me." He snuggled his face back against me, and it was a little lower than my hip that he was cuddling against.

I looked at Griffin, still gleaming and so beautiful that I wanted to shield my eyes as if I were gazing at the sun. I wanted to scream at him, things about lies and trickery, but I didn't. Anger would have convinced him that I still felt something for him. I didn't—or, rather, not what he wanted me to feel. I felt tricked and stupid and angry. "Contact the queen, Doyle," I said.

The dresser sat in front of the bed with the large mirror facing me. Doyle stood in the center of the mirror. I could still see myself in the glass. I stared back at myself and wondered why I didn't look more different. Oh, my hair needed to be brushed, the makeup needed to be retouched, the lipstick was gone completely, but my face was still the same. My innocence had vanished years ago, and there was very little surprise left in me. All I truly felt was a great numbness.

Doyle pressed his hands just above the glass. I felt his magic crawl through the room like a prickle of ants marching along my skin. Kitto raised his head to watch, resting his cheek against my thigh.

The power built to a push of pressure, as if you could clear it by making your ears pop, equalizing the pressure, but the only thing that would make the pressure ease was use. Doyle caressed the mirror, and it wavered like water. His fingertips were like stones thrown into a pool where the ripples spread outward. He made a small gesture with his hands, a flexing at wrist and hand, and the mirror was no longer clear. The surface was milky, like a cup of fog.

The mist cleared, and the queen sat on the edge of her bed, looking at us through the full-length mirror in her private quarters. She'd removed her gloves, but the rest of the outfit was intact. She'd been waiting for the call. I'd have bet a body part on it. Eamon's naked shoulder showed to one side of her. He was turned on one side as if asleep. The blond boy was kneeling beside her, propped on his elbows. He was naked, too, but he wasn't under the covers. His body was strong, but thin, a boy's body without the musculature of a man. I wondered again if he was really eighteen.

Doyle had stepped aside so that I was the first one that the queen's eyes sought. "Greetings, Meredith." Her eyes took in the scene, the half-dressed goblin and Frost on the bed with me. She smiled and it was a pleased smile. I realized that the two scenes were similar. She had two men in her bed, and I had two men in mine. I hoped she was having a better time than I was. Or maybe I didn't.

"Greetings, Aunt Andais."

"I thought you'd be all tucked into bed with one or more of your boys. You disappoint me." She stroked her hand along the boy's bare back, sweeping at the end of the oval, fingertips across his buttocks. It was an idle gesture, like you'd pet a dog.

My voice came out very neutral, carefully empty. "Griffin was here when we arrived. He says you sent him."

"I did," she said. "You agreed to sleep with my spy."

"I didn't agree to sleep with Griffin. I thought after our little talk you understood how I felt about him."

"No," Andais said. "No, I didn't understand that at all. In fact, I wasn't sure you knew how you felt about him yourself."

"I don't feel anything about him," I said. "I just want him out of my sight, and I am certainly not going to sleep with him." I realized as soon as I said the last part that she might insist on it out of sheer perversity. I added, quickly, "I want to know he's celibate again. He was freed of the geas ten years ago so he could sleep with me, but he used his freedom to fuck everyone that would have him. I want him to know that I'm sleeping with the other guards, that they're getting sex and he's not. That unless I consent to lie with him that he may never have sex again for the rest of his so unnatural life." I smiled as I spoke and realized it was the truth. Goddess bless me, it was vindictive, but it was true.

Andais laughed again. "Oh, Meredith, you may be more my bloodline than I ever dared hope. As you will. Send him back to his lonely bed."

"You heard her," I said. "Get out."

"If it's not me," Griffin said, "it will be someone else. Maybe you should ask her who she will send to replace me in your bed."

I looked at my aunt. "Who are you going to send to replace Griffin?"

She held out her hand, and a man stepped into view as if he'd been patiently waiting for his cue. His skin was the color of soft spring lilacs, his knee-length hair the color of pink Easter-egg grass. His eyes were like pools of liquid gold. It was Pasco, Rozenwyn's twin brother.

I stared at him, and he stared back. We had never been friends. In fact there was a time or two I'd thought we were enemies.

Griffin laughed. "You can't be serious, Merry. You'd let Pasco fuck you before me?"

I stared at Griffin. He'd stopped glowing and looked almost ordinary as he stood there. He was angry, so angry that there was a fine tremble in his hands as he pointed to the mirror.

"Griffin, honey," I said, "I'd let a hell of a lot of men in my bed before you."

The queen laughed, drawing Pasco down until he sat in her

lap, like a child visiting Santa Claus in the mall. She stared out at me, running her hands through Pasco's cotton-candy hair. "You agree to Pasco as my spy?"

"I agree."

Pasco's eyes widened just a bit at that, as if he'd expected at least a little protest on my part. But I just wasn't up to it tonight.

Andais caressed a hand up Pasco's clothed back. "I think you have surprised him. He told me you'd never agree to sharing a bed with him."

I shrugged. "It's not a fate worse than death."

"Very true, niece of mine."

Our eyes met through the nothing of the mirror. She nodded and pushed the man to his feet. She slapped his butt as he walked out of frame. "He'll be right over."

"Great," I said. "Now get out, Griffin."

Griffin hesitated, then walked into view of the mirror. He glanced from one to the other of us. He opened his mouth as if to say something, then closed it. Probably the wisest thing he could have done.

He bowed, "My queen." He turned to me. "I will see you again, Merry."

I shook my head. "What for?"

"You did love me once," he said, and it was almost a question, almost a plea.

I could have lied—there was no spell on me—but I didn't. "Yes, Griffin, I loved you, once."

He looked at me, eyes roving over the bed and the smorgasbord of men. "I am sorry, Merry." He sounded sincere.

"Sorry you lost me, sorry you killed my love for you, or sorry that you can't fuck me anymore?"

"All of it," he said. "I'm sorry for all of it."

"Good boy. Now get out," I said.

Something passed across his face, something close to pain, and for the first time I thought that maybe, just maybe, he understood what he'd done was wrong. He unlocked the door, stepped outside, and when the door closed behind him, I knew he was gone, gone in a way beyond simply not being around. He was not my honey bun anymore, not my special person.

I sighed and leaned back against the wall. Kitto snuggled close, sliding one bare leg up and down against mine. I wondered if there was a chance in hell of me getting any alone time tonight.

I looked at the mirror again. "You knew I wouldn't accept Griffin as your spy, not if it meant having sex with him."

She nodded. "I needed to know how you truly felt about him, Meredith. I had to be sure that you weren't still in love with him."

"Why?" I asked.

"Because love can interfere with lust. Now I'm sure that you are rid of him in your heart. I am pleased."

"I'm just tickled pink that you're pleased," I said.

"Have a care, Meredith. I don't like sarcasm directed at me."

"And I don't like having my heart cut out for your pleasure." The moment I said it, I knew it was a mistake.

Her eyes narrowed. "When I cut your heart out, Meredith, you'll know it." The mirror spilled into fog, then was suddenly reflective again. I stared at myself in the mirror, my pulse thudding in my throat.

"Having your heart cut out," Galen said. "Poor, poor choice of words."

"I know," I said.

"In the future," Doyle said, "keep your temper. Andais doesn't need any help coming up with awful ideas."

I pushed Kitto away. I lifted my foot off the bed, carefully, using the bedside table to stand up.

"What are you doing?" Doyle asked.

"I am going to clean some of this blood and dirt off, then go to bed." I looked at the men gathered in the room. "Who wants to help me run my bath?"

The silence was suddenly very thick. The men looked at one another as if not sure what to do, or say. Galen stepped forward, gave me his hand to help me stand. I took the hand, but shook my head. "You can't be with me tonight, Galen. It has to be someone who can finish what we start."

He looked at the floor for a second or two, then up. "Oh." He helped me back to the bed and I let him do it, then he walked to the chair where he'd thrown his leather jacket. "I'm going to see about getting a second room next to this one, then I'm going for a walk. Who's going with me?"

They all looked at each other again, little eye flits from one to the other. No one seemed to know how to handle the situation. "How does the queen choose between you all?" I asked.

"She simply requests the guard, or guards, she wishes to have for the evening," Doyle said.

"Don't you have a preference?" Frost asked, and there was something almost hurt in his tone.

"You say that like there's a bad choice here. There is no bad choice; you are all lovely."

"I have had my release with Meredith," Doyle said, "so I will bow out for tonight."

That got everyone's attention, and Doyle had to explain very briefly exactly what he meant by the comment. Frost and Rhys looked at each other, and suddenly there was a tension in the air that hadn't been there before.

"What's wrong?" I asked.

"You must choose, Meredith," Frost said.

"Why?" I asked.

Galen answered, "You can't bring it down to just two of us without the danger of a duel."

"It's not just two, it's three," I said.

They all looked at me, then slowly at the goblin still on the bed. He looked as surprised as they did. He stared back at us with large eyes. He looked almost frightened. "I would never presume to compete with the sidhe."

"Kitto is coming in the bathroom regardless of who else comes in," I said.

Every pair of eyes in the room swiveled back to me. "What did you say?" Doyle asked.

"You heard me. I want the alliance with the goblins sealed,

that means I have to share flesh with Kitto, and that's what I'm going to do."

Galen went for the door. "I'll be back later."

"Wait for me," Rhys said.

"You're leaving?" I asked.

"As much as I want you, Merry, I don't do goblins." He walked out with Galen; they shut the door behind them, and Doyle locked it.

"Does this mean you're staying?" I asked.

"I will guard the outer door," Doyle said.

"What if we wish to use the bed?" Frost asked.

Doyle looked thoughtful, then shrugged. "I can wait just outside the room if you feel the need of the bed."

There was a little more negotiating. Frost wanted it clear that he did not have to touch the goblin. I agreed. Frost picked me up and carried me into the bathroom. Kitto was already in the room running the water for the bath. He glanced up as we entered. He'd taken off Galen's shirt and was back to just his silver thong. He said nothing to us, just watched us with his huge blue eyes, one hand trailing under the water as it poured from the faucet.

Frost looked around the small room. He finally sat me on the counter by the sink. He stood in front of me, and suddenly it was awkward. The kiss in the car had been wonderful, but it was the first time Frost and I had ever touched each other. Now suddenly we were supposed to have sex—with an audience.

"Awkward, isn't it?" I said.

He nodded. The movement sent that thin veil of silver hair gliding around his body. He reached out, slowly, tentatively, to the dress's jacket. He pushed the velvet off my shoulders, slowly, sliding it over my arms. I started to help him with the sleeves, but he said, "No, let me."

I put my hands back at my sides, and he pulled the sleeves off one hand, then the other. He dropped the jacket to the floor. He ran the tips of his fingers down the bare skin of my shoulders. It raised goose bumps down to my fingertips.

"Undo your hair," I said.

He took out the first bone clip, then the second, and the hair fell around him in a glorious spill of Christmas-tree tinsel. I reached out and grabbed a handful of it. It looked like silver wire, but it felt soft as satin, with a texture like spun silk.

He stepped close enough that his legs brushed mine. He ran his hands over my bare arms. His touches were so tentative, as if he was afraid to caress me. "If you will lean forward, I will unzip the dress."

I did what he asked, leaning my head against his chest. The sheer material of his shirt was scratchy, but his hands as they unzipped the dress were slow, gentle. His fingertips slid inside the open dress, circling the smooth skin of my back.

I tried to pull the shirt out of his pants, but it wouldn't budge. "I can't get the shirt out."

"It is fastened so it lies smoothly," he said.

"Fastened?" I made the word a question.

"I would have to take the pants off to get the shirt off." He was blushing, a wonderful pale red rose color.

"What's wrong, Frost?"

The bathwater stopped running. Kitto said, "The water is ready, Mistress."

"Thank you, Kitto." I looked at Frost. "Answer the question, Frost. What's wrong?"

He looked down, all that shining hair acting like a curtain. He turned away from me to face the far wall, so even the goblin couldn't see his face.

"Frost, please don't make me hop down from the counter to make you look at me. I don't need to twist another ankle."

He spoke without turning around. "I do not trust myself with you."

"In what way?" I asked.

"In the way of a man with a woman."

I still wasn't understanding him. "I still don't understand, Frost."

He turned suddenly to face me, eyes a dark storm grey with anger. "I want to fall on you like some ravening beast. I don't want to be gentle. I just want."

"Are you saying you don't trust yourself not to . . ." I searched for a word, but had to settle for, "rape me?"

He nodded.

I laughed, I couldn't help it. I knew he wouldn't like the laughter, but I just couldn't help it.

His face grew arrogant, distant, eyes cold but still angry. "What do you want of me, Meredith?"

"Frost, forgive me, but you can't rape the willing."

He frowned at that, as if he didn't understand the phrasing.

"I want to have sex with you tonight. That's the plan. How can that be rape?"

He shook his head, sending the hair sliding around him, sparkling in the light. "You do not understand. I do not trust that I can control myself."

"In what way?"

"In every way!" He turned away again, hugging himself.

I finally began to get an inkling of what he was trying to say. "Are you concerned that you won't last long enough for my pleasure?"

"That and . . ."

"What, Frost, what?"

"He wants to fuck you," Kitto said.

We both looked at the goblin still kneeling by the bathtub. "I know that," I said.

Kitto shook his head. "Not sex, just fucking. He's been so long without, he just wants to do it."

I looked at Frost. He was avoiding my eyes. "Is that what you want?"

He hung his head, hiding behind all that hair. "I want to strip off your panties, put you up against the sink, and just be inside you. I don't feel gentle tonight, Meredith. I feel half-crazed."

"Then do it," I said.

He turned and stared at me. "What did you say?"

"Do it, just the way you want it. Eight hundred years, you're entitled to a little fantasy."

He frowned. "But it won't be enjoyable for you."

"Let me worry about that. You forget that I'm descended from fertility gods. As many times as you go inside me, I can bring you back to need with a touch of my hand, a tiny use of power. Just because we begin the night here, doesn't mean we have to end it here."

"You would let me do that?"

I looked at him, standing there with his broad shoulders, the swell of his chest peeking through that glorious hair, the narrow waist, the tight hips encased in those so-tight pants. I thought about him dropping those pants, of seeing him nude for the first time, of having him push himself inside me, urgent, so full of need that he would touch nothing, do nothing but shove himself inside me. I had to let my breath go in a sigh before I could speak. "Yes."

He crossed the room in two strides, lifting me off the counter, setting me on the floor. I had to balance on the bad ankle, but he didn't give me time to protest. He pulled the dress off my arms in one abrupt movement. I had to grab the edge of the counter to keep from falling. He jerked the dress down, letting it pool on the floor around my feet. He grabbed the black satin of the panties and pulled them down, too.

I could see Kitto in the foggy mirror. He watched everything with eager eyes, utterly silent, as if he didn't want to break the spell.

Frost had to unlace the pants, and it took time. He was making a small noise low in his throat by the time he had gotten them unfastened and peeled down his body. The shirt was fastened over his groin, and he ripped the material away. He was long and hard and more than ready. I had a glimpse of him over my shoulder, then his hands were on my waist, turning me to face the fogged mirror.

I had a moment of feeling him sliding against me, then he was inside me. He shoved against the tightness of my body, forcing himself into me. I'd given him permission, wanted him, but with almost no foreplay it was still pain with the pleasure. A bruising, almost tearing pressure brought my breath in a gasp that was both pain and desire. When he was sheathed inside me as far as he could go, he whispered, "You're tight—not ready for me—but you are wet."

My voice came out breathy. "I know."

He drew himself out, part way, then in, and after that there was nothing but his body inside mine. His need was large and fierce and so was he. He thrust into me as hard and as fast as he could. The sound of flesh hitting flesh punctuated every thrust of his body. It forced sounds from my throat, from the sheer force of it, and from the sensations as he moved inside me, over me, through me. My body opened to him, no longer tight, just wet.

He used his hands to force my body down on the counter, then lifted me so that most of my body was on the counter. My feet were no longer touching the ground. He pounded himself into me, as if he were trying to force his way not just into my body but through and out the other side. A tightness began to grow low in my body, my breath coming faster. Flesh into flesh, so hard and fast with such strength that it danced that thin line between pleasure and pain. I kept expecting him to finish his need in one long glorious burst, but he didn't. He hesitated, using large strong hands to move my hips along the counter, a small adjustment as if he were looking for just the right spot, then he thrust inside me again in one long hard movement, and I cried out. Frost had found that spot inside my body, and was running himself over it, and over it, and over it, as hard and as fast as before, but now he drew small sounds from me. The tightness began to grow, swell, like a warm thing growing inside me. It grew large and larger, flowing outward along my skin as if a thousand feathers were being drawn down my skin to send me shivering, twitching, drawing noises from my mouth that were wordless, thoughtless, formless. It was the song of flesh, not love, not even desire, but something more primitive, more primal.

I looked into the mirror and found my skin glowing, my eyes startled full of green-and-gold fire. I could see Frost in the mirror. He was carved of ivory and albaster; a glowing, shining play of white light pulsed against his skin as if the power would burst from him. He caught me looking at him in the mirror, and those glowing grey eyes like clouds with moonlight behind them turned angry. He put his hand on my face, turned me away so I couldn't watch him, kept his hand there, trapping me, his other hand on my back, his body pinning me. I couldn't move, couldn't get away, couldn't stop him. I didn't want to, but I understood. It was important to him that he be in control, that he say when and how, and even me looking at him was an intrusion. This was his moment—I was just the flesh that he drove himself into. He needed for me to be nothing and no one except someone to fill his need.

I heard his breathing quicken, his thrusts taking on an urgency, harder, faster, until I cried out, and still he didn't stop. I felt the rhythm of his body change, a shudder run through him, then I was gone. That swelling warmth spilled over me, through me, pulsing deep inside my body, making my body contract, jerking, unable to control it, only his hands on my body kept me still, kept me whole. But if my body couldn't move, the pleasure had to come out some way; it spilled out of my mouth in screams, deep, racking screams, over and over as fast as I could draw breath.

Frost cried out above me, sending his cries after mine. He leaned over the counter, a hand on either side of me, head down. His hair spilled over my body like warm silk. I lay totally passive, still pinned under his body, trying to relearn how to breathe.

He found his voice first, though it was a ragged whisper, "Thank you."

If I'd had enough breath I'd have laughed. My throat was so dry, that my voice sounded stiff. "Trust me on this, Frost, it was my pleasure."

He bent over and laid a kiss on my cheek. "I will try to do better next time." He moved his hands away from me, letting me move, but stayed sheathed inside me as if he were reluctant to let that go.

I looked at him, thinking he was joking, but his face was utterly serious. "It gets better than this?" I asked.

He nodded solemnly. "Oh, yes."

"The queen was a fool," I said softly.

He smiled then. "I always thought so."

Chapter 35

I WOKE TO A SPILL OF SILVER HAIR STRETCHED LIKE GLIS-
tening spider-webs across my face. I moved just my head,
leaving the hair to trail across my face. Frost lay on his
stomach, his face turned away from me. The sheets lay in a
twist around his waist, leaving his upper body bare. His hair
trailed to one side like a second body lying between us, and
half across me.

Of course, there *was* a second body in the bed, or rather a
third. Kitto lay on my other side. He was curled on his side,
facing away from me, his body huddled around itself as if he
were hiding from something in his dreams. Or maybe he was
just cold, because he lay naked beside me. His body was pale,
like some perfect china doll. I'd never been this close to a man
that brought to mind words like petite. My shoulder ached
where he'd left his mark: a perfect set of his teeth marks set in
the flesh of my shoulder. The skin had bruised wonderfully
around it, reddish purple, almost hot to the touch. It wasn't
poison, just a really deep bite. It would leave a scar, and that
was the point.

Sometime during the third or fourth time with Frost I'd invited Kitto to us. I had waited until Frost's body brought me
to a point where pain and pleasure merge, and let Kitto
choose his bit of flesh. It hadn't hurt when he did it, which
told how far gone I'd been last night. It had hurt a little as we
finally drifted off to sleep; this morning it hurt more. It wasn't
the only thing that ached. My body hurt, telling me I'd abused
it last night, or rather that I'd let Frost abuse it.

I reveled in the small pains, stretching my body, exploring

exactly what hurt. It was like the ache after a really good workout with weights and running, except the muscle soreness was in different places. I couldn't remember the last time I'd woken with the feel of sex riding my body like a silken bruise. It had been too long.

Kitto had been honored that I allowed him to mark me so that all would know I was his lover. I don't know if he realized that he was never going to get intercourse from me, but he hadn't asked last night. In fact he'd been utterly submissive, doing only what was invited, or asked, never intruding. He was the perfect audience because he simply wasn't there until called, then he followed directions better than any man I'd ever been with.

I sat up and Frost's hair spilled down my body like the brush of something alive. I ran my hands through my own woefully short hair. Now that I was outed as Princess Meredith, I could grow it out again. My wrists hurt as I touched my hair, and it had nothing to do with the sex. The bandages at my wrists hadn't survived the bath last night, and we should have re-dressed the wounds, but this morning the marks of the thorns were scabbed over, nearly healed, as if they were a week or more old, instead of hours. I ran my fingers over the healing wounds. I had never healed this fast before. Kitto must have bitten me after the fourth time, otherwise it would have healed more. Assuming that the sex was what was healing me. We still didn't know that for certain.

I had a small corner of sheet, but the rest was wrapped around Frost. He was a cover hog. It was chilly in the room. I tugged at the covers, and got only a small protesting noise for my troubles. I stared down at the smooth expanse of his back and had an idea for how to get the covers away from him.

I ran my tongue down his back, and he made a small sound. I leaned over him, drawing my tongue up his spine in a slow wet line.

Frost raised his head from the pillow, slowly, like a man drawn from a deep, dark dream. His eyes were slightly unfocused, but when he looked at me a slow, pleased smile curled his lips. "Haven't you had enough?"

I draped my naked body the length of his, though the covers kept us from touching below the waist. "Never," I said.

He laughed, a low, pleasant chuckle, and rolled onto his side, propped on one elbow to look at me. He also freed the covers. I pulled them over the bed to cover Kitto, who still seemed to be deeply asleep.

Frost's arm encircled my waist, drawing me back down on the bed. I laid back against the pillows, and he bent down to place a soft kiss across my lips. My hands slid over his shoulder, his back, pulling him against me.

His knee slid over my legs, between them, and he'd made that first movement of his hips to slide on top of me, when he froze, the look on his face totally changed to something watchful, almost frightened.

"What is it, Frost?"

"Quiet."

I was quiet. He was the bodyguard. Was it Cel's people? This was their last day to kill me without costing Cel his life. Frost rolled off the bed, snatching the sword, Winter Kiss, from the floor and crossing the room to the windows in a movement like blurred silver lightning.

I got my gun from under the pillows. Kitto was awake, looking wildly around.

Frost jerked the drapes back from the window, and his sword was in midmotion toward the glass, when he froze. A man with a camera was on the outside of the window. I had an instant to see him raise a startled face, then Frost's fist smashed through the window, and grabbed the reporter by the neck.

"Frost, no, don't kill him!" I ran across the room naked, the gun still in my hand. The door behind us burst open, and I turned, gun pointed, safety off, at the door.

Doyle stood in the doorway, sword in hand. We had a moment of eye contact where he saw the gun in my hand. I pointed the gun at the floor and he kicked the door shut behind him and strode into the room. He didn't sheathe his sword, but tossed it on the bed as he moved toward Frost.

The reporter's face had turned that violent red-purple that

said he wasn't able to breathe. Frost's face was unrecognizable, torn with fury, enraged.

"Frost, you're killing him."

Doyle came up beside him. "Frost, if you kill this reporter the queen will punish you for it."

Frost didn't seem to be hearing either of us, as if he'd gone to a distant place and all that was left was his hand on the man's throat.

Doyle stepped behind him and kicked him in the small of the back hard enough that Frost fell into the window, cracking more of the glass, but he let go of the reporter. He turned with blood running down his hand, the look in his eyes feral.

Doyle had gone into a fighting stance, bare-handed. Frost threw his sword on the floor and mirrored him. Kitto huddled in the middle of the bed and watched it all with wide eyes.

I went for the drapes, intending to close them, and I saw the reporters running like a pack of hounds toward us. Some were snapping pictures as they ran, others screaming out, "Princess, Princess Meredith!"

I closed the drapes, so there was no gap for them to peer through, but it wouldn't last. We had to get into the room next door where Galen and the rest had slept. I sighted the gun on the wooden headboard of the bed, to one side of the two guards. Kitto saw me and dived on the other side for the floor.

I fired the gun just once, the report thunderous in the room. It whirled the two men around, staring and wild-eyed. I pointed the gun at the ceiling. "There are about a hundred reporters about to descend on us. We have to get to the other room, now!"

No one argued with me. Frost, Kitto, and I grabbed sheets and clothes, and made it into the other room before the reporters started climbing in through the broken window. Doyle brought up the rear with the weapons. He, Galen, and Rhys went back for the luggage. I called the police and reported the reporters for breaking into our room.

The three of us who were naked took turns dressing in the bathroom, not for modesty's sake, but because there were no windows in the bathroom.

When I stepped out of the bathroom with an armload of toiletries, Doyle and Frost were sitting in the room's only two chairs. No one else was here. They were both doing their typical guard face, unreadable, inscrutable. But there was something about the way they held themselves, something odd.

"What's happened?" I asked. I was walking normally—I'd forgotten my ankle was supposed to be sprained until Galen had remarked on it. Neither of them spoke, and that made me nervous.

The men glanced at each other. Doyle pushed to his feet. He was wearing black jeans today, spread over the tops of ankle-high black boots. You'd almost mistake them for dress shoes if you didn't know what you were looking at. The shirt was a black dress shirt, long-sleeved. It was silk and looked it, shimmering against the blackness of his skin. The black of his shoulder holster blended in perfectly with everything. Even the gun was black. A Beretta 10 mm, the older model.

His hair gave the illusion of being very short and cut close to his head. It was in his usual tight braid, curling down his back to be lost in the blackness of his jeans. His high pointed ears gleamed with silver earrings in a shimmering display. Those and a small silver belt buckle were the only things that distracted from the total monochrome of his look. He'd added a silver chain on one ear with a small dangling ruby.

"We have a problem," he said.

"Like reporters taking pictures through the window of Frost and me in bed together. Yes, I'd say we have a problem."

"It is not just the one reporter," Frost said.

"I saw them, like a pack of sharks on the scent of blood." I started to put the small armful of toiletries away in the open suitcase that lay waiting on the bed. "I've been the subject of media attention, but never like this."

Frost crossed the legs of his grey dress slacks, showing pale grey loafers but no socks. Frost would never wear dress slacks short enough to flash sock—so déclassé. The tailored jacket matched the pants and had a small pale blue show hankie in one pocket. The shirt was white and held in place with a dove grey tie, complete with a silver tie tack. He'd pulled his hair back in a tight ponytail, leaving the strong, clean lines of his face bare to the eye. He was dazzlingly handsome without the hair to distract the eye. He looked cool, perfect, not at all the same man who'd nearly ground me into the bathroom tile last night. But I knew the other Frost was under there waiting for permission to come out.

I shoved the last of the toiletries in the suitcase, closed it, and started to zip it up. I looked at the two men. "You guys look like something really, really bad has happened. Something I don't know about yet. Where is everybody else?"

Frost answered, "They are guarding the door and the window. They are trying to keep the media at bay, but it is a losing battle, Meredith."

Doyle leaned his hands on the dresser, head hanging down. The thick braid of his hair slid around his legs like some sort of pet.

"You're scaring me. Just tell me what's happened."

Frost touched the paper that was lying on the table next to him. An idle gesture, but . . .

"Is that the *St. Louis Post-Dispatch*?" I asked.

Doyle darted a look at Frost, who raised his hands showing them empty. "She has to know."

"It is," Doyle said, voice tight.

"I talked to Barry Jenkins yesterday. He said he'd out me as the faerie princess. I assume he was as good as his threat."

Doyle turned, leaning his butt against the dresser, arms crossed, so that his right hand caressed his gun. It was a nervous gesture for him. It looked like a threat when he stood behind the queen stroking his gun, and it could be, but it was also a nervous gesture.

I walked over to the table. "What is the big deal, guys? Jenkins is an asshole, but he wouldn't actively lie, not in the *Post*."

"Read it, then tell me we have nothing to worry over," Doyle said.

The picture of Galen and me at the airport was the lead

photo, front page. But it was the caption that got me. PRINCESS MEREDITH RETURNS HOME TO FIND HUSBAND. In smaller letters under the photo, it read "Is this the one?"

I turned to Doyle and Frost. "Jenkins could be guessing. Galen and I knew there were photographers at the airport." I stared from one to the other of them, and they were still solemn, worried. "What is wrong with the two of you? We've all been in the papers before."

"Not like this," Frost said.

"It gets better," Doyle said, "or worse. Read the article."

I started to browse the article, but the first full paragraph stopped me. "Griffin gave Jenkins an interview." My voice sounded breathy, and I suddenly had to sit down on the edge of the bed. "Goddess save us."

"Yes," Doyle said.

"The queen has already been in contact with us. She will see that he is punished for having broken your trust. She's scheduled a press conference for tonight."

"Please, Meredith, read the article," Doyle said.

I read the article. I read it twice. I didn't mind that Griffin had given personal details, but that he'd done it without my permission. He'd shared my private life with everyone. The sidhe have strange rules about privacy. We don't value intimate secrets as humans do, but our own personal life is not to be spied on. Spying on us used to bring a death penalty. For Griffin, it still might. The queen would think it very déclassé to have tattled to a reporter.

I ended simply sitting on the bed staring at the newsprint but not really seeing it. I looked at the two men. "He gives details of our relationship, hints, dirty little hints. I'm just lucky it was a legitimate paper and not some tabloid."

They looked at each other.

"Oh, no, please, please tell me you're kidding."

Frost reached behind his back as if he'd been reading it as I came out of the bathroom. He held it out to me.

I let the newspaper fall to the floor in a scattered heap and took the sleek colorful paper from him. The picture on the front was one of Griffin and me together in a bed. Only his hands kept my breasts from being fully exposed. I was laughing. We were both laughing. I remembered the pictures. I remembered his desire for the pictures. I still had some of the pictures myself, but not all of them. Not all of them.

I heard my voice and it sounded calm, though far away. "How? How did they get the article out so quickly? I thought magazines didn't get out this fast."

"Apparently, it can be done," Doyle said.

I stared at the picture. The caption was PRINCESS MEREDITH AND HER SIDHE LOVER'S SEX SECRETS REVEALED.

"Please tell me that this is the only picture."

"I am so sorry," Doyle said.

Frost started to touch my hand as if to pat it, then let his hand fall back. "There are no words for how sorry I am that he did this to you."

I looked into Frost's grey eyes. I saw compassion there, but one thing I didn't see was anger. And right now that's what I wanted.

"Does the queen know about this?"

"She knows," Doyle said.

I held it in my hands, wanting to open it, wanting to see what other pictures there were, and I couldn't make myself open it. I couldn't make myself look.

I shoved the paper into Frost's hands. "How bad is it?"

He looked up at Doyle, then back to me. The arrogant, distant mask slipped a little, and the Frost that I'd woken up with peeked from his eyes. "The tabloid didn't use any full frontal nudity. Other than that, it's bad."

I hid my face in my hands, my elbows on my knees. "Oh, God, if Griffin would sell them to Jenkins, to the tabloids, then he might sell them anywhere." I raised up like a swimmer coming out of deep water. It was suddenly hard to get my breath. "There are magazines in Europe that would publish all of the pictures. I didn't mind the nude photos, but they were private—just for Griffin and me. If I'd wanted to publish photos, I'd have said yes to *Playboy* years ago. Lord and Lady, how could Griffin do this?" I had a horrible thought. I looked to Frost.

"Please tell me that you got the camera and the film from the reporter you tried to strangle this morning?"

He met my eyes, but he didn't want to. "I'm sorry, Meredith, the camera should have been my first priority, but I let my anger better my judgment. I would do anything to make this up to you."

"Frost, they'll publish the pictures, do you understand that? Pictures of you and me, and hell, Kitto, in bed together. They'll plaster them over the tabloids, and the ones with nudity will go to Europe." I would have liked to swear, or scream, but I couldn't think of anything harsh enough to make me feel better.

"Griffin would know what the queen would do to him for this," Doyle said. "He'll be lucky if she doesn't kill him."

I nodded, trying to control my breathing, forcing myself to concentrate on the rise and fall of my own chest. I fought for calm, but it wasn't happening today. I nodded again. "He'll do as much damage as he can before they catch him." I took three quick, gulping breaths, and my voice came out strained, but holding. "I assume he's fled the area."

"We will find him," Frost said. "The world is not that big."

That made me laugh, but the laughter turned into tears. I slid off the chair onto the floor among the scattered pieces of the *Post-Dispatch*. It hurt to land so hard on the floor. I was aching from the sex, bruised. The pain helped remind me that things were not that bad. Horrible, but I still had access to the men of the court. I was still welcome back in faerie. The queen had given her word—and her power—to keep me from harm. Things could be worse. Or at least that's what I kept trying to tell myself.

I got my breathing under control, but not my anger. "I did not mean him harm last night, but now . . ." I grabbed the tabloid from Frost and forced myself to look inside. It wasn't the partial nudity that really cut me up. It was the happiness in our faces, our bodies. We'd been in love and it showed. But if he could do this to me, then he'd never really loved me. He'd lusted after me, desired me, wanted to own me, maybe, but love . . . love didn't do things like this.

I threw the pages up into the air and watched them flutter slowly back to Earth. "I want him dead for this. Don't tell the queen that. In a few days I may change my mind, and I don't want her doing anything dramatic." My voice was cold with anger, the kind of anger that settles in your heart and never leaves. Hot rage runs through you, and is close kin to hot passion, but cold rage, that is close kin to hate. For this I hated Griffin, but not enough. "I don't want her to send me his head or heart in a basket. I don't want that."

"She may be planning to kill him anyway," Doyle said.

"Yes, but if she does, then it's on her head, not mine. I won't ask for his death. Let her come up with it on her own."

Frost knelt beside me, gazing up at me with those storm-grey eyes. He took my hands in his. His hands felt warm, which meant my hands were cold. Maybe I was more upset than I thought, maybe I was in shock.

"I am sure our queen has already decided his fate," Frost said.

"No," I said. I stood, pulling away from his hands, from his eyes. I hugged myself, because I knew I could trust my own arms; I was beginning to have doubts about everyone else's. "No, if she catches him right away, she might kill him. But the longer he eludes capture, the more creative she'll get."

Frost stayed kneeling on the ground looking up at me. "If I were he, I think I would prefer to be captured soon, while a quick death was still possible."

"He'll run," I said. "He'll run as far and as fast as he can. He'll delay and hope that some miracle will save him."

"You know him that well?" Frost asked.

I stared down into his face, and laughed. The laughter had a wild edge to it. "I thought I did. Maybe I never knew him at all. Maybe it was all just lies." I stared at Frost. I was glad I didn't love him, glad that it was just flesh. At that moment, I trusted lust more than I trusted love.

Doyle stood, taking my arms gently in his hands. "Don't let Griffin make you doubt yourself, Meredith. Don't let him make you doubt us."

I stared up into his dark face. "How did you know that was exactly what I was thinking?"

"Because it's exactly what I would be thinking in your place."

"No, it isn't, you'd be planning to kill him."

Doyle hugged me to him, resting his face against my hair. I stayed tense against him but didn't pull away. "Say that you wish his death and it will be so. Pick a body part of your choosing, and I will fetch it for you."

"*We* will fetch it for you," Frost said, standing.

I relaxed enough against Doyle to slide one arm around his waist. I leaned my face against the silk of his shirt. I could hear his heart beating, solid and a little fast.

There was a knock on the door. Doyle nodded and Frost moved to answer it. Doyle drew his gun, then moved me to one side, still in the curve of his arm, so his body blocked me partially from view.

"It's Galen, open up."

Frost checked the peephole, a large nickel-plated .44 in one hand. "It's him and Rhys."

Doyle nodded, lowering his gun but not putting it away. The tension level was high, very high. I think we were all expecting another attack from Cel and company. I know I was, and I was only paranoid by necessity. The guards were paranoid by profession.

Kitto came in behind the two guards. He was dressed in dark blue jeans, a pale yellow polo shirt with a little alligator on the front, and white jogging shoes. Everything looked brand-new, stiff, and fresh out of the package.

Galen glanced at the papers, then at me. "I'm so sorry, Merry."

Doyle let me slide out from behind him, so I could go to Galen. I buried my face against his chest, wrapped my arms around his waist and held on. I felt safe with Doyle, passion with Frost, but it was Galen's arms that made me feel comfortable.

I wanted to hold on to him, to close my eyes and just cling. But there was a press conference planned, and the queen wanted us at the court early so we could all discuss the version of the truth we were going to feed the media. I'd been going to press conferences since I was a child, and I'd never been to one yet where we told the truth, the whole truth, so help us Goddess. There was no way to clean up the mess that Griffin had made. He could be punished, but the story and the pictures were already out there, and nothing would change that. I still had no clue what sanitized version of the truth would account for the pictures of Frost, Kitto, and me naked together. But if anyone could come up with a necessary lie to cover it, it would be my aunt. Andais, Queen of Air and Darkness, could put a spin on any scandal that would make the media's head spin. Bedazzled by her charms, they tended to write what she told them to write, though making this particular scandal squeaky clean was going to stretch even her talents. I used to hope that I'd live to see my aunt fail badly. Now I was hoping she'd succeed brilliantly. Was that hypocritical of me? Maybe, or maybe it was just practical.

Chapter 36

BY MIDNIGHT THE LAST OF THE REPORTERS HAD DRIFTED AWAY full of old wine, expensive hors d'oeuvres, and my aunt's bullshit. But she did sling it with style. She'd dressed in a slinky black business suit and no blouse, so that her cleavage showed at the line of the jacket, call-girl chic. She was thrilled that I was home for a visit. Excited that I'd finally decided to settle down with some lucky sidhe. Saddened by Griffin's betrayal. One reporter had asked her about the alleged faerie aphrodisiac that had caused a near riot at a Los Angeles police staion. She had no knowledge of it. Andais wouldn't let anyone else but herself answer questions. I'm not sure she trusted what I'd say. The men were just window dressing—they never got to talk.

Cel sat on her right, and I sat on her left. We smiled at each other. The three of us posed for pictures. Him in his monochrome black-on-black designer suit, me in a little black designer dress with a short jacket set with hundreds of genuine jet beads, Andais in her call-girl business suit. We looked like we were going to a very expensive, very chic, funeral. If I do ever get to be queen, I'm getting the court a new color scheme, anything but black.

The court was very quiet tonight. Cel had been led away to be prepared for his punishment. The Queen had taken Doyle and Frost to her rooms for a debriefing. Galen had been limping by the time we finished the conference, so Fflur had taken him off for some ointment to help speed his healing. It left Rhys and Kitto, and Pasco, to guard me. Pasco had come to the hotel last night, but spent the night in the second room.

455

His long pink-colored hair trailed to his knees like a pale curtain. Black was not his color. It made his skin look purplish,
and his hair almost brown. In the right colors Pasco sparkled,
but not tonight. Black looked better on Rhys, but what made
the outfit was the blue shirt, a color to match his eye, that the
queen allowed him.

Rhys and Pasco paced behind me like good bodyguards.
Kitto stayed at my side like a faithful dog. He had not been allowed on camera during the conference. Goblin prejudice
runs strong in the courts. Kitto was the only one who had
been allowed to keep his jeans and T-shirt. We were staying at
the court tonight because it was the only reporter-free zone
within fifty miles. Nobody would be breaking the queen's
windows or snapping pictures through the earthen mound.

I was trying to find my old rooms, but there was a door in
the middle of the hallway, a large wooden-and-bronze door.
The Abyss of Despair lay behind the door. Last I'd seen this
room, it had been near the Hallway of Mortality—read torture room. The Abyss was supposed to be bottomless, which
was impossible had it been purely physical, but it wasn't
purely physical. One of the worst of our punishments was to
be cast into the Abyss and to fall forever, never aging, never
dying, trapped in free fall for all eternity.

I stopped in the middle of the hallway, letting Pasco and
Rhys catch up to me. Kitto moved to one side, out of Rhys's
reach, instinctively. Rhys had not so much as touched him,
just looked at him. Whatever Kitto saw in that one blue-on-
blue eye frightened the goblin.

"What's wrong?" Rhys asked.

"What is this thing doing here?"

He studied the door, frowning. "It's the door to the Abyss."

"Exactly. It should be down three levels of stairs, at the
very least. What's it doing on the main floor?"

"You say that as if the sithen made sense," Pasco said.
"The mound has decided to move the Abyss up to the top
floor. Sometimes it does major rearranging like that."

I looked at Rhys. He nodded. "It does sometimes."

"Define sometimes," I said.

"About every millennium," Rhys said.

"I just love dealing with people whose idea of sometimes is every thousand years," I said.

Pasco grabbed the huge bronze door handle. "Allow me, Princess." The door moved slowly open, proving beyond doubt that it was a very heavy door. Pasco was like most of the court in that he could have bench-pressed a small house if he could have found a convenient handhold, yet he opened this one door as if it had weight.

The room beyond was a dim greyness, as if the lights that worked in the rest of the sithen didn't quite work here. I stepped into the dimness with Kitto at my heels, darting just ahead of me, staying out of Rhys's way, like a dog that's afraid of being kicked. The room was just as I remembered it. A huge circular stone room with a round hole in the center of the floor. There was a white railing around that hole, a railing made of bones and silver wire, and magic. The railing glimmered with its own brand of glamour. Some said the railing was bespelled to keep the Abyss from flowing up through the floor and eating the world. The railing was bespelled to keep people from jumping over it, so no one could commit suicide in it, or fall by accident. There was only one way to go over the rail, and that was to be thrown over.

I gave the glowing collection of bones a wide berth, and Kitto clung to my hand like a child afraid to cross the street by himself. There was another door on the far side of the room, and we walked toward it, my high heels making clackety echoes in the huge room. The door behind us closed with a huge clang that made me jump. Kitto tugged at my hand, urging me to move faster toward the far door. I didn't need any urging, but I also wasn't going to run in the high heels. I'd healed one sprained ankle this week—one was enough.

Two things happened at once. I saw something out of the corner of my eye on the side of the Abyss opposite us, a flicker of movement where nothing stood. The other was a small sound from behind us. I turned toward the noise.

Rhys was on his knees, hands limp at his sides, an expression of bewilderment on his face. Pasco stood over him with a bloody knife in his hand. Rhys fell forward slowly, landing heavily, hands still at his side, mouth opening and closing like a fish pulled from the water.

I moved toward the door, the wall at my back, Kitto beside me. But I knew—I knew that it was too late. The flicker on the other side of the room parted like an invisible curtain to reveal Rozenwyn and Siobhan. The two women divided the room, one moving left, the other right, coming to outflank me. Siobhan all pale and ghostly like a Halloween horror, and Rozenwyn all pink and lavender like an Easter-basket doll. One tall, one short, so much opposites, yet they moved like two pieces of a whole.

I put my back against the wall, Kitto crouching beside me, as if trying to make himself smaller and more invisible. "Rhys isn't dead. Even a heart blow won't kill him," I said.

"But a trip into the Abyss will," Pasco said.

"I take it that's my fate as well," I said, my voice sounding terribly calm. My mind was racing, but my voice was calm.

"We'll kill you first," Siobhan said, "then throw you over."

"Thanks bunches, how thoughtful of you to kill me first."

"We could let you die of thirst while you fell," Rozenwyn said. "Your choice."

"Is there a third choice?" I asked.

"I'm afraid not," Siobhan said, the sibilance of her voice echoing in the room, as if it belonged here.

They'd both crossed around the edge of the railing and were coming in on either side. Pasco stayed by Rhys's gasping body. I had the two folding knives, but they had swords. I was outarmed, and about to be outflanked. "Are you so fearful of me that it takes three of you to kill me? Rozenwyn nearly killed me herself. I still bear her mark over my ribs."

Rozenwyn shook her head. "No, Meredith, you can't talk us into a one-on-one duel. We were given very strict orders that we are simply to kill you, no games, no matter how fun they would be."

Kitto had pressed himself to the floor, huddled by my leg. "What are you going to do to Kitto?"

"The goblin joins Rhys in the Abyss," Siobhan hissed.

I took out one of the folding knives, and they laughed. I
called power to the other hand, called the hand of flesh deliberately for the first time. I waited for it to hurt, but it didn't.
Power moved through me like heavy water: smooth, alive,
tilling my body, my hand, like something almost thick enough
to throw.

The two women knew I'd called some magic, because they
glanced at one another. There was a moment of hesitation,
then they moved forward again. They were only about ten feet
away, when Kitto launched himself from his crouch like a
leopard springing onto Siobhan. She stabbed him, the blade
coming clean through his body, but it missed anything vital,
and he rode her body slashing, biting, fighting like some small
elegant animal.

Rozenwyn rushed me, sword up, but I was expecting it,
and I dived to the floor feeling the rush of air as the blade
roared past me. I grabbed for her leg, touched her ankle, and
her leg collapsed in upon itself. To do what I'd done to Nerys,
I needed to hit in the center of her body, but Rozenwyn would
never give me a chance at a mid-body blow.

She fell to the ground, shrieking, watching her long beautiful leg shrivel up, roll bone and flesh in waves. I drove the
folded blade into her throat, not to kill but to distract. I
scooped the sword out of her suddenly nerveless hand. I
heard Pasco running up behind me. I dropped to my knees,
fighting the urge to look behind, but there was no time. I felt
his blade go over my head, and drove Rozenwyn's sword back
and up, desperately seeking his body and finding it. The
sword bit deep into his body and I said a quick breath of
prayer as I rolled away from him. His own body weight carried him to the floor, drove the sword in hilt deep, while he
made wet sounds deep in his throat. Then something happened that I hadn't planned. Pasco rolled onto his sister's
damaged leg, and the rolling flesh poured over his face. He
didn't even have time to scream before his sister's flesh covered his, and his body began to melt into her. His hands beat
against the floor while his head was already swallowed into
the lump of flesh that had become his sister's lower body.

Rozenwyn pulled my knife from her throat. The wound healed instantly and she began to shriek. She reached out one lavender pink hand to me. "Meredith, Princess, do not do this, I beg you!"

I backed into the wall, watching, because I could not stop it. I didn't know how. It had been an accident. They were twins, they'd shared a womb once, and that may have caused this. A freak accident in every way. If I'd had any clue where to begin I'd have tried to stop it. No one deserved this.

I tore my gaze away from the melting horror of Rozenwyn and her brother becoming one, to see Siobhan and Kitto. Siobhan was bloodied, scratched and bitten, but not really hurt. She was kneeling, though, her sword on the floor in front of her. She was surrendering her weapon to me. Kitto lay gasping beside her, the hole in his chest already beginning to close. She could have killed me while I watched Rozenwyn and Pasco melt, but Siobhan, who was the stuff of nightmares, watched with open horror as the pink-and-purple flesh consumed the two sidhe. She was too scared to risk coming close enough for a death blow. She was scared . . . of me.

Rozenwyn's face went last, screaming, as if she were trying to keep her head above quicksand, but it swallowed her, and the mass of flesh and organs pulsed on the stone floor. You could hear their screams, two voices this time, two voices trapped. My pulse pounded in my ears until all I could hear, taste, was my horror at the sight. It wasn't just Siobhan who was scared.

Rhys staggered to his feet, his own sword in his hands. Then he fell to his knees beside me, his eyes on the thing on the floor. "Lord and Lady protect us."

I could only nod. But finally my voice came, low, hoarse. "Disarm Siobhan, then kill that thing."

"How?" he asked.

"Chop it up, Rhys, chop it up until it stops moving." I stared down at Rozenwyn's sword. It was one of a kind, made for her hand, with a hilt of jeweled spring flowers. I started for the near door with the sword naked in my hand.

"Where are you going?" Rhys asked.

"I have a message to deliver." The huge bronze door opened in front of me as if moved by a great hand. I walked through it and it closed behind me. The sithen pulsed and whispered around me. I went to find Cel.

He was naked, chained to the floor of a dark room. Ezekial was there, our torturer, with surgical gloves on his hands and a bottle of Branwyn's Tears. The torture had not yet begun, which meant that the three months had not begun, so I could not demand Cel's life.

The queen saw me first, her eyes going to the sword in my hand. Doyle and Frost were with her, witnesses to her son's shame. "What has happened?" she asked.

I placed the sword across Cel's bare chest. He recognized it—I could see it in his eyes. "I would have brought you an ear from Rozenwyn and Pasco, but they don't have an ear left between them."

"What did you do to them?" He whispered it.

I raised my left hand, just above his body. The queen said, "Meredith, no, you cannot."

"They shared a womb once, now they share flesh. Should I have them thrown into the Abyss where you meant to put Rhys and Kitto? Should I let them fall forever a pulsing ball of meat?"

He stared up at me, and the fear was there, but underneath the cunning. "I did not know they were going to do this. I did not send them."

I stood up and motioned Ezekial forward. "Begin." Ezekial looked at the queen. She nodded, and he knelt beside Cel's body and began to coat him with the oil.

I turned to Andais. "For this I want him in here like this alone for six months, the full sentence."

Andais started to argue, but Doyle said, "Your Majesty, you must begin to treat him as he deserves."

She nodded. "Six months, I give my oath on it."

"Mother, no, no!"

"When you're done, Ezekial, seal the room." And she walked out while he was still screaming for her.

I watched Ezekial coat him with the oil, watched his body come alive at the touch of it. Frost and Doyle stood on either side of me. Cel looked at me while it was happening, his face saying plainly that he was thinking about me in a very uncousinlike way. "I was going to just kill you, Meredith, but not now. When I get out of here I'll fuck you, fuck you until you're with my child. The throne is mine even if I have to get it through your lily-white body."

"If you come near me again, Cel, I'll kill you." With that I turned and walked out. Doyle and Frost came behind and to either side like good bodyguards. Cel's voice followed us down the hallway. He was screaming my name, "Merry, Merry!" each time more frantic than the last.

Long after I shouldn't have been able to hear his screams, they echoed in my ears.

Chapter 37

PASCO'S DEATH MEANT THAT THE QUEEN NEEDED A NEW SPY TO send back to Los Angeles with me. She seemed unsure of herself with Cel's screams still echoing in the hallways. I was able to press until we settled on a guard who wasn't exactly one of her pets. Nicca is terrified of my aunt, so he'll report to her, but he also helped us after the thorns tried to drink me dry. Doyle trusts him, and I trust Doyle. The queen says that Nicca is not an inspired lover, but the packaging is nice. His father was one of the demi-fey, something with butterfly wings. His mother was one of the ladies of the court, a full-blooded sidhe. The queen had him strip his shirt off for me, to show that giant butterfly wings are tattooed across his shoulders, arms, down his back to vanish into his pants. The genetics tried to give him wings even though he was man-sized. No tattoo artist has ever done anything as lovely as the wings on Nicca's back. The queen would have had him strip completely so I could see just how far down the wing design went, but I opted to be left with a little mystery. Nicca had looked frightened the entire time. He watched Queen Andais the way a crippled sparrow watches a snake, just wondering when the first big bite is going to sink into its flesh. I got him out of her presence as soon as was polite. Doyle assures me that Nicca is fine as long as the queen is nowhere around. I'd love to know what she did to him in particular to make him so very afraid—or maybe I wouldn't. The older I get the more I realize that ignorance may not be bliss, but sometimes it beats the alternative.

We flew back to Los Angeles as soon as we could get a flight out. The police had to be called in to keep the press at bay. The pictures of Frost, Kitto, and me were already in the tabloids. I'm told the European tabloids were showing the full nude shots with nothing fuzzed out. The question everyone wanted to know the answer to was: Is Frost or Kitto the new fiancé. I kept answering no, and one smart reporter asked if I was into polyandry. I motioned at all the beautiful men surrounding me, and said, "Wouldn't you be?" The press laughed, and loved it. Since we can't do anything else, we're playing to it. Princess Meredith is picking a new husband, or two.

Jeremy brought Uther to the airport to meet our plane. Uther used "the glare" to clear a path through the reporters. When you're thirteen feet tall, muscular, and have a double row of wicked-looking tusks coming out of your face, even reporters will clear a path. Jeremy fielded questions that, yes, the princess did work for the Grey Detective Agency. We'd already talked on the phone, because Jeremy had pretty much expected me not to come back to work. But being a detective had made me feel better than being a faerie princess ever had. Besides, I had a lot of mouths to feed. Ringo was out of the hospital and almost completely healed from the ogre's attack in the van. Roane was back from his sea vacation. He gave me a seashell, pale, white, gleaming with opalescence like a daintier, pinker version of abalone shell. It was lovely, and meant more to me than any jewel because it meant more to Roane. He bowed out as my lover without having to be told, though I've let him know that if our having sex has made him sidhe-struck, he's welcome. He seems fine; his new sealskin seems to be a cure for sidhe-sickness. I'm glad, because truth is I have enough men in my life right now.

I have at least one bodyguard with me at all times; Doyle prefers two. It's going to be twenty-four–seven, so they rotate, and mix the rotation so no watchers can ever be sure who is going to be on duty and who isn't. I'm letting Doyle handle the details—it is his job. When they're not guarding my body, they're trying to settle into the new world I've dragged them into. Rhys, of course, wanted to work for the detective agency and be a real-life detective. Jeremy didn't argue with a full-blooded sidhe warrior coming on staff. Once the word got out, it seemed like every celebrity in the area wanted a sidhe to guard their body. Business was so good and most of the time so easy—a lot of standing around and looking decorative with no real danger—that Galen and Nicca both signed on. Doyle says he doesn't guard anyone but me. Frost seems to agree. Kitto simply wants to hang around with me and would spend most of his time under my desk if I let him. He's not adapting well to his first view of the twentieth century. The poor goblin never saw a car before, or a television—and now he spends his days in a skyscraper in one of the most modern cities in the world. If he doesn't start thriving, I'll have to send him back to Kurag, which will mean the goblin king will send a replacement. Call it a hunch: I'm betting the next goblin won't be nearly so nice.

Whatever the demi-fey did to Galen, it was more than simple injury, because he's not healing in one certain area the way he should. We've had a doctor and the best magical practitioner in the city look at him. Neither one of them was very helpful. If science and magic both keep failing us, I may have to talk to Queen Niceven herself and find out what the hell they did to him. I think he's taking to guarding other bodies because to be so close to me and still not be able to have me, when everyone else can, is just too difficult for him. Me, too. All that heat, all those years of waiting, and we're still waiting.

The Grey Detective Agency is getting so much high-profile, big-bucks business that Jeremy is interviewing new people and talking about moving to bigger offices. There were some tense moments between Jeremy and the guards, because they were Unseelie and Jeremy was still holding a grudge. Galen and Rhys took him out drinking. I don't know what was said, but the next day the tension level was better. Male bonding at its best.

Alistair Norton's widow, Frances Norton, and Naomi Phelps, his ex-mistress, are doing well. They've moved in together and if they were a heterosexual couple I'd say we might be getting a wedding invitation soon. They seem happy, and no one is mourning Alistair. The police have traced some of Alistair's fellow sidhe worshipers. Two of them died mysteriously just before the police found them. I don't have much hope for the health of any of the sidhe worshipers. The queen, or Cel's toadies, or both, are tidying up the mess. The queen assured me that there was only one bottle of Branwyn's Tears missing from her private stock, so the danger to the human public is over. She gave me her oath on it, and no sidhe would go back on their oath, not even Andais. There is almost no worse insult among the sidhe than to be an oath-breaker. No one will do business with you after that. No one will bed you, let alone marry you. Andais is on shaky ground with the sidhe right now—she would not risk it. There are whispers of revolution, and I know that Cel's followers among the court are behind it. Though some have suggested that Barinthus is behind it, that he intends to make me queen whether I bear a child or not. "Barinthus Queen-maker" is what they say behind his back. I've made him promise he's not doing anything like that, but he still refuses to come to Los Angeles, saying we need at least one powerful friend to talk to the court about me. He's probably right, but I'm beginning to wonder exactly what he's saying at court without me there to say yea or nay to it.

Doyle has shared my bed, but not our bodies. Literally we have slept together, but not had sex. He says that anticipation will make it better. I don't know what he has planned, but looking into his dark eyes I know he has a plan, a purpose. When I ask about that plan, he says, "I want only to keep you safe and see you queen after your aunt." I don't believe him. Oh, I believe he wants me safe, and I believe he wants me to rule after Andais, but there is more to it than that. When I press, he smiles and shakes his head. I should know by now that when the queen's Darkness keeps secrets there is no prying them from him until he is ready to speak them. Until we are together completely, until I know exactly what he is thinking, he is still the queen's Darkness and not truly mine. It's not the lack of sex but the wealth of secrets that keeps me from owning Doyle completely. If I cannot own him body and heart, how can I trust him? The answer, simply, is I can't.

I'm back in Los Angeles working as a detective but under my real name now. I have access to sidhe lovers and could return to faerie any time I want. I have everything I wanted, but there is a tension that never quite goes away. Because I know that, as they say, the other shoe has not dropped. Cel still lives; his followers fear that I will destroy them if I gain the throne. Revolutions have begun over less. The media is always present like a circle of sharks kept at bay only by court orders. They're chasing the sex and romance angle—if only they knew how very much more there is to the story. Griffin hasn't been found. Maybe he's dead and no one told me. Though somehow, knowing my aunt, I think she'd probably box him up and send me a few favorite parts. I should be happy, and I am, but I'm not at peace. We are in the quiet before the storm, and it is going to be a hell of a storm. I will be weathering the storm in a boat made of flesh and bone, the bodies of my guards, and with every caress, every glance, I am more and more reluctant to give any of them up. I've lost enough people in my life. I'd like to try, just this once, not to lose anyone else. I'd pretty much abandoned my religion with my family, but I've set up an altar in my room, and I'm praying again. I'm praying as hard as I can, but I know better than most that while you always get an answer to your prayer, sometimes the answer isn't what you want it to be. I don't want the throne if I have to climb over the bodies of my friends and lovers to get it. I don't want anything that badly— I never did. I always thought love was more important than power, but sometimes you can't have love without the power to keep it safe. I pray for the safety of those I care about. Maybe what I'm really praying for is power, enough power to protect them. So be it. Whatever it takes to keep them safe, even if that means being queen. I can't be queen while Cel lives, no matter what my aunt believes. I pray for the safety of those I care about, and what I'm really asking for is power, the throne, and my cousin's death. Because those three things must happen to give us all safety. They say, be careful what you wish for. Well, be even more cautious with your prayers. Make sure, very sure, it's what you want. You never know when a deity may give you exactly what you asked for.

Read on for an excerpt from

SEDUCED BY MOONLIGHT

by Laurell K. Hamilton

A LOT OF PEOPLE LOUNGE BY POOLS IN L.A., BUT FEW OF THEM are truly immortal, no matter how hard they pretend with plastic surgery and exercise. Doyle *was* truly immortal and had been for over a thousand years. A thousand years of wars, assassinations, and political intrigue, and he'd been reduced to being eye candy in a thong bathing suit by the pool of the rich and famous. He lay at the edge of the pool, wearing almost nothing. Sunlight glittered across the blue, blue water of the pool. The light broke in a jagged dance across his body, as if some invisible hand stirred the light, turning it into a dozen tiny spotlights that coaxed Doyle's dark body into colors I'd never known his skin could hold.

He wasn't black the way a human being is black, but more the way a dog is black. Watching the play of light on his skin, I realized I'd been wrong. His skin gleamed with blue highlights, a shine of midnight blue along the long muscular sweep of his calf, a flare of royal blue like a stroke of deep sky touched his back and shoulder. Purple to shame the darkest amethyst caressed his hip. How could I ever have thought his skin monochrome? He was a miracle of colors and light, strapped across a body that rippled and moved with muscles honed in wars fought centuries before I was born.

The braid of his black hair trailed across the edge of the lounge chair, fell over the side, and curled beside him on the concrete like some patient serpent. His hair was the only thing that seemed black on black. There was no play of colors, only a gleam like a black jewel. It seemed as if it

469

should have been the other way around, that his hair should have held the highlights and his body been all one color, but it wasn't.

He lay on his stomach, head turned away from me. He was pretending to be asleep, but I knew he wasn't. He was waiting. Waiting for the helicopter to fly over. The helicopter that would contain the press, people with cameras. We'd made a deal with the devil. If the press would just stay away enough for us to have some privacy, we'd make sure that at prearranged times they had something newsworthy to take pictures of. I was Princess Meredith NicEssus, heir to the throne of the Unseelie Court, and the fact that I'd surfaced in Los Angeles, California, after a three-year absence was big news. People thought I'd died. Now I was alive and well, and living in the middle of one of the biggest media empires on the planet. Then I'd gone and done something that was even better tabloid fodder.

I was looking for a husband. The only faerie princess born on American soil was looking to wed. Being fey, especially a member of the sidhe, the highest of the high royals, I wasn't allowed to marry unless I was pregnant. The fey don't breed much, and the sidhe royals breed even less. My aunt, the Queen of Air and Darkness, would not tolerate anything less than a fertile match. Since we seemed to be dying out, I guess I couldn't blame her. But somehow the tabloids had gotten wind that I wasn't just dating my bodyguards, I was fucking them. Whoever got me with child, got a wedding. Got to be king to my queen.

The tabloids even knew that the queen had made it a contest between me and her son, my cousin, Prince Cel. Whoever got a baby first, won the throne. The media had fallen on us like a cannibalistic orgy. Not pretty, not pretty at all.

What the tabloids didn't know was that Cel had tried to have me assassinated more than once. They also didn't know that he'd been imprisoned by the queen for six months as punishment. Imprisoned and tortured, for six months. Immortality and an ability to heal almost anything does have some downsides. Torture can last a very, very long time.

When Cel got out, he'd be allowed to continue the contest, unless I got pregnant first. So far, no luck, and it wasn't for lack of trying.

Doyle was one of five bodyguards, the queen's own bodyguards, who had volunteered, or been volunteered, to be my lover. Queen Andais had had a rule that her bodyguards gave their seed to her body, or nobody. Doyle had been celibate for centuries. Again, immortality, if it goes wrong, can have some downsides.

We'd chosen one of the most persistent of the tabloids and made our arrangements. Doyle thought it was rewarding bad behavior; the queen wanted us to show positive images to the media. The Unseelie Court of the sidhe has a reputation for being the bad guys. We can be, but I'd spent my fair share of time at the Seelie Court, the bright and shining court that the media think is so perfect, so joyous. Their King Taranis, the King of Light and Illusion, is my uncle. But I'm not in line to that throne. I had the bad taste to have a father who was full-blooded Unseelie sidhe, and that is a crime for which the glittering throng has no forgiveness. There was no prison that I could go to, no torture I could endure, that would cleanse me of this sin.

They can say that the Seelie Court is a beautiful place, but I learned that my blood is just as red on white marble as it is on black. The beautiful people made it very plain at a young age that I would never be one of them. I'm too short, too human looking, and, worse yet, too Unseelie looking.

My skin is as white as Doyle's is black. Moonlight skin is what I have, a mark of beauty at either court, but I am barely five feet tall. No sidhe is that short. I have curves and am a little too voluptuous for the sidhe—that pesky human blood, I guess. My eyes are tricolored, two shades of green and a circle of gold. The eyes would be welcome in the Seelie Court, but not the hair. It's blood auburn, sidhe scarlet, if you go to a good salon and get the dye job. It's not auburn, and it's not human red. It's as if you took good red garnets and spun the jewels out into hair. It has one other nickname among the glittering throng—Unseelie red. The Seelie have red hair, but it's closer to human red, orangey, golden, true auburn, or true red, but nothing as dark as mine.

My mother made sure that I knew I was less. Less beautiful, less welcome, just less. She and I don't talk much. My father died when I was younger, and there is rarely a day that I don't miss him. He taught me that I was enough, beautiful enough, tall enough, strong enough, just enough.

The time is right for another dark, sensual Meredith Gentry novel

A STROKE OF MIDNIGHT
by Laurell K. Hamilton

I am Meredith Gentry, P.I., solving cases in Los Angeles, far from the peril and deception of my real home–because I am also Princess Meredith, heir to the darkest throne faerie has to offer. Enemies watch my every move. My cousin Cel strives to have me killed even now from his prison cell. But not all the assassination attempts are his. Enemies unforeseen move against us—enemies who would murder the least among us.

I need my allies now more than ever, especially since fate will lead me into the arms of Mistral, Master of Storms, the queen's new captain of her guard. Our passion will reawaken powers long forgotten among the warriors of the sidhe. Pain and pleasure await me—and danger, as well, for some at that court seek only death. The gentlest of my guards will find new strength and break my heart. Passions undreamed of await us—and my enemies gather, for the future of both courts of faerie begins to unravel.

 Available wherever books are sold
Ballantine Books • www.laurellkhamilton.com

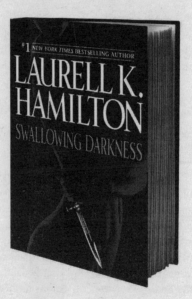